Also it causes all, both small and great, both rich and poor, both free and slave, to be marked on the right hand or the forehead, so that no one can buy or sell unless he has the mark, that is, the name of the beast or the number of its name.

<u>Rev 13 vs 16,17.</u>

Books by Alex Willis

Non-Fiction

Step by Step Guitar Making 1st and 2nd editions

Standalone fiction

The Penitent Heart

The Falcon, The Search for Horus.

The Long Road Home

Crichtons End

Buchanan Series

Book 1   The Bodies in the Marina

Book 2   The Laminated man

Book 3   The Mystery of Cabin 312

Book 4   The Reluctant Jockey

Book 5   The Missing Heiress

Book 6   The Jockey's Wife

Book 7   Death on the Cart

Book 8   Death Stalks at Night

Book 9   Death Sleeps Late

The Missing Heiress

A DCI Buchanan Mystery

By

Alex Willis

Published by Mount Pleasant Publishing 11-11-2020

ISBN-13: 978-1-913471-19-4

Text set in Garamond 12 point.

Cover photo. Nancy Willis 2019
Cover Layout © Alex Willis 2020

A big heartfelt thank you all the NHS heroes, seen and unseen. We clapped, we cheered, and we will be forever thankful to you all.

This book is dedicated to my great uncle John Eldon Porter.
1st Battalion Seaforth Highlanders
Wounded France May 9th, 1915
Died London Hospital May 15th, 1915 aged 19yrs

1

Hands

Detective Chief Inspector Buchanan rolled over and looked at the clock on the bedside table: six o'clock. He yawned, pushed the covers back and sat up. 'You know something. Karen?'

Karen, his wife, opened one eye and squinted at the daylight coming through the bedroom window, 'I know if you are going to get up this early and wake me, you can at least bring me a coffee.'

'I can do one better than that, I'll make us breakfast. What would you like?'

'I'm too tired to think, surprise me.'

♦

'It was a morning like this when we moved into our house in Glasgow,' said Buchanan. 'I remember it as though it was yesterday.'

'Hmm. I remember the day well, our first house as a married couple,' said Karen, as she mopped up the last of her poached egg.

'Was it really thirty-four years ago?'

'No, it was thirty-five. You know, if we'd had children, they'd be having their own children by now.'

Buchanan put down his cup and looked at Karen. 'I know that, and it's not for the want of trying – it's just the hand fate has dealt us. But we do have Jill, and I can't imagine anyone being more like a daughter than she has been. Don't forget, like us not having children, she has no parents; we're sort of made for each other.'

'You are so right, my dear. As usual you have just the right words.'

'Hmm, far too nice a day to work,' said Buchanan, looking out of the conservatory window.

'Don't go in then. Take the day off. We could take a trip into town.'

'Town? Where to, exactly?'

'Nowhere in particular. I thought we could just wander.'

'I'm not taking the day off in order to go window shopping.'

'Jack, come sit down and have another coffee. You're making me tired just watching you pace the floor.'

'I shall be late for work. However, you're quite right, I suppose being a senior policeman has certain privileges: I'm entitled to another cup of coffee; I'm entitled to occasionally be late for work.'

'You know, we could have many more of these breakfasts together if you weren't working,' said Karen, as she spread honey on her toast.

Buchanan put down his cup. 'Yes, we could, but –'

'But you're not ready to retire, am I right?' she said, smiling at him.

He smiled back and pulled a grape from the bunch in the fruit bowl.

'I was in town yesterday,' she continued. 'I went into Closs and Hamblin to look at fabric for the spare room curtains.'

'Did you find what you were looking for?'

'No, that's one of the reasons I wanted you to come with me. I need your opinion.'

He looked at the time display on his phone. 'I really should go to work; I have reports to complete.'

'But you're in charge, you deserve to be late occasionally.'

He grinned. 'You're quite right, I can be on time tomorrow. Would you pour me another coffee, please?'

♦

Buchanan drove into the car park at Hammonds Drive police station and parked beside an empty slot usually occupied by DS Street's car. He looked at the time and smiled; he was exactly two hours late – one of the benefits of being a senior policeman. He was puzzled though, Street was usually in the office before this; where was she?

As he walked past the reception desk he asked, 'Anyone heard from DS Street – I mean Hunter – this morning?'

The duty sergeant shook her head and said, 'Sorry Jack, no.'

It was funny he thought as he walked down the corridor, just how one gets used to the norm and finds it difficult to change. Jill Street, his partner, had been married to Constable Stephen Hunter for almost a year now, and he still couldn't get used to her new surname. But since she was known to everyone as DS Jill Street she'd decided, after discussing it with her husband, to continue with the Street surname. Besides, in her mind, she was still fifty percent of the Buchanan and Street combination.

He pushed his office door open with his foot, walked in, and placed his coffee and slice of banana bread on his desk. Like so many times previously, he took off his jacket, hung it on the back of his chair then sat down at his desk to read his copy of the *Eastbourne Herald*.

The article on county lines drug gangs moving out of major cities and into local towns, and about how vulnerable people and young children were being sucked into the mess, had him grinding his teeth. At least some of these county lines gangs' plans had been thwarted. Last week he'd been to a press conference where he had been informed that, during the previous six months, eighty-seven county lines gangs had had their plans foiled, and that had led to 133 arrests. He smiled to himself when he thought about the government's plans to substantially increase police numbers, plus provide an additional ten thousand prison places. He put down the paper thinking that it might be time to bring back national service.

There were at least two real successes for the police, albeit for the National Crime Agency. The two men who had been arrested for making untraceable firearms in a unit on Diplocks Way, Hailsham, had been found guilty. In the old days they'd have been in for twenty years at least and spend them sewing mailbags as a punishment. Instead they'd been sentenced to eighteen and eleven years in jail but would probably only serve half of those. The second was the breakup of a stolen-car chop shop in Hellingly, near Hailsham. Two local men had been arrested and soon would

3

be appearing in court charged with the dismantling and sale of stolen car parts.

Buchanan picked up his copy of the weekend incident report lying on his desk and read that a significant quantity of tools had been stolen from a construction compound by the castle at the far end of Westham village – his village. In the list of stolen tools were two spades, a toolbox containing various spanners, a hand saw, an 18-volt cordless drill and a 16-volt Makita cordless chainsaw. Closer to home, one of his local churches in Pevensey had the lead stripped from its roof. The report said it was especially sad as the church was a 13th-century building with a Grade 1 listing.

But not all was gloom and doom in Eastbourne. The previous Friday, he and Karen had gone to see a comedy stage performance of *The 39 Steps* at the Devonshire Park Theatre. When he'd purchased the tickets, he wasn't quite sure what to expect as he'd read the story many years ago and didn't remember it being that much of a comedy. That said, he and Karen had enjoyed it immensely.

It had been a busy weekend as Airbourne, Eastbourne's annual fly-by extravaganza of mostly military aircraft, took place on the seafront. The programme, including an RAF Typhoon, Chinook helicopter, wing walkers, and helicopter rides around Beachy Head, had the town buzzing. Topping off the air display was a fly-by of the Battle of Britain Memorial Flight consisting of a Lancaster, Hurricane and Spitfire.

As he read the word 'Spitfire', he glanced up at the clock and wondered, just where was Jill? She was usually in the office by now; it was extremely unusual for her to be this late. He turned on his computer to check his emails when the door opened, and an ashen-faced Street walked in.

'What's the matter, Jill? Are you all right? Come in and sit down. Would you like some water?'

'Yes, please,' she mumbled.

Buchanan got up and took a bottle of water from the office fridge.

4

'Thanks,' she said, taking a sip. 'I've felt better. Must have been something I ate last night.'

'What did you have?'

'Stephen and I went out for a curry with Morris and Debbie.'

'Where did you go?'

'We went to the Royal Indian in Hailsham, the food was great.'

'Was it spicy?'

'Not any more than usual,' she said, screwing the cap back on the bottle. 'Sorry I'm late.'

'That's all right. Do you need to go home?'

'No, I'll be fine. Could do with a coffee and something to eat, my last breakfast went down the toilet.'

'Starbucks?'

'Sounds just what I need. Would you mind driving?'

'Not at all. It's quiet today, not much happening.'

'You realise you shouldn't say that you'll jinx the day.'

'Nah, that's just an old police superstition. Nothing is going to happen today.'

♦

'Feeling better?' asked Buchanan, as he watched Street wash down the last of her bacon roll with a large cup of coffee.

'Yes thanks.'

'How is Stephen? Did he have the same food as you?'

'No, he had lamb, I had chicken.'

'If you're feeling better, I think we should be getting back to the office. I have a mountain of paperwork to attend to.'

'You go on out, I'll get my coffee in a takeaway cup and join you.'

♦

'What do we have on today?' asked Street, as she followed Buchanan along the corridor to their office.

'Mostly paperwork.'

'That will make a change, be nice to have a chance to catch up. Oh, thanks for the coffee and bacon roll.'

'You're welcome.'

'I'll just pop down to the canteen and reheat my coffee.'

Street returned a few minutes later. 'Funny how coffee never quite tastes the same after being microwaved.'

'Not to worry, we can stop by Starbucks and get a fresh one on our way to the next incident.'

'What's that?'

'Control has just called to tell us about a report from a resident, a Mrs Driscoll, in Westham.'

'And what did she report?'

'That her dog had unearthed what looked like a human hand in the flower bed.'

'See, I told you, you've jinxed the day.'

'Nonsense, that's just superstition.'

'You could say that, but I won't comment further. What did she mean by what *looked* like a human hand?'

'Apparently she didn't want the dog to go near to what it had dug up, so she stayed indoors and called 999.'

'Do we have an address?'

'Yes. Just up the road from where I live in Westham, house name Hibernia. It's on Gallows Lane, just off Rattle Road.'

'Well, since we haven't much else to do this morning, let's go have a look at the hand from the flower bed.'

♦

Hibernia was a large bungalow on the right near the top of Gallows Lane; it had been extended at the rear and the loft converted into a bedroom.

He drove up the driveway and stopped behind a blue Toyota Rav4. As they approached the front door, it opened, and a distraught Mrs Driscoll exited onto the top step. Beside her was an agitated brown Staffy Cross.

'Mrs Driscoll? Detective Sergeant Street and Detective Chief Inspector Buchanan. I understand your dog has found what appears to be a human hand in your flower bed?'

'Trust Diesel,' she said. looking down at her dog. 'He's always up to mischief, Sergeant. He's really a good dog.'

6

'I'm sure he is,' said Street, bending down to pat Diesel. 'What have you found, Diesel?'

At the sound of his name Diesel, tail wagging furiously, tried to jump up at Street.

'Down, Diesel. I'm sorry, Sergeant, he's still just a big puppy.'

'That's all right,' said Street, reaching down to scratch Diesel behind the ear. 'Could you show us where the object is?'

'Yes, of course, this way.'

As Mrs Driscoll turned to go back into the house, Diesel, sensing he was about to be the centre of attention, tail still wagging vigorously, pushed ahead.

'This way, Sergeant. It's lying on the patio. I just couldn't bring myself to touch it,' she said, stopping in front of the kitchen window and pointing at Diesel's recent find. 'The door's not locked. If you don't mind, I'll wait here with Diesel.'

'No problem, we'll take care of it,' said Buchanan, reaching for the door handle.

Street stepped out on to the patio behind Buchanan and closed the door behind them.

'What do you think, Jack, male or female?' she asked, bending down to look at Diesel's bit of buried treasure.

'Could it be a woman's hand?' wondered Buchanan, crouching down beside Street.

'I don't think so,' said Street, 'no nail polish.'

'Some men wear nail polish.'

'More likely a man who does manual work,' said Street, as she stood up and took out her phone to call control. 'DS Street. Can we have a CSI team to house name Hibernia, Gallows Lane, Westham – yes, homeowner's dog has just unearthed a human hand – which one? The right.'

Street reached for the kitchen door as Mrs Driscoll opened it a crack and asked, 'Is it real?'

'Yes, I'm afraid it is. I've asked for a CSI team to attend. I'm sorry, but it will mean quite a bit of disruption while they investigate.'

'For how long?'

'I can't answer that. It depends on what they find.'

'Oh well, I suppose I should go and put the kettle on. Tea?'

'Yes, please,' said Street.

As Mrs Driscoll went off to make the teas, Buchanan and Street returned to stare at Diesel's garden find.

'Definitely a right hand,' said Street. 'Pity there's no tattoos or rings.'

'Probably fox food,' said Buchanan. 'They like to bury their finds, then come back when it's rotted down a bit.'

Buchanan and Street returned to the kitchen and an overly excited Diesel. While Street petted Diesel, Buchanan said, 'If you don't mind, we'll wait indoors till the CSI team arrive.'

'So, it is a human hand?'

'Yes, but where it came from, I have no idea. Is there a cemetery anywhere near here?'

'Yes, behind the church at the end of the High Street. Do you think it came from there, Inspector?'

'It's a possibility, especially in the countryside. Badgers have been known to dig up graves whilst looking for human remains. I recall an incident in a graveyard, somewhere in Leicester, where badgers were creating problems by digging up old graves and leaving human bones strewn all over the ground.'

'When I was a lot younger than I am today,' said Mrs Driscoll, 'my parents took us camping. During the night a badger got into the tent and tried to steal our food.'

'I've never been camping,' said Street.

'Oh, you should try it sometime, our children loved it.'

'I don't have any,' said Street, smiling down at Diesel.

'You're still young, plenty of time for children.'

'Thanks.'

'And Inspector, you think this might be the work of a fox, or maybe a badger?'

'It's a bit early to come to that sort of conclusion.'

'Most likely scavenged by a roaming fox, there are lots of them around here. I have to keep Diesel in at night otherwise he would be out there chasing them.'

Their conversation was interrupted by Buchanan's phone ringing.

'Buchanan – they have – what's the name – Mrs Reynolds. OK, we'll get over there right now. Where is it – got that – the allotments on Rattle Road. Location – behind the telephone exchange. That's just down the road from here, thanks.'

'What's happened?'

'A report from a resident on Rattle Road. They have just unearthed a human hand on their allotment.'

'I suppose that will be the other hand,' said Mrs Driscoll. 'Will your CSI people want tea?'

'I expect so,' said Buchanan, swallowing the last of his.

'You know you can get indigestion, swallowing your tea that quick,' said Mrs Driscoll.

'Thank you for that, my wife says the same thing.'

♦

'There's the entrance, and I'll bet that is Mrs Reynolds,' said Street, as Buchanan drove up on to the grass verge by the telephone exchange.

'Mrs Reynolds?' asked Buchanan.

'Yes. Are you the police?'

'Detective Chief Inspector Buchanan and Detective Sergeant Street.'

'It's up there,' she said, indicating a path beyond the wooden gate.

They followed Mrs Reynolds up the path between a recently trimmed leylandii hedge and a chain-link fence. As they walked, she pointed and said, 'That's a fox track. No matter how often we mow the grass the fox always walks the same trail.'

'This is yours?' asked Street. 'It's huge. How do you find time to look after all this?'

'Before she died, my neighbour shared the allotment with me. But now she's no longer around I was just getting on with what I could.'

'Will you have to give up the allotment?' asked Street.

'No, my husband is going to share it with me. The hand is over there, in the new asparagus bed,' she said, nodding towards it. 'Do you think your people will dig up the whole allotment looking for a body?'

'I think not,' said Buchanan.

'Good. I only just weeded the last crop of beets, carrots and beans and it would be a pity to lose them.'

'You can relax, Mrs Reynolds. Having the police dig over the whole plot looking for bodies only happens in jokes.'

Street followed Buchanan past the sweet peas and where Mrs Reynolds had been tending her summer crop. They stopped at a small mound of fresh earth and the errant hand.

'What do you think, Jill?' said Buchanan, crouching down to get a closer look.

'Without touching it, I'd say since it's a left hand, probably the opposing hand to the one on Gallows Lane. It looks like it could do with washing.'

'Jill, would you call Henry Littlejohn and ask him to join us here at the allotments when he's finished at Gallows Lane? You can tell him we have another hand, and please, no card jokes.'

'Will do,' said Street, as they walked past a mass of sweet peas in blossom. She stopped, bent forward to smell the scent and sneezed.

'I think we'll wait here,' said Buchanan, sitting on the bench in front of the allotment shed.

'If you are going to wait here,' said Mrs Reynolds, 'would you like a cup of tea? I usually have one about this time of day.'

'Yes, please,' said Street.

'Milk and sugar in your tea?'

Street nodded. 'Yes, please.'

'And the Inspector?'

Street turned and looked at Buchanan. He was fast asleep on the bench, snoring quietly.

'Yes, please, a splash of milk and two sugars for the inspector.'

At the sound of the tea being stirred, Buchanan woke and sat up.

'Thanks for the tea.'

'You're welcome. OK if I go and do some weeding? I'll work over at the far end of the plot; I'll stay well away from the hand.'

'That should be fine,' said Buchanan.

As he sipped on his tea, he said, 'You know, Jill, this morning Karen was suggesting, in a nice way, that I should retire. What do you think of that?'

'What would you do with your time?'

'Look at Mrs Reynolds, scratching in the dirt, singing to herself quite happily. Not a care in the world.'

'Don't see you on your knees pulling weeds.'

'Maybe not pulling weeds, but just look and listen,' he said, gesturing with open arms, 'it's so peaceful – reminds me of a day long ago.'

'Long ago?'

'I guess I would have been about twelve or thirteen at the time. It was the school summer holidays and I was bored. All my friends had gone away with their families, so I went for a long bike ride up towards Eaglesham. There's a golf course up there and as long as you didn't get in the way of the golfers you could just wander. Not sure if you could do that today, though.'

'Sounds lovely.'

'It was, what memory tells me, a perfect day. It had not rained for days; the grass was green, and the fields were almost ripe for harvest. I parked my bike, climbed over the wall, and walked about a hundred yards into the long grass and lay down. I stared up at the passing clouds and imagined they were huge airships collecting thoughts and dreams of those they flew over. The only sound I heard was that of lapwings as they rose up out of the grass – look over there, see that?'

11

'See what?'

'Three feet from where Mrs Reynolds is digging, a robin waiting for her to turn up a worm. Humankind and nature working in unison.'

'Isn't that what we do? Digging in the filth of life waiting for something to turn up?'

'Talking of turning up, here's Dr Mansell with Henry Littlejohn and the CSI team.'

Buchanan stood up and waited for Mansell and Littlejohn to join them.

'Morning Buchanan. Running out of bodies, you're now dealing with parts?'

'Good morning to you too, Andrew.'

'Where is it, where is the other hand?'

'You're assuming they are from the same body?'

'How many hands – what –what's so funny, why are you laughing? Those hands belonged to a living breathing human being.'

'An old joke,' said Buchanan, 'many hands make light work – you must remember it?'

'High school was many years ago, Jack, I've grown up since then.'

'The hand is on aisle three, between the sweet peas and the beans,' continued Buchanan.

'Very funny, and I suppose you two are the checkout?'

♦

'Thank you, Mrs Reynolds,' said Mansell, taking the offered cup of tea.

'Well, Andrew, your initial thoughts?' said Buchanan.

'Initial thoughts,' said Mansell. 'Both hands are from the same body, probably male, aged between twenty and thirty. No obvious tattoos or distinguishing marks, but whoever removed them from the body was no surgeon. I'd say they have only been in the ground for two to three days. I can give you a more detailed answer when I get them back to the lab. If I were you, I'd be calling the hospitals to see if any young men have been brought in suffering from some sort of industrial accident.'

'Could he have been a tree surgeon?' pondered Buchanan.

'Possibly. There was a case a few years ago where an unfortunate tree surgeon cut his own head off with his chainsaw. Not sure how you'd cut off both hands though.'

'What about you, Henry? Have you found anything other than the hand?'

'No, nothing.'

'Good. I'll give you a call later, Andrew,' said Buchanan, as Mansell started down the path behind Littlejohn and his CSI team.

'Can I go back to weeding?' asked Mrs Reynolds.

'Certainly, and thanks for your patience and the tea.'

'What's next?' Street asked Buchanan.

'Let's go and have a look at a graveyard, see if any graves have been disturbed.

◆

Buchanan parked in the lane in front of the manse and followed Street along the narrow paths around the church building and into the graveyard.

'Graveyards always look a bit tired to me,' said Street.

'How about that one over there?'

'That's a fresh one.'

Buchanan looked at Street. 'Talking of fresh, I think one of us could do with an early night.'

'Do I look that tired?'

Buchanan nodded. 'I'll run us back to the station and drop you off. Tomorrow will probably be a paperwork day, not often we get two hands in one day.'

◆

'You know you've mellowed quite a bit since we moved down from Glasgow,' said Karen, as they sat down for dinner.

'You think so?'

'You used to come home from work and the first thing you'd do was open a beer and go sit in your chair and not speak to me for an hour.'

'And now?'

'You walk in the door, give me a kiss and ask how my day's been.'

'I hadn't realised I'd changed.'

'You have.'

'I hope that's a good sign.'

'It is, and that statement sounds like it requires a glass of wine. You go through to the lounge and I'll bring the wine.'

Buchanan leaned back in his chair and raised the footrest. Two severed hands worried him. He was well aware of the practice of kneecapping in Northern Ireland being used to send a very violent message not to step out of line. Then there was the hideous practice in certain parts of the world where thieves had their hands surgically removed as a punishment. But never both hands. This was England – it just didn't make sense.

'Your wine,' said Karen, handing Buchanan a tall wine glass half-full of red wine.

'Thanks.'

'How was your day?' she asked.

'It was a two-hand day.'

'You and Jill were playing cards?'

'No, we found two human hands.'

'No body?'

'No body.'

2
Tue AM
Amal Barazani

Buchanan drove into the police car park and parked by a shiny black series five BMW. He glanced at the registration, HEL1N and wondered what had brought Helen Markham, the Assistant Chief Constable, down from the ivory towers of police headquarters in Lewes. Surely a pair of hands didn't warrant such a visit, so what could it be? Probably just another futile attempt at getting him to retire.

As he passed the booking-in desk, the duty constable said, 'You have visitors, Jack.'

'Where is she?'

'She and the gentleman with her just popped out to McDonalds for a cup of coffee. She said they'd won't be long.'

'Gentleman? Description?'

'Greying hair, middle-aged, built like a rugby player. He was driving a green Aston Martin DB11.'

'Did you see the registration?'

'GSP1.'

Buchanan entered his office, trying to make sense of the visit of Sir Nathan Greyspear and Helen Markham at seven fifty-five on a Monday morning. Unlikely to have anything to do with hands that were found the previous day.

Other than the severed hands, he was pleased at how the town was behaving itself. Leaning back in his chair, coffee at the ready, he turned to the business at hand, patio furniture for the new house. Now that spring had passed, and with summer peeking over the horizon, Karen had decided it was time to prepare for barbeques and garden parties.

But before he had time to open the Robert Dyas summer sale brochure, the sound of approaching footsteps heralded the arrival of a distraction he could well do without this morning.

'Good morning, Jack,' said Helen.

Buchanan looked away from the brochure and at Assistant Chief Constable Helen Markham. Before she joined the police force, she'd been a Marine and had served two tours in Afghanistan; here was someone he could work with.

'Sorry to interrupt your day, but something has come up and we need to have a chat.'

'Good morning, Helen, Nathan,' replied Buchanan, realising his idea of a quiet week in Eastbourne was vanishing like the smile on Lewis Carroll's Cheshire cat.

'Good morning, Jack,' said Sir Nathan, pulling a chair over from the wall and placing it in front of Buchanan's desk for the ACC to sit.

'Thanks, Nathan,' said Markham.

Greyspear picked up a second chair and placed it beside Markham's.

'How can I help?' asked Buchanan.

'Sir Nathan contacted me yesterday about a problem one of his business friends is having with his daughter and I thought of you.'

Buchanan smiled. 'That was kind of you.'

'My friend's name is Amal Barazani,' said Greyspear. 'His daughter is missing, and he has not been able to find her.'

'Why hasn't he reported her missing through the regular channels?'

'He's concerned she has been kidnapped.'

'Then why didn't he contact the Anti Kidnap Extortion Unit?'
'What's that?' asked Greyspear.

'It's a specialist department within the National Crime Agency.'
'What do they do?'

'They work to secure the safe release of hostages and to deal covertly and professionally with any form of blackmail or

16

extortion. The unit provides specialist 24/7 strategic and tactical support to UK and international law enforcement agencies. The team also delivers specialist training to governments, police and the private sector nationally and internationally,' recited Buchanan from memory.

'Thanks. But my friend doesn't want to attract attention in case she has just run away.'

'Quite a normal reaction. Has she done that before?'

'More than once,' said Greyspear.

'So, what do you want me to do, and why?'

'Would you go and talk to him and see what is going on?' said Markham. 'Find out if it's just a simple case of a spoilt girl being a brat.'

'For your information, Jack' said Greyspear, 'Amal Barazani owns Mastrani; they are one of the top computer software development companies in the UK.'

'Mastrani? I've never heard of them.'

'That's not surprising, they tend to keep a low profile.'

'So, do you think it could be a case of kidnap for ransom?'

'Amal's company is currently working on several important government contracts,' said Greyspear. 'It's possible his daughter has been kidnapped to extort trade secrets from him.'

'So, my question remains, why hasn't he gone to the Anti Kidnap Extortion Unit?'

'That's what we want you to find out,' said Markham.

'Someone else once said that to me,' said Buchanan. 'OK, I'll go have a word with him – can I have his company address?'

'I can drive you,' said Greyspear. 'Amal is at the club waiting for me. He is reluctant to attract attention to the situation by coming to the police station.'

'That makes sense.'

♦

As they drove into Castlewood, Buchanan reminisced about the last time he was here and his fourth place in the Castlewood Cup.

'Did you ever hear anything from Cynthia Mountjoy and Pat? Did they get married?' asked Greyspear, as he drove slowly up the driveway to the clubhouse

'Not since the race. Before they left, Cynthia asked me again if I would give her away when she and Pat got married. I expect they are waiting to hear what happened to her husband before they set a date.'

'Plane crash in the channel is what you said,' said Greyspear.

'Yep, the wreckage is yet to be recovered. Before we go in, what can you tell me about your friend, Amal Barazani?'

'Amal Barazani has a conglomerate of companies connected with software. They include but are not limited to games, accounting and ant-virus software. He's known to take chances with fledgling ideas and seems to act mostly on impulse. He appears to be an excellent judge of a person's abilities. For instance, he might meet someone at a party and sign them on the spot. Sudden ideas are converted into improbable, yet highly profitable, software ventures. Games are invented that ought never to have existed, yet with skilful marketing they top the computer game league tables. He acts speedily and never flinches from taking a decision, he doesn't like to lose, and if you're not careful, he'll have you working for him.'

'An interesting character, but I already have a job and am happy doing it,' said Buchanan, as they entered the club reception.

'Amal should be waiting in the library,' said Greyspear, as he nodded at the receptionist.

♦

'Let me introduce you,' said Greyspear, as they entered the library. 'Amal, this is my friend I was telling you about, Detective Chief Inspector Jack Buchanan.'

'Hi, Jack,' said Barazani, standing.

'Amal,' said Buchanan, shaking his hand before sitting. 'Nathan has told me your daughter is missing. Can you tell me why you think so?'

'Her backpack and clothes aren't in her room.'

'Could she have just gone away for a couple of days? Have you checked with her friends?'

'Those that she has.'

'What about money?'

'She took her mother's jewellery with her.'

'Was it valuable?'

'Yes, especially the diamond ring. It is worth more than five years of your salary.'

'Could she be intending to sell them and set up home somewhere?'

Barazani shook his head. 'The jewels are priceless. Her mother's wedding band and engagement ring are precious to her. They are all she has to remember her mother by. Besides, she doesn't need to sell them to survive. She has a trust fund that, when she reaches the age of twenty-one, will keep her in comfort for the rest of her life.'

'Does she have any hobbies?'

'Not now. When she was much younger, her grandmother would take her and her cousin horse riding together.'

'So, why do you think she's disappeared?'

'That's what we would like you to find out, Jack,' said Greyspear.

'Can I have her name?' asked Buchanan, taking out his notebook.

'Zilini.'

'Same surname as you?'

'Yes.'

'The address in Eastbourne?'

'Shalom, Auckland Quay, North Harbour.'

Buchanan thought for a moment, then, 'You're a neighbour of Nathan?'

Barazani smiled at a memory. 'Yes, two doors down the road, close enough to pop round and borrow a cup of sugar.'

'And is your daughter usually there with you all week?'

Barazani flicked through a couple of screens on his phone. 'No, she's at university and lives in halls of residence during the week. Her address is Flat 1C, Paddock Field, University of Brighton, Falmer.'

'Her date of birth? And do you have a recent photo of her?'

'We just celebrated her eighteenth birthday a few weeks ago. This photo was taken at her birthday party,' he said, scrolling through his photo album on his phone. 'She's always been such a capricious child, especially since her mother died.'

'What's that one?' asked Buchanan, spotting a video.

'Ah, that was a pleasant surprise, Inspector, I recorded her singing.'

'May I have a copy of her singing?'

'Certainly, I'll message that and a photo to you. What's your phone number?'

Buchanan looked at the photo of the eighteen-year-old Zilini. Eyes sparkling, hair flying as she danced, her singing video would wait till he was elsewhere.

'Is she single – married?'

'She's single but has a boyfriend, Zac Taylor, he's a twin. Not someone I would choose for her. He came for dinner a few times, and I admit I was warming to him till one Saturday I invited him for a barbecue. Unfortunately, Zac brought his brother – what a mistake that was.'

'Why was it a mistake?'

'His brother was high on something and made a real nuisance of himself.'

'Can you describe Zac?'

'I'm five foot eight, he was probably about an inch taller than me.'

'Colour of hair?'

He shrugged. 'Dark, he had it close cropped. He did have one of those narrow beards and a pencil-thin moustache. Made him look like a 1950's spiv.'

'Any scars, tattoos?'

'None that I'm aware of.'

'Anything else?'

'No, sorry Inspector.'

'Do you have an address for him?'

'No, but my PA may have.'

'We'll need to talk with her.'

'She'll be in the office.'

'Can I have the address?'

Barazani shook his head and smiled. 'You'd think I'd remember something as simple as that but being dyslexic, numbers confuse me. My dyslexia is so bad I have to keep my bank card pin numbers in my phone as fictitious phone numbers.'

'A lot of successful people in the world are dyslexic.'

'I go to the office almost every day of the week, but I can't tell you if the number is 371 or 137 or 317. But you can't miss it, it's the large white building on the left at the end of Commercial Road in Eastbourne. The Mastrani name is in gold letters on the office door.'

'Have you talked to the boyfriend?'

'He's not answering his phone. We've left messages, but he never calls back, and when I had one of my people check at his flat, they were told no one had seen him since last week.'

'Do you have any other family living in the UK, somewhere your daughter could have gone to?'

'I have a brother, well actually a stepbrother. My mother died when I was three, and my father, Yousef, remarried Hiezabel shortly after.'

'Can I have your stepbrother's name, please?'

'His name is Nasim, his wife is Bahija and they have a son, Achmad.'

'Do they live locally?'

'Yes.'

'Can I have his address, please?'

'Just a minute,' replied Barazani, as he picked up his phone and scrolled through several screens. 'Their address is Kilmarnock,

21

Marshfoot Lane, Hailsham. They've just moved in; I don't have a phone number for them.'

'Do you have any other relatives living in the UK?'

'Sort of. My father and stepmother have a house in Meads.'

'Do you have their address?'

'Yes. Lytchett, Upper Carlisle Road, Meads, Eastbourne.'

'You remember it well,' said Buchanan, smiling as he wrote down the address.

'It's numbers I have issues with, plus my stepmother won't let us forget it.'

'Have they always lived in Meads?'

'My stepmother was born in Saudi Arabia. When the weather gets too cold for her in the UK, they visit her family in Jeddah.'

'Could your daughter have gone to stay with your father and his wife in Meads?'

'It's possible, but highly unlikely, we're not that close on my side of the family. Besides my stepmother is very traditional and likes to ridicule the way Zilini and I live our lives.'

'Do you know if they are in the country at present?'

'Yes, I talked with my father yesterday afternoon. He said he hadn't spoken to Zilini since her birthday party.'

'Could Zilini have gone to stay with the family in Hailsham?'

'I had my assistant call the house and, when asked, my sister-in-law said she hadn't seen Zilini since a week ago Thursday.'

'When did you first realise your daughter was missing?'

'Saturday morning, when the housekeeper went in with her morning coffee.'

'You have a housekeeper?'

'Yes. Since my wife became ill and sadly passed away, running a business and having a young child to look after was too much for me to handle. So, engaging a housekeeper was the ideal situation.'

'Does your daughter always have coffee brought to her room on Saturday mornings?'

'Yes, when she's here.'

'Does she come home every weekend?'

'Not every weekend. She sometimes has lectures on Saturdays and, if she does, she'll stay the weekend on campus in Falmer.'

'Did she come home last Friday evening?'

'Yes, we had dinner together before I went out.'

'What time was this?'

He shrugged. 'I went out about seven, I don't really remember an exact time.'

'What was the mood at dinner?'

'Frosty. I put my foot in it by saying her boyfriend wasn't really suitable for her.'

'Did you argue?'

'A bit, but nothing really serious.'

'And that was the last time you saw her?'

'Yes. I had to go into the office after dinner. When I got home, I watched the evening news then went to bed. As I walked along the corridor to my bedroom, I could hear music being played in her room.'

'What time was that?'

'About eleven-thirty.'

'Did you say goodnight?'

'No. I was tired and just wanted to get to bed.'

'How do you know she was home?'

'I heard her radio playing; she tends to leave it on as she is getting ready for bed.'

'Is there a current Mrs Barazani?'

'Not quite, but I have a stable relationship with someone. My first wife died fifteen years ago after a long illness. It's really just Zilini and me.'

'Could your daughter have gone to stay with your friend?'

'Unlikely, Charlotte lives comfortably and alone in her flat in Meads.'

'If your daughter had gone there, would Charlotte have let you know?'

He nodded. 'I was with Charlotte yesterday, there was no sign of Zilini.'

'Could I have Charlotte's address, just for the record?'

'Mount Road, Eastbourne. I don't know the number.'

'The housekeeper who takes Zilini her coffee, how long has she been the housekeeper?'

'She became Zilini's nursemaid after my wife became ill. Her name is Darsameen, she lives in and looks after the house, so I have now made her the housekeeper.'

'Regarding your daughter, why didn't you just make a missing person's report?'

'At first I wasn't sure she was missing.'

'Then what exactly is your concern about your daughter?'

'It's possible she may have been abducted for ransom.'

'Would you describe yourself as wealthy?'

'It isn't a simple matter of a ransom for cash,' he said, slowly shaking his head. 'No, not cash. It's more likely going to be industrial blackmail.'

'What do you mean by industrial blackmail?'

'My company is working on some sensitive projects. If details fall into the wrong hands it could put internet security back into the stone age.'

'He isn't exaggerating, Jack,' said Greyspear. 'Amal's company is working on some cutting-edge technology.'

'Have you made a will? If so, who are the beneficiaries from it?'

'My daughter Zilini is the main beneficiary, she inherits eighty percent, then there are some small bequests to a few other people.'

'Do you suspect anyone of kidnapping your daughter?'

'No one comes to mind.'

'How about employees who have been let go recently? Someone with a grudge, maybe?'

'I don't know. You'd have to ask personnel about that.'

'And where would I find your personnel department?'

'Along with my PA in my office in Eastbourne.'

'Thank you, I'll do that later. Have you heard anything from these possible abductors? Do you have a ransom note?' asked Buchanan.

Barzani reached into his jacket pocket and removed a well-fingered padded envelope. 'This arrived yesterday,' he said, passing it over to Buchanan.

Buchanan grimaced as he saw how casually Barazani handled the envelope. Forensics would have a lot of extra work checking it for prints and DNA. Buchanan held the envelope by its edges, squeezed the sides and looked inside. 'No note?'

Barazani shook his head. 'Just the empty ring box.'

Buchanan slid the bright red ring box out onto the desk and carefully opened it. 'No ring either?'

'The rings in the collection are family heirlooms.' Barazani said and, for the first time that morning, Buchanan saw a look of sadness on his face. 'The rings were a special gift for Zilini on her eighteenth birthday, a sort of coming of age present. The wedding band and engagement rings were her mother's and go back three generations. I had the jeweller resize the wedding band and the engagement ring. They were the rings her mother and own grandmother wore when they got married. Zilini can't remember her mother and never knew her own grandmother, that is why she said one day she would wear the rings at her own wedding in their honour. The rings are reputed to have come from the Romanoff jewels that were looted when the family were murdered by the Bolsheviks.'

'Do you have a photo of the rings?'

Barazani shook his head.

'How about the jewellers where the ring was altered? Are they local?'

'No. Their workshop is located in the town of Farnham.'

'Can I have their contact details?'

'I don't have that with me, my PA will have it in the office.'

'Have you talked with your daughter's friends? Have you asked them if they know where she might be?' asked Buchanan.

'She doesn't have many really close friends. The ones she has have been contacted, none of them have heard from her since last week.'

'How about her cousin, Achmad? Do you think he would know where she might be?'

'I doubt it, they don't get on. Though I believe his grandmother thinks he and Zilini would make a good match.'

'Why is that?'

'She thinks if they got married it would put an end to Zilini's petulance and at the same time reunite the family.'

'Cousins don't usually get married in this country.'

'Oh, they're not directly related. Hiezabel, my stepmother, was married before. Nasim was her son by her first husband who drowned when his fishing boat sank in the Gulf. My father adopted Nasim shortly after he married Hiezabel, hence Nasim has the same surname as me.'

'Would it bother you if Zilini decided to marry Achmad?'

'I'd be disappointed, but, if it were her wish, I'd go along with it. Ever since her mother died, I've tried to make her happy.'

'The commissioner said you have your own security people; can you explain what is meant by that?'

'I own and run a technology company that specialises in discrete software solutions. Many blue-chip companies use our products and as such we keep those solutions tightly guarded. Hence our security measures.'

'And they are?'

Barzani looked at Greyspear. 'Nathan, you assured me the police would be discrete and not ask too many questions.'

'Amal,' said Greyspear, 'Inspector Buchanan is one of Sussex CID's best detectives. If we are to find out the truth about your daughter's apparent disappearance, you will need to trust him.'

'OK. What do you want to know, Inspector?'

'You mentioned that you had a stepbrother?'

'Nasim, yes. He's the son of my father's second wife, but we don't see much of them.'

'Why is that?'

'He says they don't agree with our lifestyle.'

'They?'

'My stepmother mostly.'

'In what way?'

'We are of Jewish faith, they are Muslim. My stepbrother tells me his mother says we should convert and stop bringing the family name into disrepute.'

'Not an uncommon situation these days. How long has your family lived in the UK?'

Barazani leaned back in his chair and stared over Buchanan's shoulder at the far wall. 'There's a story that's been passed down through the generations that members of my family were descended from the Jewish tribe of Benjamin. They settled in what is now called northern modern Syria. Many years ago, our ancestors called Kurdistan in northern Syria home. When the massacre in Simele happened in 1933, the family took flight and escaped before they became part of the three thousand people who lost their lives to the Iraqi forces. It was a horrible time for those Assyrians living in northern Assyria.'

'I didn't realise Kurdistan existed,' said Buchanan.

'In memory and tradition mostly. Just before the Second World War, there was a split in our family, my side came to England and the other side went to Saudi Arabia. Though my father and his second wife spend most of the year in Eastbourne, they also have an apartment in Jeddah, Saudi Arabia.'

'What does your stepbrother do for a living?'

'He works for Al Rayan Bank in London. I believe he is a junior manager.'

'Does your father work?'

'Not full-time anymore. He had a heart attack six years ago. Before his heart attack he was involved in arranging financing for people who were setting up to make movies. Now he runs workshops for those eager to get into the film industry.'

3
Tuesday Mid-morning
Mastrani

'Amal, I think it would be helpful if I were to have a look round your office. Just to familiarise myself with your operation,' said Buchanan. 'Also, could we have a sample of your fingerprints and DNA, as well as your daughter's if possible?'

'You suspect me of getting rid of Zilini?

'No, not at all. It's just to eliminate you from our enquiries.'

'It would be my pleasure; I was just about to suggest that. You can follow me.'

'I didn't drive, Nathan brought me in his car.'

'No problem, I'll drive you.'

♦

Buchanan followed Barazani out of the club and into his Rolls-Royce.

'You don't mind if I smoke, Jack?' said Barazani, lighting a cigar as he drove sedately along the road out of Castlewood.

'It's your car,' replied Buchanan, reaching for the window button.

As Barazani drove he gave Buchanan a running commentary about how wonderful it was to be living in the UK and Eastbourne in particular. Eventually he ran out of things to say about living in Eastbourne and asked Buchanan about his life and what had led to his interest in being a policeman. He listened intently and then surprised Buchanan by saying that he had always wanted to write crime stories.

'You are going to enjoy working for me,' said Barazani. 'I have a good feeling about it. Nathan told me all about you and how you think outside the box.'

'Excuse me, Amal, but I already have a full-time job.'

'Whatever.'

◆

As they approached a large two-storey building at the end of Commercial Road, Barazani slowed and pressed a button on a remote control clipped to the sun visor. In the distance Buchanan watched as a large door at the end of a block of offices slid back revealing spaces for several cars underneath. Barazani drove serenely into his allotted space and switched off the engine. They exited the car and made their way up a flight of internal steps. At the top Barazani swiped a card over a card-reader and the door slid silently back revealing a small lobby. He turned to Buchanan and smiled, then reached for the handle on the opposite door.

They stepped out of the gloom of the underground garage into a brightly-lit reception area. To the right was the main entrance to the building. Buchanan recognised the toughened glass of a secure door. In front of them was a reception desk with two receptionists, on the left was what Buchanan reasoned was the door to the office interior. One of the receptionists was busy talking on the phone, the other was talking to a visitor. Off to the left, beside the door to the garage, a uniformed security guard stood behind a counter.

As the door slid shut, the receptionist who was on the phone looked up and said, 'Good morning, Mr Barazani.'

'Good morning, Alison, any messages?'

'No.'

'You will need to sign in, Jack,' said Barazani, pointing to a tablet on the top of the security desk.

Buchanan picked up the pen, filled in his details on the tablet, then stood back.

'Please look in the camera for me, thanks,' said the security guard, as he pressed the screen on the notepad. He smiled and, reaching under the counter, removed a plastic card the size of a credit card, complete with Buchanan's photo, and passed it to him. 'This is your visitor pass, valid for today. It clips to your lapel, please wear it wherever you go in the building.'

'You will also have to leave your phone,' said Barazani. 'Phones and all forms of electronic devices are not permitted past reception.'

'Fine with me,' said Buchanan, passing his phone to the security guard who slid it into a small cotton bag and placed it in a wall locker before handing over a receipt.

Buchanan clipped his ID card to his lapel and stood in front of the reader by the door, there was a click and the door opened revealing a brightly lit corridor. Before he could follow Barazani, the security guard scanned Buchanan with a hand-held scanner.

'This is a very secure building, Jack,' said Barazani. 'This way, follow me.'

'What's to stop me wandering off anywhere in the building?'

'Your visitor pass would alert security that you are in an unauthorised area and would prevent you from going anywhere except back to reception.'

'Hmm, like ankle tagging for criminals?'

Barazani smiled and said, 'precisely, but a lot more polite for our visitors.'

Walking along the brightly polished vinyl-covered corridor behind Barazani reminded Buchanan of being at school. The next thing he noticed was the rhythmic dance music emanating from the open doors of the offices as they passed. The atmosphere resembled that of a high school on steroids. In whole the building vibrated with youthful vigour; he felt like a fish out of water.

'The premises were once a printworks, after that a BT call centre,' said Barazani. 'The offices extend in a ramshackle way over three buildings.' He noticed Buchanan sniffing the air as they walked to his office. 'Formaldehyde, Jack. My offices are over an undertaker's premises but don't worry, it's not contagious.'

Buchanan thought it smelled of something else, something he had noticed when he and Karen had visited Amsterdam the previous year.

He smiled when he saw the pictures on the walls – not the energetic photos of fast cars and aeroplanes, but screenshots of characters from video games.

Barazani opened his office door and gestured Buchanan to follow. Mounted on the wall behind the leather-topped desk was a stuffed ferret, its teeth sunk deep into the neck of a rabbit.

'You like it?' he asked, motioning Buchanan to sit opposite him at the desk. 'I call him Mustela. The ferret is a crafty hunter, Jack. It lies in wait, then pounces. It attacks everything, and nothing gets the better of him.'

Barazani drew himself up regally in his chair. The ferret's head showed just above his, its eyes shining brightly, seeming to stare directly at Buchanan. To Buchanan, the head below looked out of place. All it needed was a *keffiyeh* to go with the beard and, with his prominent nose, Barazani would look like any Saudi prince. He was king of his own domain. Buchanan had met many interesting people in his career as a policeman, but not many as flamboyant as Amal Barazani.

Barazani got up from his desk and walked over to the sideboard. 'Coffee, Jack?'

'Please. Black, no sugar.'

Barazani poured Buchanan's coffee, set it on the desk, then began to pace the floor like a powerful caged animal. His Savile Row suit did its best to hide his muscular frame. In his breast pocket he sported a large blue silk handkerchief. Around the neck of a pale blue silk shirt with a white collar he wore a matching vivid-blue silk tie. There was a gold Rolex watch on his right wrist, a platinum Fitbit on his left, and on the pinkie of his right hand, a gold signet ring.

'Jack, it's not who knocks on your door that you need to worry about, but he who sneaks in behind you that you need to be aware of. I see you are wondering of what I'm speaking. Let me ask you a question. Have you ridden on London's wonderful underground system?'

'Yes, many times.'

'During rush hour?' he said, sitting down at his desk.

'On occasion.'

'You walk up to the gate, slide your ticket into the reader, the gate opens, and you walk through, correct?'

Buchanan decided to humour Barazani. 'Yes, but I get the ticket back if it is a travel card.'

'Have you ever had someone push through with you? Someone who obviously doesn't have a ticket?'

Buchanan nodded, realising where Barazani was going with the conversation.

'That's what I mean by my simple example.'

'Tell me more about your simple example.'

'Jack, do you know anything about ferrets?'

'My grandfather used to go rabbit hunting with them. When there was an issue on the farm with rats, he'd use the ferret to chase them out from their hiding place for the dog to catch and kill.'

'Precisely. Let me expand upon your knowledge base. Ferrets are docile animals and exhibit many instinctive behavioural characteristics. They are extremely intelligent, playful and curious...'

'Excuse me for interrupting,' said Buchanan, 'but I thought we were discussing what your company makes?'

Barazani raised his hand. 'Please be patient, Jack, all will come clear. As I was saying, ferrets show little fear when darting down dark tunnels seeking their prey, such as rabbits and mice, and according to your grandfather, will gladly also go after rats. Their eyesight is not great, but they are able to sense when something is moving close to them. When this occurs, they don't mess around, they just grab with their teeth and hold on. They spend most of the day resting in dark enclosed areas. When not resting they wander through the tunnels, exploring and seeking their next meal – are you still with me?'

'I'm assuming this is an analogy?'

Barazani nodded. 'My developers have been working on a piece of software which we have designated as Mustela. The Mustela program works like a ferret. It is uploaded to a client's intranet and sits quietly on the server watching and waiting for intruders. Also, with the advent of 5G and, in the not too distant future, 6G, mobile broadband, there is an urgent requirement for discrete software that will seek and isolate rogue software.'

'I'm sorry to disillusion you, Amal,' said Buchanan, 'but those types of software programs, such as Avast, MacAfee and Norton to name a few, are already available. Many of them free to download to your device.'

Barazani nodded. 'Quite so, but none of them work like our software. Mustela, like the other software you mentioned, lies dormant on the client server till an intruder arrives, then immediately quarantines them. Now, where Mustela differs from other programs is, once it has quarantined the intruder, it begins its unique procedures – am I losing you, Jack?'

'No, go on.'

'What Mustela will do when fully functional – that no other program can – is this. Once it has the intruder secured it begins the interrogation. First job is to identify the intruder by matching it against any others known and then leaving a message for the computer technicians.

'If it is a non-standard intruder, it is dissected and analysed. This process used to take up to several days for a team of software engineers; with Mustela it is almost instant. It is a perpetual self-learning program. With this information, and having access to top-secret government security databases, the intruder can easily be traced all the way back to its origins, and proper procedures put in place to neutralise it. Or if deemed appropriate – retaliate.'

'Is your company working on any other projects that might cause someone to kidnap your daughter?'

Barazani thought about it, then said, 'The Department for Transport is looking at ways of replacing the present system for charging motorists for driving on the roads. They have asked us come up with some ideas.'

'And have you?'

'Yes, we have.'

'Can you tell me what you've come up with?'

'Sure. I don't know why anyone hasn't thought of it before, it is so simple. The brief, as I said, was for us to devise a more efficient method of road charging.'

'And how do you propose to do that?'

'Initially our idea is to set up a system using a special driving card, much like the present tachograph cards. These cards will be registered to the individual driver, linked to their bank account, and connected to the internet through the vehicle's on-board engine management system. I'm sure you are aware that the government has announced that as of 2030 the sale of petrol and diesel cars will cease leaving a severe shortage of income from the tax on sale of petrol and diesel?'

'I am aware of that fact.'

'As part of our offering we are proposing that, since all new cars come fitted with GPS transponders as part of their on-board computer management, it will be a simple job for the computer to connect to the national road map and determine the distance driven and what the local speed limit is. To get on the road, all the driver has to do is to insert the card into the card reader built into the car and drive. The charge for driving will be based on the gross weight of the vehicle and the miles driven. Also, the cost of the driver's insurance will be included in the mileage charge. Of course, the insurance increment will be commensurate with the individual driver's history.'

'So those who use the road the most will pay the most.'

'Precisely, and there will be no more uninsured motorists.'

'Sounds like it might just work.'

'There is an additional bonus – one you as a policeman will approve of.'

'What's that?'

'If the driver exceeds the speed limit they will be fined in real time and have points added to their licence. If any driver exceeds the allowed penalty points while driving, the computer will simply turn off the engine and the car will drift to a safe halt.'

'What's to stop someone who's had their driving card suspended using a friend's card?'

'A very interesting question. Do you have time to listen to what some people call science fiction, and what others call the implementation of the Mark of the Beast?'

Buchanan looked up at the office wall clock. 'Sure.'

'In 1948, the scientist and inventor Harry Stockman created RFID technology that today is involved in almost every form of purchasing transaction. From those early days the technology has gone through several forms of development to where it is today, an injectable microchip.'

'You mean the things that are injected into dogs, cats, even horses?'

'My friend, technology has moved on from just injecting animals. There is a company in Israel developing a form of invisible tattoo that would perform the same function as an injected micro-chip. Today, if you have one of those chips in the back of your hand you can unlock secure doors, turn on computers. Soon you will be able to do shopping or eat out at restaurants without the need to carry cash or cards. All that and more, and, as a special bonus, you never have to worry about remembering your pin number for your bank card.'

'Just where is all this technology going?'

'I'll give you some examples. There is a company in the USA that has developed a chip that can monitor alcohol or drugs in your bloodstream. Another has developed a GPS version, so you can never get lost; or more importantly your child. or senior family member with dementia, will not wander far before being found.

There are benefits beyond those I have just mentioned. Imagine you have a bad heart; these microchips will be like having your own 24-hour attending physician who can link to your mobile and call the emergency services before you even experience symptoms of a heart attack. It might even prevent a diabetic person going into a coma by operating their inbuilt insulin supply.'

'That sounds like a good idea for certain people, but I doubt if it would work for the majority. We British are a proud bunch, and I don't see people having a chip implanted.'

'There might come a day when they don't have a choice, especially when the world moves over to a cashless society.'

'There has to be a catch somewhere.'

'I don't see one, it's the perfect solution for society, especially in the times of a national emergency. Just suppose there was a resurgence of SARS, or something even more virile. We've had world-wide plagues before. Doctors and nurses would be on the front line. They could be tested and if they are either clear of infection or have antibodies, they could use their implanted microchips as health passports and resume their duties without fear of spreading the infection. Also, if someone were diagnosed as having a contagious infection, their whereabouts could be traced and anyone who had been near them could be notified to immediately seek medical assistance.

'Or, and I think you'll like this idea, suppose someone has been assaulted, all they have to do is notify the police where and when the assault took place and by contact tracing, everyone who had been in the vicinity at the time of the attack could be traced and questioned.'

'I'm sorry, Amal, I just can't see any circumstances where an inserted microchip can solve a national emergency.'

'Have you ever heard of an American television presenter called Johnny Carson?'

'No.'

'Let me elucidate. Johnny Carson was a talk show host back in the 1970's and his show was called the *Tonight Show*. At the beginning of each show he would do a short humorous monologue to the audience. One night in 1973, as part of this, he mentioned and joked that he'd been reading a newspaper article that the nation was going to have a toilet tissue shortage.'

'Odd subject matter for a talk show host?'

'Yes and no. In reality there was no shortage of toilet tissue, but since Johnny Carson had said it live on television, the public believed him. By the end of the next day the shelves were empty of toilet tissue. That shortage lasted for four weeks.'

'That would never happen here in this country.'

Barazani shook his head. 'Have you heard of the FIG syndrome?'

'I've heard of the expression, *couldn't give a fig.*'

'So, have I. But FIG stands for Fear, Ignorance and Greed. During the Second World War food and certain items were rationed to prevent panic buying.'

'So how would RFID technology help prevent that today?'

'Some of my people have been working on that. Most of the technology to manage a panic of that sort already exists off the shelf. The program we have put together consists of using store loyalty cards, customer debit cards, internet and 5G, and of course the implanted microchip.'

'Go on, I'm listening.'

'OK. Firstly, all customers must have the microchip implanted. This chip, like fingerprints, will be unique to that individual, no two people will have the same registration number. This number will be stored in a central computer that will be linked to banking, medical, and designated government computers in various parts of the globe.'

'I don't see how this will prevent panic buying?'

'Wait a moment, all will become clear. In this example, when someone goes into the supermarket to purchase an inordinate quantity of goods, at checkout the shop computer will check the customer's shopping profile, their home consumption from their smart pantry, fridge and freezer and, if it deems that they have purchased too much, the sale will be denied.'

'I've heard of smart televisions – but smart fridge-freezers?'

'How about smart speakers?'

'Oh yes, we have one in the kitchen.'

'These days smart technology is in almost everything in the home; from speakers in the kitchen bringing you the news, to switching the lighting on and off, to controlling the central heating.'

'A bit Orwellian, don't you think? I can't quite see people willingly standing in line waiting to be injected with a microchip.'

'Jack, people are like sheep, they need a shepherd to show them which way to go and how to behave.'

'Let me ask a cynical question?'

'Be my guest.'

'What keeps these microchips running – I presume they require batteries?'

Barazani shook his head. 'Problem has already been solved. These chips are powered by a form of internal power, like a battery, but not as you would recognise them. Some chips have their power developed by variations in skin temperature, others by pulses of the beating of the heart.'

'I never realised. Just a minute though, what about people who have, for one reason or another, no hands? How will they, say, pay at the checkout at the grocery store?'

'Simple, they can have a microchip implanted in their forehead.'

'This sounds like 1984 on steroids!'

'This is only the beginning, Jack. Just wait and see what 6G will bring.'

'No thanks, I'll stick with what we have now.'

'Didn't take you for a Luddite.'

'Can we get back to the subject in hand? You think your daughter's possible disappearance could be someone trying to sneak in and steal your company secrets?'

'That's the advice my security people have suggested.'

'Could I talk to your security people before I go?'

'That won't be possible.'

'Why?'

'They're not here.'

'You mean they are taking the day off?'

'No, Jack, they are not taking the day off. They don't work directly for me.'

'A private company?'

'Yes.'

'Can I have their details? I would like to talk with them.'

Barazani opened a desk drawer, rummaged through some business cards, then passed one to Buchanan.

'Zhukovski Limousines?' Buchanan read the name on the card. 'Are you sure this is the correct card?'

Barazani smiled, 'Jack, you should know that not everything that you see is what it seems. Mr Zhukovski offers more than a limousine service.'

Buchanan wrote down the details in his notebook then handed the card back. 'I'll go and see him later. But, before I go, I'd like to talk to the person who could tell me about anyone who has been dismissed lately.'

'Certainly, I'll take you over to personnel.'

Buchanan followed Barazani back along through the maze of corridors till they came to a door that said, *Private – Knock Before Entering.*

Barazani knocked loudly, pushed the door open and walked over to a desk in the far corner of the crowded room overlooking the station.

'Denise, this is Inspector Buchanan. He would like to know if we've let anyone go lately?'

'Hello. Any particular days?'

'How about during the last six weeks?'

'That's easy, only two.'

'Could I have their details?'

'Yes, of course.'

Buchanan looked over the car park to the station and watched as an eight-coach train arrived and disgorged its passengers.

'These are the two who have left during the last six weeks,' said Denise, turning her computer screen for Buchanan to see the complete list of names of departed employees.

'Do you know why those two left the company?'

She looked at him, smiled and said, 'To get married. They're in the Maldives on their honeymoon just now.'

'Will they be returning to work?'

'No, they've emigrated to New Zealand.'

'Tell me, Denise, did you recommend Zhukovski Limousines to Mr Barazani?'

'Yes.'

'Can you tell me why?'

'I came across them while working at my last job.'

'Which was where?'

'GCHQ.'

'Thanks.'

♦

Buchanan took a taxi back to the office realising he'd missed lunch, while wondering just who this Zhukovski was and what his connection was to Amal Barazani.

'Anyone looking for me, Jill?'

'No, should there be?'

'Doesn't matter. Are you free? I need to go interview someone,'

'Sure, who?'

'A Russian security advisor who runs a limousine service.'

Street looked at Buchanan.

'No, it's true, c'mon, get your coat, you won't need your passport.'

'What's the hurry?'

'If this is a case of kidnapping, Jill, we've no time to waste. But if it is just a case of a missing daughter who's done a runner with her boyfriend, we must still use all efforts to return her to her kith and kin.'

'Daddy didn't approve of the match?'

'*Précisément.*'

'You're doing it again.'

'Doing what?'

'Your Poirot voice.'

◆

'Doesn't look like anyone's here,' said Street, as they drove up to and stopped in front of the office. A sign on the front door read *Zhukovski Limousines*.

'Pull into the car park,' said Buchanan. 'We'll give them a few minutes and, if I am correct, we won't have to wait too long.'

They had been sitting there for about ten minutes when a black BMW drove into the car park at the side of the building. A passenger got out and went in a side door to the office. The driver, shaped like a professional wrestler, looked at Street's car then walked over and stopped beside Buchanan's door.

Buchanan wound down the window. 'Yes, can I help?'

'Are you looking for someone?'

'We're looking for Mr Zhukovski.'

'Who's looking?'

'Detective Chief Inspector Buchanan, Sussex CID.'

'Good, come with me.'

'You have a name?'

He pondered as though divulging it might give away some national secret. 'Yuri – follow.'

'Lead on,' said Buchanan.

They entered the offices of Zhukovski Limousines and stood patiently by the reception desk as Yuri picked up a phone and called an internal number. He spoke a few words in a language they couldn't understand, then hung up. He walked back to Buchanan and Street and said, 'Follow.'

Another corridor thought Buchanan, as they walked behind Yuri.

'He was early, Boss.'

'Good work, Yuri,' said the other one. 'Who were you waiting for?' He directed his question at Buchanan.

'We were waiting for Vladimir Zhukovski.'

'I am Vladimir Zhukovski. How can I help?'

Buchanan looked at Zhukovski: at over six-foot and broad-shouldered he was an impressive sight. He had blue eyes, a white flecked crewcut, and a face that looked like it had been chiselled from a lump of stone. Buchanan could imagine Zhukovski dressed head to foot in a black leather coat, with a black fur hat, a Kalashnikov over his shoulder and a smoking pistol in his hand. He was never a chauffeur, Buchanan thought to himself.

'Mr Barazani gave us your contact details,' said Buchanan.

'I know, he said to expect a visit from you.'

'I was given to understand that your company is advising Mr Barazani's company on security matters.'

Zhukovski nodded slowly. The sound of Yuri lowering his bulk into an armchair disturbed the silence.

'What sort of advice are you providing?' asked Buchanan, turning back to look at Zhukovski.

'Please, sit and be comfortable. Can I offer you something to drink, Inspector? We have tea, coffee, or would you like a wee dram?'

'Coffee will suffice.'

'Yuri, coffees for our visitors,' said Zhukovski, as he went round his desk and sat.

'I was asking about the advice you are providing.'

'Basics.'

'Such as?'

'To make sure all their software systems are up-to- date, and that includes anti-virus software. Secure passwords used and changed frequently. Door codes changed regularly, that sort of thing.'

'Was it you who implemented the no mobile phones past reception rule?'

'That and a few other things.'

'Such as?'

'Inspector Buchanan, Mr Barazani's company pays a great deal of money for my services.'

'I'm dealing with a missing person report, Mr Zhukovski, possibly a kidnapping. Mr Barazani's daughter has gone missing.'

'So, I understand.'

'What do you understand?'

'Mr Barazani asked me to discreetly check a few things for him.'

'What sort of things?'

'The whereabouts of his daughter's boyfriend.'

'And what did you discover?'

Zhukovski moved the mouse on his desk and read from the computer screen. 'He was last seen on Wednesday afternoon, the 2nd, in town. Later that afternoon he took the five twenty train to Hastings, spent the evening in the Jenny Lind pub, then left Hastings on the ten o'clock train for Brighton. He was seen to get off the train at Pevensey and Westham station at ten thirty and was collected by taxi.'

'Which taxi company?'

'Cliff Cabs.'

'Was the taxi followed?'

'No.'

'So, you lost him?'

'He lives nearby – he was never lost when we know where he lives.'

'I live nearby, but I don't need to take a taxi home.'

'I only report what we see, Inspector.'

'Can I have his address, please?'

'Flat 8, 175 Etchingham Road, Langney.'

'Thank you. Do you follow Mr Barazani?'

'No.'

'His daughter, or her friends?'

'From time to time Mr Barazani has asked us to keep an eye on his daughter.'

'Was there a special reason for this?'

'Mr Barazani's daughter is a bit headstrong and has the habit of picking up strays.'

'Present boyfriend included?'

'He's the latest in a string of undesirable relationships.'

'What can you tell me about him? Why does Mr Barazani have reservations?'

'He's currently unemployed and, although he's on benefits, he manages to dress in the latest Nike trainers and hoodies.'

'What was your conclusion on your observations?'

'I imagine they would be the same as yours: he's dealing in drugs.'

'Did you actually see him dealing?'

'I had Yuri set him up for a sale. Stupid boy thought he was a real Mr Big.'

'How often did you observe him dealing in drugs?'

'Enough to know he was just a small-time dealer, probably selling just enough to finance his own habit.'

'How did you know it was the boyfriend?'

'What do you mean?'

'When I talked to Amal Barazani, he said the boyfriend, Zac, has a twin brother.'

'That I didn't know.'

'Did you inform Mr Barazani of your findings?'

'Yes.'

'What did he say?'

'Do you want it in Kurdish, or English?'

Buchanan smiled and shook his head. 'I can imagine. How about Mastrani employees, have you been asked to check on any of them?'

'There have been occasions.'

'Recently?'

'Yes. Two people resigned.'

'Do you have details?'

Zhukovski smiled. 'They left to get married. They have since emigrated to New Zealand.'

'Have you been asked to follow anyone else?'

'There was an occasion a few months ago, not long after we started working for Mr Barazani's company; we were asked to do DBS checks on several employees.'

'Why? What was the reason given?'

'Mr Barazani's company was about to start a new project and we were brought in to vet the list of candidates.'

'How many?'

'I seem to remember there were about twelve.'

'How many were rejected?'

'Just two.'

'Can we have a copy of the list of names, please?'

'Yuri, the Barazani file, please,' said Zhukovski.

Yuri raised his bulk from the settee and walked over to a filing cabinet and withdrew a set of keys from his pocket. He selected one key from a bunch and unlocked the second drawer. He withdrew an envelope then walked over to Zhukovski and laid the file on the desk before returning to his settee.

'Security is our business, Inspector. Yuri will you make you a copy of the list and give it to the inspector.'

'Dimitar Lupov and Toma Baretata,' said Buchanan. 'Don't recognise the names. I wonder if they feature on the Interpol list. Do you know if all these people were ever employed by Mastrani?'

'The review was done months ago, Inspector. Our recommendation was to not employ them. You will need to check with Mastrani personnel about their whereabouts.'

'Thanks, I will.'

'You will keep the document secure, Inspector?'

'Of course. Is this the only copy?'

'I have the master; you have the only copy.'

'No digital copy?'

'No, the fewer copies the better.'

'Why do you think that?'

45

'You ask a lot of questions, Inspector.'

'That's what I am paid to do.'

'In my country asking questions is sometimes not advisable. In Russia it can get you free winter swimming lessons in the Volga.'

'Well, this isn't Russia and I believe you still owe me an answer to my question.'

'A few years ago, one of your countrymen tried to steal some documents from our Finnish office.'

'Tried?'

'Yes, but he escaped.'

'Doesn't say much for your security methods.'

'He didn't get far.'

'You recaptured him?'

'No, he was eaten by a pack of wolves.'

'Did you get the documents back?'

Zhukovski shook his head. 'No. It was a SIM card and he'd swallowed it. It's now probably rotting in a big lump of wolf crap.'

'How about the boyfriend? Are you sure you don't know where I might find him?'

'No, Inspector, I don't.'

Buchanan looked back at the address for Zac Taylor: Flat 8, 175 Etchingham Road, Langney.

♦

'What did you think of Zhukovski?' Buchanan asked Street, as they drove to the last known address of Zac Taylor.

'Quite a character,' said Street. 'I'm not sure if he was pulling our leg regarding the story about the wolves. What really surprised me was he didn't know that Zac has a twin brother.'

'I thought that as well. But does he look like someone who needs to impress anyone?'

'No, he definitely doesn't.'

'I'm wondering if he really doesn't know where the boyfriend is, especially since he is supposed to be so resourceful.'

'A good question.'

'Which number?' asked Buchanan, as he turned off Langney Rise.

Street looked at her notes. '175 Etchingham Road, Flat 8. Not quite Blackwater Road,' she said, as they stood at the front door to the flats.

Buchanan reached for the handle and found the door locked. 'Do you see a door phone?'

'On the wall beside that bush.'

'Flat 8?' said Buchanan, reaching to press the call button. 'Here we go.'

The sound of a desperate bumble bee emanated from the speaker. They waited, no reaction.

'Try again,' said Street.

This time Buchanan leaned hard on the button and was rewarded by an answer.

'Who's that?'

'It's Detective Chief Inspector Buchanan, I'm looking for Zac Taylor.'

'He's not here.'

'Can we come in, please?'

'I said he's not here.'

'I can get a search warrant.'

'Just a minute.'

There was the sound of papers being rustled, then the door lock buzzed.

'After you,' said Buchanan, pushing the door open.

As they exited the lift on the third floor the door to Flat 8 clicked open and a very frightened face, razor in hand, looked out and stared at them as they approached.

'You don't look like them, do you have some sort of identification? If you don't, I'm shutting the door and calling the police.'

'I can assure you we are the police,' said Buchanan, showing his warrant card. 'Detective Chief Inspector Buchanan and Detective Sergeant Street. Your name?'

'Sam Taylor, come in,' he said, opening the door fully.

Street followed Buchanan into Flat 8.

'Sorry it's a bit of a mess. I just got in; Zac is so untidy,' he said. 'I'm Zac's brother, we're twins, we share the flat.'

'When was the last time you saw your brother?' asked Buchanan, as Street excused herself and went to have a look round the flat.

'I last saw him Wednesday evening.'

'What time was that?'

'About half eleven, we'd just got off the train. He had to go back to Hastings and collect his guitar. He missed the last train back and got a taxi home.'

'No sign of him next morning?'

'His bed was empty when I checked. I had to go into town early to see some friends. No one had seen him, so I reported him missing.'

'Why would you report him missing?'

'He has had issues with illegal substances in the past.'

'Do you know if he went straight home Wednesday evening?'

'I'm not sure.'

'Was that a normal thing for him to do, not to go home after a late night out?'

'Depends on how much he had to drink.'

'Did he drink much?'

'He lost his driving licence a few months ago. He was three times over the limit.'

'I presume he had a job?'

'He did garden jobs between driving.'

'Would you mind if we have a look in his room?'

'Why are you asking all these questions? Has there been an accident, is he all right?'

'Have you met his girlfriend, Zilini?'

'Is that her name? He did mention her a couple of times, said her old man was filthy rich.'

'And that was all?'

'Yeah, oh – he was always going on about her car.'

'What about her car?'

'He said she liked it when he drove really fast.'

'What make was it?'

'German sports car, a Mercedes SLC.'

'I thought you said he'd been banned from driving?'

'That's Zac. I told him his lifestyle would catch up with him one day. I suppose that's what you are here for?'

'We'd just like to talk to him; which bedroom is his?'

'The one on the left.'

'Have you been in there today?' asked Buchanan as Street walked over to it.

'The mess just winds me up, I make him keep the door shut.'

Street pushed the door open.

'First impressions, Jill?' said Buchanan.

'This isn't an untidy room, it's been ransacked. Someone has been looking for something.'

'Sam, could you come here for a moment?' said Buchanan.

'Wow, it's never looked this bad!'

'Could you tell if anything is missing?'

Sam shook his head.

'Is this your bedroom?' Buchanan pointed at the door opposite. Sam nodded.

'Mind if we have a look?' Buchanan reached out and pushed it open. The room could have been a twin of the one opposite, it was just as untidy.

'Did Zac ever bring his girlfriend here?'

'If he did, he kept it quiet.'

'Sam,' said Buchanan, 'when you opened the door, you said something about us not looking like them. Who were you referring to?'

'Two men looking for Zac. I saw them lurking across the road last Tuesday. They saw me come out of the building and stopped me. They thought I was Zac.'

'Did they say why they wanted to talk to him?'

'They said he owed them some money.'

'Can you describe them?'

'Well built, looked like wrestlers. Dark stubbly hair cut really short and both spoke with a foreign accent.'

'What sort of vehicle were they in?'

'I think it was a Mercedes.'

'Do you remember the licence plate?'

'No.'

'Anything else?'

Sam shook his head.

'And you say this is not the normal mess that Zac makes?'

'No, it's never like this. Something terrible has happened to Zac, I just feel it. I hope it's nothing like the last time.'

'What was that?' asked Street.

'A couple of years ago Zac had a dream about me – that I'd injured myself by falling in a ditch.'

'Was the dream real?'

'Oh yes it was. He woke, checked my room and when I wasn't there, he called me on his mobile. It took four times before I answered, I was well drunk. I told him I had been in the pub, taken a short-cut across a field and had fallen in a ditch, breaking my left leg.'

'Did he call for an ambulance?'

'Not then, I was still quite drunk and wasn't sure where I was. So, as soon as he hung up, he used the find my phone app to locate me.'

'Was your leg broken?'

'Yes, in two places. Took me months before I could walk properly again.'

'Is there anything else you can think of?'

'No. Look, will you be much longer? I need to get into town.'

'Going anywhere nice?' said Buchanan, pointing to the passport sticking out of Sam's shirt pocket.

'Oh, this? Yes, me and a friend are booking a holiday. You know how it is these days, can't book tickets without a passport.'

'When are you leaving on your holiday?'

'A week Saturday, still got to book time off at work.'

'Where is work?'

'Er, I'm a van driver, wherever I'm sent.'

'Thank you, Sam. Please let us know when you are leaving the area,' said Buchanan, handing over his business card. 'We may have further questions for you.'

♦

'Your thoughts, Jill?' asked Buchanan, as they drove along Seaside.

'He's a worried young man. Did you see what a mess he was making of shaving?'

'I had noticed. Can you hold the fort tomorrow morning? I have promised Karen I'd go with her into town to look at some curtain material for the spare bedroom. I'll come in early then go with Karen, I shouldn't be too late.'

'That works for me, I have a doctor's appointment at ten. Don't look at me like that, I'm fine, it's just a check-up.'

4

Wednesday
A body

Street returned from her doctor's appointment and walked into an empty office. She looked at Buchanan's desk and saw the remains of his coffee and a half-eaten croissant. She felt the cup: it was cold. Sitting down to await his return, Street was about to turn on her computer when she saw the note on her keyboard.

Gone into town with Karen, call me when you get this message, Jack.

Before she could call Buchanan, her phone rang.

'DS Street – a what – a bad smell? Why are they calling us, surely drain smells should the council's responsibility – it's coming from a garage. OK, I'll check it out, where is it?'

She hung up on the call from Control then called Buchanan. 'Hi, it's Jill, you said to call when I got in – yes, just a few minutes ago. Sure, I can come and collect you, where are you?'

♦

Buchanan was standing at the bus stop outside the station when Street arrived.

'Thanks, Jill,' he said, doing up his seat belt. 'Karen took me into town to see some curtain fabrics.'

'Did she find what she was looking for?'

'Who knows, curtain fabric is not quite my thing. Oh, she did ask me what you thought of this,' said Buchanan, passing her a swatch of material.

'I can see that in the spare bedroom.'

'Any news on the hands yet?'

'Nothing from Dr Mansell, but a member of the public has just called Control saying that there is a horrible smell coming from a disused garage on Gallows Lane. Stephen and Morris are on their way, I said we'd join them.'

♦

Street turned off Westham High Street onto Peelings Lane and parked by the pond behind Hunter and Dexter's patrol car. They were already waiting twenty yards up the lane, chatting.

'What have you found?' asked Street.

'Nothing yet,' said Hunter, 'but it smells like rotting fish coming from the garage. Shall we have a look?'

'Just the two of you,' said Buchanan. 'If this turns out to be a crime scene, I don't want our footsteps to confuse the issue. I've smelt that smell before.'

Hunter carefully pulled the brambles away for Dexter to pull up the rusty overhead door.

'See anything?' said Buchanan, as Dexter made his way through the brambles and under the partially-open garage door.

'Lumps of rusty metal that look like they were some sort of hydraulic drive shafts, and an old Land Rover bonnet. There's a pile of old blankets, newspapers piled up in the corner, and a cordless chainsaw that looks like it's covered in blood. Either someone had a bad accident, or something awful has taken place. Dr Mansell will feel right at home.'

'Suppose someone uses the garage to butcher sheep?' suggested Dexter, as he exited the garage. 'Sheep rustling does happen, especially out in the country, and there are a lot of sheep in the fields around here.'

'There haven't been any reports of sheep being stolen,' said Street. 'Though I did read recently about a bunch of cows being rustled down in Cornwall.'

'Right,' said Buchanan, 'Jill, will you call Henry Littlejohn and let him know we need a CSI team here as soon as possible. Then call Control and have them dispatch a patrol car; we need this site secured. Stephen, Morris, will you put up a cordon twenty yards either side of the garage and stop anyone from passing? This is now a crime scene. If anyone shows up, whether it's a dog walker or just someone being curious, make sure you take their details.

While we wait, I'm heading round to The Heron – too many cups of coffee.'

♦

'I still find it odd,' said Hunter.

'I know what you mean,' said Street. 'It's not every day we find a pair of dismembered hands and a garage that looks like a butcher's shop gone mad.'

'That's not what I mean.'

'What did you mean?'

'Us being married, Jack being our boss, and him being sort of my father-in-law.'

'You don't like that?'

'Oh no, don't get me wrong. I'm not complaining, he's the best of both worlds. It's just odd, that's all.'

'I understand. The first time we met I thought he was just another one of those self-important prats we get stuck working for.'

'What happened to change your mind?'

'Two things. You remember me telling you the story about my midnight visit to Beachy Head?'

'Do I – and second?'

'The second was when he took me back to his house and introduced me to Karen. As you know, my parents died when I was a child and I never really knew what it was like to have a mother or father. With them being childless, we've sort of just adopted each other.'

'You're one of the fortunate ones. There must be thousands of children with no parents, all waiting to be adopted.'

'We could do that.'

Stephen nodded. 'Yes, we could. But –'

'You'd rather we have our own?'

He smiled at her. 'Much more fun.'

'Enough of that talk, we're at work, remember?'

'Something else has just occurred to me.'

'What's that?'

'We have both hands, just wondering if the body is close by?'

'Well, it's certainly not in the garage, though according to what Morris saw, it looks like parts of it could be.'

♦

'Feeling better, Jack?' asked Street, as Buchanan returned with two uniformed policemen.

'Yes thanks. Do you know PC's Dick Strawbridge and Ken Storey?'

'We've met before,' said Hunter. 'Hi Dick, still racing your old Triumph?'

'Got married, what do you think?'

'Dick and Ken will keep an eye on the garage till the CSI team arrive,' said Buchanan. 'This is the garage in question.'

'Someone had to know the garage was there, someone local,' said Ken. 'Look at all the brambles and bushes covering the door, you'd never even know there was a garage there, especially in the dark.'

'Good point, what do you want us to do?' asked Dick.

'Since this is now a crime scene, I want you and Ken to set up a cordon up the hill, just before the farm entrance,' said Buchanan, looking back towards the village. 'Set the other end up just past the gate to that house. I don't want the scene to get contaminated with nosey bystanders. Though this lane, being as quiet as it is, probably only has the occasional dog walkers and residents.'

'OK. Ken – you take the top of the hill, I'll head down towards the pond,' said Dick.

'OK.'

'What do you want us to do?' asked Dexter.

'How about you and Stephen head up the lane and knock on the doors, see if anyone has seen anything suspicious during the last few days. Jill and I will head down towards the pond.'

'Where shall we meet?' asked Hunter.

Buchanan looked at the time. 'Littlejohn said the CSI team won't be here for at least two hours, how about The Heron? It's going to be late before we are done. I think we could justify dinner on expenses.'

'OK, see you in The Heron,' said Hunter.

♦

When Buchanan and Street walked into The Heron, Dexter and Hunter were already seated at the corner table underneath the silent television. Two empty half-pint glasses were on the table in front of them.

'Anything?' asked Buchanan, as he sat.

'The CSI's just arrived as we walked past,' said Hunter.

'Was Dr Mansell with them?'

'Yes.'

'How about the door to door?'

'Nothing from the door to door, but a chap at the bar said he'd been out walking his dog early on Saturday morning and thought it odd to see workmen at work that early and on a Saturday.'

'Did you get his name?'

'Mike Hanson.'

'Which one is Hanson?' asked Buchanan.

Hunter looked towards the bar. 'He was there a few minutes ago, must have gone to the toilet, that's his dog.'

'OK, we'll wait for him. In the meantime, Jill, do you want something to drink?'

'Could I have a lime and soda, please?'

'Fine. I suppose neither of you have eaten?' he addressed Dexter and Hunter.

They shook their heads.

'I'll get some menus.'

Buchanan returned with his and Street's drinks and was about to sit when Hunter said, 'That's him, the chap with the walking stick.'

'Thanks,' said Buchanan.

'Excuse me, Mr Hanson?'

'Yes?'

'DCI Buchanan. My constable said you saw something strange last Saturday morning?'

'Yes. I thought it was odd at the time.'

'Can you explain?'

'I was out walking with Jess.'

At the sound of her name, the Labrador looked up from her docile position at the foot of the bar stool and wagged her tail. Hanson bent down and gave Jess a biscuit.

'As I was saying, I was out walking when Jess and I saw two workmen working in the pit.'

'What pit?'

'The one by Peelings Lane. Contractors have been installing a sewer pipe for the new houses being built up in Stone Cross. It runs right down the village High Street. To do this they dug pits to gain access to the pipe joints. Well, they usually fill in the pits after the pipe has been pulled through. The odd part is the filling-in is normally done during the day.'

'And did they do this to the pit you are referring to?'

'Yes, very early Saturday morning.'

'What time was that?'

'Jess wouldn't sleep, kept pacing the floor, so I took her for a walk to get her to relax. It must have been somewhere about five o'clock. The sun wasn't quite up yet and there was an almost full moon with a cloudless sky; an absolutely lovely morning to be out walking. Oh, I just remembered, the first train of the day had just gone down to Hastings as we walked past The Swan.'

'Were the men in the habit of working so early in the morning?'

'I don't know, you'd have to ask them.'

'But you're sure they were filling the pit in?'

'Oh yes.'

'What did you actually see?'

'There were two workmen wearing orange tabards standing in the pit.'

'What were they doing?'

57

'There they were, a-digging this hole, a hole in the ground, so big and sort of round, and there was I, asking why. Sorry, Inspector, couldn't resist, Bernard Cribbins' song.'

'The hole in the ground song?'

'Yes, I'll be singing it the rest of the day now.'

'Did you talk to them, ask them why they were working so early on a Saturday morning?'

'Yes, I did. One of them said there had been a leak and they had just repaired it and were filling the pit back in.'

'Can you show me where this pit in the road is?'

'Oh, it's not in the road.'

'Then where is it?'

'On the verge on the corner where Peelings Lane meets the High Street.'

'Please wait here.'

Buchanan walked over to the table. 'Sorry to interrupt dinner, but we have a hole in the ground to investigate.'

They followed Hanson and Jess along the High Street to where it met with Peelings Lane.

'It's over there,' said Hanson. 'Where the grass hasn't grown back.'

'They did a good job of filling it in,' said Hunter.

'Is there something wrong?' asked Hanson.

Buchanan shook his head. 'I'm sure it's nothing to worry about. Thank you, Mr Hanson.'

'Well, if you're sure, I'm off home.'

'Not quite yet, Mr Hanson. We will need a statement from you, and a complete description of the two men you saw working in the pit. Detective Sergeant Street will take your details, Jill?'

♦

'What do you think, Jack?' asked Street, as they walked slowly up Peelings Lane to the garage and the CSI team.

'I've only ever heard of workmen digging holes or filling them at five-thirty on a Saturday morning when there has been some sort of emergency repair needed. I wonder who the contractor is for this job?'

'It's Connors,' said Dexter. 'Their yard is down by the castle.'

'Right. There's bound to be a phone number for them somewhere, would you go get it for me? I want to talk to the foreman in charge.'

'Will do,' said Dexter.

While Dexter went off for the phone number, Buchanan, Street and Hunter continued up Peelings Lane to where the CSI team were working. At the cordon Buchanan approached the PCSO standing guard.

'This is a crime scene, sir; you can't go beyond the tape.'

'DCI Buchanan,' he said, showing his warrant card. 'Is Dr Mansell still here?'

'He's in the garage with the CSI team, sir. Would you like me to give him a message? He's quite busy.'

Buchanan nodded. 'Will you tell him DCI Buchanan would like a quick word?'

While they waited for Dr Mansell, Dexter returned with the phone number for Connors.

'That didn't take you long,' said Buchanan.

'I didn't have to go all the way to the compound,' said Dexter. 'I popped into The Heron for the toilet and the barmaid said she had the foreman's business card. His name is Calum.'

Buchanan looked at the card.

'The foreman gave it to her when they were working in the High Street, just in case something went wrong after they had pulled the new pipe through.'

Buchanan dialled the number and waited. 'Is this Calum – Detective Chief Inspector Buchanan here. Are you the foreman in charge of the new sewer pipe being installed in the village of Westham – sorry, no, we haven't found your stolen tools. The reason I'm calling is I wanted to know if you had men working last Saturday morning – Why? Because one of the residents of the village says they saw two of your men filling in a pit at five-thirty on Saturday morning – You didn't? I'm sorry to disturb your evening but I need you to come here and confirm this – because we may have to dig it up – You will? Good, we'll be in The Heron waiting for you.'

Buchanan smiled as he hung up.

'What did he say?' asked Dexter.

'He said he didn't have any workmen filling in pits last Saturday morning. I've asked him to come over and confirm that we are talking about the same pit.'

'Is he coming?' asked Hunter.

'Yes, and if my hunch is correct, before today is out, we will be heading down the road with Dr Mansell and Henry Littlejohn's CSI team.'

'In that case, I need to call my wife and let her know I'll be late getting home,' said Dexter.

'Good man.'

'Who's a good man?' said Dr Mansell, as he approached the cordon tape with Henry Littlejohn.

'Sorry to mess up your evening, Andrew,' said Buchanan. 'How bad is it?'

'I've seen worse, looks like an abattoir,' said Dr Mansell. 'Unfortunately, there's no body for me to look at, just viscera.'

'There are blood spatters everywhere,' said Littlejohn. 'Blooded newspapers in heaps on the ground, and a chainsaw that looks like it was the weapon of choice.'

'Is that what you have in there?'

Littlejohn nodded. 'I've had a look at the chainsaw. There's some body tissue and bone chips on the chainsaw blade, but not much else. I'm almost finished here.'

'So, could it be sheep rustling and butchery?'

'You tell me, you're the policeman,' said Littlejohn.

'I'll wait for your report,' replied Buchanan.

'Excuse me, Henry,' said one of the white-suited CSI's, 'we're almost done in there; should we load up the evidence?'

'Jack? Your call,' said Littlejohn.

'If you've got everything, OK. I'll maintain the crime scene for a couple of days, just in case.'

'Fine, do you need us for anything else?'

'Yes, I'm afraid so. Would you mind waiting for a bit? I've another possible crime scene just down the road.'

'Is that imminent?'

'Probably, but not for at least an hour. I'm waiting for someone to arrive to inspect the potential crime scene.'

'Good, that will give us time to change into clean suits, and hopefully get something to eat,' said Littlejohn. 'Although we may need a clean van if there is any evidence to recover. Any idea where we could get something to eat around here?'

'We've been eating in The Heron. For something lighter there's Kendal's Coffee Shop across the road, they do sandwiches and pastries, its late so they may not be open. Down by the roundabout there's the restaurant Simply Fish, with The Swan fish and chip shop next door.'

'The Heron sounds fine.'

'But before you head off for dinner, Henry, what did you find here?' queried Buchanan.

'The usual collection of cigarette stubs, two of which could be marijuana, an empty cigarette package, one cigar stub, a single size nine blue well-worn flip-flop and a couple of empty Coke cans. There were also some rusty bits of machinery and what appears to be a Land Rover bonnet.'

'Did you find the cigar stub in the garage?'

'No, just outside the door.'

'What about footprints?'

'Apart from your police officers, three clear sets. I took plaster casts of them. Sorry, there was no body.'

'That's OK, I think I know where we'll find that.'

'Near here I hope,' said Mansell, looking at his watch.

'If I'm correct, you won't have to wait long, though we'll have to wait for it to be exhumed.'

'From the graveyard?'

'No, not in a graveyard. I believe it's buried with a new sewer pipe.'

'A sewer pipe! I realise policing is a dirty job, but why a body in a sewer pipe?'

'It won't actually be in the pipe, at least I hope it isn't. I'm waiting to talk to the contractor whose company has been installing the sewer pipe.'

'Let's hope he gives us time to eat, I've missed my dinner again,' said Mansell.

'I'm sure The Heron could find something suitable for you and the CSI team.'

◆

'How was the weekend, Jack?' asked Mansell, as the waitress cleared their plates from the table.

'Perfect. Saturday, we went to see a play at the Devonshire Park Theatre, we were lucky to get tickets. After the play Karen and I went out for a late dinner. Sunday, I managed to sleep in and despite the sound of the jets at Airbourne spent the rest of the day lounging in my chair and reading *The Telegraph*.'

'What was the play?' asked Littlejohn.

'*The 39 Steps*, but not as you might know it.'

'What do you mean?'

'It was a comedy version based on the movie made by Alfred Hitchcock of the book written by John Buchan. It had only four actors playing all the characters, it was absolutely hilarious.'

'Sounds like you enjoyed it.'

'I couldn't stop laughing.'

'Excuse me, Inspector,' said the barman, 'I just saw Calum drive into the car park.'

'Thanks, Christian. Right everyone, it's time to get back to work.'

They followed Buchanan out of The Heron and into the car park.

'Calum?' said Buchanan, as a tall man climbed out of a Ford Transit van.

'Inspector Buchanan?'

'Yes. Thanks for coming out.'

'All in a day's work,' he said, looking at the display on his phone. 'Which pit were you referring to?'

'I'll show you, it's just down the road by Peelings Lane.'

'I don't understand,' said Calum, as the seven of them stood looking at a partially filled-in pit. 'We haven't worked this pit for two weeks, there's no reason for anyone to have been working in it.'

'You're absolutely certain of that?' said Buchanan.

'Of course, I am. The pipe is all the way through, and this pit was empty last Friday. If they'd been a bit more patient, we would have filled it in after we had installed an inspection pit. Looks like someone has been impatient to get us out of the village and they have filled it in for us.'

'Calum, I'm sorry to say that this area is now a potential crime scene. I'm going to have it excavated. Is there anything in the pit that could pose a safety hazard?'

'No, but I can help if all that is needed is to dig it up.'

'How?'

'We have an excavator in the yard. I have the keys to both. It's only just down the road.'

'Have you ever done this sort of work before? It takes a careful hand not to damage what is under the ground,' said Buchanan.

'Digging for a 400 KVA cable focusses the mind, Inspector, and I can assure you there's nothing like that around here.'

'That's not what we will be looking for,' said Buchanan.

'What will you be looking for?'

'It's possible that someone is buried in the pit.'

'Oh, I've never dug for one of those before! I'll go get the excavator.'

'Stephen,' said Buchanan, 'would you get your high-viz jacket and escort Calum along the High Street?'

'OK. You go on, Calum, I'll catch you up – my jacket's in the squad car.'

As Calum and Hunter left, Buchanan sent Dexter back to The Heron to tell Littlejohn and the CSI team they would soon be needed down at the High Street.

'Shall I organise a crime scene perimeter?' asked Street.

'Yes, that's a good idea' said Buchanan. 'Though there is not much to protect at the moment, as soon as we start digging, plus the railway crossing closing every twenty minutes, I imagine we'll attract quite a crowd. With that in mind, could you call Control and get a traffic car here to the High Street?'

As Street was calling Control, the sound of the excavator rattling up the High Street could be heard. As it approached, Buchanan signalled Calum to turn off the High Street and park on the corner of Peelings Lane, directly beside the pit.

Within ten minutes of the excavator arriving, one of the neighbours showed up demanding to talk to whoever was in charge.

'I am,' said Buchanan.

'We've just about had enough of you lot! What are you up to working at this time of the night? We've had weeks of disruption with you blocking the High Street and –'

'Detective Chief Inspector Buchanan, sir. Would you mind stepping back a couple of yards, you are contaminating a crime scene.'

The man stood for a moment staring at Buchanan, then stepped back on to the pavement.

'Crime scene, what's happened?'

'Just part of an ongoing investigation sir,' replied Buchanan. 'You are?'

'James Harvey, I live just round the corner by the pond. I tell you, Inspector, we've really had it up to here. First it was the pond with tractors, pumps, and dead fish, then – then the chaos caused by the sewer pipe from the new houses on Stone Cross coming through here. It's bad enough with the school traffic in the mornings, but this takes the cake. I'm calling my MP in the morning; this has to stop.'

'That's your democratic right, Mr Harvey. Now if you'll just wait here for a moment, Jill, would you take Mr Harvey's details, please?'

'What? Why, are you accusing me of something? This is the limit; I'm calling my MP!'

'Excuse me, I have business to attend to,' said Buchanan, as a blue Vauxhall Astra pulled up at the kerb across the road.

'So, this is where we search next?' said Mansell. 'What will it be, a pair of feet?'

'Probably,' replied Buchanan, 'and I'm hoping the body will be attached.'

'Is that who I think it is?' said Street, as a tall, thin, individual walked across the High Street. 'I've never actually met him.'

'Inspector Buchanan,' said Miasma.

'What is it you want, Mr Miasma?' asked Buchanan, thinking he could well do without the crime reporter for the *Herald* asking questions.

'Is it true you have found a body floating in the pond?'

'I'm sorry to disappoint you, Mr Miasma, but there has been no body found floating in the pond.'

'Well, what can you tell me?'

'We are in the early stages of a possible murder investigation.'

'Male or female?' interrupted Miasma.

'We are appealing for anyone who has any information about suspicious activity in Peelings Lane during the last week to come forward. Even if they think the details may be insignificant,' continued Buchanan, ignoring Miasma's question.

'Standard statement, Inspector. It won't fill many column inches in my newspaper.'

'May I inform you that we're not here to help you sell newspapers.'

'How about, why is the CSI team still here?'

'Relax, Mr Miasma, it's only Wednesday. As soon as we have anything, you will be informed. You have plenty of time to submit your report before tomorrow's deadline. Now if you'll excuse me,

I have work to do. Stephen, Jill, can you assist Morris in keeping the public back from the crime scene?'

Calum came over and said, 'Ready when you are, Inspector. Where shall I start digging?'

'Can you park on the corner so that you can still reach into the pit without getting in the way of the CSI team? You probably won't have to dig very deep.'

'OK.'

The CSI team, under the watchful eyes of Street and Littlejohn, put up a perimeter of blue and white tape as Calum crept forward with the excavator.

'Where exactly do you want me to dig?' said Calum.

'Could you start by just scraping the surface? We need to look at the debris as you dig it up,' said Littlejohn.

As Calum, under the direction of the CSI team, began to dig, Dexter came over to Buchanan. 'Excuse me, Jack, some late evening dog-walkers have just told me they'd seen a white van parked outside the garage on Peelings Lane late Friday evening.'

'Great! Can you get a full statement from them?'

'Already done.'

Inch by inch Calum kept scraping till one of the CSI's indicated that he saw what looked like orange tabards. During the next hour of digging, three rubber gloves, a lone cigarette package and a battered mobile phone were recovered from the pit. It wasn't till they dug down a further two feet that a piece of bloodied bed sheet appeared.

For the next forty minutes, using hand tools, two of the CSI team carefully worked their way down till the outline of a human torso wrapped in the white bedsheet was exposed.

'Will you need me further, Inspector?' asked Calum.

'I don't think so,' said Buchanan. 'The CSI's will take it from here, but just in case would you mind parking your excavator round the corner on the verge?'

As Calum manoeuvred his excavator onto the grass verge, the CSI team put up a tent over the pit and began the gruesome task of hand-digging the remaining earth from around the body.

'What do you make of that, Jack?' said Mansell. 'Why go to the trouble to cut the body in half then just stick both parts in the same hole?'

'Whoever did the burying of the body must have got spooked and instead of disposing of two sections in separate graves, just dumped them in the same grave.'

'I suppose we should be grateful for whoever disturbed them,' said Mansell.

'Yes, I suppose we should.'

After measurements and photos had been taken, the body parts, still draped in the bedsheet, were lifted out of the pit revealing a Tesco shopping bag stuffed full of male clothing.

'I was wondering what was done with his clothes,' said Buchanan, as the body was laid on a plastic sheet on the path. The CSI's, under the watchful eye of Dr Mansell, unwrapped the bedsheet revealing a headless, handless, naked male corpse in two sections, minus its reproductive appendages.

Further measurements and photos were taken, then the corpse was covered with its blooded sheet, placed in a body bag and loaded into a private ambulance for transportation to the morgue.

'Jill,' said Buchanan. 'I think I'm soon to become the village's most disliked person.'

'Why is that?'

'This is now a primary crime scene and I'm going to close this side of the High Street to the public.'

'That will probably require traffic lights – the High Street is quite narrow.'

'Good point. I would also like you to arrange for the left side of Peelings Lane to be cordoned off from the High Street up to the entrance to Mortain Road and also along the left side of Mortain Road to the end of the pond.'

'How far up Peelings Lane do you want closed?'

'From the right side of Mortain Road up to the entrance to the farm. That should at least allow the locals to get down to the village'.

'That's going to require a lot of manpower.'

'I should think no more than three uniformed police officers will suffice. Besides, I think we'll only need to keep it closed for a couple of days. Would you work as the CSM for this?'

'Sure, but I've never managed a crime scene before.'

'It shouldn't be an issue for you, in fact it'll be good experience. Just keep me appraised of what the CSI's find.'

'OK. When do you want me to start?'

'No time like the present. I'm going to have the pond searched at first light and I'd like you to be here when they start. Who knows what they'll find?'

'A head?'

'Possibly.'

5

Thursday Morning
The Boyfriend

'You eat breakfast here?' said Buchanan, as he entered Dr Mansell's office.

'This?' he said, looking at his bacon sandwich. 'I need to eat when I can. These last few days have been manic.'

'We haven't seen any of it.'

'You wouldn't. It was a fire in a squat. Five people died from smoke inhalation. The report should be in next week's *Herald*.'

'Not sure if I want to read that.'

Mansell smiled. 'And you a big, tough, Glasgow cop.'

'Not anymore.'

'Well, I think you still have it.'

'Have what?'

'The ability to dig up corpses, just like a dog after a bone. Though we are still missing the head on this one.'

'It's on its way,' replied Buchanan. 'Jill just called to say the team of police divers found a head in the village pond thirty minutes ago.'

'Let's hope it's the head to the body we have already.'

'Me too. The divers have been going through the village pond since just before sun-up this morning. Apparently, it was quite a task, the silt in the pond is more than a metre deep in places.'

'Great, I'll get started on the corpse as soon as the head gets here. In the meantime, I've got another over-the-cliff body to look at.'

'Fine, I'll check back with you this afternoon.'

◆

'What time did you finish last night?' said Mansell, as he unzipped the body bag revealing the body parts laid on the autopsy table.

69

'We'd wrapped up by three, I was in bed by three-fifteen. Jill got the short straw, she was back on scene at sun-up to oversee the divers, she's my CSM in this case.'

'You realise this is the second time you've been living within walking distance of the crime scene?'

'No, I haven't had time to think of that, been a bit busy digging up bodies – do you have something for me to go on with?'

'Male in early twenties, five foot ten inches tall, with a chinstrap beard and small moustache. Shaved head showing black stubble. Missing molars upper and lower-right, scar on right forearm, indicative of a knife wound. His last meal was fish and chips.

'Can you tell when he died?'

'I'd say by looking at the body, late Wednesday night, early Thursday morning. He died while tied to a chair and left there for about forty-eight hours. This might be of interest to you,' said Mansell, pointing to a small tattoo on the right hand.

'Five dots: he did time,' said Buchanan.

'His fingernails are chewed short on both hands,' continued Mansell. 'Blue eyes. There are marks of surgery on the left leg. I opened it up, a bad break at one time, nice job of pinning the bone. Reminds me of the work done by Anstruther before he retired. There is extensive bruising and cigar burn marks on the upper torso indicating torture prior to death and dismemberment. He is also missing his reproductive organs, removed by what could have been a dull saw or bread knife. You'll have to wait for the bloodwork'

'And the cause of death?'

'Strangulation.'

Buchanan stared at the body, then said, 'Cigar burns, not cigarette?'

'Yes, I'd say they were cigar burns, but don't waste your time waiting for me to tell you the make of the cigar, only Sherlock Holmes could do that.'

'He's a fictional character.'

'So was his ability to determine cigar makes from their ash. In spite of that, you can determine certain things from cigar ash.'

'Such as?'

'Such as where the tobacco was grown, how the cigar was assembled, and the quality of the tobacco used in its manufacture. I have been able to get an ash sample for analysis, but don't hold your breath for anything too revealing. Forensics should be able to give you some basic info on the cigar and have the results for you later today. Is he known to you?'

'Could be the boyfriend of someone who's just been reported as missing.'

'Should I expect another body to go with this one?'

'I sincerely hope not.'

'What will you do now?'

'Since we now we have a body, and we still have a missing person, I think a council of war is in order.'

Buchanan took out his phone and called Street.

'Jill, are Stephen and Morris available – they are, good. Will you call them for me and ask them to meet us in my office in half an hour – yes, I think it is.'

♦

Buchanan was pleased to see Hunter and Dexter walking across the car park as he drove into the police compound. He parked his car and followed them into the building and his office.

'Before we get started,' said Buchanan, 'Stephen and Morris, are you free for the next couple of days? We have a lot of investigating to do.'

'I'm available,' said Hunter. 'The jury has just retired on the case I was giving evidence on, so as long as we don't have anything like the recent climate change protests, I'm all yours.'

'My latest little one has just started sleeping through the night,' said Dexter, 'so I have returned to regular duties.'

'Any pictures?' asked Street.

'Are you on Tiny Beans?'

'No, what's that?'

'It's a private app for families to share baby pictures, sort of like WhatsApp. You have to be invited to see the photos. Would you like an invitation?'

'Yes, please.'

Buchanan looked at Street and thought, could it just be possible? No. He shrugged and put it down to her being a woman.

'Can we get to the business in hand?' asked Buchanan, interrupting Street and Dexter's tête-à-tête about how cute babies look.

'What did Dr Mansell have to say?' asked Street, as she took one last glance at Dexter's latest.

'From his description I'd say we've found Zac Taylor.'

'Who is Zac Taylor?' asked Dexter.

'He's the boyfriend of the missing girl, Zilini Barazani,' said Street.

'If I can have everyone's undivided attention,' said Buchanan, 'I'll bring you all up to date on what has transpired, then I'll get to the autopsy report. First, we're going to give this case the code name, *The Missing Heiress.*'

'That will keep Miasma happy,' said Hunter.

'Tuesday this week, when I entered my office, I was waylaid by the ACC and Sir Nathan Greyspear,' said Buchanan. 'Sir Nathan had approached the ACC on behalf of a business acquaintance of his, Amal Barazani. He has asked for help in locating his daughter.

'Sir Nathan drove me out to Castlewood to meet Amal Barazani, where he informed me his daughter hasn't been seen since last Friday evening. She attends Brighton University. During the week she stays in halls of residence but comes home for the weekend on Friday evenings. She has, or I should say, had, a boyfriend, one Zac Taylor whose dismembered body I believe is now residing in the Eastbourne morgue.'

'Do we have an autopsy report yet?' asked Dexter.

'Yes, let me read Doctor Mansell's initial report: Torso found in shallow grave, torso cut in two at the waist by industrial chainsaw, viscera partially intact, reproduction appendages missing and severed by a blade with serrated edge, possibly a narrow-bladed saw or long-bladed bread knife. Hands severed by industrial chainsaw found at crime scene two. Hands found at various sites in village. Head severed by same chainsaw and disposed of in village pond. Investigation of stomach revealed the deceased had a meal of fish and chips about two hours prior to death. About four hours prior he had eaten a substantial slice of fruit cake. Gastric tract contained twenty-two belladonna seeds. Toxicity blood test revealed an equivalent dose of 2 grains of atropine. Actual cause of death was manual strangulation.'

'I wonder why no one heard the noise of the chainsaw,' said Hunter. 'Must have made a real racket. Are we sure it's the boyfriend?'

'It was a cordless electric chainsaw, and we've yet to make a positive identification,' said Buchanan.

'Any suspects in mind?'

'The obvious one would be Amal Barazani, the missing girl's father. He told me he didn't approve of the relationship between the boyfriend and his daughter. He also has a stepbrother, the son of his father's second wife – they live in Hailsham. Then there's the grandparents.'

'Grandparents?' said Dexter.

'I don't have a first name yet, but Barazani says his stepmother doesn't agree with his lifestyle, and especially the daughter's, says it brings the family into disrepute.'

'Why would that be a factor?' asked Street.

'The stepmother, Amal Barazani's father's second wife, is of the Muslim faith. They have a house in Meads but visit Saudi Arabia for part of the winter.'

'So, it could be an honour killing?' asked Hunter.

'That is one possibility.'

'Whoever did it must have had transportation to get the body to the garage,' said Street, 'then down to the High Street. I'll have a look through the database for missing or stolen vehicles.'

'I wonder if Barazani's company owns a van?' said Hunter. 'We have a witness statement about a white van being seen in the Lane late on Friday evening.'

'You can make that one of your priorities,' said Buchanan. 'But before we get involved in missing vehicles, we need to focus of the whereabouts of Zac Taylor before his untimely demise.'

'Anything else?' said Dexter.

'Barazani smokes cigars, and the body had several cigar-burns on the torso. Dr Mansell's report said the victim had been tortured before being strangled and dismembered, that would take more than one person.'

'Have we heard from forensics yet?' said Hunter.

'Not a full report,' said Buchanan. 'They just completed the crime scene search a couple of hours ago. Macalister said he hoped to get a full report through sometime tomorrow. In the meantime, he's sent through the preliminary results for us to look at. Jill, could you pass a copy to Stephen and Morris?'

'I'm impressed,' said Hunter.

'In the meantime, let's see what we have to go on,' said Buchanan. He read aloud, 'Cigarette ends match cigarette package found in pit. Brand of cigarettes is Gauloise, French cigarettes made in Germany and freely available across Europe. Chainsaw from the garage, Makita 18-volt, serial number matches the one listed as reported stolen from contractor's compound sometime Friday evening. Tissue samples removed from saw sent for DNA matching.

'Orange tabards, non-descript type and well worn. Typically used by railway contractors and the like. Both tabards have initials hand printed on inside at neck location. Tabard A initials TB, tabard B initials DL. Mobile phone smashed beyond use with SIM card installed. Phone and SIM card sent off for analysis.

'Three pairs of nitrile gloves, typically worn by decorators and mechanics, sent off for fingerprint and DNA testing. There were several sets of tyre tracks with only one set matching both crime scene one and crime scene two. Both tyre mark locations contained oak tree leaves from the tree adjacent to crime scene one. Tyre tread pattern is a Firestone brand, size 215/65 R15, usually fitted to commercial vehicles. Four identifiable shoe imprints at crime scene one. There were only three at crime scene two where the body was found, and they did match the ones at crime scene number one. The deceased's clothes were found under the body.'

Buchanan continued, 'Macalister is on the ball. It's unusual to get results this quickly.'

'Must be something to do with who and what we are investigating,' said Street. 'Didn't you say Amal Barazani's company is working on a special government contract to design bespoke software for the security services?'

'Yes, that's what he said. Supposed to be a hush-hush job.'

'Sounds like there were at least two people with a motive for the murder,' said Dexter.

'Let's not forget there's also probably someone behind the scenes pulling the strings,' said Hunter.

'A Mr Big?' queried Street.

'When I interviewed him, Barazani referred to his security people,' said Buchanan.

'He employs his own internal security people?' said Dexter.

'No. He contracts that out to a private company called Zhukovski Limousines. The boss is a Russian,' said Buchanan. 'Jill and I interviewed him on Tuesday and he's quite a character. He looks like he could have stepped straight out of a John le Carré novel. He said he saw Zac Taylor get off the train on Wednesday evening and get into a taxi but didn't follow him.'

'That doesn't add up,' said Hunter. 'If this Zhukovski said he watched Zac Taylor get in a taxi on Wednesday night, why didn't he just follow him home?'

'An excellent question, Stephen. Jill, I think it would be a good idea if you and I go back and have further words with Mr Zhukovski. We need to find out just what security services his company actually provides for Mastrani. Especially since his people checked Zac Taylor's flat, but found no one home.'

'So, where do you want me and Morris to start?' said Hunter.

'As soon as we are done here, would you and Morris start by getting Sam Taylor to ID his brother? Then would you go to the university and see if you can dig up any background information on Zilini Barazani? Her university residence address is in the file, as is her home address. Next, if you get time today, see if you can trace the boyfriend's movements. Zhukovski says they tracked him last Wednesday from Eastbourne to Hastings and back to Westham by train. Zhukovski said Zac Taylor got off the train at Pevensey and Westham station then took a taxi, which I know for a fact is unusual – there is no taxi rank there.'

'It would be helpful if we had a photo of Zac Taylor,' said Dexter.

'Jill, would you mind calling Dr Mansell and asking him to take a photo of the head? Then if you could touch up the photo so we don't scare people.'

'Will do.'

'Did Zhukovski say where the taxi dropped Zac Taylor off?' asked Dexter.

'No. Zhukovski assumed it took him to his home address.'

'That's a bit odd. He tracked Zac Taylor all day, but assumed he'd gone home in a taxi. Do we have the name of the taxi firm?'

'Yes, they're in the file. But leave Zac Taylor's address for now, Jill and I will go back and talk with the brother.'

'Jill, any luck with Dr Mansell?'

'Yes. He said he'd anticipated you asking and has taken one from the front and a second shot of the side of the face. He said he would email it over. Let me check,' said Street, as she clicked on her email account. 'The doctor is good; he should be doing make-up on TV. Zac almost looks like he's alive. I'll touch it up and print a few copies for us.'

A few minutes later, the printer whirled into action. Street printed six copies and handed them out.

♦

As they drove along Seaside, Street asked, 'Do you miss your Evo?'

'Not really. It was fun to drive for a while but explaining why I was using so much petrol on my expenses was getting to be a chore. No, I'm quite happy with my BMW.'

Street parked at the side of the Barazani office.

'Didn't this use to be the *Herald* offices?' asked Street, as they climbed the steps.

'Before my time,' replied Buchanan, opening the front door.

'Can I help?' asked the lone receptionist.

'Detective Chief Inspector Buchanan and Detective Sergeant Street. We'd like to have a word with Mr Barazani.'

The receptionist smiled. 'If you'll take a seat, I'll see if Mr Barazani is available.'

'We do a lot of this,' said Street, as they sat and watched the comings and goings of Barazani's busy office. 'I don't think I've seen anyone over the age of forty come in or go out while we've been here.'

'It's the modern world of computer games and programming; a young person's world,' said Buchanan. 'I'd be lost in it.'

Their attention was diverted as the door to the corridor opened and a tall well-dressed lady wearing a white dress shirt and a tan pencil skirt entered.

'She looks a bit out of place here,' said Street, as the lady walked across to the reception desk. She said something to the receptionist, who nodded at Buchanan and Street. Buchanan stood as she turned towards them.

'Mr Barazani's apologies, Inspector. He's chairing a meeting and is unable to get away. He asked me to give you this information – he said you may find it useful in your investigation. Mr Barazani said he will be available later this afternoon if you still need to talk to him.'

'Thanks, er –?'

'Charlotte Murray, I'm Mr Barazani's personal assistant.'

'Thank you, Charlotte,' said Buchanan, glancing at the list of names and addresses. 'I don't see your address on here?' He smiled up at her.

'But – why would you want my address?'

'You are more than Mr Barazani's personal assistant, aren't you?'

'We are friends, yes.'

'Please add your address for me,' said Buchanan, handing back the typed sheet.

'One minute,' she said, turning to walk over to the reception desk.

She returned a moment later and passed the sheet back to Buchanan, who smiled when he saw the address she'd written was in Meads

♦

As they navigated their way through the traffic jam on Cavendish Road, Street read down the list of names and addresses. 'Amal Barazani, Shalom, Auckland Drive, North Harbour. No wonder he knows Nathan Greyspear, they must be neighbours,' she said. 'Zac Taylor's address is Flat 8, 175 Etchingham Road, Langney. Nasim Barazani, Kilmarnock, Marshfoot Lane, Hailsham.

Zhukovski Limousines 559 Seaside, Charlotte Murray, Mount Road, Meads?'

'No house number or name?'

'She didn't give us one?'

'Why don't you give her a call and ask? I'm sure she'll be delighted to tell us.'

As Buchanan drove, Street called Mastrani and asked to speak to Charlotte Murray.

'And the answer is?' said Buchanan, as Street hung up from the call.

'Just Mount Road, she said it was the only residence there.'

'She's cagey, wonder what she's trying to hide?' said Buchanan. 'Before we're done for today, let's go have a chat with Nasim Barazani.'

♦

'Good someone's home,' said Buchanan, as Street turned off Marshfoot Lane into the private driveway for Nasim Barazani's house. Buchanan rang the doorbell and waited for a response. What he got was the incessant barking of a dog.

'Do you ever count up how many dogs we come into contact with during an investigation?'

Buchanan's answer was interrupted by the front door being opened by a lady of eastern appearance wearing a blue headscarf.

'Yes, can I help?'

'Good morning. Detective Chief Inspector Buchanan and Detective Sergeant Street, we would like to talk to Nasim Barazani, if he's home.'

'What do you want with my son?'

'We're making enquiries as to the whereabouts of Zilini Barazani.'

'You'd better come in and wait.'

Buchanan followed Street into the hallway.

'You can wait in here,' she said, ushering Buchanan and Street into the living room. 'I'll let him know you're waiting.'

'We do this a lot as well,' said Street.

'Waiting?'

She nodded. 'Remember the first time?'

'That would have been – Rodney Richardson.'

'Yes, what a surprise he turned out to be.'

Their conversation was interrupted by a stocky young man in his mid to late forties coming through the door.

'Inspector Buchanan?'

'Yes, are you Nasim Barazani?'

'Yes. How can I help?'

'It's about your stepniece, Zilini.'

'She's come home?'

'Not as far as we know. Have you seen or talked to her recently?'

'Not sure, hang on, it was two weeks ago.'

'Where was that?'

'In town, I was visiting my stepbrother, Amal.'

'Your reason for visiting your stepbrother?'

'It was a private matter.'

'You met him in his office?'

'Yes.'

'What was the private matter?'

'I needed his signature on a document.'

'What was the document?'

'Inspector, I don't see what this document has to do with Zilini's disappearance.'

'Just standard police procedures, Mr Barazani.'

'Standard procedures my hat! I don't believe there is such a thing as standard procedures. I think you are just making all this up. Has my stepbrother put you up to this?'

Buchanan shook his head. 'No, nothing of the kind. Is your stepbrother in the habit of causing you trouble?'

'It's a game we sometimes play,' he said, smiling at a memory. 'He once sent a load of sheep to our door.'

'Already butchered?'

'No, live. I'd been chatting to him the previous day and I said our lawn mower had died and the grass needed cutting.'

'What did you do?'

'I sent him a ham sandwich.'

'Was he angry?'

'No, he called me and said he enjoyed it with his afternoon tea.'

'Your occupation is junior banker for the Al Rayan bank?'

'Certainly not. I'm head of domestic business investment.'

'What does that entail?'

'I deal with corporate finance.'

'You handle loan applications?'

'Must you be so crude, Inspector? We who work at the bank would never refer to financing business requirements as handling loan applications.'

'Was that what you and your stepbrother were discussing?'

'Amal was arranging some short-term financing for a special project his company was undertaking for a client.'

'Who was the client?'

'That is confidential information and nothing to do with Zilini going missing.'

'Was Zilini in the office when you were discussing the financial arrangements?'

'Yes and no. She opened the door and barged right into me.'

'Did you say hello?'

'I might have done – yes, I'm sure I did.'

'What was her demeanour?'

'Her demeanour? I'd say she was angry about something, she looked at me, smiled, and marched off down the corridor.'

'Do you know why she was angry?'

'Amal said she'd asked him if she could take a couple of weeks off college and go on a hiking trip to Europe with friends.'

'Why would that be a problem?'

'Amal said it was just an excuse to go travelling with her boyfriend.'

'Zac Taylor?'

'That's his name. I believe he is a folk musician.'

'Have you heard him play?'

'Yes, but folk is not my style.'

'What about her eighteenth birthday party? I thought the whole family were there?'

'I had to leave early. Achmad called to say he crashed his motorcycle and needed a ride home from the hospital.'

'Achmad?'

'He's our son.'

'Was he injured?'

'No. Apparently he was trying to talk on his phone while stopped in a lay-by and got hit from behind by a drunk driver. He was fine but the motorcycle was a write-off.'

'What was your impression of Zilini's lifestyle?'

'A trollop, that's what she is,' said Nasim's mother, who'd been eavesdropping at the door.

'Mother, this is a private meeting, I do wish you wouldn't interrupt.'

'Now there's a word I haven't heard in a long time,' said Buchanan. 'Why would you describe Zilini as a trollop, Mrs Barazani?'

'Have you seen the way she dresses? Skirt up to her navel, looks like a whore. And the company she keeps! She needs to be given a good whipping and locked in her room till she behaves like a Barazani should.'

'Hitting children is illegal in this country, Mrs Barazani.'

'Not where I come from it isn't.'

'Do you live with your son, Mrs Barazani?'

'No, we have a house in Meads.'

'Could we have the address, please?'

'Why?'

'Just standard police procedures, Mrs Barazani.'

'Lytchett, Upper Carlisle Road, Meads, Eastbourne, is there anything else you want to know?'

'Thank you, Mrs Barazani, that will be all for now.'

Street looked at Buchanan and stifled a smile.

'Good, I need to get back to the kitchen.'

'Nasim, can you tell us when you last saw your stepniece?'

'Please excuse my mother, Inspector,' said Nasim as the door closed with bang. 'She grew up in Saudi Arabia where women are treated as mere possessions, unlike here in England. You ask when Zilini was last here, she was here a week ago last Thursday. She comes to see my wife each week for music lessons.'

'What kind of music lessons?'

'Singing.'

'Does she come alone?' asked Buchanan.

'No, she comes with her boyfriend, they are good together.'

'I thought you didn't like his music?'

'That was for my mother's ears, Inspector. She likes to listen at the door when I have someone visit. No, he is a very good musician, and with Zilini having such a good voice for jazz my wife is encouraging them to become a duet and go on the road. She has been coaching them, they really are very good together.'

'Does your mother agree with this?'

He laughed. 'It doesn't make any sense, but she must do. Every time they visit, she bakes them a cake.'

♦

'Excellent job, Jill.'

'But I didn't say anything.'

'No, but you sat there taking notes, makes the witnesses nervous, makes them say more than they intend. Did you get the bit where the grandmother said Zilini should be whipped and locked up till she behaved?' said Buchanan, as he parked in the police compound.

'Strange thing to say, but then she's from Saudi Arabia, they have different standards for women than we do here. What do you want to do next?' asked Street.

'You look exhausted – why don't we have an early night? I think we're in for some long days ahead. I'll see you back here in the morning.'

Street's face relaxed. 'Thanks, see you tomorrow.'

♦

'How was your day?' asked Karen, as Buchanan entered the kitchen.

'Like it always is at the beginning of an investigation.'

'Like that is it? Why don't you go put your feet up and I'll pour you a glass of red.'

Buchanan looked at Karen for a minute, then said, 'What is it? We've been married too long for you to try and keep surprises from me.'

'I had an email from Shelly this afternoon.'

'Shelly?'

83

'Married to Travis – you remember him, don't you? You almost accused him of beating up Harry, Nathan's assistant stable manager.'

'I never accused him. That was DI Hanbury in one of his exuberant moods. So, what was so special about the email?'

'She says Travis is coming over to the UK for a Bible Conference. He's the keynote speaker.'

'So?'

'He's bringing Poppy with him.'

Buchanan smiled. 'And you've invited them to stay with us, is that it?'

'Do you mind? It will only be for a few days.'

'No, of course not. When?'

Karen smiled. 'They fly in on Virgin Atlantic, Friday morning.'

'That's tomorrow, a bit short on notice.'

'Shelly said they were booked into the Claremont.'

'Ah, that was unfortunate. I heard the fire department are keeping an eye on what's left of the building. The seafront is closed to traffic and the gas company engineers are having to dig up the roads to lay a temporary gas main for the nearby hotels.'

'Why?'

'They had difficulty finding the gas shut-off valve for the Claremont, so they dug down to the main gas pipe and shut it off.'

'The news report said the rear of the building had just collapsed.'

'That's sad, another one of Eastbourne's landmarks gone up in flames.'

'So, will you go to collect Travis and Poppy from the airport?'

'Of course I will. What time does their plane land?'

'It's an overnight flight that arrives at eight forty-five.'

'That will mean an early start for me.'

'I'll give Jill a call and let her know you'll not be in till after lunch tomorrow.'

'Did Shelly say what terminal?'

'No.'

84

'Not to worry, I'll check before I leave. Now, you said something about a glass of wine?'

6

Friday AM
Travis and Poppy

Leaving at six o'clock, Buchanan was ahead of most of the London-bound commuter traffic and had plenty of time to stop in at the Hickstead services for his morning Starbucks coffee. He parked in the airport car park and went through to the arrival's hall; thankful he had made an early start.

He'd forgotten just how tall and broad-shouldered Travis was. But there was no escaping the excitement on Poppy's face – she was here to see her fiancé, Harry.

Buchanan had previously met Travis and Shelly Grant at Castlewood, Sir Nathan Greyspear's country club. Poppy, their daughter, had fallen head over heels in love with Harry, the assistant stable manager, causing great consternation for her father.

It had been love at first sight and initially a tenuous one. Harry being on probation had not gone down well with Travis who, as Karen reminded Buchanan, had once been a suspect in a serious assault on Harry.

'Jack, good to see you again,' said Travis, giving Buchanan a bear hug. 'How are you?'

'I'm fine.'

'Still busy locking up criminals?'

Buchanan smiled. 'When we catch them. Hello, Poppy.'

'Hi.'

'She's disappointed Harry couldn't be here,' said Travis.

'He's gone to Manchester to collect a horse for Sir Nathan,' said Poppy, 'but he said he'll be home Saturday. Oh, that's tomorrow.'

'The car's this way,' said Buchanan, nodding to the garage sign.

♦

'Working on anything interesting at the moment?' asked Travis, as they approached the A27 junction with the A23.

'We're working on a case of a dismembered body with the related case of a missing young woman.'

'You say a related case – do you mean the dismembered body and the missing person are related?'

'The dismembered body of a young man is possibly the boyfriend of the missing girl.'

'Do you think she's in danger, gone into hiding?'

'That's one avenue of investigation.'

'You don't seem so sure.'

'It's a complicated matter. The missing girl is the daughter of a wealthy businessman. . .'

'And dear old pop didn't agree with the relationship?' interrupted Poppy.

'That's one scenario,' said Buchanan, smiling in the rear-view mirror at Poppy.

'What was wrong with the boyfriend?' asked Poppy.

'We know little about the boyfriend at this time. When we interviewed the twin brother, he thought something terrible might have happened.'

'Sort of twin telepathy,' said Poppy.

'I've heard about that,' said Travis.

'We have recovered a body that could be the missing boyfriend. Other than that, and his name and description, we know very little. Though there is the fact the girl's father did not approve of his lifestyle,' said Buchanan.

'What was wrong with his lifestyle?' said Poppy.

'We're not sure of that either. The body was only discovered on Wednesday evening. We've yet to get a positive identification.'

'You said the father of the missing girl is wealthy?' asked Travis.

'Runs a bespoke software company,' said Buchanan. 'He told me his company, amongst several other projects, is currently working on a special anti-virus program for the government.'

'Could the daughter have been kidnapped for ransom?'

'That is another avenue to explore.'

'What's the other – or are there more?' said Travis.

'The father is Jewish.'

'I don't follow,' said Travis.

'There is another branch of the family: an uncle, the father's stepbrother. I think they are Muslim,' said Buchanan. 'A modern version of Cain and Abel?'

'You need to read your Bible, my friend,' said Travis. 'Cain and Abel were brothers, sons of Adam. But I think you are referring to another set of brothers. Jacob and Esau, and the world has lived with the problems ever since.'

Buchanan shook his head as they entered onto the A27.

'Let me explain,' said Travis. 'In simple terms, the Jews trace their spiritual heritage to God the creator, all the way back to Adam and Eve through the lineage of Jacob. The Muslims do that through Esau.'

'So why would that be an issue?'

'Have you ever heard of honour killings?'

'Yes.'

'In some families, if a sibling brings dishonour to the family name, that person can be put to death.'

'Murdered, you mean,' said Poppy.

'That's the way it is,' said Travis.

'I don't quite understand,' said Buchanan. 'Zac Taylor, that's the boyfriend's name, wasn't a member of the family.'

'It's possible that since the daughter was in hiding, killing the boyfriend was the alternative solution.'

'So, the daughter is safe, she can come home,' said Poppy.

'Not if the father was involved,' said Buchanan. 'Don't forget, he was the last person to see his daughter alive.'

'I remember a case of a young Saudi woman who fled her family while passing through Bangkok airport,' said Travis. 'She refused to leave the hotel and board her flight back to Kuwait. Instead she barricaded herself in her airport hotel room. According to the newspaper report, she said she feared her family would kill her if she returned home, as she'd recently renounced Islam.'

'That's barbaric!' said Poppy.

'What happened to her?' asked Buchanan, as they drove down Rattle Road into the village of Westham.

'I'm surprised you didn't hear about it,' said Travis, 'it was all over the news in Dallas. The Thai government referred the situation to the UN Human Rights Refugee Agency.'

'So, what happened in the end?'

'I believe she was given refugee status in Canada.'

'I'm glad for her,' said Poppy.

'So, this is home, Jack,' said Travis, stretching as he climbed out of Buchanan's car.

'Yes. We just moved in a few months ago,' said Buchanan, as the front door was opened by Karen.

'Hi Karen,' said Travis, as he picked up his suitcase.

'Hello Travis, Poppy.'

'If you'll excuse me,' said Buchanan, 'I need to get back to work.'

'Sure thing, Jack,' said Travis. 'See you later.'

♦

'Everything OK?' asked Street, as Buchanan entered his office. 'Karen said you'd gone to the airport to pick someone up.'

'Everything is fine. You remember the Grants?'

'The American family you met at Castlewood?'

'The very same. Travis is here on business with his daughter, Poppy. They were booked into the Claremont, but since it's a burnt-out shell, Karen suggested they stay with us.'

'That must be nice, your first house guests.'

Buchanan paused by his desk for a moment, 'I suppose it is, hadn't really thought about it like that.'

'I'll bet Karen did,' said Street smiling.

'Where are Stephen and Morris?' said Buchanan, taking off his jacket and sitting at his desk.

'Gone to deal with an RTA on Seaside Road. Stephen just called and said they should be done within the hour.'

'Good. How are you feeling today? The colour is back in your cheeks.'

'I feel great. Had an early night, slept nine hours straight.'

'Glad to hear that. Have we heard from forensics?'

'Yes, where do you want me to start?'

'At the beginning?'

'OK. In no particular order...'

Buchanan looked at Street and smiled. 'This isn't *Strictly Come Dancing.*'

'Sorry, my joke. The DNA on the cigarette ends at the garage match the DNA on those found beside the pit. The cigar ash on the body matches the cigar stub and there are three sets of DNA on the cigar stub which do not match anything else. There is a clean set of prints on the Coke can, plus DNA that matches one of the cigarette stubs. It's a pity the prints show no record on our database.'

'What about the envelope that contained the empty ring box?'

'You're not going to like this; I'll start with the postal details. It was only traceable back to the Gatwick sorting office and delivered from the Westham sorting office. Two of the four sets of fingerprints on the envelope match Zilini's and her father's, but none of the others match any taken from the garage on Peelings Lane. I'm assuming they are probably the postman's prints.'

'Any DNA?'

'It says too many people have handled the envelope.'

'What about the ring box?'

'Same as the envelope.'

Buchanan reached into his jacket pocket and stopped. There were no cigarettes there anymore, he no longer smoked. Instead he took out a withered tube of fruit gums, took one and offered the tube to Street.

'No thanks.'

'Anything else?'

'The envelope had been used before and as such can't be considered reliable for forensic purposes in this case. There was dust inside it and the envelope revealed an outline of something about the size and shape of a CD box. The dust is a similar consistency to what you'd find in the inside of a handbag, plus traces of a generic hand lotion. The old postal information showed it was posted in Paris two months ago and sent to the Mastrani office in Eastbourne.'

'Sounds like she's being held in an old handbag,' said Hunter, who'd just returned from the RTA.

'I hadn't thought of that one,' said Buchanan. 'Any of you know of any old handbags?'

'There must be dozens of them,' said Hunter.

'Enough of that, we have work to do. Anything on the van?' said Buchanan.

'I checked all the local rental agencies this morning,' said Street. 'Nothing, all vans accounted for. Next, I went through the stolen vehicle reports, especially white vans and there I think we have a lead. During the last two weeks there have been three reported stolen in the area. Two of those have been recovered, the third – a white Ford Transit – is still missing.'

'A local owner?'

'You're going to love this. It's a contractor who keeps his van at the Hankham industrial estate; and he worked on the pipeline in the village.'

'I didn't realise there was an industrial estate in Hankham.'

'It's a former poultry farm that has been subdivided into small rental units. I think it's used more for office space and storage than anything really industrial.'

'Were you able to talk with the owner of the van?'

'Eventually. He wasn't very pleased when I told him we hadn't located his van yet. He was especially angry because, he informed me, he'd just invested a small fortune fitting new tyres to the van and was getting ready to convert it into a camper van. I asked him what type of tyres. He said Firestone, 215/65 R15's.'

'Would you call our friends in CSI, Jill? Ask if they have anyone available to go up to Hankham and check the tyre tracks to see if they match the ones at the crime scene.'

'You are assuming there will be tyre tracks?'

While Street called the CSI office, Buchanan stood and walked over to the window.

Street hung up. 'Someone will be out there within the hour.'

'Good. I've been thinking, Jill. If you were trying to hide something as big and obvious as a white van, where would you hide it?'

'Down a country lane, there's loads of them around here.'

'Yes, that is one option.'

'So where would you hide it?'

'With a load of other white vans.'

'You mean on a used car lot?'

'No, that wouldn't work, it would be spotted immediately someone asked to go for a test drive. Where else would you expect to see white vans? Think about Saturday mornings.'

'Car boot sales?'

'That's the idea. But since it's not Saturday till tomorrow and whoever had the van will have already got rid of it, I think an alternative to hiding in plain sight should be investigated.'

'Any ideas?'

Buchanan nodded. 'Building sites. Who's going to notice another white van parked on a building site?'

'Shall I ask Morris and Stephen to have a look?' said Street.

'No, you and I are going to do that, it's about time I found out what is happening to my neighbourhood.'

♦

'I never realised just how many houses were being built around here,' said Buchanan, as they left the last of five building sites on Rattle Road.

'Or just how many white vans there are,' said Street.

'Yes – hang-on,' said Buchanan, pressing the call answer button on his steering wheel. 'Buchanan. Who's this?'

'Hi, it's Jade in Control. We've just had a call about your missing white van. One of the traffic cars has had a hit on its NPR camera.'

'Did they stop it?'

'They didn't have to, it's already stopped.'

'Where?'

'Pevensey Starbucks car park. The manager mentioned to one of the traffic guys when they came in for coffee that people keep ridesharing and use the coffee shop car park to leave their vehicles. The traffic cop ran the plates and found out the van was on the wanted list.'

'Why would parking be an issue? They have a large car park.'

'The van is tucked round the back and blocking access to the mobile phone mast. There are two angry engineers and a mobile crane who require access to the mast.'

'Where is the patrol car?'

'They're parked in the garage car park keeping an eye on the errant van.'

'No sign of a driver?'

'Not while they've been watching.'

'Thanks, Jade, we'll be right there.'

♦

Buchanan turned off the A27, into the BP garage and parked beside the patrol car.

'I wonder why we didn't notice the van when we were here for coffee last week?' pondered Street, as she parked beside the hedge separating the garage from Starbucks.

'That's because it's tucked round the corner behind the coffee shop and also we weren't looking for one at the time.'

Buchanan and Street got out, walked over to the patrol car and introduced themselves to the driver.

'DCI Buchanan and DS Street. Has anyone approached the van?'

'A couple of the baristas looked in the through the driver's window, nothing else.'

93

'Thanks, we can take it from here if you need to get on.'

'I was just going to suggest that. Happy hunting!'

'Jill, I think we'll stand by the front door of M&S and watch the van for a few minutes. See if the patrol car leaving brings anyone over to have a look.'

'Fine with me.'

'Fancy a coffee?' said Buchanan, as they stood beside the newspaper stand. 'Starbucks is open.'

'Sure,' said Street. 'But mind if I pop inside while we're here? I promised Stephen we'd have steak for dinner.'

'OK, while you are doing that, I'll have a chat with the Starbucks manager.'

Street returned twenty minutes later to find Buchanan sitting at a table outside Starbucks talking on the phone. He hung up as she approached.

'You look like the cat that swallowed the canary, what's up?'

'While you were at M&S buying steaks for you and Stephen, I had a nice chat with the Starbucks manager. Apparently, some kind-hearted citizen has paid forward our next ten cups of coffee.'

'That's lovely, did you ask her about the CCTV?'

'The manager says she'll have a look at the footage, but not to hold our breath.'

'Is that the one we are looking for?' she said, pointing to a rather dirty white van.

'Yes. I was just about to have a look.'

'OK, lead on.'

Street followed Buchanan over to the van and stood beside him as he looked through the driver's door.

'What a tip,' he said. 'Typical contractor's van, driver's door is unlocked, but I think we'll leave the opening for the CSI's.'

'Blood stains on the steering wheel aren't what you'd expect in any vehicle,' observed Street.

'Let's try the back.'

They walked round the van to the sliding door. Street put on a cotton glove and tried the door; it was locked.

'If the steering wheel is anything to go by this is our murder wagon. I'll call and get a CSI team here,' said Buchanan.

'What about the locked doors?'

'I think we'll call a locksmith; I doubt if the CSI team will have keys for this.'

While Buchanan made his phone calls, Street took down the details of the occasional curious customers as they enquired about the van.

'CSI team are on their way,' said Buchanan, putting his phone back in his pocket.

'It's quite ironic,' said Street.

'Why?'

'This is only a couple of miles from where it was reported stolen.'

'That thought had crossed my mind.'

'How are you going to be with house guests?'

'Not sure. Karen and I are sort of used to just each other's company.'

'Doesn't Karen's family visit?'

'When we were living in Glasgow her sister and husband would sometimes come to stay for the week.'

'What about Karen's mum?'

'Once or twice, but she said the weather was too cold and wet for her.'

'Is that why Karen goes to France often to visit her mum?

'Yes. Ever since her dad died, she's been even closer to her mum.'

'Talking of parents, how are your mum and dad?'

'Talked to them last weekend, both are fine, though Dad says his knees are bothering him.'

♦

Buchanan and Street stood near the van sipping on their coffees watching to see if the van attracted any attention from the passers-by. Since it was late in the day, if someone was using it for work, they might come and collect it to go home. They had just finished their coffees when a white van with a CSI team arrived.

'Is this the vehicle?' asked the civilian who exited the van.

'Yes. Go carefully, it looks messy inside,' said Buchanan.

'I don't suppose you have the key?'

'Nope.'

'Is it locked?'

'We tried the side and back doors, they're both locked. The cab appears to be unlocked. I was leaving the opening of the back to you.'

'Been really busy I see,' said the taller of the two CSI's, nodding at Buchanan and Street's empty coffee cups.

'Somebody's got to do it, Chris. How are you? How are the kids?' said Street.

'Fine. Young George has just started crawling and Grace now walks like a little princess.'

'How about you, Harry? Has Liz got over her morning sickness?'

'Excuse me,' said Buchanan. 'Could we get back to work? I have a killer to catch.'

'OK, let's get dressed first,' said Chris.

Buchanan and Street watched as the team donned their white coveralls and set up a police cordon around the van. The one Jill referred to as Chris reached for the side door of the van and, like she had, found it locked.

'Do you want us to force it or call for a locksmith?' asked Chris.

'A locksmith is on his way.'

'Who did you call?'

'I opted for Fast Fixings; they specialise in automobile locks.'

'Good, they know their way around vehicles.'

While they waited for the locksmith, the CSI's took photographs, fingerprints and bagged various pieces of builder's van detritus from the front cab of the van.

'Inspector,' said Chris, 'if the back of the van is anything like the front. I suggest we treat this as a crime scene prior to recovering it to a secure location.'

'That bad?'

'Not only is there blood on the steering wheel, it's also on the seats and floor mats,' said Henry. 'Must have been quite a fight for all that blood to be shed. We also have glove prints in the dried blood on the inside door handles, not sure if we can get prints from them. There are also blooded shoe prints on the floor mats. We've found three sets of fingerprints from the back and side doors.'

'Just as well the locksmith has arrived then,' said Buchanan, waving him over.

'Someone reported a locked van door?' asked the locksmith. 'Who's the driver?'

'None of us,' said Buchanan, taking out his warrant badge. 'I'm Detective Chief Inspector Buchanan. The van in front of you is suspected of being involved in a crime and we need to see in the back. Are you able to open it without damaging the lock?'

''05 Ford Transit, shouldn't be too much trouble.'

'OK,' said Chris, 'but before you start, could you wear these gloves? Can't have you contaminating the scene by adding your prints to the samples we've already lifted from the doors.'

'Don't need them,' said the locksmith, taking a pair of black nitrile gloves from a box on the passenger seat of his van.

While the locksmith set about opening the van door, Street stood outside the cordon and chatted with Chris and George about children; Buchanan sucked on a fruit gum. The locksmith was as good as his word and fifteen minutes later he pulled the door open to reveal a pile of blood-soaked newspapers and plastic tarps.

'Woah, what's gone on here?' he asked.

'Let's hope you never have to see anything like it again,' said Buchanan. 'Are you OK?'

'I am now, thanks,' he said, stepping under the cordon tape. 'Whew, that gave me quite a turn. Haven't seen anything that bad since dogs got in with the sheep when they were lambing on my dad's farm.'

'I think I'll pass on that,' said Buchanan.

♦

'Glad this is someone else's job?' asked Street. She and Buchanan watched as Chris and the CSI team carefully photographed, tagged and bagged the contents of the rear of the van.

'Someone has to do it.'

'They're very efficient, looks like they are done.'

'No body parts, that's good.'

'Why?'

'Dr Mansell has a full body currently laying in the morgue, any more parts and we'd be looking for a second body, possible female.'

'All done, Chris?' asked Street.

'Yes, are you the CSM?'

'I am. Could you send me the list of what you've found as soon as you can and any samples to the lab for blood matching? Were you able to get many sets of prints?'

'Several.'

'Excellent.'

'What about the van?' asked Chris.

'I'll arrange to have it removed to a secure location,' said Buchanan, looking at the time on his phone.

'Back to the office?' asked Street.

Buchanan shook his head. 'The forensics from the van won't be ready till tomorrow at the earliest. Have you heard from Stephen and Morris?'

'Not so far. Stephen said they were going to Falmer first thing this morning to talk to the friends of Zilini Barazani, then on to Hastings to check on the movements of Zac Taylor.'

'In sorry to do this as tomorrow is Saturday. Would you let Stephen and Morris know I'd like to see you all about ten in the office tomorrow morning? We need to go over the facts of the case.'

♦

Buchanan parked his car on his driveway and went into the house.

'One of those days?' said Karen, as he walked into the kitchen.

'It shows?'

'Why don't you go freshen up and I'll make you a cup of tea.'

Buchanan frowned.

'OK, whisky and water.'

♦

Buchanan reclined in his chair and waited for his glass of whisky. Things were getting worse, but then they always did in the early stages of a case. As he waited, he looked out of the conservatory windows at the small vegetable plot he'd started. Where there once was barren earth, there now grew a single tomato plant.

'Where are our guests?' he asked, as Karen put his whisky on the side table.

'Travis took the train to Brighton. He said since he is one of the keynote speakers, he wanted to go over the timings with the organisers.'

'And Poppy?'

'As soon as she'd unpacked, she called Harry. He'd just got in but still found time to drive down and collect her. I don't expect we'll see them till dinner time.'

'Harry's coming to dinner?'

Karen looked at Buchanan. 'What do you think? Of course, he's coming to dinner.'

Buchanan smiled. 'That will be a nice ending to the day. How was Harry?'

'He was like a cat on a hot tin roof, couldn't wait to whisk his intended off for a romantic walk.'

'Did she say where they were going?'

'Poppy said they'd talked about taking a walk along the promenade and having a late afternoon tea at the Beach Deck.'

'It's been a lovely day for it. What's for dinner?'

'Do you think lasagne will be OK?'

'With garlic bread and salad?'

'And apple pie for dessert.'

'Mrs Buchanan, you still amaze me. Is there anything I can do to help?'

'No thanks. The table is set, and the lasagne is in the oven cooking.'

'Bread – shall I get some French sticks out of the freezer?'

'That's OK. I've wrapped the bread in foil, all it needs is ten minutes in the oven to warm, and the apple pie just needs heating; so that just leaves the salad. From the look on your face, I deduce you have a lot to ponder upon.'

'Thanks.'

'Are you getting any closer to finding the missing girl?'

'It's early days. Finding the boyfriend's dismembered body worries me. The last thing Eastbourne needs is some sort of internecine war between family factions.'

'I'm glad all I have to worry about is have I have made enough for dinner? You know how Americans enjoy their food.'

'I'm sure that won't be an issue. I've seen how well you prepare.'

'Thanks, I'll leave you to your thoughts.'

Buchanan took a sip of his whisky and tried to make sense out of what was known so far in the case of 'The Missing Heiress'.

Zac Taylor, the boyfriend of Zilini Barazani, was last seen alive late on Wednesday evening. Zac's twin brother, Sam, said two men had been looking for Zac; could it have been them who ransacked Zac's bedroom? Could they have been Zhukovski's men, or relations on Zilini's father's stepbrother's side of the family? Something just didn't add up.

Amal Barazani said he last saw his daughter at dinner on the Friday evening. He further added that he'd heard music from Zilini's bedroom when he went to bed. If she was still in her room, when did she leave, and did she leave alone?

It was now a certain fact that Zac Taylor had been killed and dismembered sometime during Friday evening and his remains buried in the early hours of Saturday morning.

The van used to transport Zac's remains had been stolen from Hankham sometime Friday evening and left in the Starbucks car park. Question, who knew where the van was kept, and who knew to leave it hidden in plain sight in the Starbucks car park? Also, did anyone see it being driven or who was driving it? Unfortunately, the Starbucks CCTV wasn't very helpful.

What was the purpose of sending Zilini's empty ring box to her father? Was it her way to say she was safe, or a cryptic message from her abductors?

Buchanan put down his glass and picked up his phone to take notes. Item one: first thing tomorrow morning was to find out what Stephen and Morris had discovered from Zilini's friends. Item two: had they found out who owned and operated Cliff Taxis? Item three: the movements of Zac Taylor during the days prior to his death needed to be ascertained.

He sighed, put down his phone and picked up the newspaper. He had only managed to read the headlines when his musings were interrupted by the sound of the doorbell, followed by the unmistakable sound of Travis's voice as Karen opened the front door. Buchanan stood and walked through to the kitchen. On his way to greet Travis, he left his empty whisky glass on the kitchen counter.

'Hi Jack,' said Travis smiling at his comment.

Buchanan shook his head. 'The old ones get you every time. How was Brighton?'

'Glad I don't have to drive there, it's a mad house. Poppy still out with Harry?'

'They said they'd be back for dinner,' said Karen. 'Why don't you two go and sit down in the conservatory? Travis, what would you like to drink?'

'What's Jack drinking?'

Karen noticed the empty whisky glass on the counter and said, 'Nothing, at the moment.'

Travis smiled. 'Is there any coffee?'

'I'll make a pot. You two go through and I'll bring it in when it's ready.'

'Thanks, Karen. No need for milk or sugar for me.'

Travis followed Buchanan through to the conservatory.

'I presume this is where you are sitting, Jack?' said Travis, indicating the *Eastbourne Herald* lying on the chair. 'I'll sit over here, wouldn't want to deprive the head of house of his prerogative.'

'When I get the chance,' replied Buchanan, folding the newspaper and putting it on the coffee table. 'I've been so busy since we moved in.'

'Interesting,' said Travis. 'Have you ever tried reading the newspaper online?'

'I tried it a couple of times, but I found the pop-up advertisements too distracting.'

'Your coffees,' said Karen, moving the newspaper and placing a tray down on the coffee table. 'There's some shortbread to go with it, but don't let it spoil your appetite.'

'You've made a real home for yourselves here,' said Travis, leaning back into the recliner chair, 'the colour choices are perfect, so relaxing.'

'That's Karen's doing. If it were down to me the walls would be magnolia and the ceilings white.'

'Back in the States most homes that I've been in are simply painted white, floor to ceiling.'

'I suppose that helps to make them seem cool in the summer?'

Travis nodded. 'So, Jack, how was your day? Find the missing girl?'

Buchanan shook his head. 'Still early days in the investigation.'

'What about the dead man?'

'Not much other than what I told you earlier. I have two constables investigating both their backgrounds this afternoon;

hopefully they will have some good news for me when we meet in the office tomorrow.'

'Do you have a theory that you are working on?'

'I'm working on two strands of investigation. The first, that the daughter has been kidnapped to coerce the father into turning over the dongle code which unlocks the anti-virus software his company is developing.'

'But to what purpose would that be? If they knew the coding it would make the product unviable. Of course, they could launch the software as their own and reap the profit for little expense.'

'I had thought that myself. If it is the stepbrother who is behind the extortion attempt, he would exact a revenge most sweet.'

'And the other strand?'

'Your idea of an honour killing. When I asked the father about a ransom note he denied there was one.'

'Anything else?'

'There is the issue of the ring box.'

'What's that?'

'The girl's father received an envelope, and the only content was an empty ring box.'

'What's the significance of that?'

'I'm not sure. The missing ring was her mother's wedding ring, the daughter hoped one day to wear it at her own wedding. It was an 18th birthday present from her father, a sort of coming of age present.'

'Was the ring valuable?'

'The wedding ring came from one of the Romanoff jewels that were looted when the family were murdered by the Bolsheviks during the Russian revolution.'

'That must have made it quite valuable.'

'Her father told me the ring was a family heirloom and was worth more than five years of my salary.'

'Not the sort of thing you'd find for sale on eBay.'

'I wouldn't know about that; I've never sold anything on eBay.'

'So, what do you think is behind the sending of the empty ring box?'

'I'd say it's a message to the father, but who sent it and what's the message behind it, is what I'm trying to understand.'

'Could she have just run away from home and the empty ring box was her way of saying, *I'm going it alone*?'

'That's one way of looking at it. But the issue of her boyfriend being murdered makes that unlikely. To my mind, it's probably the other way round. The boyfriend was killed, and she ran away because she was frightened, thinking quite reasonably she might be next.'

'So, the ring box is her way of getting in touch with her father to say she is all right?'

'Or, if she felt threatened by her father, it was her way of saying she was gone and not to look for her.'

7
Saturday Morning
Meeting time

'You haven't slept this late in a long time, what time did you come to bed?' asked Karen, as she placed a cup of coffee and newspaper on the bedside table.

'It must have been about three. Travis likes to talk.'

'Well, it's Saturday, you can take it easy.'

'Not today, I have a killer to catch, and a team meeting at ten o'clock.'

'You'd better hurry then, it's almost eight o'clock. Why don't you get dressed and I'll make your breakfast? Can't have you going to work hungry. Scrambled eggs on toast sound OK?'

'No thanks. I'll get breakfast at The Beach café,' he said, looking at the bedside clock. 'They open at eight-thirty.'

'You'll need to let Jill know you'll be late.'

'Thanks, I will. Is Travis up?'

'He left an hour ago. He said there's an executive team meeting at eleven that he needs to attend.'

'And Poppy?'

'She's in her room getting ready. She and Harry are off to Hickstead showground later this morning. They are going with Nathan to look at some horses going through their paces. And you, what will you and the three musketeers be doing today?'

'Still looking for Zilini Barazani.'

'Do you really think her dad is responsible for her disappearance?'

Buchanan yawned as he stood up. 'I really don't know. One minute he's the obvious contender for the position, then the evidence points to possibly the uncle, or even a third party.'

'What did the uncle say when you talked to him?'

Buchanan shook his head. 'It didn't make sense. He said that Zilini came to the house most Thursdays with her boyfriend for singing lessons.'

♦

'How was breakfast?' asked Street, as Buchanan entered his office.

'Just what I needed, we should have a meeting there one day, they even do black pudding with breakfast. Stephen and Morris – any sign of them this morning?'

'Stephen went to pick up Morris, Debbie's car has gone in for a MOT and she needs his car to go and see her parents. He said they will be here by ten-thirty.'

'Good. We do need to get on top of this case before it blows up in our face.'

'How was dinner last night?'

'Did you meet the Grants when they were here a few months ago?'

'Briefly at Castlewood.'

'Karen made a lasagne, and I drank too much wine. Always happens when we spend the evening with interesting people.'

'What about the daughter, Poppy?'

'She was there with Harry, her fiancé. We didn't get much out of them though; they spent the evening chatting to each other and making plans for their wedding.'

'Have they set a date yet?'

'No, it's not that simple. Especially when you consider the facts Poppy lives and attends university in the USA and Harry works full time at Castlewood.'

Their conversation was curtailed with the arrival of Hunter and Dexter.

'Morning, Boss,' said Dexter.

'Good morning; grab a seat both of you. How was the identification?'

'Very interesting,' said Hunter. We left the office and, since it was going to be a long day, stopped in at Morrisons for petrol and a sandwich. I went in to pay and got a big surprise. Standing three customers in front of me was Sam Taylor! I stopped him as he was leaving and told him we wanted to have a quick word with him.'

'How did he react?' said Buchanan.

'Surprised, and a bit shaken. He did calm down a bit when we said we only wanted to tell him something.'

'How did he take the news?'

'We suggested he got in the car as it would be a bit more private.'

'What did you tell him?'

'I said his brother had been assaulted and died as the result of his injuries. I went on to say that whoever had killed him had buried his body in a construction pit.'

'How did he take the news?'

'He just sat silently in the back of the squad car staring at his hands. Eventually as the news sunk in, he started sobbing. We asked if there was anything we could do for him. He just shook his head and asked if he could see his brother,' said Hunter.

'I drove us to the morgue,' said Dexter. 'Dr Mansell did a good job of making the corpse look like it was in one piece. 'It was uncanny how the two brothers looked alike, even when one was dead.'

'What was Sam's reaction.'

'He looked at Zac, smiled and said, *'sleep well bro, see you in eternity. Yes, that's my brother.'*

'So, he identified Zac?'

'Yes. Sam identified his brother,' said Hunter.

'I wonder what he was doing at Morrisons? The Langney shops are much closer to his flat,' said Buchanan.

'I asked him that same question,' said Dexter. 'He said he was meeting a friend who lived nearby. We dropped him back at Morrisons on our way out of town.'

'Good. Finally, a solid fact to build on,' said Buchanan, standing and walking over to the window.

'How did you two get on at Falmer?'

'We drove over to Lewes and interviewed as many of the residents of the halls of residence we could find. Most of those who knew Zilini Barazani said they hadn't seen her recently. Only one said she'd talked to her, and that was on Friday afternoon.'

'Where was that?'

'On the train to Eastbourne.'

'What did she say?'

'They talked mostly about the upcoming exams.'

'Did she say anything about Zilini's demeanour?'

'No.'

'Did the boyfriend's name come up in conversation?'

'I did ask,' said Dexter. 'She said she thought there had been a bit of a misunderstanding about a party they were supposed to be going to.'

'Did she say what the misunderstanding was?'

'Zilini and her friend had arranged to do some studying together for the upcoming exams and the date conflicted with the party.'

'Where and when was the party to be held?'

'She thought it was to be in a flat of a friend of Zac's. I asked where the flat was, she thought it might be somewhere in Hastings, near the Jenny Lind pub.'

'Didn't Zhukovski say they followed Zac Taylor to the Jenny Lind pub on the Wednesday?' pondered Street.

Buchanan nodded. 'What about Zac Taylor's movements?'

'Nothing in Falmer,' said Hunter. 'We were planning on going to Hastings later this morning.'

'Good,' said Buchanan. 'How about forensics, Jill? Anything in from them this morning?'

'While you were eating breakfast. Want me to read?'

'Go ahead.'

'It's mostly about the crushed phone found in the pit. The call record for the last four weeks shows he called a lot of numbers in the London area. I checked some of them and they were all companies looking for delivery drivers.'

'Sounds like he was looking for work,' said Dexter.

'What about local numbers?'

'Several. A couple to McDonald's, one to the cinema, several to a local betting office, and the rest to a number we know to be that of a local escort service.'

'Stephen, remind me again exactly what Sam Taylor said when he identified the corpse?'

Hunter consulted his notebook and read. *Sleep well Bro, see you in eternity. Yes, that's my brother.*'

'Not, *yep that's Zac?*'

Hunter looked back at his notebook. 'That's what he said. *Sleep well Bro, see you in eternity. Yes, that's my brother.* Why?'

Buchanan smiled. 'Nothing, just thinking out loud. OK, let me know immediately if anything turns up in Hastings.'

'Will you need us for anything else today?'

'Probably not,' said Buchanan, looking up at the office clock. 'You'd better get your skates on if you're to get to Hastings and back before we knock-off for the day.'

'Bye. See you later, Jill,' said Hunter, as he and Dexter walked out the door.

'Jill, do we have any samples of Zac Taylor's fingerprints?'

'Yes, from the corpse.'

'Nothing independent from that?'

'Why?'

'Just wondering about something. Jill, will you call Dr Mansell? No, don't bother, I'll do that. In the meantime, while Stephen and Morris are in Hastings, can you arrange for a CSI team to meet us at Zac Taylor's flat and do a complete search?'

'What should they be looking for?'

'Anything that will have Zac Taylor's prints on it. While you do that, I'll call Dr Mansell.'

Buchanan hung up from his call and waited for Street to complete hers to the CSI office.

'The receptionist said they should have a team at Zac Taylor's in an hour. How did you do with the doctor?'

'He confirmed my suspicions.'

'And they are?'

'I'm the prince of fools, Jill.'

'You, a fool? I don't think so.'

'Don't you? Do you remember the actual words used by Sam Taylor when he did the identification of his brother?'

Street thought for a moment, then said, '*Yes, that's my brother.*'

'*Précisément, ma chérie,*' said Buchanan. 'He said, *that's my brother.*'

'I don't follow you.'

'He did say that the body on the table was his brother, but what he didn't say was, *yes that's Zac, my brother.* Did he?'

She shook her head. 'I still don't follow you.'

'When we interviewed Sam Taylor on Tuesday, he told us about an incident several years ago when Zac was returning from a party and fell in a ditch and broke his left leg.'

'I remember.'

'Well, when I talked to Dr Mansell about the body, I asked him to check hospital records. He came back to me and said there was no record of a Zac Taylor being brought in with a broken leg, but there was one for a Sam Taylor.'

'So, the other day when we talked to Sam Taylor, we were actually talking to Zac Taylor. Zac is still alive, and it's Sam who's lying in the morgue?'

Buchanan nodded his head. 'Jill, we need to go and see Sam, I mean Zac Taylor.'

'Why?'

'Before he ends up in the morgue like his brother, Sam.'

'Suppose he's not home?'

'That's a possibility I've been contemplating.'

♦

'I hope we're not too late,' said Buchanan, as they parked behind a white van in front of Zac Taylor's flat.

Buchanan pressed the doorbell. After no answer on the third ring he pressed all the others. 'That should wake someone.'

'Who's that?' came a voice from the speaker.

'Police,' replied Buchanan. 'We're looking for Zac or Sam Taylor.'

'Lazy buggers, can't be bothered to answer their own bell, come in.'

Buchanan smiled at Street as the door lock buzzed.

'Interesting scene,' said Street, as they stepped out of the lift, they saw two uniformed bailiffs standing on the landing. 'I wonder if those bailiffs are looking for the Taylor brothers?'

'Let's find out,' said Buchanan, approaching the two bailiffs.

'Zac Taylor?' asked the shorter of the two.

'No. Detective Chief Inspector Buchanan and Detective Sergeant Street. What's your interest in Zac Taylor?'

The bailiff looked at his paperwork. 'We have a county court judgement to collect seven hundred and fifty pounds.'

'What's it for?'

The bailiff looked back at his paperwork. 'Zac Taylor had an unpaid bill at a local music shop. He paid with a credit card and forgot to pay Visa when the bill came in. I deduce by your presence we are unlikely to collect today, Inspector?'

'That is a possibility,' said Buchanan, knocking on the door.

'We've tried that,' said the bailiff, when Buchanan's third hammering on the door received no reply.

'We have a warrant to enter and recover goods to the value of the outstanding amount,' said the bailiff. 'We're just waiting for a locksmith.'

'Good, we'll wait with you.'

Twenty minutes later, the locksmith had the door to the Taylor brothers' flat unlocked.

'Would you mind waiting here on the landing?' said Buchanan to the bailiffs. 'I have a CSI team coming. You can go in as soon as they have completed their search.'

'Sure, as long as it doesn't take all morning, we have a lot of addresses to collect from before we're done today.'

'Do you think Amal Barazani's stepbrother was on the level with us?' Street asked Buchanan.

'I hope so, though his stepmother is quite something.'
She nodded. 'I wouldn't want her for my mother.'

> 'The Queen of Hearts,
> she made some tarts,
> to keep Zilini in line,
> but what a shame
> when the time came
> Zilini did depart.'

'Another Buchanan masterpiece,' said Street. 'I take it you don't care for her either?'

Buchanan smiled. 'I couldn't make a comment.'

Their conversation was disturbed by the arrival of the CSI team.

'Good morning Jack, Jill. What are we looking for?' asked Littlejohn.

'Fingerprints to start with, Henry. The flat is lived in by twin brothers and there is at least one girlfriend who visits occasionally. We already have the prints from one of the brothers, he's currently in the morgue. Wallets, chequebooks, credit cards would be appreciated. Also, mobile phones and memory cards would be most useful.'

'How about post?'

'I doubt if you'll find much of that, but collect what you find,' said Buchanan, looking in through the door at the tight confines of what passed for a hallway. 'We'll wait outside with the bailiffs while you search.'

♦

'That didn't take long,' said Buchanan, as the CSI team exited the flat. 'Did you find much, Henry?'

'Nothing of any value. It's a busy place, we found seven distinct sets of prints, four sets in the rear bedroom. We've logged where the prints were taken from, made me think the room might have been searched. You were correct about the post, mostly circulars, and one demanding payment from a music shop. There was also a letter from the rental agency saying that there had been some complaints about noise.'

'How about mobile phones?'

'You're in luck there, we found two. They were stuffed under the mattress in the left-hand bedroom. Both have flat batteries.'

'Any musical instruments?'

'No, nothing like that. But now you ask, there were several short lengths of what looks like fishing line and piano wire lying on the floor. Ted says they look like the ends of guitar strings.'

'Thanks.'

'Can we go in now?' asked one of the bailiffs.

'I'm sorry, no. This is now a crime scene, and besides, you heard what the CSI said about valuables,' replied Buchanan. 'Here's my card. If you still wish to gain access, give me a call in a couple of weeks.'

'OK, no point in trying to get blood from a stone.'

'Where next?' asked Street.

'Back to the office, hopefully Stephen and Morris will be back from Hastings and have some information for us.'

♦

'What did you two find out?' asked Buchanan.

'The Jenny Lind isn't just a pub,' said Morris, reading from a brochure. 'It's also a hotel,

> We are perfectly located in the midst of the medieval Cinque Port of Hastings Old Town, two minutes' walk from the beach and the Stade, with its iconic, tall black net huts and the largest beach-launched fishing fleet in Europe. Come explore our wonderful town and make your base with us at The Jenny Lind Inn. Our delightful Hotel Manager, Eloise, is dedicated to looking after our guests and ensuring that you are happy, comfortable and well-informed during your stay with us.

According to the brochure they have guest ales and live music.'

'Quite a local attraction. Did you find anyone who recognised the photo?'

'Yes, and that was a bit of a surprise. Apparently, Zac was a regular at their open mike evenings.'

'What did he perform?'

'Folk music, he was best known for his rendition of Bob Dylan songs.'

Buchanan smiled. 'That makes sense.'

'What does?' asked Street.

'Remember what the CSI's said they found in the Taylor brothers' flat, short lengths of fishing line and piano wire?'

'Yes.'

'Those probably were the cut ends of guitar strings.'

'So where is Zac Taylor's guitar then?' asked Street.

'Probably in a pawn shop somewhere,' said Hunter. looking at his watch.

'Jill,' said Buchanan, 'did you put a rush on with forensics with what was found in the Taylor brothers' flat?'

'I got the usual, *you'll just have to wait, we're so busy*, answer.'

'What did you say to that?'

'I asked them if they'd like my boss to come over and give them a hand.'

'I'll bet that made them laugh.'

'Only till I told them who my boss was – you do have a bit of a reputation! They'll have the fingerprint results over to us first thing Monday morning. Mobile phone details may take a bit longer. All depends how much information there is on the phones and how long it takes to fully charge the batteries.'

'Jill, before we end for the day, would you get on to the transport police and see if you can get copies of the CCTV videos from Hastings and Pevensey & Westham stations for last Wednesday? Also, while you are asking, see if they have any videos of Zac Taylor or Zilini Barazani in Eastbourne and Hastings stations?'

'I'll try.'

'Stephen, Morris, what did you find out about Cliff Cabs?'

114

'They have no record of collecting a fare from Pevensey and Westham station last Wednesday evening,' said Dexter.

'Interesting. Zhukovski's surveillance report says Zac Taylor was picked up by a Cliff Cab Mercedes taxi.'

'The dispatcher at Cliff Cabs said one of their drivers reported someone had pinched the magnetic door signs off his taxi, and none of the drivers has a Mercedes.'

'What about the actual operator's licence? All taxis have to have an operator's licence attached to the rear of the vehicle beside the vehicle's licence plate?'

'That was still there, that's why the driver didn't make a fuss. He figured it was just kids having a laugh.'

'That is interesting, Zhukovski's people must just have looked at the door signs on the taxi,' said Buchanan. 'Anything else?'

Three heads shook no.

'In that case, I'll see you all back here first thing Monday morning.'

♦

Buchanan parked his car on the driveway and went into his quiet house wondering just how quiet it would be with Poppy and Travis staying with them for the weekend. He took off his jacket and walked through to the kitchen.

'Hiya, how was your day?' He kissed Karen on the back of the neck.

'Absolutely fine, I'm having so much fun thinking we have our first house guests.'

'Has Travis returned from Brighton?'

'No, it's a bit early for that. I think he said he would catch the five o'clock train from Brighton, it gets into Pevensey and Westham about six. I asked him if he wanted to be picked up from the station, he declined and said he'd prefer to walk up'

'Poppy and Harry?'

'They went for a walk up to Hankham.'

'Any post?'

'A bank statement, oh, also your greenhouse catalogue is here. I put it on the coffee table beside your chair.'

'Thanks.'

'I just made a fresh pot of coffee, or would you like something stronger?'

'Coffee will be fine. Can I help with anything?'

'No, it's all in hand. Why don't you go and sit down and I'll bring you your coffee?'

'Thanks; on the coffee table you said?'

'Yes.'

Buchanan was looking at aluminium shelving for the eight by twelve-foot greenhouse he was planning on purchasing when Poppy and Harry returned.

'Hi Jack,' said Poppy.

'Hello Poppy, Harry.'

'How are you doing on the search for the missing girl?' asked Poppy.

'Still looking. How was your day?'

'Fantastic. Since there weren't any events going on at Hickstead, we were able to walk all round the grounds. I think being the guests of Sir Nathan helped.'

'You said he was going to look at some horses?'

'Yes,' said Harry. 'Sometimes he will go to look at horses for sale on behalf of friends.'

'Did he find any suitable horses?'

'Yes, he said he was spoilt for choice, they were such fine animals.'

'If you'll excuse me,' said Poppy, 'I'm going to freshen up before dinner.'

As Poppy left the room, Buchanan gestured to Harry to sit.

'How are you doing, Harry?'

'Fine.'

'Any issues about what happened to you at Castlewood?'

'No. I'm completely recovered.'

'How was your visit to Dallas?'

Harry smiled and thought before answering. 'Unsettling. I thought I had all I wanted working and living at Castlewood, now – I don't know.'

'What's made you so unsure, or should I guess at the cause?'

'I think Poppy would live anywhere we were together. It's just I don't want to let Nathan down, especially since he did so much to help me when I was in trouble.'

'I take it you are thinking about moving to Dallas after you get married?'

'Yes. I've been offered a job as stable manager at a horse ranch near where Poppy's family live. We'd only be thirty minutes' drive from her parents. There's also a three-bedroom ranch-house and a huge 4-wheel drive Ford pickup that goes with the job.'

'Have you talked to Nathan about the job offer?'

Harry shook his head.

'Would you like me to say something to him?'

'No thanks, that's my job.'

'I wouldn't worry about it, Harry. I'm sure Nathan will understand.'

'Who wouldn't worry?' asked Poppy, who'd just walked into the conservatory.

'I was just telling Jack about my job offer in Dallas,' said Harry.

'Oh, it's so perfect, Jack. Our first home together and only a short drive from Mom and Dad's house.'

'Have you set a date for the wedding?'

'It all depends on Harry's visa application,' said Poppy. 'Mom and Dad are sponsoring Harry, and with his confirmed job offer we are hoping his visa will come through before I have to go back to college next January. Unfortunately, he's not allowed to live in the country while he waits for the visa.'

'You don't start back till January?'

'I'm taking the fall term off. It will put my graduation off a year, but I don't mind, just as long as Harry and I can be together. We're hoping for a spring wedding.'

117

Buchanan smiled 'Sounds like you two have everything worked out,' he said, rising from his chair. 'If you'll excuse me, I need to have a quick word with Karen.'

♦

'It's so sad, Dad and I fly home Friday morning and I'll have to say goodbye to Harry again,' said Poppy, as Karen stood to clear the dinner dishes from the table.

'I'll come over for a few days in October,' said Harry.

Buchanan looked at Karen and nodded.

'Jack and I have been talking,' said Karen. 'Poppy, you said you were thinking about putting off going back to college till next January?'

'Yes, didn't think I could get my mind round studying and not being with Harry.'

'Can I make a suggestion?' said Karen.

'Yes.'

'Suppose you stayed with us till Christmas? You should be able to do a distance learning course at Brighton University and see Harry at the weekends.'

'Dad, could I? That would mean I wouldn't have to delay my graduating.'

'Are you sure it wouldn't be too much trouble, Karen? Jack is a very busy man and probably needs space to unwind.'

'Relax Travis,' said Buchanan. 'It was mostly my idea.'

'If you're sure? It's just till Christmas?'

'I'm sure we're sure,' said Karen,

'OK, I'll give Shelly a call and let her know what's happening. Though I'm not sure what she is going to say when I tell her.'

'Oh, Dad, thanks,' said Poppy.

'Not sure I had a choice in the matter. I suppose I'd better get on to the Dean of Admissions and make the necessary arrangements.'

'We can come for visits,' said Poppy, her head resting on Harry's shoulder. 'We could have a Thanksgiving meal and invite Jack and Karen.'

'When and what is Thanksgiving?' asked Buchanan, 'is it like our Harvest Festival in September?'

'Thanksgiving is the last Thursday in November,' said Travis. 'To Americans it is seen as the great gathering of the families. Though the holiday is on the Thursday, most spread the festivities over the whole weekend. Families travel from all over the States to be together for the holiday, be great to have you and Karen come for a visit. You can even watch football, non-stop, from Thursday morning till Monday night. American football, Jack, not what you call football.'

'Thanks, we'd love to come for a visit. Though it might depend on what I'm working on at the time.'

'Surely Jill could stand in for you if there's a case under investigation?' suggested Karen.

Buchanan nodded. 'You're right, Jill is more than capable of running things while I'm gone for a few days. Thanks Travis, we'd love to come for a visit.'

'Do you hear that, Harry?' said Poppy, as she sat up and looked into his face. 'I can stay here till your visa comes through.'

'Yes, I did, and I also know I have an early start at the stables tomorrow morning. I'm going to say thank you for a lovely evening Mrs Buchanan, and head off home to Castlewood.'

'You're welcome, Harry.'

'I'll see you to the door,' said Poppy.

'Would either of you like something to drink before you turn in?' Karen asked Travis and Buchanan.

'Yes, could I have a – Horlicks?' said Buchanan.

'I'll have a coffee if there's any left,' said Travis, 'and I'm sure Jack would like something stronger than Horlicks.'

'That's all right Travis, I remember the last time we shared a drink together – it wouldn't feel right to put you through that again.'

'Thanks, but it's OK with me if you want a drink.'

Buchanan shook his head, 'I'm fine with Horlicks.'

'OK one coffee and a Horlicks coming up,' said Karen.

'I'm sorry you had to go through that ordeal with DI Hanbury, Travis. It must have been terrible for you, a church pastor, to have been arrested for attempted murder when all the time you were innocent.'

'That was how Inspector Hanbury saw it. I wouldn't lose any sleep over it, he was only doing his job. You may have seen my circumstances as something bad, but I believe it was for my good.'

'But you were innocent. I felt it was my fault, I should have acted quicker.'

'Don't be angry with yourself because I had to spend a few hours in a jail cell, Jack; it was God who sent me there. I needed to have a change of heart; I was an arrogant, self-centred egotist. I judged Harry as being unworthy for Poppy because he had a criminal record. How else was God going to show me what it was like to be accused of a heinous crime, when all the time I was innocent? You may think it was done as an evil act, not so, I see it was for good.'

'Are you going to Brighton tomorrow?'

'No. Part of the purpose of the conference is to find out how other churches do Sunday service, so I'm going with you and Karen to your church tomorrow. Plenty of time to sleep in.'

'Er – I don't actually go to church, and it's time for me to go to bed. I've a mountain of paperwork to catch up on tomorrow.'

'Excuse me,' said Karen, as she picked up the empty cups. 'You're wasting your time, Travis. I've been trying for years to get him to come to church,'

'Jack, come to church with us tomorrow, what do you have to lose?'

'Two hours of work, that's what.'

'Please, Jack,' said Karen. 'Poppy and Harry will be going as well.'

'Tell you what,' said Travis, taking out his wallet and opening it. 'Here's two one-hundred-dollar bills, no. I wasn't going to give it to you. I'm going to give them to any charity you name if you come with us in the morning.'

'And if I don't come with you?'

'I'll eat them with my dinner.'

'That doesn't make any sense, Travis.'

'And neither does your fear of going to church.'

'I'm not afraid of going to church, it's just as I said, I'm too busy.'

'OK, I'll extend my offer. You spend two hours with us at church and I will spend two hours with you helping you on your latest case.'

'But you're a church minister – what do you know about crime and human nature?'

'Where would you suggest I begin?'

Buchanan shrugged.

'All right. How about the story of Joseph, youngest son in the family, sold into slavery by his brothers, only to become prime minister of Egypt? Or the story of Ruth and her mother-in-law, Naomi. Then there's the classic one, David, the loyal subject of King Saul, born as a shepherd boy, destined to become a giant slayer and finally King of Judah.'

'All right, I'll go to church with you, but I will want my pound of flesh.'

'Jack, you show thy mercy and remorse more strange than is thy strange apparent cruelty, where thou now exacts the penalty, which is a pound of this poor pastor's flesh.'

Buchanan smiled. 'The quality of mercy is not strained. It drops as the gentle rain from heaven upon the place beneath. It is twice blest: it blesses him that gives and him that takes.'

'Touché,' replied Travis. 'I see you read Shakespeare.'

'As a schoolboy, Travis. See you in the morning.'

8

Sunday evening
Bedtime Story

'Well now, that wasn't so bad,' said Travis, as he sipped his after-dinner coffee. 'No thunderbolts for you today, Jack.'

'I will admit the preacher did a good job; his talk was very well presented. Pity about the music, a bit loud for me.'

Travis smiled. *'Make a joyful shout to the Lord, all you lands; serve the Lord with gladness.*

Come before His presence with singing – Psalm 100, Jack.'

'My church was Church of Scotland; my grandmother was the church organist.'

'We have an organ back home, but the members prefer the modern worship songs. So, this morning was the first time in a long time that you were in church?'

'As I said last night, I don't actually go to church, that's Karen's thing,' said Buchanan, easing into his recliner.

'You amaze me,' said Travis.

'Why?'

'You deal with all aspects of human life, from child murders to bank robberies and serious and complex investigations, yet you rely on your own strength to get you through.'

'You sound like you're trying to make me the CID poster boy. Yes, I've had my fair share of the issues you described.'

'Yet when it comes to time to defend yourself against the great evils of our days, you neglect the one great strength available to everyone.'

'Unlike your American police, except for the armed response teams, the British police don't carry firearms.'

'Jack, I'm not talking about guns, I'm talking about prayer. Ephesians chapter six verse twelve says: *For we do not wrestle against flesh and blood, but against principalities, against powers, against the rulers of the darkness of this age, against spiritual hosts of wickedness in the heavenly places.'*

Buchanan smiled. 'I suppose there's a bit of truth in what you say there. I've had to deal with people who, for the want of any other description, could be described as having a demonic wickedness in them.'

'That's exactly what I'm getting at, and that is how I would describe those ISIS, Boko Haram, Taliban, Hamas and other terrorist groups running loose in various parts of the world. They are nothing but demons in human form.'

'That's fine for you, you're a minister, you deal with abstracts. I'm a policeman – I have to deal with the real world.'

Travis looked over at Buchanan's cup and saw he had barely tasted his Horlicks.

'Let me tell you a story about someone you might find interesting.'

'Good, I like bedtime stories,' said Buchanan, picking up his cup.

'Just over two and half thousand years ago in the land called Assyria, which is now part of Iraq and modern-day Syria, their leader, Nebuchadnezzar, ruled with an iron fist. It is said when he caught a cold, the whole country sneezed. His authority was absolute – if he didn't like you, he'd cut you into pieces and make your house a dung heap.'

'Sounds a bit like the former Iraqi leader, Saddam Hussein.'

'An apt comparison. While he was dictator of Iraq, Saddam Hussein so admired Nebuchadnezzar he decided he would restore the ancient city of Babylon.'

'I thought Babylon was just a myth?'

'It is very real, and up till a few years ago you could go and inspect the ruins. During one of Nebuchadnezzar's campaigns, he pillaged the land of Canaan and, as part of his way of conquering foreign lands and people, he brought back treasure and people – including their royalty.'

'There are ruins all over the world. Archaeologists make up all sorts of stories to keep them in work.'

'Not so, Jack. Have you ever been to the British Museum?'

'Years ago, why?'

'If you weren't so busy on Monday, I'd take you there and show you physical proof that the Bible stories are real. There's a whole section on Assyrian history recorded in stone wall reliefs and. excellent records detail the sacking of the city of Lachish by Sennacherib, mentioned in the Bible. So detailed, you can read them like a book.'

'Maybe I'll pay the museum a visit one day and see for myself this story about Sennacherib. But wait a minute, are you inferring I'm like the Nebuchadnezzar you mentioned earlier?'

'No, of course not. As I was saying, when Nebuchadnezzar returned from conquering Canaan, some of the people he brought back were four names you will probably remember: Shadrach, Meshach, Abednego and Daniel.'

'I remember the lion's den stories from Sunday school.'

'And the one about the furnace?'

'Vaguely.'

'Let me refresh your memory. Shadrach, Meshach and Abednego were fellow princes with Daniel. They were devout Jews and refused to bow down and worship the enormous gold statue that Nebuchadnezzar had the palace foundry cast of himself. It was reputed to be about ninety feet tall.

'They were given a second chance to bow down and worship the statue, but refused to do so, or to worship any of the Babylonian gods. So, when they were confronted with the choice of bowing down or being thrown into the furnace – probably the one that was used to smelt the gold for the statue – they said that their God would save them and, even if he didn't, they would still not bow down and worship the gold statue.'

Buchanan nodded. 'That is how I remember Mrs England, the Sunday School teacher, telling it. Didn't they get chucked in?'

'It's amazing what comes to mind from distant memories when we dig for them. Yes, but before they were thrown in, Nebuchadnezzar, who by now was incandescent with rage, ordered the furnace to be heated up seven times hotter. I don't know if you know at what temperature gold melts but let me say it is somewhere around 1000 degrees Fahrenheit.'

'Wait a minute, are you saying the furnace was 7000 degrees? There's no furnace that can get that hot, it would melt itself.'

'Not true, tungsten melts at just over 6000 degrees and there are furnaces that get hotter than that.'

'But you're talking about something that happened thousands of years ago.'

'They knew things then that we are now only discovering, Jack.'

'If you say so.'

'I do, and back to what I was saying. Water boils at 212 degrees Fahrenheit and, if it were possible to heat it to even 1000 degrees, it would instantly evaporate. Can you imagine what would happen to the human body, which is sixty percent water?'

'I imagine it would just disappear in a flash.'

'The soldiers tasked with throwing Shadrach, Meshach and Abednego into the furnace were instantly killed with the heat, yet when Nebuchadnezzar looked into the furnace, he saw four people walking around in it.

'Nebuchadnezzar was so stunned that he called Shadrach, Meshach and Abednego to come out of the furnace. To everyone's amazement when the three came out, they were not burnt, or did not even smell of smoke. They were perfectly unscathed by their ordeal.'

'I'm confused. You said there were four of them in the furnace. Was the fourth one Daniel?'

'No, it was Jesus. You said you have memories from Sunday School?'

'Yes, from time to time some of the songs we used to sing pop into my mind.'

'Do you remember reading the twenty-third Psalm?'

'The Lord is my shepherd, is that the one?'

Travis nodded. '*Yeah though I walk through the shadow of the valley of death, you are with me, your rod and your staff comfort me.* Jesus is with us through all troubles in this life. He promises us that he will never leave us or forsake us.'

'Well, if he's always available, I could do with some help on my present case.'

'I'm all ears. How can we help?'

'It's about the missing girl case. The father sounds like he's one of your crowd.'

'I thought you said he was Jewish?'

'He is. What I meant was, he went on about people getting microchips injected into the backs of their hands. Sounded a bit Orwellian to me.'

'Revelation thirteen. *He causes all, both small and great, rich and poor, free and slave, to receive a mark on their right hand or on their foreheads, and that no one may buy or sell except one who has the mark or the name of the beast, or the number of his name.*'

'That's what he was saying, but not quite so eloquently as you put it.'

'How about you start from the beginning and tell me what you know.'

'Not sure if I can match any of your Bible verses but here goes. A couple of weeks ago, mid-Monday morning, we had a report of a human hand being dug up in a resident's flower bed by their pet dog. Doctor Mansell verified that the hand was human.'

'Doctor Mansell?'

'Yes, he's the local forensic medical examiner. He works with us on cases of suspicious death. Later that morning we had a subsequent report that a second hand had been dug up on an allotment garden.'

'How close were the two hands?'

'Less than half a mile if you were to walk round the roads, much shorter if you were a fox.'

''That's quite logical, go on.'

'Foxes and badgers have been known to dig shallow graves looking for bones. On Tuesday I was introduced to Amal Barazani. He told me he was concerned for his daughter, who he thought had been abducted. She had not been seen since the previous Friday. I questioned the father, and he mentioned his daughter had a boyfriend who he did not approve of. Later that day I attended an abandoned garage, which we have since determined was the scene of a human dismemberment.'

'The remains of the body?'

'No. Just blooded newspapers, clothes and the remains of viscera.'

'Viscera?'

'Sorry, been around the doctor too much. Viscera means internal organs. At first it was thought it might have been a case of sheep rustling, but upon examination of the remains the doctor determined they were human.'

'Have you found the body?'

'Later the same day we were informed of a suspicious encounter on the previous Saturday morning with two workmen filling in a pit at the side of the High Street. With the finding of the garage being used as an abattoir, I had the pit dug up and that is where we found the remains of the body, minus the head.'

'Was it the missing girl, or her boyfriend?'

'Neither, as it has turned out. The boyfriend has, or should I say had, a twin brother. We are thinking along the lines that the brother was mistaken for the boyfriend and was killed by mistake. That is the outline of the case.'

'You said in the car on the way from the airport the girl's father was Jewish?'

'That's correct.'

'And he has a brother who is a Muslim?'

Buchanan nodded. 'It's actually a stepbrother.'

'Is the missing girl's father wealthy?'

'I assume so. Runs a software development company. He has some strange ideas of where society is going, though.'

'In what way?'

'I mentioned earlier, microchips injected into the hand for shopping, cash eliminated.'

'Ah, yes – the mark of the beast. I remember having to put quite a few of my congregation right about the matter. This idea is not new, it has its origins in the book of Revelation. A variation of it rose to great prominence a few years ago in the US with talk of the introduction of a national ID card. The card was to be a combination of health, entitlement to work, payment, ID, and driving licence, which could also be used as a domestic passport. One of the great proponents of the ID card said the idea of a national ID card was benign, imagine that!'

'Gives me the shivers.'

'But this thing about having a microchip injected into the hand does sound feasible and might just have acceptance in our modern society.'

'Why do you say that?'

'Identity theft and online fraud costs the American society millions every year. So, I suppose a case could be made for microchipping everyone, but I pity the society that accepts this loss of freedom.'

'What you say is very interesting, but I don't think that is what is behind the death of the young man or the disappearance of Amal Barazani's daughter. Let me be a little cheeky and quote a Bible verse to you, not sure where it is, but it goes like this: *the love of money is the root of all evil.*'

'Ah, yes. One Timothy, chapter six, verse ten.'

'It has been my experience, through my thirty-five years as a policeman, that after you work your way through the fog of evidence, lies, innuendos and anger, you end up with money being the basis for the crime.'

'So, if the father is unmarried and not in the picture and the daughter has been killed, who stands to inherit her money?'

'I imagine the girl's grandfather would be next in line. Then the stepbrother and, after him, his son.'

'If the daughter is dead, then I'd say the father is in the line of sights of the killer.'

'That is a workable scenario, and something like this has happened before. A few years ago, a desperate young man was convicted for murdering his parents. His first attempt at engineering a car accident failed, so he later shot them both dead with a shotgun and tried to make it look like a murder suicide.'

'Why don't people just get jobs and play their parts in society?'

'Someone once worked out that the wages from petty crime never rise to that of a criminal working legally as, say, a short order cook in a burger restaurant.'

'And you say the murder victim usually knows the killer?'

'Usually, in Agatha Christie stories, though in the case of Sam Taylor, I don't think that adage applies.'

'You said the father disagreed with his daughter's choice of boyfriend. Why was that?'

'The boyfriend, Zac Taylor, was an itinerant musician. He made his living as a Bob Dylan tribute singer, and from what I was told the daughter was working with him to start a jazz duet. His last sighting was at the railway station, though we now think that was his twin, Sam. I'm hoping that tomorrow we will have the autopsy report from the doctor and video evidence from the transport police.'

'I'm thinking about what you said about the murder victim usually knowing their killer.'

'Not in this case. I'm sure Sam wasn't the intended victim.'

'Hang on a minute. If, as you say, Zac was the intended victim, who would you think could be a killer candidate?'

'Ah, you should be a policeman, you ask all the right questions. The obvious one is the father, Amal Barazani, though the stepbrother could be a candidate, in spite of his glowing testimonial of his niece and Zac becoming a singing duo.'

'Why would he be a candidate?'

'What you said earlier about the rivalry between brothers, especially since the stepbrother may also have disagreed with Zilini's choice of boyfriend.'

'Anyone else?'

'Not in the family, and now, if you don't mind,' said Buchanan yawning, 'I need to go to bed, Tomorrow is going to be a very busy day for me and my team.'

9
Monday Morning
Text Me

'Another late night?' Street asked Buchanan.

'Travis is on Dallas time, so our midnight is his six o'clock.'

'Did he keep you up talking again?'

'Yep. He's quite a man, really lives by what he believes.'

'And what does he believe?'

'I think he believes I'm a sinner destined for hell if I don't accept his way of thinking.'

'Really, he said that?'

'Not in those actual words, but I think that's what he meant.'

'So, what did he say?'

'He said everyone is a sinner trying to work out their own salvation, but Christians are sinners saved by grace, not by works.'

'I'm sure he means well. After all it's his job, being a pastor, to say those things.'

'I suppose you are right. Still bugs me though, he is so sincere in what he believes.'

'Maybe the world needs more men like Travis.'

'Talking of men, where's Stephen and Morris?'

'Morris called and asked for a lift, his wife's car broke down and she had to use his to take the children to school. Stephen went to pick him up.'

Buchanan smiled. 'Again, maybe it's time he replaced his wife's car with a more reliable one.'

'They've just had another child. I think another car is not in the plans just now.'

'That makes sense. Anything from forensics?'

'Yep. Forensics emailed the fingerprint details and phone records, also Doctor Mansell called to say he's coming over with his autopsy report. Littlejohn called and said he will be here as well.'

'That'll make a first; I'd better pop over to Tesco's, you know how Andrew likes his doughnuts.'

'I know someone else who likes their doughnuts.'

'You do? I wonder just who that might be? Forensics report?'

'I've made copies for us all, yours is on your desk,' she said, pointing.

'What time should we be expecting the illustrious doctor?'

'Twenty minutes. He said, he'll bring the coffees.'

'Better get my skates on.'

'While you're out getting the doctor's supplies, I left my charger cable in my car.'

♦

Buchanan was placing the doughnuts on a paper plate when the sound of chattering voices announced the arrival of Hunter, Dexter and Dr Mansell plus Littlejohn from CSI.

'Thanks for the coffees, Andrew,' said Buchanan.

'You're welcome. Jill says you have info from forensics?'

'Jill, would you pass round the copies of the forensics report?' said Buchanan, as he reclined in his chair.

'Will do. We also have CCTV from the transport police for Falmer, Eastbourne, Pevensey and Westham, and Hastings stations,' said Street, as she passed out copies of the forensics report.

'Excellent,' said Buchanan, 'but before we discuss the forensics report, I'd like to hear the autopsy report from Andrew.'

'Thanks. I'll start with the hands retrieved from the garden on Gallows Lane and the Westham allotments. Both were from the body found in the pit. I found animal DNA from saliva on the hands, probably from the foxes that found and buried them. The deceased was left-handed and a heavy smoker. I found a small, dotted tattoo in the web of the left hand, usually depicts time spent in prison.'

'We saw that,' said Street.

'I examined the palms of the hands and I would say looking at the calluses he spent a great deal of time driving heavy goods vehicles. He was of a nervous disposition; his fingernails were chewed almost back to the quick. First and second digits of the right hand were heavily stained with nicotine. The wrists showed signs of friction burns caused by him struggling, possibly when he was stripped to the waist and tied to a chair.'

'Sounds weird,' said Street. 'I wonder why he was tied to a chair, stripped from the waist down?'

'He died from strangulation and was dead about forty-eight hours before he was dismembered and buried. He probably wouldn't have lived much longer because someone was trying to poison him. I found twenty-three belladonna seeds in the upper digestive track.'

'Belladonna – isn't that another name for deadly nightshade?' asked Dexter.

'Exactly. About twenty-four hours before he died, he'd eaten a meal of cod fried in batter with chips and mushy peas washed down with Coca-Cola. I'd say he smoked between ten to twenty cigarettes a day, plus whatever else was being shared around at the time. Both hands were roughly separated from the arms by a chainsaw, his reproductive appendage by something similar to a bread knife,' said Mansell.

'How could anyone be so evil?' said Street. 'Why would the murderer try and disguise the victim's sex?'

'A quick but brutal amputation by someone with no anatomical experience,' said Mansell. 'The body parts were removed from the pit beside the High Street in Westham, the body you now refer to as Sam Taylor's.'

'That doesn't make much sense,' said Dexter. 'Why poison someone then strangle them?'

'Sounds like it was a murder attempt by two separate people,' said Hunter.

'Or someone wanted to make sure he died,' said Street.

'That's for you to ascertain,' said Mansell. 'My job is to tell you how he died, not who did the deed. He wasn't killed where he was dismembered, the marks on his throat and the livor mortis body marks showed signs of him being strangled while seated, then left slumped on a chair. His hyoid bone was crushed. He was left in the chair for about twenty-four hours. His heels showed signs of the body being dragged backwards down a flight of steps before being dumped in some sort of workshop or factory area where he was then stripped of his remaining clothing. Not an easy task when rigor mortis has set in.'

'What effect would the belladonna have on him?' asked Buchanan.

'Early effects would be a dry mouth, difficulty swallowing, then becoming hoarse and finding it difficult to speak,' said Mansell. 'Next, the face would become flushed and the victim would appear to be drunk.'

'So, if someone was trying to question him, he wouldn't make much sense?'

'Absolutely.'

'Poor sod. Wrongly abducted, poisoned by who knows who, then strangled by someone who probably got angry with what they thought was his refusal to answer questions.'

'I made a microscopic examination of the clothes,' said Littlejohn, 'and I'd say the type of chair he was sitting in when killed was an office chair with green polyester fabric covering.'

'The marks on his wrists showed a struggle,' said Mansell, 'and I found chair cloth fibres embedded in them.

'Amongst the items detected on his clothes were fibres that matched the bedding in bedroom number two and the lounge chair in the living room from the flat in Langney,' said Littlejohn. 'I also found a fine selection of rodent and fox hair. There were splashes of grease from the frying pan in his kitchen on the front of his trousers and shirt. The bottom edges of his shirt were blood-stained, probably from his ordeal with the bread knife. I'd also add that his near-naked body was dragged across the workshop floor before being dumped. I found short lengths of copper wire and even shorter lengths of multi-coloured plastic insulation, probably stripped from the wire, trapped in the fabric of the shirt he'd been wearing. I googled the wire size and insulation colours and found they match the CW1308 telecommunication colour code. He must have had his jeans down round his ankles when dragged as they were also stained with automobile engine oil and grease.'

'Sounds like he was killed in an office then dragged into a garage somewhere. Not sure what the telephone wire has to do with it,' said Buchanan. 'Henry, what about the phone found in the pit, did you look at it?'

'I found a positive DNA match with the corpse. Something to consider, that is the only place where that particular DNA has appeared.'

'Do we have a sample of Amal Barazani's DNA?'

'Yes, we got that earlier,' said Street. 'Are you thinking he might have been there when Sam was buried?'

'It's a possibility. Jill, can you tell us about the phone call records for the last month?'

'Yes. Most calls were to a job agency. I called them and was informed that they hire commercial drivers on short-term contracts to cover the UK and sometimes across the channel. There were five to Domino's Pizza, the remainder were random numbers. When I dialled them, they all went through to what I suspected were sex for sale numbers. Only one of them answered and, when I asked if they knew Sam Taylor, they denied ever having met him.'

'I've seen telephone equipment rooms in large offices,' said Hunter. 'There are quite a few of them dotted round the Eastbourne area. Remember the case of *the laminated man*: he was killed in a factory that probably would have had its own telephone equipment room.'

'Barazani has a large office, and there is a set of stairs leading down from the office to the garage,' said Street. 'I wonder if they have green office chairs and a telephone equipment room somewhere in the building?'

'A good question, Jill,' said Buchanan. 'I think a further visit to see Mr Amal Barazani will be necessary.'

'You're quite a detective, Doctor,' said Hunter. 'What does it take to become a forensics medical examiner?'

Mansell smiled and wiped the sugar from his lips. 'Firstly, a good grounding in chemistry, biology and law. Then on to medical school to get a medical degree, preferably a medical school where forensics is emphasised. It is also helpful to possess the power of observation, deduction, a wide range of exact knowledge, and a constructive imagination.'

'Sort of being able to see things from the outside looking in, just like Sherlock Holmes?' queried Dexter.

'Precisely, Morris. Interesting you mentioned Sherlock Holmes – Conan Doyle, the man who wrote the Sherlock Holmes stories, modelled his detective on a real doctor who taught at Edinburgh Medical School while Doyle was a student. His name was Joseph Bell, a real-life medical sleuth. In addition to me being an MD, I am also a Fellow of the Royal Society of Physicians.'

'So, you're not just a doctor?'

'No, Morris, I'm not just a doctor.'

'Are you married? Sorry, that's being nosey.'

'Not at all, Jill. And to answer your question, yes, I am very happily married to Katherine. We have two children, Sydney and Keith, both studying medicine at Edinburgh University. Since you have asked about forensic medicine, I'd say the greatest ever to have stared into a microscope was Sydney Smith. He was born in New Zealand and served many years as a medical examiner in Egypt. He wrote two excellent books, both of which I have in my personal library and one especially which I still consult.'

'What are their titles?' asked Street, picking up her pen.

'The first is his biography, *Mostly Murder*, still available to purchase, and I would say, amongst others, it should be required reading by anyone who aspires to be a competent detective; and to point you in the direction of an answer to your earlier question, I suggest you read up on the Buck Ruxton case, one of many investigated by Sydney Smith.'

'And the other?'

'*Forensic Murder.* That book is out of print now, though you should be able to find second-hand copies from book dealers.'

'Henry,' said Buchanan, 'can you go over the forensics report? Start with the details gathered from the flat, please.'

'Zac's bedroom, the one on the left as you enter the flat, had five sets of prints, four of them non-identifiable; the fifth matched a set in Sam's bedroom on the right, where there were two sets of prints. One set identified as Sam's, the other matched a set from Zac's bedroom, assumed to be Zac's. There is a DNA match taken from the fingerprints that back this up,' said Henry, 'The DNA from the bedroom on the right also matches the DNA samples taken from the chainsaw, viscera found in the garage, bloodstained materials found in the van and the body parts exhumed from the pit on the High Street in the village of Westham.'

'So, we can be sure that it is Sam's body we have in the morgue and not of that of Zac?' asked Buchanan.

'Yes.'

'What about the mobile phones that were found in the flat?'

'There were two found under the mattress in Zac's room,' said Street. 'From the calls made and the tracking information, I'd say one was Zac's and the other was Zilini's. They called and texted each other several times a day.'

'What about the Friday they went missing?'

'I've printed a timeline of texts for us. I thought it would be more helpful if I just typed a day by day and time of texts that are pertinent to our case. The first set of texts were sent and received on Monday two weeks prior to our involvement.'

Monday evening 24th

Zilini	22:15	Thanks for the great weekend.
Zac	22:21	No, thank you. You were great. You really

		nailed Moondance, the crowd loved your rendition
Zilini	22:30	I couldn't have done it without you and your guitar accompaniment. I don't know how you manage to remember all those chords.
Zac	22:35	Practise, my dear, practise. Are we still going for a music lesson with your aunt on Thursday afternoon?
Zilini	22:37	Yes five o'clock, don't be late.
Zac	22:38	Fine. I'll meet you at the bus stop outside the station. Wonder what your great-aunt will have baked for me this time? Doesn't she know I'm a coeliac sufferer?
Zilini	22:40	She makes such a fuss about baking them I don't have the heart to tell her, you don't mind, do you?
Zac	22:42	They're not my thing, I usually give them to Sam. Are you sure you don't want to tell your dad about our plans?
Zilini	22:37	Absolutely not. You've seen how he behaves towards you. Any time I try and raise the subject about taking time out from Uni, he gets mad.
Zac	22:40	What you doing?
Zilini	22:45	Getting ready for bed, I have a test in the morning and need to be awake for It, besides, I need to keep up appearances for the big day.
Zac	22:48	It won't be long now, sleep tight, talk to you tomorrow.
Zilini	22:51	I like the name for our duo, Zac and Zil, it's cute. Night, night.

'The next set of text messages were sent and received Wednesday 26th through to Sunday morning 30th.

Wednesday evening 26th

| Zilini | 21:35 | Hi, what did the agent say when he heard the demo disc? |
| Zac | 23:30 | Hi. Just got in. He didn't have time to listen to it when I was there, he said he'd listen to it on the way home and get back to me. |

Thursday morning 27th

Zilini	08:27	Morning, I'd gone to bed when you texted. Just read your text, bit of a bummer, going all the way to London to see him in person then he didn't have time to listen, are you sure he's the right person?
Zac	10:33	Yes, he's one of the best. We are going to have to stop meeting like this.
Zilini	10:35	One day soon, we'll be together all the time, not long now.
Zac	10:37	Can't wait.
Zilini	10:39	I'll be on the six-eighteen train tomorrow, don't be late. I need time to practise.
Zac	10:46	I'd never be late for you. Where are you going tonight?
Zilini	10:51	Judith and I are going to see a movie, not sure what's playing. Oh, I've bought a new dress for the act, nice and short and sparkly, should look good on stage. Got to go now, see you at five for the lesson.

Saturday late 29th

Zilini	18:20	On the train, see you in ten minutes.
Zilini	23:25	You cheeky pup, why didn't you tell me the agent would be there this evening?
Zac	23:57	I wanted it to be a surprise.
Zilini	23:59	It certainly was. Did you get a copy of the contract?

Sunday early 30th

Zac	00:03	No. He said he'd get it copied Monday and post me a copy by the end of the day.
Zilini	00:05	We've got to do it soon, wow, I've just realised now it's going to be a week Saturday.
Zac	00:11	I think I'm being followed. There were two men waiting in the car park when I got off the train. They stared at me as I walked out of the car park and asked me if I wanted a lift.
Zilini	00:12	What did you do?
Zac	00:14	Ignored them. They've just driven past me and headed up the hill past the crematorium.
Zilini	00:16	Oh dear, I wonder if they are working for my father, he can be quite ruthless when he wants to be. Be careful my love. Oh, what did Sam mean when he said he would soon be very rich, has he got a new job?
Zac	00:18	I'm not sure, he's been acting really strange lately. He actually shaves every day and wears a clean shirt when he goes out, he's also got plenty of money.
Zilini	00:21	Do you think he's got a rich girlfriend who buys his clothes for him?

Zac	00:25	He must have, I've never seen him look so tidy.
Zilini	00:27	You don't suppose he's being, you know, sort of being kept?
Zac	01:03	I'm safely home now, talk to you tomorrow, oh that's today.

'I've moved us on to the following Wednesday,' said Street, 'the evening Zhukovski says his people recorded seeing Zac Taylor getting in a taxi.'

Wednesday late 2nd.

Zac	23:31	On the train back to Hastings, I left Sam to make his own way home.
		Don't know how I managed to leave my guitar in the pub. Dave said he'd meet me at the station so I can catch the last train back.
Zilini	22:35	Great, hope Sam makes it home OK, he didn't look that good.
Zac	22:37	He'll be fine, never could hold his drink, half a pint and he'd be under the table babbling like a baby.

Thursday 3rd

Zac	01:43	I'm worried, had to get a taxi home, missed the last train back. When I got home there was no sign of Sam. I hope he's not gone back on the stuff, he promised me he'd quit.
Zilini	08:21	Morning, just saw your text, did you find Sam? Called my father last night. He was too busy to pick up, as per usual.
Zac	08:25	I've reported Sam missing, police say they'll keep an eye out for him. I'm

going into town to see if any of his friends know where he is.

Zilini	16:23	Have you found Sam?
Zac	17:21	There's no sign of him anywhere, none of his mates have heard from him. His phone just goes to the answering machine. Also, I just looked out the window and there are two men sitting in a car parked outside the flat.
Zilini	17:25	Has Sam gone missing before?
Zac	17:26	A couple of times, especially when he's on the stuff, but not recently.
Zilini	17:28	Do you think it could be those men who tried to give you a lift on Wednesday night?
Zac	17:29	Not sure. They're still down at the front of the flat, the doorbell buzzed a few minutes ago, I think it was them.
Zilini	17:31	Zac, be careful.
Zac	17:43	It's OK, they've just left.
Zilini	17:45	What will you do? They might come back. Oh, do you think it could be something to do with my father? He has some strange friends.
Zac	17:53	I think I need to go somewhere and do some serious thinking.
Zilini	18:01	Where will you go? Wait, I have a suggestion. Why don't you come and stay here with me for a few days, just till next weekend?
Zac	18:03	What, move in with you? Where would I sleep?
Zilini	18:04	On the couch, my bed is too small for both of us.
Zac	18:07	That won't work, I need to stay close to my flat. I have a new pickup for my guitar being delivered next Tuesday.

| Zilini | 18:09 | You're safe for the moment in the flat. I'll be home tomorrow for the weekend. After dinner I'll make an excuse to go out. Watch for me about seven, I'll pick you up in my car then we can head back by train to my flat to think things over. Pack a bag, and don't forget your guitar. Got to go, battery almost flat, talk to you tomorrow. |

Friday 4th

Zilini	19:28	Just getting in the car. Just realised my Uni digs probably aren't safe for us now, but I do have a great idea where we can stay until we head off to the gig. My father has gone out, perfect timing for me to disappear. He's really angry about something.
Zac	19:30	At you?
Zilini	19:31	No, I think it's something to do with the project they are working on. See you in fifteen. Shall I come up? Will you need a hand with your stuff?
Zac	18:03	No, I'll be fine. Best I meet you somewhere away from the flat.
Zilini	18:05	Good idea, how about the station? If I drop my car at the garage, I can walk round to the station main entrance and meet you there.
Zac	18.07	No, not the main entrance, too well lit. How about beside the NHS trailer in the car park, we'll watch for the train then dash round and get on it?
Zilini	18:09	OK see you there. Bring your charger, my phone battery is almost flat again, I think I need a new phone.

'So, they were planning all along to do a runner and set up as a jazz duo,' said Buchanan. 'Jill, are there any contact details for the agent Zac was talking about?'

'Not directly. There are several unidentified phone calls. I could call each of them and see what turns up.'

'Please do. Damn, we were talking to Zac just a few days ago, he must be really scared.'

'He was quick off the mark to pretend to be Sam,' said Street.

'He was probably worried about his girlfriend,' said Dexter.

'In that case she must be somewhere else, but where? Who's hiding her?'

'Could it be her aunt, she seems to be quite welcome at her house?'

Buchanan shook his head, 'I don't think so, Morris. Nasim's mother had some disparaging words for Zilini and her dress code.'

'Does Nasim's mother live in Eastbourne?' asked Dexter.

'We have an address for her in Meads.'

'Do you want us to go and ask her if Zilini is there?'

'No, I'll take care of that. Jill, do we know who the phones are registered to?'

'The one we are assuming was Zilini's phone is registered to the Mastrani company; the other, which we think was Zac's, was a paygo phone, as was the one found in the pit.'

'Excuse me one moment,' said Mansell, 'just what is a paygo phone?'

'Paygo is a contraction for pay-as-you-go,' said Street.

'Well, you learn something every minute.'

'I wonder if Zilini realised her phone could be monitored?' said Buchanan. 'I also wonder if Amal Barazani was the one monitoring the phone. Stephen, when you and Morris went to Falmer to talk to Zilini's friends, did you get into her room?'

'No,' Hunter said, consulting his notebook. 'We talked to a Sandy, an Emma, a Nancy, a Judith, a Kate and a Pat. Also, when we knocked on Zilini's door, there was no reply.'

'Is it possible they were in there and just not answering the door?' said Buchanan. 'As soon as we are done here, Stephen, I'd like you and Morris to go back over to Falmer and see if you can gain entry to the flat, hopefully by having someone open the door.'

'Should we get a search warrant first?' asked Dexter.

'An excellent idea, you might have to force an entry. And while you two are in Falmer, Jill and I will be paying Amal Barazani a return visit at his office. I don't think he's been forthcoming with the whole truth about the disappearance of his daughter. Jill, could we now have the CCTV evidence?'

'I've put the clips together to coincide with the telephone text messages as best I could. If you look at the monitor on the wall, I'll give you a running commentary.

'This shot is the evening of the 29th of Zac and Zilini boarding the ten-seventeen train at Hastings. Zac gets off at Pevensey and Westham and Zilini gets off at Eastbourne.'

'What about CCTV at Pevensey and Westham station, any suspicious characters hanging around?' asked Dexter.

'That's the next clip and, as you can see, the only one in the video is Zac pulling his jacket on and walking off with his guitar.

'According to Zac's text he said someone offered him a lift home. There are several cameras at the station, and we can see a taxi arriving at ten-twenty. The driver must have been trying to avoid the cameras, see how he parks against the fence.'

'Very interesting,' said Buchanan. 'We can clearly see the taxi company signs on the door of the taxi, but when you look at the back, the required taxi licence is missing. Jill, did you check the taxi registration number?'

'Yes, and unfortunately it's a cloned plate, registered to a Nissan Micra which was, according to the DVLA, an insurance write-off and has been destroyed.'

'Might be interesting to track the vehicle with the ANPR cameras, especially if it's using cloned plates.'

'I'll do that while we watch the videos,' said Hunter.

'If you watch the video you can see Zac looking over at the car,' said Street,' he shakes his head, then walks off. The taxi leaves a few minutes later.'

'Anything, Stephen?'

'Not yet, still looking.'

'OK, Jill, back to you.'

'Our next set of videos come from Wednesday evening of the 2nd. And for the first time we see the Taylor twins together. They board the seven-nineteen to Hastings at Pevensey and Westham. All three of them return on the ten-sixteen to Eastbourne. Zac and Sam get off at Pevensey and Westham station at ten past eleven, go to walk over the footbridge – and this is where Zac realises, he's left his guitar behind. They both go over the footbridge, Sam not looking very steady on his feet.'

'That would be the atropine starting to take effect,' said Mansell. 'Without any medical intervention he'd be dead within twenty-four hours.'

'We can see Zac sitting on a bench waiting for the half past eleven train to Hastings,' continued Street, 'and if we look at the car park cameras, we can see two cars waiting. One is the suspicious taxi from the previous Saturday night, and another car, a black BMW, is parked in the back corner of the car park. Sam exits the station and is distracted by the taxi driver. Sam goes over and leans down to the front passenger window. He says something, shakes his head, then shrugs and opens the front passenger door and gets in. The taxi leaves with Sam as a passenger, followed by the BMW. We have video of the taxi crossing the railway line, but no sign of the BMW.'

'I wonder why Zhukovski's people didn't follow the taxi?' said Morris.

'Anything more on the CCTV, Jill?' asked Buchanan.

'No.'

'Anything showing them getting on the train at Eastbourne for Falmer on the Friday evening?'

'I looked from seven-thirty all the way through to the last train just after midnight. There were a couple of possibilities, but nothing definite. But that's not surprising, Eastbourne is a very busy railway station.'

'So, there we have it,' said Buchanan. 'Sam Taylor was mistaken for his brother Zac Taylor and was abducted on Wednesday the 2nd. After an attempt at questioning him, he was subsequently strangled, then two days later transported to and dismembered in the garage on Peelings Lane in the village of Westham. The body, minus hands and head, was buried in a construction pit during the early hours of Saturday morning of the 5th by two, yet unidentified, males.

'In an effort to confuse the identity of the body, the head was removed and thrown in the local village pond. The hands, having been severed from the arms, were probably just tossed into a convenient hedge where roaming foxes picked them up and buried them.'

'Amateurs, absolute amateurs,' said Mansell.

'So, what do you want us to do?' asked Hunter.

'I still would still like you and Morris to go to Falmer and check Zilini's flat. Pity we don't have her bank cards; we might have a chance of catching up with her and Zac if we did. When you're done with that, if you have time, see if you can track down the bogus taxi. It might be connected to the chop shop that was discovered recently in Hellingly.'

'We'll have a good look while we're there,' said Hunter.

'Good. Jill and I are going to have another word with Amal Barazani.'

'What about me?' asked Dr Mansell. 'Will you be finding any more bodies today?'

'Let's hope not, Andrew,' said Buchanan. 'We have enough pieces as it is. Was there anything else?'

'Yes,' said Littlejohn, 'a small detail: the DNA on the wire clippings found in the Taylors' flat is not the same as those on the body and they are guitar strings manufactured by Rotosound. The set size was number 13 acoustic, quite a heavy gauge, available worldwide, and used by folk guitar players.'

♦

'Penny for your thoughts,' said Buchanan, as they drove through Eastbourne on the way to Mastrani and a hoped fruitful conversation with Amal Barazani.

'I like Doctor Mansell,' replied Street, 'he'd make a good GP.'

'Oh, why hadn't I thought of that before?'

'What, about Doctor Mansell being a good GP?'

'No, that's not what I'm talking about,' Buchanan said, shaking his head. 'What good reason would a young woman Zilini's age have for running away from a happy home?'

'You don't think she could be pregnant, do you?'

'It would sort of make sense. Just imagine, Dad finds out that his precious jewel has been taken advantage of by some ne'er do well musician. He blows up in a rage, hires hitmen to eliminate the boyfriend and then threatens the daughter with an abortion. Jill, before we get to Mastrani, would you call Stephen and tell them while they are in Zilini's flat to be on the lookout for anything that could point to Zilini being pregnant? You know the sort of things they should be looking for.'

'Yep. Doctor's appointment cards or letters from the clinic, pregnancy test kits, the usual stuff. I'll let them know.'

♦

'I wonder if he's in the office today,' said Street, as Buchanan parked on the double yellow lines outside the Mastrani office.

'Good morning, how may I help?' asked the receptionist.

'Detective Chief Inspector Buchanan and Detective Sergeant Street to see Mr Barazani,' replied Buchanan, showing his warrant card.

'Oh, I'm not sure if he's available at the moment.'

'He is in, isn't he?'

'I think so.'

'It's about his daughter, Zilini.'

'Has she been found?'

148

'Not yet, we're still looking for her. Would you please call him and let him know we would like to have a quick word with him?'

'Just a moment please, I'll call his PA.'

'Thank you.'

'Inspector,' said the receptionist after making the call, 'I've had a word with Mr Barazani's personal assistant, and she said if you'd like to wait a moment she will be right out to see you. Would you like coffee while you wait?'

Buchanan nodded. 'Coffee black, no sugar, Jill?'

'Yes please.'

'Fine,' said the receptionist, 'if you'd like to take a seat, I'll have them brought out to you.'

'Tell me, Avril,' said Buchanan, reading the receptionist's ID badge, 'did Zilini's boyfriend ever come here?'

'Once, maybe twice, but that was months ago.' She leaned forward and lowered her voice. 'Between you and me, I don't think he and Mr Barazani got along very well.'

'Why do you think that?'

'The young man looked scruffy and was very outspoken, two things that annoy Mr Barazani.'

'Thank you, Avril, I'll do my best to stay smart.'

The phone rang interrupting their conversation. 'Excuse me, Inspector. Mastrani, how may I help?'

'What was that all about?' asked Street, as Buchanan sat in the other reception chair.

'I asked if Zac had ever been here. I get the impression that it's common knowledge Barazani and Zac didn't quite see eye to eye.'

The inner office door opened and a young man, carrying a tray, walked over to Buchanan and Street.

'No milk? Was that right?' he asked, as he set the tray down.

'Yes, thank you.' said Street.

As the inner door closed, Street asked, 'Do you think we'll get anywhere with Barazani?'

'Maybe,' he said, smiling and rubbing his hands.

'You're up to something.'

'Maybe.'

The inner door opened, and Charlotte came out. 'Inspector Buchanan, Mr Barazani's apologies. He's going to be about another twenty minutes. Is there anything I can help you with?'

'It's a bit public out here, Charlotte. Is there anywhere we can be a little more private?'

'Certainly, if you'll sign in first, please.'

Once again Buchanan and Street filled in the visitor register and handed their mobile phones to the security guard. Buchanan smiled as he saw the love-hate tattoos on the guard's knuckles.

'Ready? Then please follow me,' said Charlotte.

Buchanan and Street followed Charlotte along the same corridor as before and into a small plain office. It contained a simple desk with four chairs.

'It's a bit spartan in here,' said Charlotte, gesturing to the green cloth-covered chairs, 'but it should give us the privacy you asked for. Now how can I help?'

'These chairs look comfortable,' said Buchanan. 'Do you know where they were purchased?'

'They're just plain office chairs,' said Charlotte. 'They were here when we bought the building. Now, how may I help?'

'Firstly, do you have the name of Zilini's doctor's clinic?'

'Why would you want that information?'

'Don't look so worried, Charlotte. It's just a standard question when someone goes missing.'

'But Zilini wasn't sick.'

'Nonetheless, could we have the name of the clinic?'

'Yes. It's the Harbour Medical Centre.'

'And her doctor's name?'

'Doctor Ambrose, Doctor Harriet Ambrose.'

'Thank you. Now where were you two weeks ago Wednesday evening? That would be the 2nd.'

'Probably working. The company is extremely busy at the moment, we have lots of deadlines to meet.'

'Would you have been working here, in this building?'

'Most likely. I can consult my diary to be precise if you want?'

'That would be extremely helpful.'

Buchanan smiled and winked at Street as Charlotte consulted her phone.

'Yes, Inspector. I was here with Mr Barazani on the evening of the 2nd.'

'Charlotte, I'm curious about something.'

'What's that?'

'I was under the impression that everyone who enters the building has to hand over their mobile phones at reception. Yet you just consulted the diary on your phone and you also told me you took a call on Amal's phone.'

'Ah, yes. Inspector, Mr Barazani is a law unto himself. He and I are the only two who are allowed to bring our phones past reception.'

'Were you working together?'

'Yes.'

'All the time?'

'I don't understand your question.'

'Let me ask it a different way. You said that you and Amal were working together, was he in your company all the time, excluding, say, trips to the toilet?'

She shrugged. 'I'm not sure. As I said we've been extremely busy these past few weeks, the days all melt into each other. We have been working late every day for over three weeks now.'

'So, you don't remember answering a call from Zilini on Amal's phone?'

'I remember a phone call, just not the day. You say it was Wednesday the 2nd?'

'Yes.'

She nodded. 'I do remember Zilini calling. She wanted to talk to her father about something.'

'Did she say what it was about?'

'I don't remember, I don't think so.'

'Did she get to talk to her father?'

'No, she hung up before he came back.'

'Where did he come back from?'

'I don't know.'

'Where were you when Zilini called?'

'I was in my office; I'd just typed up a letter.'

'Can you tell me why Amal's mobile was in your office and not with him?'

'He dictated the letter in his office then we went through into my office for me to type the letter. It was a very important letter and he wanted to sign it immediately; he probably just forgot his phone.'

'What was so important about the letter?'

'You'll need to address that question to Mr Barazani.'

'Where is your office in relation to Amal's?'

'Next to his, we have an adjoining door.'

'So, would you know if he left his office?'

'Yes, he'd have to walk past my door to go down the corridor.'

'And did he at any time of the evening go past your door?'

'Not that I remember.'

'And you don't know why Zilini called?'

'No.'

'How was her demeanour, was she happy, angry?'

'She sounded impatient.'

'Is there any other way out of Amal's office down to the garage that would allow him not to have to go through the front reception?'

'Yes. This end of the building used to be a separate office and the then tenants had their own access from the garage. The office is reached by climbing a flight of stairs from the back of the garage. It used to open into a large open-plan office, but now it is in the back of a small anteroom in Mr Barazani's office.'

'Let me ask you one more question. Do you know where the telephone equipment room is in this building?'

'No. Office space is at a premium on this floor, I'm sure I would have seen it if there is one. You could ask Mr Barazani when you see him. He was heavily involved in the purchase of the building.'

'Thank you, Charlotte. I wonder if you would find out if Amal is available to talk to us now?'

'If you'll wait here, I'll go and see if he is available.'

As the meeting room door closed, Buchanan said to Street, 'What do you think of the chairs? Green polyester fabric.'

Street smiled. 'Same type of chairs and colour as in my doctor's surgery.'

'Yes, I've seen the same in our local community library.'

'What had you smiling when we handed in our phones?'

'Did you see the guard's knuckles?'

She nodded. 'Were those prison tattoos?'

He shrugged. 'Possibly?'

Buchanan was standing, looking out the window at the arriving and departing trains from Eastbourne station, when Charlotte opened the door and announced that Amal Barazani was now ready to see them.

'Is he in his office?' Buchanan asked, as they walked down a long corridor behind Charlotte.

'No, he's in the boardroom. This way,' she said, opening a large polished oak door to reveal an expansive, classically decorated boardroom. Seated at the head of the polished mahogany table was Amal Barazani.

There hadn't had been time to clear away the coffee cups from the meeting. Buchanan counted seven empty cups, a large coffee jug and a plate of three uneaten sandwiches. At the sound of the door closing, Barazani looked up and smiled. 'You like it, Jack?' said Barazani, waving his arm in a welcoming gesture. 'I got the idea from a visit to Syon House and its great entrance hall. I even managed to get the wall and ceiling colours matched.'

The decor reminded Buchanan of the interior of Culzean Castle; it too was a Robert Adam design. The black and white checkered floor tiles made him think of the floor of a masonic hall he'd visited as a young police cadet.

'You have fine taste in decor, Mr Barazani,' said Street.

'That was down to the decorators. I just told them what I wanted.'

'They did a nice job.'

'Yes, I think they did. A local firm, Pace Decorators.'

Buchanan remembered the name; they'd played a key role in a previous investigation.

'Do you have news about Zilini?'

'I'm sorry, no, not at this time.'

'Then why are you here? Why aren't you out looking for her?'

'We are, Amal, and her disappearance is the reason for our visit.'

Barazani leaned back and his shoulders slumped as he relaxed into his chair. 'You want a coffee?'

'No thank you.'

'Charlotte, would you get me some paracetamol and water, please?'

'Certainly.'

As the door closed Buchanan said, 'A busy time for you?'

Barazani exhaled slowly and pushed his hair back with his hand. 'Never known anything like it. You'd think the country was getting ready for war.'

'Would you mind explaining that statement?'

'The Mustela project, the Department of Transport's project, and the microchip project are coming along nicely. What is causing us grief is the government suddenly wants us to accelerate the development of the microchip project. Something is up, Jack. The government is keeping something from all of us, and I don't like it.'

'Is it a money issue?' asked Buchanan, remembering his discussion regarding Barazani talking about financing with his stepbrother, Nasim.

'No, as long as the results of the stress test are successful, the government will finance the whole project. Do you realise that if we are successful, Mastrani could become more powerful and profitable than Microsoft, Google and Amazon all rolled into one?'

'No, I was not aware of that fact. Tell me, who owns Mastrani?'

'I do.'

'And Zilini – will she inherit the company if you die?'

'Yes. Zilini will inherit Mastrani,' said Charlotte, as she placed Barazani's paracetamol and glass of water on the table in front of him.

'Have you had any correspondence from her since her disappearance, other that the empty ring box?'

He swallowed his paracetamol and shook his head as he washed them down. 'No, nothing.'

'Will that be all, Mr Barazani?' asked Charlotte.

'Yes, thanks.'

Buchanan waited for Charlotte to leave the room and shut the door before he asked, 'What do you know about Zilini's life at university?'

'I presume she goes to lectures and studies.'

'What about her friends? What do you know about them?' said Buchanan, looking at his notebook. 'How about someone called Sandy?'

Barazani shook his head.

'Or a Nancy, Emma, Pat, Kate or Judith?

Barazani once more shook his head.

'What about her grades, is she doing well?'

'She's on target for a 2.1.'

'What about her social life?'

'We've never talked about that.'

'Not even about her boyfriend, Zac Taylor?'

'We decided not to discuss it, we just end up arguing over it.'

'Does Zilini have any hobbies?'

'I don't think she has time for hobbies, she's studying for her degree.'

'You said she stays in halls of residence during the week and only comes home on the weekends – is that every weekend?'

'Yes, I think so. Inspector – Jack – I'm a very busy man. Many people depend on me for their livelihoods. Sometimes running a business like Mastrani is akin to riding a horse in the Grand National without a saddle.'

'I see, a great responsibility sits on your shoulders.'

'Sometimes I have to be quite ruthless. Mustn't let the horse get its head.'

'Was it you who found this building for your company?'

'Yes. I'd been in town, I don't remember why, and as I walked back to my car I passed the building and saw it was available. I called the agents and arranged for an inspection. I had a good look round and felt it would be perfect for my needs.'

'It has only one entrance?'

'Yes. I had a security firm survey the building and they made the recommendations on the building's layout.'

'And there is only one way into the offices?'

'Yes, through the reception.'

'You said you were involved in the decoration of the offices?'

'Yes.'

'Who undertook the building works?'

'Bournes, they're a local family business.'

'Did Bournes also do the interior building works, under your supervision?'

'Yes, they took care of everything.'

'You agreed to all the alterations to the building?'

'Yes, I've already told you I designed the whole layout of the building. I gave Bournes architects my requirements and sketches of how I wanted the building laid out.'

'From the garage up?'

'Yes.'

'What about the furniture, did you select that?'

'Ah, now that did become an issue. By the time I got round to choosing furniture the project was over budget, so I decided to just reuse the furniture that was left by the previous tenants. Turns out it wasn't such a bad idea, green is the corporate colour, and considering how most youngsters use desk chairs I won't have lost much money on the deal.'

'Is there a telecom room in the building?'

'Yes, downstairs in the garage. The room contains the telephone system and the servers. Look, why are you asking all these questions about how the office was constructed? How will it help to find Zilini?'

'When we first met, you said you last saw Zilini on the Friday evening when you had dinner together.'

'That is so.'

'You also said she went out on Friday evening after dinner. Do you know where she went and what time she returned?'

'No. I presumed it was to see her boyfriend.'

'And later that evening you heard music coming from her bedroom?'

'Yes.'

'Yet when you got up Saturday morning you noticed she had gone; what time was that?'

'I seem to remember Darsameen mentioning it when she served me coffee about ten.'

'Was it normal for Zilini to go out early on a Saturday and not say where she was going?'

'She was always a late riser on Saturdays, on account of how late she stayed out on the Friday.'

'So, going out early on Saturday wasn't normal for her?'

'Not that early.'

'Zilini's phone is registered to Mastrani – did you monitor her calls?'

'How do you know who it is registered to?'

'We have our ways. Did you monitor her calls?'

'No, just the phone bills.'

'I wonder if we might come round to your house and have a look in her bedroom?'

'It's a bit late for that, she's gone. Her room will have been tidied and the bed made.'

'All the same, could we have a look?'

'I suppose so. I'll call the house and let Darsameen know you'll be stopping by. Now, if there are no more questions, I have work to do.'

'Yes, just one.'

'And your question is?'

'When we last talked you mentioned something about injectable microchips.'

'I remember.'

'Is your company going to be making these chips?'

'No, we are only working on developing the software that will enable the chips to function.'

'Can you explain?'

'I can't but I know someone who can explain it better than me,' he said, pressing the speaker button on the phone. It rang four times before being answered.

'Michael, it's Amal. Listen, I have two police officers here who want you to explain how the microchip program will work. I already covered the RFID development with them and explained the benefits. We're in the boardroom.'

'OK, be right there.'

Barazani smiled and said, 'Michael heads up our software development team, he also looks after security. If he doesn't know the answers to your questions, no one will.'

Almost immediately the door opened, and tall, slender, young man entered. 'Michael Levitt, you must be the police?'

'DCI Buchanan and DS Street.'

'What is it you want to know?' he asked, as he sat in one of the chairs draping his right leg over the arm rest.

'Mr Barazani already gave me a brief explanation of what Mastrani is developing. Can you explain how these microchips will help society be a better place to live in?'

'The microchip has its limitations on how much and what information it can contain. Development has gone in the direction of creating an incorruptible injectable chip with a totally unique serial number matched with some very sophisticated software. The unique number is made from certain bio markers, such as your blood type, fingerprints, iris scan, and your DNA coding sequence. This unique number will be stored on the chip and in a totally secure government data vault.'

'Yes, I already know that, but what is the practical outcome of this? Will I be able to buy a bag of potatoes with this chip?' asked Buchanan.

'Of course you will, and here is the great thing about it. When you walk into the supermarket to buy your bag of potatoes, the RFID reader at the entrance will read your hand and know who you are. All you have to do is to walk over to the potato bin, remove the potatoes, then do the remainder of your shopping. Each time you remove an item from the shelf and place it in your shopping bag, the shelf reader scans your hand and, as you walk out the store, the RFID reader recognises that you have completed your shopping and charges your bank account, simple. The same will go for driving your car, riding the train, flying out of the country to go on holiday – no passports or visas required.'

'So, no more checkout staff in shops, no need for traffic policemen keeping order on the roads, uninsured drivers a thing of the past, and immigration staff at our ports of entry all on the beach relaxing in their deckchairs?'

'Jack, use your imagination,' said Barazani. 'You as a policeman should see the obvious advantage of such a system. The days of criminals hiding in plain sight will be over, all the police need to do is search online using the criminal's ID and instantly their location will be displayed. As will the tracking details of everywhere they have been, alibis smashed.'

'Cash will be a thing of the past,' said Michael. 'No more fake bank notes - just think how much money the treasury will save by not printing banknotes, which currently, I may add, is estimated at about forty million pounds annually.'

'Crimes involving cash will cease,' said Barazani. 'Drug dealing and prostitution will be seriously curbed if there is no cash. Money laundering will almost be wiped out overnight. No more doing jobs for cash – just think how much money will be raised by the exchequer. Tax rates could even fall because of the increased revenue received by the treasury. Satisfied, Jack?'

'And this is the big project that will make Mastrani one of the world's richest companies?'

'Precisely.'

'Tell me,' said Buchanan, 'what's to stop one of your employees, say young Michael here, just making a copy of the program and walking out the door with it?'

'He could do, but without the dongle code, it would be useless.'

'And I suppose you have that locked away in a safe?'

'Better than a safe. It is kept in a digital safe with a 12-digit code that has three separate sections, and each section has been given to a trustworthy individual.'

'I suppose you are one of the three individuals?'

'Yes, and before you ask Zilini is another, and someone whose name I am not going to reveal is the third.'

Buchanan nodded. 'Before we go, I wonder if we could have a look inside the telecom room?'

'Why not? How about the staff kitchen and toilets while you are at it? Sorry, my Zilini going missing is upsetting me. Michael has a key to the room; he can show you.'

'Oh, you haven't told us where your private staircase to the garage is?'

'Who told you about that?'

'How often do you use it?'

'I don't see what that's got to do with the disappearance of Zilini.'

'Please answer my question.'

'It's over there, behind the door. It's more convenient for me and I can also avoid the plethora of questions I get every time I walk through the office. It's also closer to where I park my car.'

'We'd still like to see it.'

'There's no need to, all guests use the main entrance. But since you insist on seeing the telecom room, Michael will take you down by my private staircase.'

'Thanks,' said Buchanan, as Michael went over to the door leading to the garage staircase.

'Please follow,' he said, unlocking the door.

As they descended Buchanan looked carefully at the steps wondering if these were the steps the body of Sam Taylor had been dragged down.

At the bottom Michael pointed to a door. 'That's the comms room over there, follow me.'

They squeezed between Barazani's Rolls Royce and a yellow Mercedes and crossed over to a door marked, *No Unauthorised Entry*.

'Not many people come in here,' said Michael, turning on the light. 'Except those who think it's a place to store their treasured possessions – that's junk to you and me.' He threw an empty cardboard box out the door. 'It may look a mess now, but you should have seen it when we moved in. Damn, I told Hanse to throw those old chairs out. Really Inspector, no one respects the IT department till their laptop freezes. This used to be the comms room for a call centre. The frame was a real rat's nest of patch leads and wires. Thankfully, since the new server was installed, most of the mess has now gone.'

'By frame, I deduce you are referring to a telephone frame?' said Buchanan.

'Yes, it's over there,' he said, pointing to a large grey metal box fastened to the far wall.

Buchanan made his way over and, looking on the floor under the box, saw short lengths of blue and white, yellow, and red and black wire.

'Is this room kept locked?' asked Buchanan.

'Mostly. The key is kept with reception. I also have my own copy.'

'How about your boss, Amal Barazani?'

'He might have, it's his company.'

'These chairs,' said Buchanan, indicating a group of green cloth-covered chairs piled up in the back corner of the room.

'You can have them if you want. They're broken and supposed to be in the skip, they were left over from the previous tenants.'

'You said this building used to be a call centre?'

'Yes. I think BT also used it as a DR training centre.'

'DR?'

'Disaster Recovery. Most large companies have one somewhere. A DR centre would be used in case of emergency, such as a fire or a flood and the main office cannot be accessed. Is there anything else?'

'How many people keep their cars in the garage?' Buchanan asked, looking round at the parked cars.

'There's only room for twelve, so just the senior managers get to do that. The rest of us get to keep our bicycles in here.'

'Do you know who owns the yellow Mercedes, the one parked beside the Rolls Royce?'

'I believe that belongs to Mr Barazani's daughter, Zilini. It spends most of its time here.'

'She doesn't drive it to university?'

'I believe parking on campus is an issue, so she keeps it here during the week. I think she comes home on the train then drives the car to the house.'

'Is the building open 24 hours?'

'Yes. We run a 24-hour helpdesk for our client networks.'

'Does everyone who uses the garage have a key?'

'They have an infrared fob. One click, and the garage door opens.'

'Are the fobs unique?'

'Yes, but sometimes if several people show up at the same time, only one fob is needed to let everyone in.'

'And the only way into the offices from the garage is up those stairs and through reception?'

'Access to the reception is by using your ID card, and when you get there, everyone has to sign in using their ID cards. Mr Barazani is looking into doing away with them and having everyone injected with a microchip. I see that idea doesn't appeal to you.'

'No, it certainly doesn't.'

'Is there anything else?'

'Is that CCTV camera working?' said Buchanan, pointing to the ceiling camera trained on the garage door.

'Yes, and to pre-empt your next question, we keep the videos for thirty days.'

'Good, I'd like a copy of the video from the main garage door and any others that show access to the reception and Mr Barazani's private stairs.'

'OK, if you'll follow me up to reception, I'll get a copy for you.'

'Is there anything else?' asked Michael, as he handed Buchanan a USB stick.

'Not for just now, thanks, Michael.'

10
Monday
A Dream

Buchanan drove into the Harbour Medical Centre and parked between a white van and a Peugeot.

At first glance on entering, the Centre looked empty of patients. The only occupant in the waiting room was a young woman holding a crying baby. Buchanan approached the reception desk and asked to speak with Doctor Harriet Ambrose.

'Do you have an appointment?'

'No. I am Detective Chief Inspector Buchanan, and this is Detective Sergeant Street. We need to have a quick word with Doctor Ambrose – it's police business.'

'One moment, I'll see if she has time to talk to you. Please take a seat.'

Buchanan followed Street into the waiting room. Street sat beside the young mother with the crying baby while Buchanan sat by the door, watching for the receptionist to return.

'How old is your baby?' Street asked, while looking down at the baby.

'She's just three months. Would you mind holding her for me for a moment? I need to get her bottle out of the bag.'

'Sure.'

Buchanan turned away from his vigil and watched as Street cradled the baby in her arms. Would she one day hold her own baby, and if he would one day be a grandfather.

'Inspector Buchanan,' said the receptionist. 'Doctor Ambrose can see you now, but she asks if you could keep your visit short, she is very busy this morning.'

'Thanks.'

He stood and looked at Street cooing at the baby; she was lost in another world.

'Jill –'

'Oh.'

'Never mind, you're busy.'

'Doctor Ambrose is in consulting room three, Inspector.'

'Thanks.'

◆

'Good morning Doctor,' said Buchanan, as he closed the consulting room door behind him. 'Thank you for taking time to talk to me.'

'How can I help?'

'I understand that you are Zilini Barazani's GP?'

'Yes, I am.'

'Are you aware of her disappearance from her home?'

'No.'

'She has been missing for several days. When was the last time you saw her?'

'Let me check,' she said, consulting her computer. 'She came in seven weeks ago.'

'Can you tell me if you are aware of any issues that might make her want to disappear?'

'I'm sorry, Inspector, but that is asking me to break patient confidentiality rules.'

'Doctor Ambrose. The need for you to protect your patient confidentiality I understand, but for your patient's safety, I need to know if there are any reasons why she may have had to go into hiding.'

'What sort of safety issues are you referring to?'

'Someone she knew was brutally murdered not long after she disappeared.'

'And you think she might be dead?'

'We don't know at this time; we are still investigating.'

Doctor Ambrose looked back at her screen and said, 'As far as Zilini's health is concerned, there was nothing wrong with her.'

'What was the reason for her visit?'

'She needed a prescription renewing.'

'When you saw her, was there any indications she had been assaulted?'

'Her demeanour didn't make me think of her being assaulted in any way. Is there anything else?' she said, looking at her watch.

'No, that will be all for now. Thank you for your time, Doctor.'

♦

'Sorry. I got involved with Marsha,' said Street, as they drove along Pacific Drive towards Tasmania Way.

'Marsha?'

'I was holding her baby.'

'Remember the first time we drove along here?' said Buchanan, as they turned onto Hobart Quay.

'Yes, and you thought Sir Nathan was a mass murderer.'

'Really? Is that what you thought I thought?'

'No, not really. Remember it was our first case together and you were just down from Glasgow.'

'What a difference working down here is.'

'Do you miss working in Glasgow?'

'It's a completely different world, and yes I do miss it a bit. But I'm very happy working here in Eastbourne.'

'Good. Learn much from Doctor Ambrose?'

'Zilini Barazani was in full health when she last visited her doctor.'

'What else?'

'Zilini Barazani saw Doctor Ambrose about getting a prescription renewed.'

'There goes one reason for her to run away.'

'The appointment was seven weeks ago; a lot can happen in seven weeks.'

'Yes, you are right, so it can.'

♦

'It'll be a late one for me tomorrow,' said Buchanan, as they drove along Hobart Quay towards Amal Barazani's house.

'Why is that?'

'I'm driving Travis to the airport, his flight leaves at nine thirty-five in the evening. He doesn't get into Dallas till six twenty-three the following evening.'

'That's a long flight.'

'He has an overnight stopover in New York.'

'Is Poppy going with you?'

'I don't think so. She and Harry are checking out the Falmer area. I think he wants to show her Brighton and where she will be going to college.'

'You realise you will be in the minority in your house, one man and two women?' said Street.

'The thought had crossed my mind,' said Buchanan, as they parked outside Barazani's house.

The front door opened just as Buchanan was about to ring the doorbell.

'Darsameen?'

'Yes.'

'Good afternoon. Detective Chief Inspector Buchanan and Detective Sergeant Street,' said Buchanan, showing his warrant card. 'Mr Barazani said we could have a look at Zilini's bedroom.'

'Yes, he called. This way.'

They followed Darsameen up the stairs to Zilini's bedroom. 'Have you made any changes to the room since Zilini left?' asked Buchanan.

'No. Mr Barazani said to tidy up the room, but I just couldn't bring myself to sweep away all traces of Zilini.'

'So, the room is exactly as you found it?'

'Yes.'

'You've looked after her since her mother became ill?' queried Buchanan.

'Yes.'

'You and Zilini are quite close, Darsameen?' asked Street, seeing tears in her eyes.

'I lost my family in Afghanistan; our house was bombed by the Taliban as a reprisal for my father helping the Americans. I alone escaped and made my way to this country.'

'So Zilini became like a daughter to you?'

Darsameen nodded. 'The Barazanis are the only family I have.'

'What was Zilini like as a child?'

'Precocious, but she was a joy to look after and full of mischief. It was difficult for me in the early days. My only experience in looking after children was taking care of my younger sisters. I soon realised that Zilini wasn't just any normal child, she was highly intelligent for her age.'

'In what way?'

'I can remember one incident when she was about three years old. She had a large piece jigsaw of a zoo scene, and after I helped her to do it a few times she got cross with me. She had even learned and remembered the names of all the animals. She was a precious little imp with wisdom above her years, a real chatterbox. She had the Barazani temper, and when she didn't want to do something, no amount of reasoning or cajoling would get her to change her mind, she was a real minx in curls.'

'Was Mr Barazani any help? Or was it you who brought Zilini up?'

'Mr Barazani was just starting his business when I joined the family. Often he would leave early in the morning for work and not return till long after Zilini had gone to bed.'

'You put her to bed each night?'

'Yes. I would bathe her and then read her a bedtime story. When she couldn't go to sleep, I'd sing her Afghani nursery rhymes. As she grew older, we would sing duets together in Pashto. She has such a lovely voice.'

'How did you manage with looking after the house and taking care of the needs of a three-year-old?'

'I managed. Mr Barazani's relatives helped as well. Bahija, Mr Barazani's stepbrother's wife, was a great help when I was very busy. Later on, for Zilini's tenth birthday, her grandmother gave her a set of horse-riding lessons. I think she might have had ulterior motives.'

'Why would you say that?'

'Bahija's son, Achmad, is just a year older than Zilini. Mrs Barazani took them both riding. I think she was match-making at an early stage.'

'That happens. I take it they didn't hit it off?'

'Zilini told me Achmad used to hit his pony. She said she couldn't like anyone who was cruel to animals.'

'Where were the stables?'

'Near the village of Hankham. I would go collect her sometimes when her grandmother had to go somewhere and couldn't bring Zilini home.'

'Are you and Zilini still close?'

'Yes.'

'What was your reaction when you heard she was missing?'

'Shock, though she'd gone missing before.'

'When was this?'

'Just before she started university, it was only for a few days though.'

'Where did she go?'

'She and Mr Barazani had an argument. I think it was all about Zilini going to university.'

'Why would that be an issue? Lots of girls her age would love to get out the house and be on their own.'

'I suppose with it being the first time she was going to be living away from home she didn't quite know what to do, so she went to her friend Judith's house. When Judith's mother found out that Mr Barazani didn't know about Zilini coming to stay, she called and told me where Zilini was. As a compromise, it was decided that Zilini would come home every weekend.'

'You must have liked that?'

Darsameen smiled and nodded.

'You brought her a cup of coffee on the Saturday she disappeared?'

'Yes. It was my way of keeping in touch.'

'What time was that?'

'Half-past-nine.'

'The same time as always?'

'Yes.'

'When you entered the room, what was your first impression?'

She thought for a minute then said, 'The room felt empty, her fragrance was missing. It was just as though she'd never been there.'

'Did you look for her, call out her name?'

'Yes. I checked her bathroom. There was one occasion, when she'd been to a party, I found her asleep on the bathroom floor.'

'Was that a regular occurrence?'

'Oh no. She rarely touched alcohol. We thought afterwards her drink might have been spiked with something.'

'What did you do next?'

'I went downstairs to see if she was in the front room. More than once she'd curled up on the settee to watch a film and had fallen asleep.'

'I take it there was no sign of her in the front room?'

'No. Oh, now I remember, the bedroom window was open, and her laundry and backpack were gone.'

'Her laundry and backpack?' said Buchanan, as he walked over to the window.

'Yes. I'd washed and ironed her clothes Friday evening and placed them on the dresser beside her backpack.'

'What time was that?'

'Shortly before seven.'

'Was Zilini in her room?'

'No, she was in the kitchen.'

'Was doing her laundry a normal thing to do?'

'Yes. I know she has a laundry facility at university, but I think she does it to make me feel needed, and it does.'

'You said nothing to Mr Barazani on Saturday morning when you saw the open window?'

'No. I just thought Zilini had gone out early for a walk before the house was awake and had forgotten to close it.'

'What sort of security arrangements does the house have?' asked Buchanan.

'I'm not sure. I do know there is an alarm on the front door and all the windows have devices to tell when a window has been opened, also there are movement detectors in the hallway at the front and back doors. Those I have to keep clear of spider's webs. Mr Barazani doesn't like to be wakened in the middle of the night by a spider building a web in front of the sensors.'

'So, the alarm system is turned on a night?'

'Yes.'

'And if someone were to walk down a hallway towards the front or back doors, the alarm would sound?'

She shrugged. 'I suppose so; unless it's before eleven-thirty in the evening and after five thirty in the morning. The alarm is only used during the night, or when there is no one in the house.'

'Why didn't the alarm go off in Zilini's bedroom when she opened the window?'

'The alarm for the window in Zilini's room is always turned off. She said she wanted to keep the window open at night because she liked to hear the sound of the seagulls when she wakes. So, Mr Barazani had the alarm company turn that window device off.'

Buchanan looked out of the window and smiled.

'Did Zilini confide in you, tell you her innermost secrets?' asked Street.

'Sometimes. When she was little, we used to tell each other stories while I brushed her hair before she went to bed.'

'Do you still brush her hair?' asked Street.

'Not very often. She's a grown woman, has a boyfriend.'

'What did she tell you about him?'

'It was difficult for her; her father didn't approve of him.'

'Why was that?'

'I think Mr Barazani hoped that Zilini would find a nice young businessman to marry and provide him with lots of grandchildren.'

'What did you think of the boyfriend?'

'I thought he was a nice young man, a bit outspoken, but always polite. He was such an encouragement for Zilini.'

'In what way?'

'She used to be very shy and withdrawn.'

'And now?'

'Have you seen her when she's on stage with him?'

'No, we haven't had that pleasure, Darsameen. I presume you have?' said Buchanan, remembering he hadn't yet watched the video of Zilini singing.

'Oh yes.'

'Where and when did you see them?'

'It was at her university about four weeks ago. I think it was on a Wednesday evening. They are so talented.'

'Did she ever bring her boyfriend here to the house?'

'When Mr Barazani was away on business trips, or in London for the weekend, Zilini used to invite her university friends, including her boyfriend, over for a party.'

'Did Mr Barazani know about these parties?'

'I don't think so. I used to tidy up afterwards.'

'Did her boyfriend stay overnight?'

'No, never.'

'And the room is exactly as you found it?'

'Yes.'

'The Friday of the weekend she disappeared; did she drive her car home from the station?'

'I suppose so, she did every other weekend.'

'When you looked for her, did you check to see if her car was outside in the driveway?'

'Yes, I did look. It wasn't there.'

'Do you have Zilini's friend Judith's home address?'

'No. Judith's parents moved back to California.'

'So, Judith is an American?'

'Yes, but she stayed behind to complete her studies. Is there anything else? I have the washing machine to empty and I don't want the sheets to wrinkle.'

'No, I think we've seen enough.'

◆

'Well, Jill, what are your impressions of the Barazani family so far?' asked Buchanan, as they drove out of the harbour.

'It always surprises me how impressions change when you get to know a family. My initial impression of the Barazani family was of a financially stable but dysfunctional family.'

'And now?'

'I think the father loves his daughter but is so wrapped up in what he does, he's lost what being a father really is.'

'And the daughter, Zilini?'

'I get the impression she respects her father but is torn between love for him and that of her boyfriend. Her disappearing is her way of avoiding a decision, sort of not facing up to the situation by running away from it.'

'If what I think is on the video from the garage, we should see Zilini enter the garage sometime after four-fifteen Friday afternoon then coming back after five-thirty on Saturday morning to drop off the car.'

'Should we do forensic checks on the car?'

'Yes. Though I doubt it will show much, but you never know. The great forensic medical examiner, Sir Sidney Smith, once said, *No one can go to a place, commit a crime, and come away again without two things happening: he leaves behind him some trace by which he can be identified, and he carries away with him certain traces by which he can be connected with the crime.* I took Dr Mansell's advice and I've been reading Sidney Smith's autobiography.'

'Good for you. I'm hungry,' said Street, as they passed the memorial roundabout.

'Would a sandwich do?'

'Yes.'

'Good. I'll stop at Poppyseed Bakery - it's just down Gildredge Road, my treat.'

♦

'What did you get?' asked Street, as she unwrapped her sandwich.

'Cheese and pickle on sourdough.'

'Why did you smile when you looked out of Zilini's window?'

'I was thinking of two other lovers, thwarted by family traditions.'

'Romeo and Juliet? Were you thinking about a ladder at the bedroom window?'

'It had crossed my mind. I saw you pick up the bedside alarm-clock radio, why was that?'

'I used to have one at the boarding school. Zilini's alarm was set for ten-thirty in the evening.'

'So, she'd set the time on the clock-radio to come on at ten-thirty to make her father think she was home, when all the time she'd driven her car to the Mastrani garage, then gone off somewhere. Well done, Jill. But where did she go?'

'Maybe the CCTV from the Mastrani garage will be helpful, at least it will provide us with a time when she was last seen.'

'Yes, it will. But, in the meantime, we have work to do,' said Buchanan, as they drove out of Hyde Gardens and back onto Gildredge Road.

♦

'That's the stepgrandmother's house,' said Street, as they drove slowly past the entrance on Upper Carlisle Road.

'I'll park a few doors down then we can walk slowly back,' said Buchanan. 'Give us a chance to chat with the neighbours.'

'If they are out and about,' said Street.

'They won't need to be, I'll knock on the doors and pretend we don't know which house the Barazanis live in.'

Buchanan parked four houses away from the Barazani residence and beckoned Street to follow him as he walked up the first driveway they came to. He didn't have to knock on the door as the resident was about to get into her car.

'Excuse me,' said Buchanan, 'Mrs Barazani?'

'No, Joyce Whitfield. The Barazanis live three houses down the road. The one with the fir tree in the front garden.'

'Thank you, Mrs Whitfield. Would you happen to know if they are around?'

'I think so, I saw Mrs Barazani two days ago getting into her car. Are you Jehovah's Witnesses? If you are, you'll be wasting your time there.'

'Why is that?'

'They're foreign, at least Mrs Barazani is.'

'No, we're not Jehovah's Witnesses.'

'Oh, then you'll be from the council, about the parking?'

'No, it's not about the parking.'

'Pity.'

'Why is it a pity?'

'When they have their parties, their guests park both sides of the road, almost blocking it. Sometimes we can't even turn into our own driveway or even park in front of our own house.'

'Does that happen very often?'

'Not since I had a word with Mrs Barazani on the phone. She was ever so apologetic about the matter.'

'Do you speak to her very often?'

'Not really, she keeps mainly to herself. My George talks to the husband sometimes.'

'Have you ever been invited to their parties?'

'No. I don't quite think we'd fit in.'

'Why is that?'

'Different generation, mostly college age.'

'Mostly?'

'It reminded me of when I was at university and it was the end of term. After all the stress of the term we'd have a faculty and student picnic. A great excuse to let the hair down and drink a bit more than usual.'

'I remember those days,' said Buchanan, nodding slowly. 'Well, thank you, Mrs Whitfield, sorry to have disturbed you.'

She looked at Buchanan, then to Street and back at Buchanan, bit her lip then asked, 'Are you from the immigration office?'

Buchanan smiled. 'No Mrs Whitfield, we're nothing to do with the immigration office. It's just a simple family matter, nothing for you to get concerned about. Goodbye.'

'Nicely done,' said Street, when they were out of earshot of Mrs Whitfield.

> 'We slip through the air
> Unnoticed as a breeze
> To uncover the truth
> With not even a sneeze'

'I've missed your rhymes,' said Street, as they turned into the Barazani driveway. 'I can see why the guests would park in the road; the steepness of this driveway would put most drivers off.'

They walked slowly up the drive taking the time to turn and admire the view over the rooftops of the Meads houses, to the town of Eastbourne and on to the bay.

'You know,' said Street, 'we're quite lucky to live in such a beautiful part of the country as this.'

'As beautiful as this view is,' said Buchanan, 'I have many memories of standing on Lyle Hill behind Greenock and looking out over the Firth of Clyde to the hills beyond.'

'Has the Clyde changed that much since you were a boy?'

'My dad once told me you could stand on the river front of Port Glasgow and while looking down the river, all you would see were ships being built – now it's nothing but bloody roads and car parks. All that history dug up and chucked in the river. Glasgow has changed as well, especially now since they have built the M8 right round the west end of the city. St Enoch station is gone, replaced by a hideous glass-roofed chamber of nothingness, sort of like the Arndale Shopping Centre extension here in Eastbourne.'

'Times change, and we must change with them,' said Street. 'We can't live in the past.'

'You're being very philosophical, is there something on your mind?'

'No, it's just sort of just popped into my head. I think I'm spending too much time hanging around with you.'

'C'mon, let's get the interview over with,' said Buchanan. looking at the time on his phone. 'It will soon be time for dinner.'

He knocked on the door and waited. It was opened by a young woman – the maid, he assumed.

'Good afternoon,' said Buchanan, showing his warrant card. 'Detective Chief Inspector Buchanan and Detective Sergeant Street. We would like to talk with Mr or Mrs Barazani if they are in.'

'Please come in, I'm Mr Barazani's PA.'

They followed her along a hallway with a polished oak floor to the rear of the house and were shown into a large room decorated with an Arabic theme. The polished oak floor extended into the room and in the centre, there was what looked to Buchanan like a hand-woven carpet. Situated exactly in the middle was a square coffee table – its top, inlaid with tiny dots of different coloured veneers, recreated a desert scene with camels resting at a water hole.

'Please take a seat. I'll let Mrs Barazani know you are waiting,' she said, as she closed the door quietly behind her.

'I'm impressed,' said Buchanan. 'Yousef Barazani has a PA.'

'It happens,' said Street, looking round the room. 'We certainly get to see some spectacular interiors in our job.'

Buchanan looked at the seating arrangement. On one side of the coffee table were two white leather chairs without arms, opposite was a two-seater settee covered in off-white jacquard fabric. In front of the wide French windows was a three-seater settee in the same fabric. Draped at each end of the windows were white muslin curtains.

'There's money here,' said Buchanan. 'I'll bet you none of this furniture came from John Lewis's.'

'I believe you. Makes me feel like we're in some rich Arab's home. This room is bigger than our whole flat.'

'The sideboard looks Eastern, though that painting somehow looks a bit out of place.'

Further discussing was pre-empted by the opening of the door and the entrance of Hiezabel Barazani.

'Inspector Buchanan, I'm sorry but my husband is away just now. How can I help?'

'Could you tell me, when was the last time you saw your granddaughter, Zilini?'

'That would have been a week ago, Saturday afternoon, the 29th. I was in town shopping and I saw her going into the railway station.'

'Can you remember what time that was?'

'Must have been about five forty-five. I was rushing to get to my car; I'd parked it in the Enterprise car park and didn't want to get a ticket for being overdue.'

'Was she alone?'

'I think so.'

'And you haven't seen her since?'

'Oh, there was one other time, at my son's house.'

'When was that?'

'It would have been the following Thursday afternoon. She showed up with her boyfriend, a really scruffy individual.'

'Do you visit your son very often?'

'Of course, he's my son.'

'Every day?'

'No, I have my own affairs to take care of.'

'Mrs Barazani, when we met last week at your son's house, you made some remarks about Zilini. Could you explain what you meant by them?'

'Nothing, I was having a bad day and spoke without thinking, that is all.'

'How often do you visit your son?'

'Once a week.'

'Always on Thursdays?'

'Yes, mostly on Thursdays.'

'Why Thursdays?'

'On Thursdays, my son works from home.'

'Is Zilini always there when you visit?'

'Most Thursdays.'

'Why was she there?'

'She comes most Thursday afternoon for a music lesson.'

'What sort of music lesson?'

'Singing.'

'When you are there, when she comes for her singing lesson, do you get to hear her sing?'

'Unfortunately, yes.'

'She's not musical?'

'Quite the opposite. She has an excellent singing voice.'

'But you don't agree with her singing?'

'It's not so much her singing, it's the boyfriend.'

'Do you know the name of the boyfriend?'

'She called him Zac.'

'How about the surname? Do you know that?'

'I think it's Taylor.'

'Thank you. Is it just because he's scruffy he's not a suitable person to be her boyfriend?'

'No. He's not one of us, and he's not one of the family.'

'Sorry, but I don't understand.'

'Inspector, in my country, young women are not allowed to go wandering about without a guardian.'

'Why do you think the boyfriend comes along with Zilini?'

'My son's wife is teaching them both.'

'As a duet?'

'Yes.'

'What does the family think about the relationship between Zilini and her boyfriend?'

'As I said, he's not one of us.'

'Not a Barazani?'

'No, not that. You English – you know so little about us. In our culture young women must dress respectfully, and they certainly are not allowed to have male relationships not approved of by their family. If they wish to travel, they must get a guardian's permission and be accompanied by a male family member. They are expected to keep the house tidy and, as far as going off to study at university, well, it's almost unheard of.'

'Have you discussed your feelings with her father?'

'Amal? You must be joking.'

'Why not?'

'He's a Jew.'

'By that I assume you consider him not to be *one of us*?'

'Precisely. Though I believe he didn't like the boyfriend any more than I did.'

'Does your husband think like you do about the boyfriend?'

'No,' she said, shaking her head.

'What about Bahija?'

'She adores Zilini.'

'Why?'

'She says Zilini is a natural, just like the boyfriend.'

'How did you and your husband meet?'

For the first time during the interview, she smiled. 'We met at Foodex Saudi.'

'What is Foodex Saudi?'

'It is Saudi Arabia's leading International Food and Drink Trade Exhibition. There are anywhere up to six hundred exhibitors in attendance.'

'I never knew there was such a thing. Were you visiting at the time you met your husband?'

'No, my family owns a hotel in Jeddah. My father was there representing the family hotel and I was there to hand out literature.'

'What does your husband do?'

'Before he suffered his heart attack, he was involved in financing movie making.'

'Does he enjoy retirement?'

'He tried it for a few months, but we got in each other's way so much he went back to work.'

'What does he do now?'

'He still travels in Europe seeking investors for movie production. We also run workshops here at the house on Saturdays.'

'Does he go abroad often?'

'Most weeks. When he goes it's usually on a Monday evening by train and returns on Thursday mornings.'

'Is that where he is at the moment?'

'You've just missed him, he's off to Bulgaria. He'll be back on Thursday.'

'I see,' said Buchanan. 'I can understand why you'd want your son to go into business on his own.'

'It's a family tradition.'

'And Zac Taylor wasn't considered a suitable partner for Zilini?'

'What do you think?'

'You son's wife is in business on her own, yet I deduce you're not too happy about that?'

'My son's wife deems it fit to work when my son is perfectly capable of providing for them both.'

'Do they have financial worries?'

'No, it's just – Inspector, if my son has a fault, it is he lacks ambition. When it comes to making business decisions at the bank, he's held in high regard. But when we try to suggest he leaves and sets up on his own, he just shrugs and says he is happy where he is. We've offered to help him get set up as a financial advisor, but he just keeps on saying money isn't important to him.'

'I see. Must make you very frustrated to have ambitions for your son that he doesn't share.'

'Just like his stepbrother.'

'Do they get along?'

'Yes, in spite of their differences. Do you have children, Inspector?'

Buchanan turned to Street and winked, then looked back at Hiezabel Barazani. 'Yes, I have a married daughter.'

'Ah, not a problem for you then. I expect she's at home looking after the affairs of the house.'

'No, in fact she's standing in front of you – Detective Sergeant Street. What time will your husband be home on Thursday?' I'd really like to talk to him.'

'It depends on what train he catches, you'll just have to call.'

'You said being in business is a family tradition. Do you share that tradition?'

'My position is as a housewife, Inspector. My focus is to fulfil the requests of my husband and my son. I take care of the cleanliness of the house, organise the cooking of the food and the entertaining of visitors when my husband has clients visit the house.'

'Do you do a lot of entertaining?'

'When he's not travelling, my husband offers private workshops here at home.'

'Workshops?'

'Introduction to film-making. The one-day course covers the basic aspects of film production.'

'Do many people attend?'

'Oh yes, the courses are extremely popular events.'

'Are these courses residential?'

'No, this house only has five bedrooms. The courses are held mostly on Saturdays. The attendees arrive early Saturday morning and depart Saturday evening.'

'That's a long day, the students must be exhausted at the end.'

'My husband likes it that way, he says it creates a sense of reality, just like it would be on the set.'

'In what way?'

'The final test involves role-playing. At the beginning of the day the students are given a script to learn, and parts to play. After dinner they get to put into practice what they have learnt during the day.'

'All that in one day?' asked Street.

'Yes, but as I said, the course is only an introduction to film production.'

'Are meals included?'

'Yes. A buffet breakfast, a light lunch, and dinner before the evening session.'

'Who takes care of the catering?'

'That is one of my responsibilities.'

'You cook for all those people?'

'No, Sergeant, I have the food catered in. I only do a bit of family baking when I get time.'

'Where are the courses held?'

'We have a summer house in the rear garden, with enough room for up to twenty people.'

'Must be a bit cramped,' said Buchanan, 'the summer houses I've seen usually only hold six, maybe eight, people.'

'This is no ordinary summer house, Inspector, it is where my husband does his teaching. Even though it is quite large, it sits nicely in our back garden. It has turned out to be very useful, especially when we have family come to stay. There's a washroom, a small bedroom and a large open-plan living room with a small kitchen counter.'

'Sounds ideal, especially if it is decorated as tastefully as this room.'

'You like it?' she said, smiling and visibly relaxing. 'That was my idea. I also laid out the gardens.'

'If the gardens are as magnificent as this room, they must really be beautiful,' said Buchanan, looking at Street.

'Would you like to see the gardens?'

Buchanan looked at the clock on the wall. 'I'm not sure, we are really pressed for time, would it take long?'

'No.'

'In that case we'd love to.'

♦

'We're really pressed for time,' said Street, as they drove back to the office. 'What was that all about?'

'My niggler was niggling, there's something not right about that setup. Did you see what I saw?'

'The room was lovely, I wouldn't mind that sort of furniture in my flat, except it wouldn't fit.'

'That's not what I am getting at. Suppose I asked you what you were doing at three in the afternoon two weeks ago Wednesday, how would you answer?'

'I couldn't. I'd need to look at my diary.'

'Precisely. How about the garden, what did you think of it?'

'Huge, wasn't it? Must be great to have direct access to the Downs at the bottom of the garden.'

'Anything else?'

'It's very secluded with all those trees along the garden fences, they looked like leylandii to me.'

'Go on.'

'It wasn't till she said the house and gardens were at one time used as a Hare Krishna retreat. that the paths meandering past the flower beds and the tall leylandii hedges made sense to me. Anyone could run naked through the garden and none of the neighbours would be any of the wiser.'

'Precisely.'

'Precisely, what?'

He shook his head as he parked in the police compound. 'What I think is, that's enough for one day. I need time to ponder what we discovered today, let us reconvene this discussion back here tomorrow morning at eight.'

'You're up to something, I know you too well.'

♦

'You look bushed,' said Karen, as Buchanan entered the kitchen. 'Are you getting anywhere with the investigation?'

'I do believe we are. Is Travis here?'

'No. He called to say he was staying in Brighton for a meeting and won't be back till extremely late.'

'Poppy?'

'She and Harry have been invited to dinner with Nathan and Susan.'

'So, it's just you and me?'

'Disappointed?'

'Not at all. How about cuddling up on the sofa and watching a movie after dinner this evening?'

'With popcorn?'

He smiled. 'Sounds lovely. Can I help with dinner?'

11
Tuesday 15th
Zilini

Buchanan yawned and looked at the bedside clock, six-thirteen, it was going to be a long day. He got out of bed quietly and dressed.

'What time is it?' asked Karen.

'Six-twenty. Travis and Poppy will probably sleep late, why don't you take advantage of the quiet, and sleep in? I'll make my own breakfast.'

'If you're sure?'

'I'll be fine.'

'Don't forget you're driving Travis to the airport this afternoon.'

'I won't.'

Buchanan kissed his wife goodbye and went downstairs to make his breakfast. As he waited for his toast, he reflected on the case. So far, they were no closer to finding the whereabouts of Barazani's daughter, Zilini, or her boyfriend, Zac Taylor. He was still sure that money was the motive behind what was going on, but to whose benefit? If the program Barazani's company was involved in were to work as designed, it would make Zilini a very wealthy heiress. But her inheritance would, of course, require the demise of Amal Barazani.

Then there was the master dongle code, securely secreted in an online vault with the password divided into three sections for security. So, as long as those three password sections remained separate, no one was likely to benefit financially.

As far as suspects were concerned, just about any members of the family could fit that bill. All would, at one juncture or another, benefit from the death of Amal Barazani. But of course, that was just speculation at this point: Amal Barazani seemed to be currently in perfect health.

First on the list of beneficiaries was Zilini and, if she were married at the time of Amal Barazani's demise, her husband would also stand to gain.

Next in line, assuming both Amal and Zilini were deceased, was Yousef. Lastly it was Nasim Barazani, whose mother had already said that money wasn't a motivator in his life; he was quite content climbing the corporate ladder. The son, Achmad, being a typical teenager, was only interested in playing games, not owning a company that designed them.

Therefore, assuming a scenario where Zilini and or Nasim were not part of the equation, who else stood to benefit? Buchanan realised this train of thought was just like trying to find out where he stood in the line of accession. A fruitless thought, or was it? The Barazani family was quite compact, and without that many members. With Zilini and her father out of the way, and Nasim and his son showing a disdain of inheriting the family fortunes, that would leave Barazani senior and wife Hiezabel inheriting.

Buchanan speculated for a moment and was about to reject the thought outright when he remembered the adage told to him by an old Glasgow detective. *When you have investigated and eliminated all the improbable and the impossible scenarios, whatever is left, no matter how improbable, must be given serious consideration.* Could Hiezabel Barazani and her husband be behind Zilini's disappearance? Or maybe Amal Barazani was behind his daughter's disappearance and was trying to cover it up by diverting suspicion elsewhere – now there was an improbable situation if ever there was one. He continued his musings, wondering what other improbable scenarios that he hadn't yet considered. Amal Barazani's former wife and mother to Zilini – what had she died of? He shook his head at the conundrum and, picking up his jacket from the back of the chair, left for work.

♦

'Morning all,' said Buchanan, as he walked into his office with a tray of coffees. 'I thought we'd think better with a cup of

Starbucks' finest. First, Stephen and Morris, did you have any success with the taxi registration?'

'Yes and no,' said Hunter. 'The registration belonged to one of the cars involved in the chop-shop operation. Apparently, the registration plates were part of a batch of scrapped registrations sold two months ago in a pub in Greenwich. The Met have CCTV of the transaction but haven't been able to trace either the buyer or the seller. We had no joy in getting any further with finding the car until Morris suggested we try the fire station. The watch commander said on Tuesday last week they responded to a report of a car on fire on Pevensey levels. I asked what make the car was and was told it was a late model Mercedes. Unfortunately, it was well alight by the time they got there. When we're done here we are going to check out the wreck before it gets crushed; I called Ripley's and told them to hold on to it till we've had a look at it, though I doubt there will be much to look at other than its VIN.'

'Good. Any chance we can get a copy of the video of the plates being sold?' asked Buchanan. 'We might get lucky and get a facial image.'

'I asked and a copy is en route, should be with us by the end of the day,' said Hunter.

'Good. How about Zilini's accommodation?'

'As we expected, there was no reply when we knocked on the door,' said Hunter. 'So, while we waited for the caretaker, we tried a few of the other rooms.'

'We managed to find Judith,' said Dexter. 'She corroborated Zilini's text message to Zac. They went to a late showing of *Last Christmas*, then back home to the university where they shared a bottle of rosé wine and sang with Sally from room 221. Quite an uneventful evening for them.'

'What about Zilini's flat?' said Buchanan.

'We didn't need a court order or a search warrant in the end. The caretaker, Mrs Ross, is a bit of a mother hen to the students and simply adores Zilini. As soon as we explained the situation, she was only too eager to be helpful. She stood by the door and watched as we went through the flat. It was in quite a mess.'

'Had the room been searched?' asked Buchanan.

'That was our initial thought when the caretaker opened it up,' said Hunter. 'We asked her to stand at the open door and tell us what she thought. She said Zilini wasn't the tidiest of students but did have her own system of organised chaos. She showed us where to look for Zilini's personal effects.'

'She wasn't trying to put you off the scent by being over helpful?' said Buchanan.

'I don't think so. We looked in all the places she suggested then she left us to get on with our search.'

'So, what did you find?'

'Other than clothes, not much. In the bedside drawer we found a half-empty pack of paracetamol, two pencils, a tear-off notepad, three packs of tissues and an empty strip of birth control pills. On top of the dresser there was a small flat-screen TV, piles of textbooks, a 13-inch laptop with a cracked screen and three out of date copies of *Jazzwise* music magazines. The dresser drawers were mainly empty but there was a pregnancy test kit under some underwear in the top drawer, it showed a negative test. There was no sign of a suitcase, backpack or handbag, nor a purse, wallet, cash or cards. We already know where her mobile phone was left.'

'Did the caretaker have anything to add when you told her of your findings?'

'She said there never was a suitcase, but there was a small backpack that Zilini used to take with her when she went home for the weekend. Apparently, the laundry facilities on the student floor weren't up to her standards, so she'd take her laundry home at the weekends for the housekeeper to wash and iron.'

Buchanan nodded as he remembered Darsameen's comment about being a mother to Zilini and how she'd bring her laundry home. The memory of the backpack triggered a thought. 'Did we ever check on the orange tabards found in the pit?'

Three heads turned to Buchanan and shook no.

'I wonder,' said Buchanan, looking at the Barazani file on his computer. He scrolled to the photos of the tabards. 'Ah, there it is.'

'Is what?' said Street.

'The initials on the tabards. Morris, do you still have the number for Calum, the foreman in charge of the sewer pipeline installation?'

'The phone number is in the file under Contacts – Civil.'

Buchanan scrolled through the HOLMES database looking for Contacts – Civil until he found the copy of Calum's business card and made a note of the number to call him later.

'Stephen, Morris, do you have anything on the go at the moment?' said Buchanan.

'No. We could go and look at the taxi if you don't have anything else for us.'

'Good idea. You probably won't learn much, but it's a good idea to tie up the loose ends.'

'Are you staying, Jack?' asked Street, as Hunter and Dexter left for Ripley's scrapyard.

'Just for a minute, something is niggling my niggler. Why?'

'I don't feel too good; would you mind if I went home early today?'

'Not at all, you go on home and I'll see you back here in the morning.'

♦

Buchanan walked down to the canteen, made himself a cup of instant coffee, then returned to his office. He unwrapped a KitKat, pressed the speaker button on his phone and called Calum.

'Calum, it's Inspector Buchanan, how are you?'

'I'm fine, any word when I can have my tools back? They're not cheap to replace.'

'As soon as the investigation is over, you can have your tools back. Listen, I have a question for you. The two orange tabards found in the pit with the unfortunate man, could they have belonged to any of your men?'

'Any particular men? I have twenty on our local gang.'

'Initials of TB and DL.'

'TB, that's got to be Toma, Toma Baretata, and you said DL?'

'Yes.'

'That has to be Dimi, Dimitar Lupov.'

'How long have they worked for you?'

'We hired them for the project.'

'Are they British?'

'No, Bulgarian.'

'Are they still working for you?'

'I'll need to get back to you on that, there's no one in the office till tomorrow morning.'

'Thanks. Calum, do you have any photos of Baretata and Lupov?'

'I might have on my phone, we had a bit of a celebration in The Heron when we'd completed the pull. Let me have a look.'

While Calum scrolled through his photos, Buchanan checked his emails and noticed one from Inspector Klaus Bierman of the DNR – another wedding invitation. Karen would be pleased.

'Inspector,' said Calum, 'I have one clear photo of Baretata and Lupov, how do you want them?'

'Text them to my mobile.'

'Will do. Do you think they stole my tools and killed the man in the pit?'

'Too early to say. Got it, which one is which?'

'Lupov is the shorter of the two.'

'Tough-looking characters, they didn't look to keen at having their photos taken. When they were on site, did they mix with others on the crew?'

'Now I come to think about it, they mostly worked together, their English wasn't very good.'

'You never saw them talk to others on the crew?'

'Big Richard used to talk to them, but then he'd talk to anyone.'

'Big Richard?'

'My site foreman.'

'His surname? And do you have his contact details?'

'Yes. His full name is Richard Bull. He likes to joke about his name, he says Bull by name, bull by nature. Anything else, Inspector?'

'No, not just now. Thanks for your help, Calum.'

♦

'Are you ready to go, Travis?' asked Buchanan, picking the car keys up from the table.

'Dad, you will be alright travelling on your own?'

'Yes Poppy, I shall be absolutely fine.'

'And you don't mind me not coming to the airport with you?'

'No, of course not. Jack and I will have a good chat in the car.'

'OK, love you, Dad, see you in November.'

♦

'You're very quiet,' said Travis, as they drove up the A23 towards Gatwick airport.

'I had a weird dream last night that is really bugging me.'

'I'm not surprised you have weird dreams, especially with what you do for a living. Want to share?'

'It wasn't anything to do with the day job, that's why it bugs me so much. In the dream I was standing at the edge of a forest and directly in front of me was a massive oak tree. It was so big that it touched the clouds. Made me think of the tree in the Enid Blyton *Faraway Tree* stories my dad used to read to us when we were kids. In those stories lots of strange people lived in the tree and would climb up a ladder into the cloud from the tree and have adventures.'

'Is that what happened in your dream?'

'Not quite. In my dream, the houses were perched on the branches and had rope bridges linking them to other houses, shops, and schools. The outer branches had fruit on them, all sorts of fruit. I was surprised to see most people didn't touch the fruit but instead climbed down the tree to dig in the dirt for their food. Does any of this make sense to you?'

'A little, is there more?'

'Just before the end of the dream I saw someone climb down from the clouds into the tree and, as they did, it started to rain. Little rivers began to run down the branches creating a lake under the tree. Next the tree started to grow backwards, like a time-lapse video going in reverse. As the tree shrunk, the tree people were frantically trying to stop it shrinking. Eventually the tree was just an acorn floating on the lake surrounded by all the tree-people waist-deep in the lake, looking lost.'

'And it shall come to pass afterward that I will pour out My Spirit on all flesh; Your sons and your daughters shall prophesy, your old men shall dream dreams, your young men shall see visions.'

'Not sure what you are talking about?'

'That was a quote from the book of Joel, he was an Old Testament prophet. He also had dreams and visions.'

'Ah, I think I understand. My mother is fey, as we say in Scotland, she has the gift of the spirit. I must have inherited it from her. But what does my dream mean?'

'I'd suggest you pray to God and ask him to explain it to you, after all, it was He who gave it to you.'

'But can't you?'

'It's your dream, not mine,' said Travis, smiling and gently shaking his head.

'It feels like I'm losing my marbles. Maybe it's time I retired and let the young ones take over. It's probably just this case of the missing girl we are working on that's screwing with my sleep.'

'When God takes away from you something you really want, Jack, it is to prepare you for what He really wants for you.'

'Thanks, that's a big help.'

'You're welcome,' said Travis, as they arrived at the departure drop-off at Gatwick Airport.

♦

'You're back early,' said Karen.

193

'There wasn't much traffic, the A23 was almost empty. I think this Chinese bat virus is scaring a lot of people into staying at home.'

12

Wednesday 16th
The Bulgarians

'Good morning, Jill, you're a bit early.'

'In spite of being so tired, I couldn't sleep.'

'Where are Stephen and Morris?'

'Stephen got called to attend court to give evidence on a case that goes back two years, and Morris has a tummy bug. He said he thinks he got it from one of his little ones, they've all been poorly.'

Buchanan frowned. 'That means it's just the two of us. Fancy a coffee?'

'Starbucks?'

'Where else?'

♦

'Thanks,' said Street, as Buchanan placed her coffee on the table.

'I have fresh information on the case,' he said. 'After you all left last night, I called Calum, the contractor in charge of installing the new sewer pipe in the village. I asked him about the initials on the tabards and he told me that two of his operatives had those initials.'

'Did he give you the names?'

'Toma Baretata and Dimitar Lupov, both Bulgarians. Calum said to call him this morning when he gets into his office, hopefully he will have an address for them.'

'Will he have any photos of them?'

'I already do – here,' he said, passing his phone over.

'Perfect.'

'What's perfect?'

'One of the things I did when I came in this morning was to run through the video the MET police sent us, the ones showing the sale of the stolen licence plates.'

'And?'

'Here,' she said, taking a photo from her jacket pocket. 'Do they look familiar?'

'They certainly do, hold on while I call Calum.'

'While you do that, I need the toilet.'

'Success?' asked Street on her return.

'We'll see.'

'We'll see what?'

'Calum said they haven't turned up for work since the pipe installation was completed. Finish your coffee, we have a date with two Bulgarians.'

'Where is it?' Street asked, as she slid her arm into her jacket.

'A flat on Pevensey Road, I've called for an unlit silent backup.'

♦

'I often wonder why people who live in towns own cars,' said Street, as she squeezed the car in between a blue Renault and a rusty VW Golf. 'By the look of the detritus in the gutter, I doubt if these vehicles have moved in months.'

Buchanan stopped beside a row of wheelie bins. 'Let's wait here for our backup, I don't fancy having to deal with two angry Bulgarians on our own.'

He was drumming his fingers on the top of a wheelie bin when a police wagon arrived with six uniformed constables.

'Hi, Jill,' said one of the constables, 'How's Morris? I hear he caught something from the kids.'

'Seems like it, Andy. How's young Robby?'

'Fine. I told him it was no good pretending, both the doctor and his mother said he was fine and that was good enough for me. I dropped him off at school this morning.'

'Excuse me,' interrupted Buchanan. 'We have a job to do.'

'Sorry,' said Andy.

'I would like two of you to go round the back before we enter,' said Buchanan. 'You two at the front watch the windows, that bay would make an easy escape from the first floor, and you two

196

follow Street and me. You have the enforcer with you in case we have to force an entry?'

'In the van.'

'Better bring it with you, just in case. It is quite possible that the flat will be empty, but we still need to be careful.'

Buchanan walked up the steps to the main front door and tried pushing it open. It swung inwards, slowly revealing an uncarpeted hallway leading to the back of the flats. On the right there was a staircase going up to the first floor and Flat 3. He turned to Street, smiled, then nodded to the two constables to follow them up the stairs.

The door to Flat 3 was shut. Buchanan knocked loudly and shouted, 'Police! Open the door!'

He tried once more with still no reply or the door being opened. He stood to the side and said, 'Right, Constable, do your worst.'

The constable stepped forward and began to slam at the door with the enforcer. The door, being old, didn't stand up to the constant hammering and soon gave way in a shower of splinters.

'Police!' yelled the constable, as he and his partner burst into the room. 'No one here, sir,' he said, exiting from the bedroom.

'Thanks,' said Buchanan, as he and Street entered the flat. 'Could you hang around for a bit in case anyone returns?'

'We'll be in the van if you need us.'

'OK. First impression, Jill?'

Street scanned the room. 'First impression is someone has been here recently; I can smell fresh cigarette smoke,' she said, sniffing the air. 'Reminds me of something, not pot, that's a different smell.'

'Gauloise,' said Buchanan. 'I used to smoke them in my youth when I wanted to look sophisticated.'

Street looked at Buchanan. 'I'm glad you quit.'

'So am I. What else do you see?'

'I see no one likes to do housework. Those dishes in the sink look like they have been sitting there for several days.'

'Anything in the fridge?'

Street stepped round a settee to get to the kitchen area. She pulled on a pair of gloves and looked inside the freezer compartment. 'I wonder why they left this behind?' she said, pulling out a Ziploc bag containing smaller bags each with an amount of white powder.

'Any cash in there?' said Buchanan.

'Not that I can see,' said Street, replacing the plastic bag and closing the freezer door. She picked up a milk carton. 'Wouldn't want to pour any of this on my cereal, it's a week out of date.'

'I'll have a look in the bedroom,' said Buchanan.

He returned five minutes later. 'Two unmade single beds, dresser drawers are empty except for a couple of pairs of socks, and a pile of dirty laundry in the bottom of the cupboard. No green chairs. You find anything else?'

'This,' said Street, handing Buchanan a well-read newspaper.

'*24 Yuaca?*'

'I googled the title, it's the most widely-circulated Bulgarian-language daily newspaper, and this copy is only ten days old. Just wondering if we should have a CSI team here to take prints and DNA samples. That way we would have a definite connection between the bogus taxi, the scene at the garage, and the two men in the pit.'

'I was just about to suggest that,' said Buchanan. 'Would you make the arrangements? I'll go down to the van and, since we have six constables at our disposal, I'll get them to canvas the street and local shops to see what can be found out about the occupants of Flat 3.'

He returned twenty minutes later. 'I've got coffee waiting for us downstairs.'

'Good. I could do with some fresh air.'

'Any luck?' he said, passing Street one of the cups.

'Half an hour. Thanks, where did you get the coffee?'

'Cavendish Bakery. The lads looked bored, so I decided to treat them in exchange for a lift.'

◆

'I'm looking forward to the results,' said Buchanan to Street, as the CSI team prepared to leave the flat with several bags of evidence. 'By late tomorrow we should have a complete identity profile of two of the perpetrators in this case.'

'Suppose we got the wrong flat and the occupants have gone off on holiday?' mused Street, as she downed the last dregs of her coffee.

'It happens. But in this case, I'm sure we have the correct address.'

As the CSI's began to carry the bagged evidence out of the flat, Buchanan said to the leader, 'This is a murder case we are working on, could you put a rush on with the results, please?'

'As always, we aim to please.'

'Thanks.'

Buchanan and Street waited till the flat door was boarded up before going downstairs to enquire if any of the constables had found anything about the occupants of Flat 3. Only one had any information.

'What did you find out?' asked Buchanan.

'One of the punters in Ladbrokes said he remembers the two Bulgarians betting heavily.'

'Why would he remember that in particular?'

'The punter said he used to sneak a look at what they were betting on and do the same. He won nine times out of ten. But he stopped when one of the Bulgarians threatened to break his arm if he continued to be nosey.'

'You get his details?'

'Yes, sir.'

'Good man. Send me a copy when you get back to the station.'

'Anyone else?' said Buchanan.

Six heads shook no.

'Thanks for trying guys.'

'Where to now?' asked Street, as the police van drove off.

'Lunch, my place if that's all right with you. Karen made a huge pot of vegetable soup last night and I'm dying to taste it.'

Street's face lit up with a smile.

'I'll give Karen a call and let her know we are on our way.'

♦

The front door opened, and Karen stepped out as Buchanan stopped the car in their driveway.

'Jill, how nice to see you!' she said, moving forward and hugging Street.

'Hope we're not troubling you with this impromptu visit, Karen?'

'Are you kidding? Two of my most favourite people show up for lunch – it's made my day!'

'Don't I get a hug?' asked Buchanan.

'Of course you do, come here.'

Buchanan followed Street and Karen into the house, through the conservatory and out onto the patio.

'I thought since it was such a nice day, we could eat lunch out here,' said Karen.

'Do you need a hand with anything?' asked Street.

'You could slice and butter the bread for me.'

Buchanan understood that they wanted to chat and he would just be in the way. Plenty of time to catch up later.

He was looking at the Interpol red notice list on his phone when the sound of the letter box announced the arrival of post.

'I'll get it,' said Buchanan, walking down the hall. He picked up the post and returned to his chair in the conservatory.

'Anything of interest?' asked Karen.

'A personal letter,' he said, holding it up for Karen to see.

'You have an admirer,' said Karen, sniffing at the hand-addressed envelope. 'Very feminine handwriting – what have you been up to?' she added, passing it back to Buchanan.

'I know that scent,' he said, smiling as he carefully opened the envelope and extracted the letter.

'Well?' said Karen, who'd been joined by Street, 'Who's the fair maiden whose heart you've enflamed?'

He chuckled. 'You remember Cynthia Mountjoy?'

'I do,' replied Karen. 'Caused you a great deal of bother at Castlewood.'

'She's getting married to Pat. Here,' he said, passing the letter to Karen.

Street looked over Karen's shoulder and read the letter with her.

'She wants you to give her away at her wedding to Pat McCall. That's got to be one for the books. Did they ever find her husband's body?' asked Karen, passing the page back to Buchanan.

'All I remember from the case was Victor Mountjoy died in Julian Du Marchon's plane when it was presumed to have run out of fuel over the English Channel. As far as I know the case is still open. But she does say that she has been given a declaration of presumed death for Victor.'

'Reminds me of that poor footballer, Emiliano Sala,' said Street. 'He died when the plane he was flying in crashed in the channel. I remember they found the plane and the body of the footballer, but not the pilot.'

'Hmm, the coroner must have been satisfied that Victor Mountjoy was dead for him to issue a presumption of death certificate, otherwise Cynthia would be committing bigamy,' said Buchanan, turning to the second page of the letter.

'That makes sense,' said Street.

'Does she say when they are getting married?' asked Karen.

'Saturday the 10th of October.'

'That's a bit short notice, it's only two weeks away,' said Karen. 'How on earth will I find a hat in time?'

'She says they chose that date so as not to conflict with the start of the jump season at the end of the month,' said Buchanan. 'She says it is especially important since Pat has got his professional licence and he will be riding both Rambler and Turpin at Cheltenham during the October weekend of the 23rd and 24th.'

'We are going to be busy.'

'Oh, I nearly forgot. I had an email from Klaus Bierman; he and Irene Adler are getting married, and we've been invited.'

'Did he say when?'

'The 21st of November.'

'That's going to make it an extremely busy six months for us,' said Karen. 'What with Pat and Cynthia's wedding in two weeks, and our invitation to spend the Thanksgiving weekend in Dallas with Poppy's parents, plus I would like to see something of Texas while we're there. Then there's Harry and Poppy's wedding. Now, in the meantime, lunch is ready.'

'That's three weddings – just hope there's no funerals to spoil the day,' said Buchanan.

'Let's hope the Sussex criminal fraternity behave then,' said Karen.

♦

'That was just what I needed,' said Street, as she fastened her seatbelt. 'I wish I could cook as well as Karen does.'

'That's what thirty-four years of feeding a policeman brings, you'll get there.'

'Where to next?'

'Castlewood. I want to run some ideas past Nathan. Since he's a business acquaintance of Amal Barazani, he may give us some insight into the family that we are not yet aware of.'

'Do you think Zilini is still alive?' asked Street, as they turned off Arlington Road and into Castlewood Country Club drive.

'Since we have no body, I'm going on the assumption that she is,' replied Buchanan, as they pulled up in front of the entrance to Castlewood.

'Good afternoon, Mr Buchanan,' said the receptionist, as he stopped in front of her desk. 'Sir Nathan is waiting for you in his office, shall I see you through?'

'That's OK, I know my way.'

Street followed Buchanan down a short passageway to Greyspear's office. Buchanan knocked and opened the door.

'Jack,' said Greyspear, standing. 'Jill, lovely to see you. What brings you here?'

'We'd like to ask you about Amal Barazani.'

'What can I tell you that I haven't already said?'

'I'm interested in how he finances his company.'

'Did you ask him?'

'Not yet. I hoped to get some background information from you, before I enter the lion's den.'

'OK. Coffee before I begin?'

'Not for me – Jill?'

'Could I have a glass of water, please?'

'Of course.'

'Well, to begin,' said Greyspear, 'Mastrani has five investors on the board, each with thirteen percent – me being one of them. The other four are Hugo Trent, John Lake, Jean Randal and Nasim Barazani, Amal's stepbrother. Amal has the controlling thirty-five percent,'

'So, any three of them could outvote him?'

'Exactly.'

'Where would you stand in the event of the board trying to oust Amal?'

'I would act on my own and take advice.'

'What can you tell me about the other investors?'

'Hugo Trent is an entrepreneur who invests in start-up enterprises, as is John Lake. Jean Randal inherited a bunch of cash from a distant aunt. Nasim Barazani's money is mostly family.'

'You say Amal Barazani is using family money – he's not borrowing from the bank?'

'That's what he told me.'

'How did you two come to meet?'

'At a Rotary dinner, I was the after-dinner speaker.'

'He approached you?'

'We got chatting in the bar after dinner. In my speech I mentioned that I'd twice been widowed, he told me he'd lost his wife when his daughter was only three. We've kept in contact since. Are you making progress with finding his daughter?'

'We have a video of her parking her car in the Mastrani car park early on the Friday evening she disappeared,' said Street.

'I thought she went out early Saturday morning – Amal said her radio was on in her bedroom when he went to bed?'

'The alarm clock-radio in her bedroom was set to turn on at ten thirty Friday evening.'

'So, she planned to disappear?'

'It looks that way,' said Buchanan.

'Did you ever meet Zilini?' Street asked Greyspear.

'Never to talk to. She came with her father a couple of times, and she had her eighteenth birthday party here.'

'Were you a guest at the party?'

'No, I just looked in a couple of times to make sure all was well.'

'Do you remember who was at the party?'

'Not off hand. The room holds two hundred guests when seated, and I seem to remember it looked full.'

'And why would you remember that?'

'Just after dinner, before the band came on, Zilini and Zac sang a duet.'

'What sort of duet?'

'She sang and he played guitar.'

'How were they?'

'They got a standing ovation.'

'What was Amal's reaction?'

'I couldn't see, I was at the back of the room.'

'Do you remember anything else about the evening?'

'No, all went well.'

'Thank you, Nathan,' said Buchanan, standing. 'My regards to Susan.'

♦

'The party must have cost Amal Barazani a small fortune,' said Street, as they drove down the A22 towards Polegate. 'I picked up a copy of the menu for the evening, including the wine list. I know for a fact that Ridgeway champagne cost at least thirty pounds a bottle.'

'Would you like to hear Zilini sing?'

'Yes, but we'd have to find her first.'

'Not necessary. Amal gave me a copy of the video he took at her birthday party. Here, it's in my email folder.'

'Have you seen it?'

'Not yet, been too busy. Bluetooth it to the car radio, we can listen as we drive.' He said passing his phone to Street.

'She has such a lovely voice,' said Street.

'She certainly can sing.'

'Where are we headed?' asked Street,

'Nasim Barazani's.'

'Any particular reason?'

'I'm following the money trail.'

Buchanan parked on the driveway, walked up to the front door and pressed the doorbell. The door was opened by Bahija Barazani.

'Good afternoon, Mrs Barazani. I wonder if your husband is in?'

'Yes, he is.'

'Could we come in and ask him some questions? It's about Zilini.'

'Certainly,' she said, stepping to the side to let Buchanan and Street enter. 'If you'll follow me, he and Achmad are playing games on the patio this afternoon.'

Buchanan and Street followed her along the entrance hall, through a spacious living room, into a conservatory and out on to the patio. Nasim was seated at a large round patio table, shielded from the afternoon sun by a large umbrella. He was typing frantically on his laptop, while his son Achmad was yelling, 'Got you!'

'Nasim, these two police officers want to talk to you.'

Nasim looked up from his laptop and placed his half-smoked cigar in the ashtray. 'Ah, Inspector Buchanan, to what do we owe this visit?'

'Sorry to interrupt.'

Nasim shook his head. 'Not a problem, the east has shut down for their afternoon *qayloulah* – that is siesta to you and your companion. I'm just playing Fortnite with Achmad till everyone wakes up and goes back to work. How may I help?'

'We would like to know what your actual involvement is with Mastrani?'

At the asking of the question, Achmad slammed his laptop shut and walked into the house.

Nasim shook his head at his son's departure. 'Children, Inspector. They irritate you no end when they're around and cause you sleepless nights when they're not. You have children?'

Buchanan looked at Street and smiled. 'Yes, a grown daughter.'

'So, I suppose you are still looking for Zilini?'

'Yes.'

'You're wasting your time, she's eighteen and all grown up. If she wants to get lost, that's her business.'

'About Mastrani – what is your connection with the company?'

'Could we offer you something to drink, Inspector? It's quite hot out here on the patio.'

'A glass of water would be welcome.'

'And your partner, sorry, I don't know your name?'

'Detective Sergeant Street. Water would be fine for me as well.'

'Bahija, water for our guests, please. Why don't you two take a seat? You look decidedly uncomfortable standing there in the sun.'

'Thanks, we will,' said Buchanan, nodding to Jill to take the seat on the left of Nasim.

Nasim leaned forward and picked up his cigar from amongst the three stubs already in the ashtray then relit it. Bahija placed a tray with a jug of iced water and two glasses on the table and poured Street and Buchanan each a glass.

'What exactly do you want to know, Inspector?'

'Do you own shares in the company?'

Nasim nodded.

'How many?'

'I'm not sure what this has to do with Zilini being missing, but I'll answer your question. I have a thirteen percent share.'

'Are you and your stepbrother the only shareholders?'

'No, there are others, four to be precise.'

'Do you have any interest in the company, other than your thirteen percent?'

'I oversee the finances.'

'I thought you worked for the bank?'

'I do. The bank finances most of Mastrani's activities these days. Mastrani is one of my accounts at the bank.'

'Isn't there a bit of conflict of interest going on?'

'Inspector, the bank prefers it that way. If Mastrani fails, it is my neck on the block. It's all above board, even down to the stipulations in the contract.'

'And what are these stipulations?'

'If Mastrani fails in any way, I carry the loss for the bank.'

'You're the guarantor of the loan?'

'Yes.'

'How many other shareholders are there?'

'Other than Amal, there are five in total.'

'I would like to talk to them, just in case Zilini has been in contact.'

'I don't see why not; the list is in my office. I'll go and get it.'

As Nasim went into the house, Street said, 'You're up to something, I can tell.'

Buchanan's reply was prevented by the appearance of Hiezabel Barazani,

'Have you finished with your drinks?' she asked.

'Almost,' said Buchanan, reaching for his glass. He took a sip, almost emptying the glass and returned it clumsily to the table beside the ashtray, spilling some of the contents, and knocking three of the cigar stubs onto the table.

'Oh, clumsy me,' he said, leaning over the table and dabbing at the spill with his napkin. 'Do you have another tissue?'

'Here, use this,' said Hiezabel, pulling a paper tissue from the sleeve of her blouse. 'Don't worry, it's clean.'

'Thank you,' said Buchanan, as he dabbed at the spilt water and at the same time wrapped up one of the cigar stubs in the tissue and slipped it into his pocket. 'Sorry, made a bit of a mess,' he said, scrunching up his napkin and placing it on the ashtray.

'That's all right, Inspector, we can't all be tidy,' said Hiezabel as Nasim returned.

'Nasim, I'm curious about something, do you think your stepbrother is able to run Mastrani and make a success of the current projects?'

'Huh.'

'Mother!'

'If it was up to me, I'd replace him,' said Hiezabel.

'Mother! The inspector doesn't want to hear about our family squabbles.'

'No, that's all right, Nasim. I'd like to hear what your mother has to say, go on Mrs Barazani.'

'Well, my stepson is nothing more than a glamorous, flashy, bejewelled playboy, who has charmed and cajoled investors into going against their best interests and investing in his crazy schemes.'

'But, Mother, he has made us lots of money with his schemes and, with his latest project, we all stand to make quite a tidy sum.'

'If you were in charge, we'd make a great deal more. You don't drive a Rolls Royce, do you, live in a fancy Marina, or go hob-knobbing with the country-club elite, trying to live up to their extravagant lifestyles?'

'No, Mother, I don't. But it might be nice to occasionally taste some of that exotic fruit.'

'Is there anything else, Inspector?' asked Hiezabel. 'My son is a very busy man and has a lot of responsibilities.'

'Thank you, Mother, I'm perfectly able to organise my own schedule. You said you wanted to be helpful, why don't you go and help Bahija in the kitchen? We have guests for dinner this evening.'

Buchanan smiled at Street as Hiezabel Barazani went to join her daughter-in-law in preparing dinner.

'Nasim, when we were here previously, you said you last saw your niece at your stepbrother's office in town.'

'Yes.'

'And before that?'

Nasim leaned back into his chair, took a draw on his cigar, and thought for a moment. 'It was a few weeks before, at her eighteenth birthday party.'

'Where was that?'

'Castlewood Country Club,' he said, blowing out a cloud of Cuban cigar smoke. 'It's just off the A22. I don't suppose you, being a policeman, have ever been there?'

Buchanan smiled. 'I am aware of its location. How was the party?'

'Quite pleasant really, though my mother wasn't too pleased at the event.'

'Why was that?'

'At the end of the dinner, Zilini and her boyfriend sang for us.'

'What did you think of the performance?'

'Zilini has such a beautiful voice, my wife was ecstatic, she's been coaching them.'

'Why would that cause your mother to be displeased?'

'You should have seen what she was wearing, or I should say, not wearing,' said Hiezabel, who'd just stepped out onto the patio.

'Mother, you're eavesdropping again.'

209

'Dress up to her navel and her top just as low. I don't know why she just didn't go up on stage naked.'

'Mother, she's a chanteuse, that's how they dress.'

'If you were to ask me, whore would be a better description.'

'You'll have to forgive my mother, Inspector. She was brought up in a very strict Saudi home and her views don't necessarily reflect those of the rest of the family.'

'I understand completely. At least in this country we are free to express our thoughts. Nasim, could you tell me where you were Thursday the third?'

'Visiting clients, all day.'

'And the Friday?'

'Fridays I also work from home.'

'Mrs Barazani, could you tell me where you were on Thursday the third?'

'I would have been here; I always visit on a Thursday.'

'Are you sure, Mother? I didn't see you.'

'I was late, you'd already gone out.'

'And on the Friday?' said Buchanan.

'Fridays, I go to pray, not like someone I know,' she said, staring at Nasim.

Nasim shook his head slowly. 'Mother, you know I perform my ablutions at home every Friday.'

'You go to pray – that would be at what time, Mrs Barazani?'

'Just after twelve.'

'And the rest of the day?'

'Shopping, of course, for the family.'

'And in the evening?'

'Two weeks ago, Friday, that would have been out to dinner. Then on to the theatre, then home and, before you ask, I was with my husband, my son and my daughter-in-law. Satisfied, Inspector?'

'Did you all go in one car?'

'No,' said Hiezabel. 'My husband and I took a taxi.'

◆

'You're up to something,' said Street, as she did up her seatbelt. 'No one else did, but I saw you slip the cigar stub into your pocket. You do realise you can't use the DNA from the cigar stub as evidence?'

'Maybe not. Jill. Would you call Mastrani and see where Amal Barazani is currently? I'd like to talk to him again.'

As they turned onto the Polegate bypass, Street hung up from her call. 'He's at home.'

'Good, let's go talk to him.'

◆

As previously the front door was opened by Darsameen.

'Good afternoon, Inspector, Sergeant.'

'Good afternoon, Darsameen, we're here to see Mr Barazani.'

'He's in his study. I believe he's on the phone. Would you like to wait in here and I'll let him know?'

'Here we go again,' said Street, as she looked round the room. 'When offered, why do you always accept a drink?'

'Firstly, you are accepting their offer of friendship, helps make them feel more at ease, and, secondly, it takes time to make tea or coffee, giving you more time to ask questions. See, simple.'

The door opened and Charlotte entered. 'Inspector, Mr Barazani will see you now. If you'll follow me, I'll take you through to his study.'

'Inspector, you have news for me?' said Barazani.

'No, sorry, we're still looking.'

'Pity, the house feels quite empty without Zilini around. I suppose you have more questions?'

'Just a couple, shouldn't take up too much of your time.'

'Time is all I seem to have these days. Would you like something to drink?'

Buchanan glanced at Street, she smiled back.

'Yes please.'

'What will you have?'

211

'Coffee would be fine.'

'Charlotte,' said Barazani, 'coffees for our guests, please. Sergeant, Inspector, please be seated and we can have a chat while we wait for our coffees. Since you haven't found Zilini yet, what have you found?'

'It's still early days in the investigation.'

'Hmm, early days, more like ten to midnight if you ask me. What do you want to know?'

'Could I ask you about how Mastrani is financed?'

'Why would you want to know that?'

'Is it self-financed, or do you have investors?'

Amal's reply was interrupted by the return of Charlotte with a tray, a large cafetière and four cups.

'I seem to remember you don't take milk or sugar, Inspector,' said Charlotte, as she placed the tray in the middle of Barazani's substantial desk.

'Only in my tea. Nice of you to remember.'

'I remember a great deal, Inspector. It is my job to remember.'

'You asked about how Mastrani is financed,' said Barazani. 'Up till a few years ago it was completely self-financing, but with the expansion ideas we have had to bring in fresh capital.'

'How many shareholders do you have?'

'Five.'

'I would like to talk to them, could I have their details, please?'

'But why would you want to talk to them?'

'In cases like this, we must examine all avenues. It would be helpful to the investigation to be able to talk to them. Are they local?'

'Yes, sort of. I suppose you'd like a list of their names and addresses?'

'That would be most helpful.'

'I'll get it,' said Charlotte, as she went over to the printer.

'I'm reluctant to give you this list, Inspector. I don't want you to go and make any of them nervous about their investments.'

'Why do you think they would get nervous?'

Barazani looked at Charlotte then back to Buchanan. 'We've just run a stress test on one of the key sections of phase one. The program wasn't live, but we did have a couple of hiccups – all now sorted.'

'I see. What about banks? I don't see any reference to banks on this list.'

'You only asked for a list of investors.'

'All the same, could I have the name of the bank you use, and if possible, a contact name?'

'Inspector, if it wasn't for our mutual friend, Sir Nathan, recommending your integrity, I would not be forthcoming with this information. It is the Al Rayan Bank, and my stepbrother Nasim is your contact name.'

'Does he ever suggest to you are over-extending your company's ability to service its debts?'

'Certainly not, Inspector. I am in complete control of everything at Mastrani.'

'Amal, when we first talked, you said you had to go into the office on the Friday evening your daughter went missing.'

'Yes, that is so.'

'Did you drive yourself?'

'Yes.'

'And you parked in the garage in your regular slot, just like the day you drove me into your office?'

'Yes.'

'Does Zilini park her car in the same garage, next to your car?'

'Yes.'

'Did you see Zilini's car in the garage on the Friday evening when you arrived?'

Barazani was silent for a moment. 'Yes, but not when I arrived, although it was there when I left. But that doesn't make sense. I'd swear it was there when I left at ten forty-five to go home; yet when I went to bed at eleven-thirty, I could plainly hear her radio playing in her bedroom and there was no sign of her car in the driveway.'

'Why would you just now remember that?'

'Inspector – Jack, I have been under a great deal of pressure to complete phase one of the program on time.'

'What sort of pressure?'

'If phase one doesn't complete on time, there are financial penalties that increase with every week it is delayed.'

'Is phase one nearly complete?'

'We still have to analyse the results of the stress test.'

'When did you do the test?'

'Last night.'

'Did it work?'

'Mostly, there were a few issues, but we soon sorted them out.'

'When has it to be ready by?'

'The end of the month.'

'This month?'

'No, last month.'

'So, you are a few days into penalty time?'

'This is not a football game, Jack. The issues have now been resolved and we are moving on with phase two.'

'I'm not a technical man, but what sort of issues were there?'

'Just a couple of lines of coding needing to be changed.'

'Is that normal, were you expecting issues?'

'Michael was puzzled about it. He couldn't understand how someone had forgotten to save one of the changes they had made the previous day.'

'You said you thought it odd that Zilini's car was in the garage when you left.'

'She usually leaves her car in the garage during the week and collects it on Friday afternoon when she gets off the train. So how did the car get back to the garage on Friday night when she was still at home? I just don't understand.'

'Why did you go into the office?'

'Nasim called and said he needed to talk.'

'Why meet at the office and not here at the house?'

'There were papers in the safe that he needed to look at.'

214

'Was he alone?'

'No, his wife was with him. Yousef and Hiezabel were behind us in their taxi'

'Does his wife usually drive him?'

'Yes.'

'Why is that?'

Barazani smiled. 'He lost his licence because of an incident involving alcohol.'

'When was this?'

'Two years ago, on the M6; three people died in the accident. He's now got his licence back, but since the accident he's decided not to drive any time he has alcohol to drink.'

'Thank you for your help,' said Buchanan, as he stood to leave. 'If we find out anything, we'll be in touch right away.'

'Where to first?' asked Street, looking at the dashboard clock.

'I think we've done enough digging for today. I'll see you in the office tomorrow morning. Before I go home, I'll send the cigar stub off to forensics for DNA analysis.'

♦

'How was your day?' asked Karen.

'Very illuminating. I'm finding out just what makes the Barazani family tick.'

'And does it tick like a bomb?'

'I hope not. I'm beginning to like Amal and Nasim.'

'Would you like something to drink? Dinner is still an hour away.'

'Not at the moment, thanks. I'm going for a shower, see you in ten.'

As he let the steaming hot water run down his head, he thought about the Barazani family and their foibles.

Amal was turning out to be just what you saw: a big gruff teddy bear with a soft centre and Charlotte faithfully at his side. Zilini, a young lady trying to assert her individuality to the point of running away from home with her boyfriend. Nasim, Amal's stepbrother,

215

standing in the middle as a buffer between Amal and his mother, Hiezabel.

Now Hiezabel, she was a formidable one, stuck with tradition while trying to live in what to her was a hostile environment. Buchanan almost pitied her and her inability to assimilate into modern British culture. But wasn't that true for most immigrants – himself to a certain degree. He well remembered the parting words of the Assistant Chief Constable in Glasgow, *It's your use of English, or should I say Glaswegian. If you want to get ahead down south, you'll have to moderate how you speak; they don't provide interpreters for staff.*

Finally, there was Amal's father, Yousef. Where was he, and what influence did he have in the family? A job for tomorrow, along with interviewing the Mastrani investors.

◆

'Feeling better?' asked Karen, as Buchanan entered the kitchen.

'Yes thanks. I think I will have that drink you offered. Is that bottle of red still available?'

'It's on the counter in the utility room. While you are at it, would you pour me a glass of prosecco, there's an open bottle in the fridge.'

'What's for dinner?' asked Buchanan, as he placed Karen's drink on the counter.

'Something special for Poppy, taco salad. She said it was one of her favourites.'

'Sounds great. Where is she?'

'Harry's taken her to PC World to look for a charger for her laptop. They said they'll be back in time for dinner. Oh, do you need Jill on Saturday?'

'No, not at the moment, why?'

'I was thinking about asking her if she would like to go with me and Poppy to Tonbridge to do some clothes shopping. Poppy only brought enough clothes with her for a long weekend.'

13
Thursday 17th
An Invitation

'Has Karen called you this morning?' Buchanan asked Street, as he hung his jacket on the back of his chair.

'Not this morning, but she did call last night; asked me if I wanted to go shopping with her and Poppy on Saturday,'

'What did you say?'

'I said yes, as long as are we aren't working. Are we working?'

Buchanan shook his head. 'No, you go shopping.'

'Thanks – I have some good news.'

'Oh, and what is this good news?'

'I looked at the CCTV video that Michael provided of the Mastrani garage for the Friday evening.'

'Oh, and what has it told us?'

'Watch,' she said, switching the view from her PC to the large monitor on the wall. 'This view is from the inside of the Mastrani garage facing the main garage door. The time is twenty past four and we see Zilini walking away from the stairs. She takes off her backpack, puts it in the boot. See how she looks around – is she worried someone is following her? Then she gets into her car and leaves. The next images are at ten past five, where we see Amal Barazani coming out of his private staircase, placing his briefcase on the back seat, getting into his car then leaving.'

'Now that is good news, anything else?'

'There is nothing else till just after seven-thirty. Amal Barazani returns, parks his car rather badly and goes up to his office. Then twenty minutes later, Zilini arrives and parks her car, better than her father did. She opens the boot, takes out her backpack and leaves by the side entrance fire door.'

'No sign of Zac Taylor? That's a worrying development.'

'His text message said to meet in the station car park, remember?'

'Ah, yes. But where? Do you think the NHS trailer is some sort of code between them?'

'No, it does exist. It's an NHS mobile screening unit parked in the station car park just outside the Enterprise Centre entrance.'

'Pity we don't have CCTV of that area.'

'But we do. When I requested CCTV coverage, the transport police gave me all they had for the days in question. Give me a moment while I look the video up for that day and time.'

'OK, and while you do that, I'll get the coffees.'

It took Street twenty minutes to find the relevant time and camera.

'Can't work without a coffee,' said Buchanan, placing a McDonalds' coffee and pastry in front of her.

'Thanks.'

'Progress?'

'Yes. It took a bit of digging through the numerous cameras, but I think this video gives us the best view. I've started it thirty minutes before we see Zilini parking her car.'

Buchanan settled into his chair to watch the grainy images of Eastbourne station car park showing there were still quite a few cars dotted around. At seven twenty-three an inbound train from London arrived and disgorged its passengers. Buchanan and Street watched as some of the homeward-bound passengers made their way out of the station and over to their cars.

'Ah, what do we have here?' said Buchanan. 'Can you enlarge the screen and focus on the lad carrying the guitar?'

'That doesn't make sense,' said Street. 'Why would he have been on the train from London?'

'Maybe he wasn't. He could have just got off the bus from Langney and walked through the station. Sort of a smart move, using the commuters as cover to walk across the car park unobserved.'

'Or the train from Hastings,' said Street. 'When I realised we'd be watching hours of the station CCTV, I jotted down the train arrival times.'

'Very thorough.'

'Thanks. He'll be rather obvious when everyone gets in their cars and leaves him standing alone.'

'Let's watch and see what he does,' said Buchanan. 'According to your timing, Zilini should be showing up in a few minutes, the Mastrani garage is just round the corner at the far end of the car park.'

However, nothing happened during the next twenty minutes, except for the arrival of two more trains and the inevitable crowd of passengers exiting the station and heading for their cars.

'Boy, he's got a nerve, how many young men carrying a guitar would saunter over to an NHS screening trailer and stand beside it in the shadows? He looks so furtive standing there in an almost empty car park. If I were on CCTV duty, I would be inclined to have a patrol car stop by and ask a few questions.'

'I'd do the same.'

Buchanan and Street sipped on their coffees while waiting for something to develop. At seven fifty-five, camera three, the camera pointing at the far end of the car park, showed the image of an approaching taxi.

'I know that profile,' said Buchanan. 'Isn't that our bogus taxi from the Pevensey and Westham station?'

'It looks like it.'

'Can you zoom in on the registration?'

'Yep, just a second.'

'Got them,' said Buchanan.

'Except we haven't really – this was two weeks ago, remember?'

'That's a pity. Let's see what they got up to. Did you see where Zac went to?'

'Camera two,' said Street. 'See, he's seen the taxi and slid round the back of the trailer looking to hide under it.'

'He must have realised he'd be seen under the trailer; look he's climbing over that low wall and is hiding in the bushes. Good, I don't think they saw him.'

'I hope they didn't, but I wonder why they would come in here looking for him, unless – unless they knew he'd be here.'

'But how could they know he was waiting there for Zilini?'

'Remember, we once wondered if her father was monitoring her phone calls and messages.'

'But that would mean he was behind Sam Taylor being kidnapped and murdered; no, that doesn't make sense,' said Street. 'If he were, then why would he ask for help in finding his daughter in the first place?'

'An alternative to that scenario,' said Buchanan, 'would be much worse. How about this as a scenario: we know Zilini had previously arranged to meet Zac by the NHS trailer in the station car park. She planned to slip out of the house unnoticed and, when her father went out to the office, she took advantage of that moment and drove to the Mastrani building, parked her car then left by the fire door. But unknown to her, she'd been followed and grabbed as she left the building and at that moment was tied up in the back of the bogus taxi hoping she hadn't inadvertently given away Zac's location.'

'That works. Let's keep watching and see what they do.'

As they watched, the bogus taxi drove slowly along the line of parked cars towards the station. At the end of the row of empty spaces it turned to the right and stopped twenty feet from the NHS trailer. The passenger door opened, and the passenger got out. He scanned the area and then walked over to the NHS trailer. He looked under the trailer and at the far end then back to the taxi. He gestured with his hands to the driver to say there was no one around. The car drove slowly forward till it came abreast of the far end of the trailer, where it stopped and the driver got out. They stood and chatted for a minute before the driver made a call on his phone. There followed a short, but agitated conversation that ended when the driver nodded and hung up. He returned to the car while the other walked around the trailer but was disturbed when a trainload of passengers exited the station and headed for the few remaining cars dotted around Empty-handed, the lone passenger then got back in the taxi which sped off.

'Good and bad,' said Buchanan. 'Why were they looking for Zac? It must be assumed they had Zilini in the car and failed to catch Zac, which we already knew because the following Monday we talked to him in his flat pretending to be his brother Sam.'

'Then, if Zilini was abducted outside the Mastrani office, she may be dead by now.'

Buchanan shook his head. 'I don't think that is likely, yet. If she was killed by whoever was behind what is going on, then they wouldn't have any leverage to get Amal Barazani to do what they want.'

'That makes sense, but what if something happens to change the scenario, and she no longer is useful?' said Street.

'Stephen never found any ANPR sightings of the taxi, did he?'

'No, and now it's a burnt-out hulk it's not much use to us,' said Street.

'There is something we can follow up on.'

'What's that?'

'Amal Barazani said the reason for him going into the office was to get some documents for Nasim to look at, and Nasim was driven to the office by his wife. I wonder if either of them observed Zilini coming out of the garage and, if they did, why didn't they mention it to us when we talked to them?'

'Shall I call and see if either of them is home?'

'No, if we let them know we are coming, they'll have time to think of their answers.'

'You suspect them of involvement in Zilini's disappearance?'

'Who knows? At this point, I'm just following my nose.'

◆

Buchanan turned off Marshfoot Lane and onto the short driveway of Nasim Barazani's house. There was a note on the front door saying the doorbell wasn't working and to come round to the side door and knock loudly. Street followed Buchanan past the wrought-iron garden gate and along the path to the side door. The door was partially open and the sound of someone playing a cello could be heard. Buchanan took the note literally and hammered on the door with his fist. The cello stopped and the a few minutes later the door was opened by Bahija.

'Good morning, Mrs Barazani, sorry to disturb you, is your husband at home?'

'No, sorry. He's gone to the office in London.'

'Do you have his office number?'

'You'll need to come in. I don't remember the number but it will be in his office somewhere. I have a student at the moment, should be through in fifteen minutes. If you'll wait in the lounge, I'll be right with you. I'll ask Hiezabel to get you something to drink while you wait.'

'Thank you, Bahija,' said Buchanan, glancing at Street and winking.

As the door closed, the sound of voices could be heard coming from the hall, the door handle turned, and Hiezabel entered.

'Good morning, Inspector, Sergeant. My daughter-in-law said you required something to drink. What can I get you?'

'A coffee would be fine,' said Street.

'Inspector?'

'If it's not too much trouble, could I have tea, please?'

'Milk and sugar?'

'A splash of milk and two sugars, please.'

'Stretching the hospitality, a bit,' whispered Street, as Hiezabel closed the door behind her shutting out the sound of the cello.

Buchanan smiled back.

'They have a new picture,' said Street, pointing at a painting hanging on the opposite wall.

Buchanan got up from his chair and went over to examine it.

'I thought so. It's an Osborne. Aaron Silverstein has two of them hanging in his office in town.'

Just as Buchanan sat the door opened and Hiezabel, carrying a tray, entered. She put the tray on the coffee table and stood back. 'I'll let you add your own milk and sugar, Inspector. Is there anything else?'

'Yes. When we last talked, you said you went to the theatre on Friday the 4th.'

'Yes, I believe I did.'

'You also said you went to dinner prior to attending the theatre.'

'Yes.'

'Where did you go to dinner?'

'Seeracha's. They do wonderful Thai food.'

'What time was that?'

'Dinner time.'

'Mrs Barazani, dinner time for a policeman is anywhere between six o'clock and midnight. Could you tell me what time you had dinner on the evening of Friday the 4th?'

'The table was booked for six o'clock.'

'Which theatre were you going to?'

'The Devonshire Park Theatre.'

'What was the show?'

'*The 39 Steps.*'

'I've seen all three film versions,' said Buchanan. 'My favourite was the one with Robert Donat as Richard Hannay.'

'I've only seen the stage version.'

'And what time did the performance start?'

'I think we had to be in our seats by eight o'clock.'

'What did you think of the performance?'

'It was OK, the actors all seemed to remember their lines.'

'Was it a large cast? I seem to remember the stage is quite small at the Devonshire Park Theatre.'

'They managed.'

'What about the scene when Hannay was being chased by the police across the moors? Getting six policemen and Hannay and his girlfriend on stage must have been an interesting sight.'

'Inspector, I don't have time to stand here talking about stage shows. Now, if that is all, I have a cake in the oven that will burn if I don't return to the kitchen.'

'Thank you for your time. We'll just wait here for your daughter-in-law to finish with her lesson.'

'You've gone fishing again, haven't you?' said Street.

Buchanan nodded, 'Just chumming, I'll drop the hook later.'

Street's next question was thwarted as the door opened and Bahija entered. 'Here is my husband's business card, Inspector.'

'Upper Richmond Road, Putney,' read Buchanan. 'Thank you, Bahija.'

'Is there anything else?'

'I was just chatting with Hiezabel about Seeracha's. Does your family eat there very often?'

'Sometimes, though we usually eat at the Thai Marina in the harbour.'

'Ah, yes, I know it well. We used to eat there quite often when we lived in the harbour. You went to the theatre afterwards?'

'Yes.'

'*The 39 Steps*?'

'Yes, what a hoot. All those parts played by only four actors.'

'Did you all go to dinner together?'

'We drove separate cars to the restaurant. Nasim chooses not to drive, so I drove the both of us. Hiezabel and Yousef came in a taxi.'

'How about after dinner, did the four of you go in your car?'

'No, they had the taxi booked for the evening.'

'That must have cost quite a bit.'

'I think the taxi company owner owes Yousef a favour, a leftover from the days when he was in the movie business.'

'Did you all go into the theatre at the same time?'

'No. Nasim needed a document from Amal's safe, so we stopped by the Mastrani office on the way.'

'All of you?'

'The theatre is sort of on the way so Hiezabel and Yousef followed us.'

'Did you go in with him?'

'No, there was no reason for me to.'

'Was Amal there when you arrived?'

'Yes, he opened the door for Nasim.'

'How long was Nasim in the office with Amal?'

'No longer than five minutes.'

'Did you see anyone else while you waited for Nasim?'

'No, but I wasn't looking for anyone.'

'So, you were on time for the play?'

'Yes.'

'How about Hiezabel and Yousef?'

'They were late, apparently the taxi driver took a wrong turn.'

'So, you missed the beginning of the play?'

'No, we didn't. Nasim and I went in for the curtain up, Hiezabel and Yousef joined us a few minutes later, but Hiezabel left before the play ended. She whispered to me that she wasn't feeling well, something to do with the dinner being too spicy for her.'

'What time was curtain up?'

'I seem to remember we had to be seated for eight o'clock.'

'Ah,' said Buchanan, 'now it makes sense.'

'What does?'

'The fact that Hiezabel didn't know much about the play, or how many actors were in the cast. How far into the play was it when she left?'

'I'm sorry, Inspector, I was so wrapped up in the play, I couldn't tell you. But it wasn't long after the beginning, maybe fifteen, thirty minutes.'

'Did Hiezabel take the taxi home?'

'She must have done. We had to give Yousef a ride home.'

'Do you know the name of the taxi company that your step-father-in-law has an interest in?'

'No, I think it is based in London.'

'Your mother-in-law made some remarks about you working.'

'Hmm, she's always going on about the fact I should be spending my time looking after the home and stop demeaning myself by teaching music to rich kids.'

'Do you have a lot of students?' asked Street.

'I have about twenty, ranging in age from six up to nineteen. I also do speech therapy. I have one student, an elderly gentleman who recently had a stroke.'

'You already told us you teach your niece and her boyfriend.'

'Yes, another arrow in Hiezabel's quiver to shoot at me. But I don't care, those two are very talented and will someday have a very successful career as performers.'

'They come here every Thursday afternoon for lessons?'

'Most Thursdays, Zilini doesn't have university classes on Thursday afternoons.'

'Did Zac's brother ever come with them?'

Bahija smiled. 'There was one occasion that I remember, about this time last year. Zilini showed up with Zac for their lesson, but I soon realised something wasn't as it should be.'

'Why was that?'

'Zac and his brother Sam were identical twins, and both quite musically gifted. It wasn't till they began to perform that I realised what was going on. Zac had been working on a new arrangement of *Smoke Gets in Your Eyes* and, as I watched his guitar playing, I saw the subterfuge. Zac plays jazz style: by that I mean he holds the neck in his left hand and rolls his thumb over the edge of the fretboard to stop the bass notes. What I saw was someone who was classically trained, resting his thumb on the back of the neck – that's when I realised, they were trying to fool me. All in good fun, I might add.'

'We didn't know Sam could play the guitar,' said Street. 'Didn't the fact that Zac had a beard give you an indication something wasn't what it should be?'

'No – neither of them had beards when I first met them. I think Zac decided to grow one when he saw a photo of Eric Clapton playing at the Royal Albert Hall.'

'Did Sam ever come here at other times, without his brother?'

'Not here, but I did see him at my mother-in-law's house.'

'What was he doing there?'

'Cutting the grass. I asked Zac about it and he said Sam used to do odd jobs till the next driving contract came along.'

'Do you know how often this happened?'

'No.'

'How often does your mother-in-law come to visit?'

'Mostly on Thursdays, but she comes at other times to help when we have a dinner party. I think she gets lonely when Yousef is traveling abroad.'

'And she bakes each Thursday?'

'I think it's her way of saying I should be doing the same.'

'How often do you visit her?'

'I do her nails the first Tuesday of the month.'

'How about on the weekends?'

'Rarely. My stepfather-in-law runs film-making workshops on most Saturdays; we'd only be in the way.'

'Has it always been that way?'

'No, just since Yousef had his heart attack. He used to travel a lot more than he does now.'

'Do you know how often he travels?'

'I'm not sure.'

'We've yet to meet him. Do you think he's home just now?'

'I'm not sure. What have these questions got to do with Zilini being missing?'

'Please excuse me, it's being a policeman for over thirty years. Asking questions has become a habit, sometimes an annoying one, my wife tells me.'

'What has Zac said? You have talked to him, haven't you?'

'We talked to him last week, but we didn't know he was Zac – we thought we were talking to Sam at the time.'

227

'Well, I hope you find Zilini soon, she and Zac have an album to record.'

'Do you know who with?'

'No, all I know is it was with a small studio near here.'

'Excuse me, Bahija, your student has just arrived,' said Hiezabel, poking her head round the door.

'Thank you, I'll be right with them.'

'Just one more question, if you don't mind. The night you went to the theatre, you stopped outside the Mastrani building, did you see anyone coming out of the carpark?'

'No. Is there anything else, Inspector?'

'No, not at this time. Thank you for your patience.'

'Do you think Zilini is in danger?'

'I'm not sure.'

'I'll show you to the door, Inspector,' said Hiezabel.

As Buchanan was about to walk out, he asked her, 'Mrs Barazani, is your husband at home just now?'

'He was when I left. He' just returned and may be sleeping, why would you want to know?'

'We're asking every member of the family about the last time they saw Zilini.'

'You'll be wasting your time asking him, he's a very busy man.'

'All the same, just a couple of questions.'

'I suppose you could try the house.'

'Thank you, Mrs Barazani, you have been extremely helpful.'

◆

'Do you think she'll call her husband and warn him we are on our way?' asked Street, as they drove down the A22 towards Eastbourne.

'I'm counting on it. I want him to have time to think about why we want to talk to him.'

'You suspect him of being involved in Zilini's disappearance?'

'I'm not sure at this point. I just think it odd that any time we talk to any members of the family he's always absent.'

'For someone who recently suffered a heart attack, he seems to keep very busy.'

'Heart attacks aren't that debilitating. There was a sergeant back in Glasgow who was out on patrol on a hot summer day. He saw someone grab a lady's purse, so he gave chase. He managed to grab the thief, but in the process had to let them go as he was in extreme pain with his chest. Thankfully he wasn't on his own and was in hospital within thirty minutes. By the time he returned to duty he'd lost four stone, had changed his diet and took up running marathons.'

'Lucky him,' said Street, as they drove up to the house. 'Is that who we are looking for, the one weeding the flower bed?'

'Let's find out,' said Buchanan, stopping the car and getting out.

'Yousef Barazani?'

'Yes.'

'Detective Chief Inspector Buchanan and Detective Sergeant Street. We'd like to ask you a couple of questions about the disappearance of your granddaughter, Zilini.'

'Disappearance? I thought she'd just run away with her boyfriend,' he said, standing up and walking towards Buchanan.

'That is why we are here. Can you tell me when the last time was you saw Zilini?'

Yousef put his trowel in the bucket he was holding and placed it on the ground.

'It's been weeks, I've been out of the country on business. I suppose it would have been at her eighteenth birthday party.'

'What sort of business are you involved in?'

'Most of my time is spent trying to separate rich people from their money. Financing movies takes a lot of investment. I also do a bit of lecturing abroad, and we run workshops here at the house on Saturdays.'

'What sort of workshops? Are they residential?'

'Nothing grand. What we offer are workshops for people wanting to get into the film industry. They are one day only, usually on a Saturday.'

'Are they popular?' asked Street.

'I have a two-month waiting list.'

'Would there be anyone I might know?' queried Street.

Yousef Barazani smiled and gently shook his head. 'Probably none you would recognise, Sergeant.'

'I know nothing about the film business,' said Street. 'What sort of things do you lecture on?'

'All phases of the industry, which might not be obvious to the person looking to make a career in it. We start with the basics, such as how to go about preparing a CV and how to present your film ideas to investors; movie making is an extremely cash-hungry industry, Sergeant. Some of the other things we look at are how to gain experience and working on other people's films; film-making is not just about directors, cameras, and lights.'

'Do you ever miss being at the forefront of the film industry?'

'Yes, but my days of working seven days a week on set, up to fourteen hours a day, are long over. I have no desire to return to the cut and thrust of competitive business.'

'So, what inspires you these days?' queried Street.

'See over there, see those roses? That is what inspires me. I spend my days trying to grow specimen quality blooms to show.'

'Did you ever meet Zilini's boyfriend?' asked Buchanan.

'At her eighteenth birthday party. He and Zilini entertained us after the dinner.'

'What about the boyfriend's brother, Sam?'

'Yes. While I was recovering from my heart attack, he did some gardening for us.'

'Was that something he did regularly?' said Street.

'I don't think so. His profession was lorry driver.'

'You own a taxi firm?' said Buchanan.

'Not quite. I helped a friend get started in the business. Amongst character references, he needed some start-up funding.'

'Where is the taxi firm?' said Buchanan.

'East End, London. It's not a black-cab operation – to get a taxi, you have to call and book one.'

'Is that what you did two weeks ago?'

Yousef thought for a moment before replying. 'Two weeks ago? I suppose you are referring to the Friday night?'

'Yes, Friday the 4th.'

'We had dinner at Seeracha's, then went on to The Devonshire Park Theatre to see a play.'

'Was the play *The 39 Steps*?' asked Buchanan.

'Ah, yes, it was. Had me in stitches.'

'And Mrs Barazani, your wife?'

'Sadly, she missed most of it. Dinner didn't sit well for her and she went home early.'

'Do you remember how she got home?'

'I suppose she took the taxi.'

'Hiring a taxi by the day must have been very expensive.'

He shrugged.' I wouldn't know, Hiezabel arranged it all.'

'Some friend you have there,' remarked Street.

'It is the way things are done in Bulgaria.'

'Your friend is Bulgarian?'

'Yes.'

'Does he employ Bulgarian drivers?'

'I don't know. I think his drivers are all self-employed and have their own cars.'

'What does she do when you are away, does she have any hobbies?'

'Yes. In spite of her disdain for women working she keeps busy selling odds and ends on eBay. Sometimes, when I'm in Europe, she will text me to say she's just purchased something from a shop near where I am staying, and would I collect it and bring it home with me.'

'Lot's of people sell on eBay.'

'It gives her something to do when I'm not home.'

'What time did you get home after the theatre?'

'Bahija dropped me off at the house just before midnight. We'd gone out for a late drink.'

'How was Hiezabel when you got home?'

'She was in bed. She'd been sick, put her clothes in the washing machine, then decided to have a bath to relax.'

'What did you do?'

'It was late, I went to bed.'

'Did you help your son, Amal, set up Mastrani?'

'We offered but, like his daughter Zilini, he is very headstrong. He turned us down and set it up using his own resources.'

'What about his recent ventures? I understand Nasim has been arranging short-term financing?'

Yousef nodded. 'Yes, that is what Nasim told me.'

'I also understand Mastrani stands to make a great deal of money if the projects they are working on succeed.'

'If they pass government inspection,' said Yousef, smiling. 'I heard that there was an issue with one of the programs.'

'I believe that has been resolved,' said Buchanan.

'Then you know more than I do. I was told that the development funds were running low and Nasim had to go cap-in-hand to the bank for more time and capital.'

'Do you know if they gave him what he needed?'

'No.'

'So, even now at the eleventh hour, he's in trouble?'

'It's of his own making. We've extended a helping hand, it's up to him to accept or refuse.'

'Before we go, how did you come to know Sam Taylor?'

'It was just after my heart attack when I realised that, to keep the garden tidy, I needed help. You see, other than my wife, my love is for my garden. My wife mentioned to my granddaughter that I was looking for someone to help and she recommended Sam.'

'When was the last time you saw him?'

'Three weeks ago, maybe. He told me he was signing up with a new agency and they had lots of work for him.'

'Did he say which agency?'

'No.'

♦

'Is the arm rising out of the pond? Is the mist clearing?' asked Street, as they walked over to the car. Street remembered an earlier utterance of Buchanan's.

'Not quite, but the mist is clearing. Would you drive? I need to think.'

Street had worked long enough with Buchanan to know not to interrupt him when he was deep in thought, so it was a quiet drive back to the office.

'It might just work,' said Buchanan, as they approached the Tesco roundabout.

'What might just work?'

'Oh, sorry, my mind is running a thousand miles an hour. Just an idea, I'll explain later. No need to cloud the issues with my musings.'

'Are we stopping for lunch?'

Buchanan looked at the dashboard clock. 'Didn't realise it was that time. Did you bring anything to eat?'

'Yes, but it's only a yoghurt, I'm not that hungry these days. What about you?'

'Karen packed me a sandwich, said I was spending too much time at Tesco's eating their food.'

♦

'Do you have the list of Mastrani investors to hand?' asked Buchanan.

'Yes, somewhere on my desk,' Street said, shuffling through a stack of papers, 'Here it is.'

'Are they local?'

Street looked at the list. 'Yes, sort of. Jean Randal lives in Bexhill, Hugo Trent lives in Westham, just round the corner from you, John Lake lives in Hailsham. You know where Sir Nathan lives and last on the list is Nasim Barazani.'

'Fine. As soon as you finish your yoghurt we'll start with Jean Randal in Bexhill and work backwards, though I think we'll leave Nasim out of the list for today. Would you call them and see if they are going to be in? Not much point in driving to Bexhill for nothing.'

'Will do.'

'While you are doing that, I'm going to pop round to Tesco's for some fruit gums. Can I get you anything?'

'No thanks, I'm fine.'

Buchanan returned twenty minutes later. 'Success?'

'Yes. Jean Randal said she had to go out to collect her cat from the vet's but would be back in half an hour.'

'That's fine, takes that long to drive to Bexhill from here. Did you get through to any of the others?'

'John Lake said he would be out till about four, and Hugo Trent said come anytime, he's waiting for an estate agent to come to see the house. Sir Nathan is at Castlewood.'

'Well done, could you do the driving? I need to do some more thinking.'

♦

'There's money here,' said Buchanan, as Street pulled up behind a wrought-iron gate.

Street pressed the intercom button and waited.

'Yes?' came a questioning voice from the speaker.

'Detective Chief Inspector Buchanan and Detective Sergeant Street to see Jean Randal.'

'Come in,' replied the voice, as the gates swung open in unison.

Street parked in front of the house at the end of the driveway. The front door opened, and Jean Randal appeared, holding a large, long-haired white cat.'

'You're on time, Inspector, I admire a man who's always on time,' she said, smiling while stroking the cat.

'We do our best,' said Buchanan, following Street up the steps to the front door.

Jean Randal ushered them into the hallway. 'We'll be more comfortable in here,' she said, leading them into the living room. She walked over to a chair beside the fireplace and sat down. 'How may I help?'

'We understand you hold shares in the Mastrani company?''

'Yes, I do.'

'Can you tell us what brought you to do that?'

'It was my late husband actually, bless his soul. The dear man knew he was dying and wanted to make sure I was well taken care of. We were introduced to the company by our financial advisor. The company was sound, and it looked like a good, safe investment, so my husband bought into the deal.'

'Do you know how many shares he bought?'

'Not offhand.'

'Have you kept up with how the company is doing?'

'Not till recently.'

'What changed?'

'A week ago, I received a letter inviting me to sell my shares. I'm not sure who it was from. I still have the letter if you'd like to read it, maybe you could help make sense of it.'

Buchanan took the offered letter and looked at the postmark over the first-class stamp, the 11th. He extracted the letter and looked at the date: it was dated the 10th.

Dear Investor in Mastrani

I just wanted to inform you that several other investors in Mastrani are considering selling their shares and I would like to offer you the opportunity to cash in your investment at a most advantageous return.

You may wonder why I am making this offer. Well, it is because, unlike you, I am in a position to take a long-term view on my investments and will be able to ride out the inevitable storm that is soon to hit Mastrani. I am unable to disclose the issues preventing a successful outcome of the latest program that Mastrani is preparing for the

235

government, and the impending scandal about to befall the owner of Mastrani, Amal Barazani.

This offer is open for seven days from the date of the offer, please use the enclosed reply slip and pre-paid envelope.

Sincerely yours

One Who Knows

'Have you replied to this letter?'

'How could I? There wasn't any reply slip or prepaid envelope in with the letter.'

'What do you plan to do about it?'

'I definitely won't be purchasing any more shares or selling what I have till I talk to my financial advisor. I have an appointment with her booked for next Thursday.'

'A very wise move. Could we borrow the letter? There might be useful fingerprints on it, we'll let you have it back when we're done with it.'

'Keep it. Is there anything else, Inspector?'

'No, not for the moment. If you think of anything, here's my card, you can call or email.'

◆

While Street navigated the traffic on the A259, Buchanan continued to contemplate. As they approached the Pevensey roundabout Street interrupted his musings and said, 'Do you fancy a coffee? Starbucks is just off the roundabout.'

Buchanan looked at the time on the dashboard and nodded. 'Yes, I'll buy.'

'So where are you?' asked Street, as Buchanan placed her drink in front of her.

'Following the money trail. I said earlier that following the money trail is quite often the road to take when trying to figure out what is behind the crime, and, to my way of thinking, this one is no different.'

'I can see that.'

'But what you don't see is what's behind it all. I think it is a classic struggle between those who have and those who have not.'

'Who do you see as the protagonists in this struggle?'

'Amal Barazani is the one who has, and his stepbrother, Nasim, is the has not.'

'That would work if it were not for the fact that Nasim's mother said his only ambition in life is to climb the greasy pole to senior management at the bank. Also, don't forget the fact that he has been working to raise financing for Mastrani to continue with the projects. If Mastrani were to fail, it would scupper any chance for Nasim to go anywhere with the bank, except maybe a one-way trip out the door.'

'There is that, but it doesn't shake my thinking that this is all about a family in turmoil over control of a very lucrative business.'

'So, what is it?' asked Street. 'Nasim doesn't want to have anything to do with Mastrani. Yousef can't, or won't, because it would be too stressful and bad for his heart. So who does that leave? Of course, there is Zilini, but all she has to do is wait for her father to die and she inherits it all. I can't think of any reason why she'd do anything to jeopardise her future inheritance.'

'Have you considered Zac Taylor? You haven't included him in your deliberations.'

'I had thought of that, but I don't think he fits into the equation. From the information we have gathered so far, all he has to do is to marry Zilini then sit back and wait for her to inherit.'

'OK, but suppose his intentions were not honourable, suppose he only wants Zilini for her inheritance? Suppose it was all a ruse between Zac and his brother, Sam? They could have been working together on this. The family found out, killed Sam and were about to catch Zac when he saw the taxi coming for him. Zilini went into hiding till it all blew over and sent her dad the empty ring-box to let him know she was all right,' suggested Buchanan.

'Whew, sounds like a plot for a murder-mystery story! When we get back to the office, I'll see what, if anything more, I can find out about the Taylor twins.'

'Good, finished with your drink?'

'No, I'll take it with me, your turn to drive.'

♦

'Which house is it?' said Buchanan, as they drove slowly along Peelings Lane.

'No number, the house name is Yardley.'

'It had to be the last one,' said Buchanan, as he pulled up by the wooden gate. 'The garden is a bit sparse.'

'That's what John Lake said when I talked to him on the phone. At least it has wonderful views of the Downs.'

As they reached the bottom step, the front door opened and a curly-haired poodle shot out and stood on the top step, barking.

'Quiet, Biff, they are friends,' said John Lake.

'Detective Chief Inspector Buchanan and Detective Sergeant Street, we called earlier.'

'Sorry, Inspector, Biff's just doing what he's trained to do. Come on up, Biff won't bite.'

They were shown into the living room, Biff keeping a constant vigil at the door.

'What can I help you with, Inspector? Your sergeant said something on the phone about the Mastrani company?'

'Yes,' said Street. 'We are interviewing all Mastrani investors asking if they are aware of anyone trying to sell them bogus shares in the company.'

'No, no one has tried to sell me shares. The opposite is the case. Last week I received a letter from someone seeking to buy my shares.'

'Could we see the letter?'

'Sure, I'll just get it.'

Biff was in a quandary, should he follow his master, or keep an eye on the interlopers? His worry soon ended by the return of John Lake.

'Here it is, silly idiot forgot to include his details.'

Street read the letter, nodded, then passed it on to Buchanan.

'What are you planning to do about the letter, will you sell your shares?' asked Buchanan.

'Ignore it. If they can't be bothered to make sure they included their details, how am I supposed to trust them to come through with the money? What I will do is to check and see if Mastrani really does have an issue with the programs they are developing. If they do, I might just be inclined to dump my shares quickly and discreetly. You know what they say, there's no smoke without fire.'

'Thank you, Mr Lake. If you hear any more about this, would you let us know, please?' said Buchanan, handing him his card.

♦

'The picture is becoming clearer,' said Buchanan, as they drove through Hankham village on their way to Hailsham. 'Someone is trying to cause concern about the solidity of Mastrani, spreading rumours to bring down the perceived value of the company.'

'I know we already discounted him, but what about Yousef Barazani? Maybe he's doing it as a present for his son, Nasim? Remember also, Sam was involved in this case. Suppose Sam found out what was being planned and saw it as a way to make some easy money by blackmailing Yousef?'

'That works, but I think there is more to the story which we haven't yet discovered,' said Buchanan. 'All that is indeed possible, but we would need to build a substantial bridge between Yousef fixing the program stress-test and spreading malicious lies to enable him to acquire the shares of the Mastrani investors. Remember he would have to own a majority share to wield enough power to oust Amal Barazani.

'Then there is the issue of Sam Taylor's murder. Killing someone in a heated argument, is one thing, but to kill someone in cold blood is quite another. Next there are the people who actually did the killing. They will need to be taken care of one way or another. Either by suffering a similar fate to that of the victim or being paid off with a substantial amount of cash.'

'I get your point, especially if we take into consideration what Yousef said about roses. He's not exactly a front runner for the position of murderer.'

'That's food for thought though. Where are we headed?'

'Hugo Trent lives on Hempstead Lane; his house is just off the A22.'

'We seem to be going up and down the A22 like a yo-yo these days,' said Buchanan, as he turned off the A22 and on to Hempstead Lane.

'That's his house,' said Street, pointing to a For Sale board outside an overgrown driveway to a dilapidated house.

'Are you sure this is the house?' asked Buchanan, as he turned off the engine and got out of the car.

Before he could take a step, an Alsatian ran out of the open garage door and stood four feet from Buchanan, barking incessantly. Street reached for her pepper spray and was about to go to Buchanan's rescue when Buchanan did something totally unexpected. He took a step forward and offered the back of his hand to the dog. The dog backed up and stopped barking.

'Here, fellow,' said Buchanan, still holding out his hand, 'come, let's be friends, I'm not here to do any mischief.'

The dog came forward, sniffed at the back of Buchanan's hand, then took two steps back and recommenced barking.

'He's not dangerous,' said Buchanan to Street as he stood up. 'Look at his face, he's smiling.'

'Jock, you silly sausage, you're not fooling anyone,' said a voice from the interior of the garage. 'You've been rumbled, come here and stop that barking. Are you from the estate agency?'

'No, we're from the police station. DCI Buchanan and DS Street. Sergeant Street called earlier.'

'Ah, yes, my wife said someone from your office called. How can we help?'

'I understand you are a venture capitalist?'

'You didn't come all this way to ask for advice, did you?'

'No, it was about your involvement with the Mastrani company.'

'Not for much longer. In case you haven't noticed, this house is for sale, or has been for the last year. The estate agent said if we really want it to sell, we need to fix the roof properly, paint the outside and sort out the garden.'

'That sounds like good advice.'

'Roofs, paint and gardeners don't come cheap, Inspector.'

'Have you received a letter offering to purchase your shares in Mastrani?'

'Yes, oh damn, I thought it was too good to be true.'

'Why do you think that?'

'There were no contact details with the letter. But never mind, my golfing friend Nathan says he knows of a developer who would be willing to buy the house at the asking price just for the land alone, even though there is no planning permission in place.'

'Nathan?'

'Yes, Nathan Greyspear, heard of him?'

'We are acquainted.'

'Anything else, Inspector?'

'No, that will be all for now, thank you for your time.'

◆

'Castlewood next stop?' said Street, sliding the pepper-spray aerosol back into the glove-box.

'You were actually going to use that?' said Buchanan.

'Of course, I was. I've seen pictures of what damage an angry dog can do to human flesh.'

'What you failed to see was his wagging tail and the glint in his eyes.'

'No, I didn't. All I could see was you about to be bitten by an angry dog – you scared the daylights out of me doing what you did back there.'

'Nah, it was nothing, and to answer your question, yes, next stop Castlewood.'

♦

Buchanan turned off Arlington Road and onto the gravelled driveway that led up to the Castlewood Country Club. He stopped in the visitor parking space in the front of the club building. As he did, his car door was opened by one of the club valets.

'Good afternoon, Jack. Nathan is waiting for you in the library.'

'Thanks, Bob.'

'They're very informal here,' said Street. 'He addressed you by your forename.'

Buchanan smiled and said, 'That was Bob Lewis, he is head of security here, and used to be one of us till someone decided to use his leg as an anvil.'

'That sounds awful.'

Buchanan led Street through the members' bar and stopped at the entrance to the library.

One of the waiters came over and asked, 'Are you a member, sir?'

'No, but I have an appointment with Sir Nathan, I was told he would be in the library.'

'Ah yes, Sir Nathan said he was expecting visitors this afternoon. If you'll follow me, I'll show you to where he's seated.'

Buchanan and Street followed the waiter between the groups of high-backed Windsor chairs. 'Your visitors, Sir Nathan.'

'Thank you, Karl. Something to drink Jill, Jack?'

'Could I have a lime and soda?' asked Street.

'Coffee for me,' said Buchanan.

'I'll have a coffee as well, Karl.'

'Yes, sir.'

'I thought this would be a more comfortable place to sit than my office,' said Greyspear. 'Now, I suppose this is about Amal's daughter, Zilini. Has she been found?'

'No, not yet,' said Buchanan as Karl returned with their drinks. 'When we last talked, you said you had taken shares in Mastrani?'

'Yes.'

'Do you still own them?'

242

'Yes, I do, and I suppose this visit is about a letter with an offer to purchase said shares before they lost their current value?'

Buchanan nodded. 'Have you made any decisions about the offer?'

'No, don't need to. The letter is a hoax, probably from some disgruntled employee. So, Jack, when are we going to see you back here at Castlewood? Mercury really misses you.'

Buchanan craned his neck to look at the clock over the mantelpiece. 'Why not now? I suppose a quick walk over to the stable to see Mercury won't have anyone sending out a search party for us.'

'Good, I'll grab an apple from the kitchen, you can't go empty-handed.'

♦

'Oh, what does she want?' said Buchanan, noticing a very distinctive licence plate in the police car park.

'Who?' asked Street.

'Over there in the visitor bay, HEL1N.'

'That's the ACC's car, you think she's here to talk to us?'

'Who else?'

'Shall I go first?' asked Street, poking Buchanan gently in the ribs with her elbow.

'That's all right,' said Buchanan, as they walked along the corridor to their office. 'I'm a big boy now, I even brush my teeth by myself.'

'Are you all right?'

'Never felt better.'

Helen Markham, the ACC, was standing looking out of the window when Buchanan and Street entered their office.

'I've been waiting half an hour for you two to show up. Where have you been?' she asked, continuing to look out of the window.

'Hastings and back via Hailsham, Ma'am,' explained Street.

Markham turned round with a smile on her face. 'Sorry to shake you up a bit. I've wanted to do that for years. I know where you've been, I just got off the phone with Nathan. I was in

243

Eastbourne and thought I would get the latest on the Barazani case. Please sit, you don't have to stand in front of me.'

Buchanan went behind his desk and waited for Street and Markham to sit.

'I will recount the events as we know them,' said Buchanan. 'Zac and Sam Taylor are identical twins and Zac is the boyfriend of Zilini.

'On the Wednesday in question, Zilini and the Taylor twins were in Hastings, Zac and Zilini were singing at an open mike evening. As Zac and Sam got off the train on the way home, Zac realised he had left his guitar behind. He called the manager, who said he would get the guitar up to Hastings station for Zac to collect. Zac got on the next train back to Hastings, but he missed the last train home and had to get a taxi. OK so far?'

'Yes, I think I have it,' replied Markham.

'When he got home, Sam wasn't in the flat. Later in the day Zac texted Zilini saying he was worried about Sam and had tried Sam's friends, but no one had seen him. At this point Zac expresses his concern about Sam, because he says to Zilini that the two men he saw at the station on the previous Wednesday are outside the flat. Zilini suggested that Zac pack a bag, bring his guitar and move into her student accommodation.'

'An offer he had to decline,' said Street. 'On the Friday evening Zilini says in her text that she will make an excuse after dinner to go out and meet Zac in the station car park.'

'I wonder why she didn't confide in her dad?' mused Markham.

'Because she thought her father was trying to get rid of Zac,' said Buchanan.

'And you took this as an indication she was planning to run away?' asked Markham.

'That's what we're going on,' said Buchanan.

'We have CCTV video of Zilini parking her car in the Mastrani garage,' said Street, 'then leaving by the fire escape door. That's the last we have seen of her.'

'I thought her father said she was in her room when she when he went to bed?'

'She had set her alarm radio to come on at ten thirty,' said Street.

'Anything else?' asked Markham.

'We have station CCTV of where they were to meet. We see Zac holding his guitar, then him disappearing into the bushes. The reason he disappeared into the bushes was because the same two men showed up in the bogus taxi that had offered Zac a lift the previous Wednesday.'

'Have you been able to track down the taxi?'

'Yes, as a burnt-out wreck sitting in Ripley's scrapyard. The licence plates were stolen from a car that had been an insurance write-off.'

'Do you have any suspects in the Sam Taylor murder?' said Markham.

'Not yet.'

'What about a motive for Sam Taylor's murder?'

'Just vague ideas. But the main thought is that it was a case of mistaken identity.'

'So, Zac Taylor was the intended victim?'

'We believe so, but the reason is still unclear. The main thought is, since the father didn't agree with the relationship with Zilini, he put out a contract on Zac Taylor. Though there's a strange event that doesn't make sense. According to Doctor Mansell's autopsy report someone was trying to poison Sam Taylor. Dr Mansell's autopsy report said he found belladonna seeds in his intestine, and if he hadn't been strangled, he would have been dead within the next 24 hours from Atropine poisoning.'

'You're right, that doesn't make any sense,' said Markham. 'Any other surprises?'

'Yes. As part of the investigation into the disappearance of Zilini Barazani, we have discovered there are five main investors in Mastrani, including Nathan Greyspear.'

'Do you know who they are, and how much each investor owns?'

'I have a list,' said Street, passing it over to Markham.

'Looks like none of them has a majority,' she said, handing the list back to Street.

'Also, each investor has received a letter offering to purchase their shares before they get devalued.'

'What would cause them to be devalued?' asked Markham.

'The writer of the letter intimated there was an issue with the compliance of the program that was about to be handed over to the government. But when we talked to the senior developer at Mastrani he didn't give any reason to believe it wasn't something they couldn't resolve.'

'A family squabble over money perhaps and, when there is a lot of money, they can go to war over it. How much is involved?'

'Amal Barazani said if all the projects came online, his company could be bigger than Amazon Microsoft and Google combined.'

'That's enough to go to war over. Who in the family would benefit the most?' queried Markham.

'We've been discussing that exact subject, but there is no obvious contender. Everyone could be considered as having a motive.'

'Is there anyone who doesn't have a motive?'

'The daughter, Zilini, she's Amal Barazani's next of kin. When her father dies, she gets the lot, unless of course he's already made alternative arrangements.'

'I think it might help you if you were to find out if there is a will, and who stands to inherit and who doesn't,' said Markham.

'There is. Amal said his daughter is the main beneficiary,' said Buchanan

'Is there anything else I should be aware of before I leave?'

'Yes, there's a Bulgarian connection. The two suspects in the taxi that abducted Sam Taylor we believe were also involved in his murder. They first came to our attention through CCTV videos from the Pevensey and Westham station where we were able to get the vehicle licence plate. Our next break came when the body of Sam Taylor was exhumed; we found two sets of orange PPE with initials stamped inside the jackets. The contractor in charge of the sewer pipe installation gave us the names and address of the two individuals who the PPE belonged to. We raided the address in Eastbourne, but they have since disappeared.'

'What about the taxi firm, did you talk to them?'

'Yes, turns out the magnetic taxi door signs had been pinched from one of their taxis the week before. The manager put that down to childish vandalism.'

'You mentioned something about the taxi's bogus licence plates?'

'The plates were taken from a written-off car that had been discovered when the serious crime agency raided a vehicle chop shop in Hellingly. The plates from that car had been in a group of plates sold in a pub in London. We managed to get facial images from the CCTV video the MET sent through. They in turn were shown to our witness who saw Sam Taylor being buried. From there we connected them to the company installing the sewer pipe, and the foreman gave us their names.'

'Where are you going next in the investigation?'

'I think we're going to start back at the beginning and make sure we haven't overlooked anything. But that will have to wait till tomorrow, we will need to have our wits about us, otherwise this case could just turn into a Brian Rix farce – before your time, Jill.'

14
Friday 18th
Breaking Windows

Buchanan turned on his side to look at the clock: three o'clock. Why always three o'clock, why not seven o'clock? But he knew why his body woke him at three. In Belgium it was four o'clock and during the First World War it would be time for the troops to wake before standing-to at five o'clock. It was the quiet hour before they would go over the top for that day's fruitless attempt to deprive some mother of her son. He remembered from childhood his great-uncle talking about life in the trenches, mostly after he'd drunk half a bottle of his father's best whisky. Before he got very far with his narration he'd break down in tears and spend the rest of the evening sobbing quietly in his chair. Was there something in the genes that passed these momentous thoughts down through the generations? He shook his head. Why was he thinking of his great-uncle John, what was going on in his life to bring up those memories?

Of course, it could have been his latest dream. In the dream he was standing outside the Royal Albert Hall. He was to be the main event but when he went to open the door, it was locked. He looked through the window and saw Amal Barazani standing in the lobby; Buchanan knocked on the door, but Amal just ignored him. He tried the next door, also locked, and when he looked through the window Charlotte, Amal's PA, just waved at him. He went round the building trying all the doors, each with a member of the Barazani clan in view. All ignored him and remained behind the locked doors. He returned to the front door and, in a fit of desperation, smashed the glass in the door. That was when he woke.

He'd tried to get back to sleep but after an hour of tossing and turning he gave up, put on his dressing gown and went downstairs to make his first coffee of the day. As he descended the stairs, he mused that if DCI Morse had as many pints of beer during the day as he had cups of coffee, how would he ever manage to stay sober enough to do his crossword?

He stepped into the kitchen wondering why the lights were still on.

'Sorry, did I wake you? I dropped my coffee and broke the cup,' apologised Poppy.

'Now it makes sense,' said Buchanan.

'What does?' Poppy asked.

'My dream. The sound of you dropping the cup mingled with my dream. I'd just smashed a window in a door at the Royal Albert Hall. Don't worry about the cup, we have plenty. Is there any coffee left?'

'Yes, I made a whole pot, it's what happens in our house. No one just makes a cup, hot or cold it all ends up being drunk. Do you usually get up this early?'

'No, do you usually stay up this late?'

'No. I'm still trying to adjust to the time difference here to that of Dallas. Back home it's only eleven-thirty in the evening.'

'Have you heard from your dad?'

'Yes, he said the flight was quiet, and the sleepover at New York refreshed him.'

'How about your mum?' asked Buchanan, as he dropped a frozen bagel into the toaster. 'Would you like one?'

'No thanks, it's a bit late for me to be eating. I just finished a Zoom call with my mom.'

'How is she? I bet she's missing you.'

'Excited and missing me, both at the same time. She has booked the main hall at church for the reception and my dad will be doing the ceremony. You, Karen, Stephen and Jill, will all come to the wedding, won't you?'

Buchanan smiled. 'Karen and I would be honoured to come to your wedding, and I'm sure Stephen and Jill would love to come as well. Have you and Harry decided when you are getting married?'

'It won't be till after he gets his visa. Dad's friend at church is an immigration lawyer and says in Harry's case it should be just a formality. We're looking at a spring wedding.'

'What about Harry's job?'

'No problems, the stables have given him a contract and left the start date open. They have even paid for him to visit to see how the stables are run and he has regular online discussions about how he is going to run the stables when he gets there.'

'Won't that contravene his visa application?'

'No, Dad's friend says as long as Harry doesn't actually do any work while he is visiting, it shouldn't be a problem.'

'How did Nathan take the news of Harry's departure?'

'He wrote Harry a character reference and has even been out to Dallas to look over the stables. They run a breeding programme and I think they are going to do business with each other.'

'And this even though Harry has a criminal conviction?'

'Thanks to your and Nathan's character references, when Harry went to the embassy for his interview, he was told there wouldn't be any issues with his past convictions.'

'I'm glad to hear that.'

Poppy yawned and went over to the dishwasher with her empty cup. 'I guess I am tired. See you in the morning – oh, it *is* morning – bye for now.'

Buchanan spread butter and a thin layer of cream cheese on his bagel and sat down with his coffee to think. In spite of the nonsense of his dream, there was a certain element that did make sense. He had been going in circles, people were staying locked behind the facade of family unity, they were ignoring him, but why? It was time to break a few windows, it was time to go over the top; let the battle begin. But first he needed to reply to Cynthia's letter.

It wasn't very often he got to actually use a pen to write, so with a fresh cup of coffee he went through to his study. He turned on his desk lamp, took a piece of writing paper, unscrewed the top from his Conway Stewart 388 and began to write,

Dear Cynthia and Pat

It was with great joy that I read your letter. Karen and I are so excited about your news. Certainly, I will give you away, it will be an honour, give me a call and we can discuss your arrangements. Karen has already started to think about what to wear and has even been out looking for a hat.

Your marriage to Pat will be the beginning of a busy season for us. I don't know if you remember the Grant family? Travis came third in the Castlewood cup. Their daughter, Poppy, is staying with us till the end of the year. In November we have been invited to Dallas, Texas, to share Thanksgiving with her family. Next spring, we will be returning to Dallas for Poppy and Harry's wedding. You may remember Harry, he's the assistant stable manager at Castlewood stables.

Yours, Jack Buchanan.

He put down his pen and smiled at the thought how much life had changed since he had come down from Glasgow, even his use of the English language had changed. Would he still be understood if he went back to Glasgow? Of course, the odds of him returning to Glasgow to do investigating was as good as him winning the lottery three weeks in a row.

He leaned back in his chair, two cups of coffee had revived him; it was time to go break a few windows, shake a few trees, and see what fell out.

◆

Being a policeman of thirty-five years' experience, he found going into the office before anyone else stimulating. Though it was still full of the furniture of the previous day, there was a difference in the atmosphere: it was empty of thoughts. Like a clean whiteboard, he could write what he wanted without clearing others' thoughts from the surface first?

As he stared across the office at the sun rising over the warehouses, he wondered where to begin, which tree to shake. Zilini Barazani was the obvious one. Was she free and hiding somewhere, or was she a captive, tied to a green chair like Sam had been? Had she been taken captive by the two Bulgarians as she left the Mastrani garage? If so, how did they know she would be there? Had she been followed from home?

In either case, where was she? If free, who was she with? Did Zac manage to escape, and did they meet up somewhere? Could they have managed to get to the station and board a train? He got up from his desk and went over to the whiteboard and created a to-do list. Item one. Do we have station CCTV of Zilini and Zac getting on a train, and if so, which train? Item two. Check with Michael Levitt of Mastrani and find out what happened during the stress-test of the software. Item three. Has Jill found out who is the agent for Zac and Zilini? Item four. Check with forensics regarding the cigar stub purloined from Nasim Barazani. Item five. What were the results of the evidence found at the Bulgarians' flat? Item six. Figure out why the empty ring box was sent to Amal Barazani.

♦

'You're up early,' said Street, as she entered the office. 'I got you a coffee, oh, you already have one.'

'In this job you can never have too much coffee, thanks.'

'Are you all right? You look a bit tired.'

'I woke from a crazy dream; I'd just smashed glass in the main entrance door of the Royal Albert Hall.'

'That is a wild dream, can you figure out what caused it?'

'Poppy, she'd just dropped her cup on the kitchen floor.'

Street shook her head. 'You've lost me on that one.'

'Poppy has trouble adjusting to the time zone, and before she went to bed made herself a cup of coffee. She accidentally dropped it and broke the cup. That was the sound I heard in my dream.'

'That makes sense now you explain it. What do you want me to start with?'

'I've been thinking about Zac and Zilini. Do we have CCTV of the station interior for the time shortly after we see Zilini park her car and Zac jumps into the bushes?'

'I'll have a look. I'll put what we have up on the screen.'

Buchanan watched as camera after camera showed different views of the interior of Eastbourne station. 'Never realised just how busy Eastbourne station can be. Can you see anyone resembling our couple?'

'I saw these two earlier but discounted them,' said Street, zooming in on one of the cameras. 'They were just two amongst many hurrying across the concourse, followed by a third. They could be anyone, especially wearing hoodies like they are.'

'That third figure, the one following closely behind, is he following them, or just heading for the same train?'

'Not sure,' said Street. 'Could that be one of the Bulgarian thugs?'

'I don't think so, they were shorter. Can you tell which train they got on?'

'Hang on, I'll zoom in on the departure board. Three departures are shown within the next thirty minutes, there's the seven forty-four to Hastings, the seven forty to Brighton and the seven thirty-five to Victoria.'

'That's helpful. Can we follow them to see which train they got on?'

'I'll switch to the camera in front of the barrier.'

'Hmm, that's not much help either,' said Buchanan. 'The Victoria train goes through Lewes; they could get off there and change for Falmer. Where have they gone, did you see which train they got on?'

'No, too many people milling around the gates. If they got on the Victoria train, they could also change at Lewes for Newhaven and the ferry to Dieppe, or the train to Brighton and get off at Falmer,' said Street.

Buchanan shook his head. 'Not Falmer – remember Stephen and Morris checked her room. Of course, they could get off at any one of the stations in between Eastbourne and Victoria, including Gatwick Airport,' he said. 'Did you see if their shadow got on a train? I wasn't able to see from the camera angle.'

'They could have, I don't see them on the concourse, nor anyone with a guitar. Difficult to tell if that was Zilini and Zac.'

'If it were them, I especially would like to know if they were being followed, and if so, by whom.'

'What next?'

'Could you see if you can find out who is Zac and Zilini's agent? While you are doing that, I'm going to have another word with Michael Levitt at Mastrani. I would like to know what went wrong with the stress test on the software they are working on.'

'OK, see you when you get back.'

♦

Buchanan parked directly outside the Mastrani office and went up the steps into the reception.

'Hello, can I help you?'

'DCI Buchanan. Is Michael Levitt in? I would like a quick word with him, please.'

'One moment and I'll check. Hi Michael, there's a policeman in reception for you – yes, the same one. OK, I'll tell him.' She turned to Buchanan. 'Michael said he'd be about twenty to thirty minutes.'

'Thanks, I'll wait.'

'Would you like a coffee while you wait?'

Number four so far today, thought Buchanan. 'Any chance of a cup of tea?'

'Certainly.'

Buchanan walked over to the security desk and the security guard. 'Morning, busy today?'

'Yes, you're DCI Buchanan?'

'Yes.'

'I'm a friend of Morris, he's told me all about you.'

'All bad I hope?' said Buchanan, smiling at his apparent notoriety

'No, he says you're not bad to work for.'

'Reg,' said Buchanan, looking at the security guard's ID badge, 'do you keep a record of everyone who enters and leaves the building?'

'CCTV, you mean?'

'No, I was talking about when visitors sign in. Do you keep a log of those visits?'

'Yes, how far back?'

'The last four weeks would be helpful.'

'Could you keep an eye on the desk and I'll have a look in the back office? If anyone shows up, just tell them I'll be back in a minute.'

Buchanan was spared the duty of acting security guard as Reg returned a couple of minutes later with an A4 folder containing a printout of the daily visitor log sheets.

'I only have the last ten weeks, apparently the log sheets get shredded after then. What are you looking for?'

'Not sure, just wondered if they were still available,' said Buchanan, flicking through the pages. 'Do all visitors have to sign in and get a visitor pass?'

'Absolutely.'

'No exceptions?'

'None. Only employees who already have passes are exempt from logging in at the desk. Once through reception, everyone is tracked all-round the building, even to the toilet. It would be my job on the line if I didn't follow company rules.'

'Ah, yes, company rules, one must always adhere to company rules,' said Buchanan, watching as an employee entered reception, walked over to the internal door, swiped their ID card and entered the office. 'I get the picture. What about Barazani family members?'

'The same as everyone else – no ID, they have to sign in and get a pass.'

'How accurate are the visitor pass records?'

'Accurate to the minute.'

'Would you mind if I had a look at them while I wait for Michael?'

'No problem, as long as they stay here. You can use my office,' said Reg, pointing to a cupboard-sized room behind the security desk. You can watch for Michael while you are in there, the mirror is one-way glass.'

'Are these in any sort of order?'

'By date,' said Reg, as he leaned round the doorframe.

The office was just big enough for a small table and chair – green fabric, noticed Buchanan. He stirred his mug of tea, being careful not to knock it off the edge of the table. He was holding the end of a strand of spider silk of an idea. He was following the tramlines to a yet unknown destination. Entry by entry, he studied the names till he came to the name he was looking for: Nasim Barazani.

He took note of the page number and date and continued through the pages. It soon became apparent that Nasim visited Amal regularly each Thursday afternoon. There was a change in the proceedings about eight weeks prior. For every Nasim entry, there was also one for Achmad. This continued right up to the entry for the previous Thursday.

'Reg, a question?'

'Yes?' said Reg, leaning round the doorframe.

'Did Zilini Barazani have an employee pass?'

'Yes.'

'Thanks.'

'Sorry to keep bothering you, Reg, but are there any secure areas in the building where visitors aren't permitted to enter?'

'As long as visitors have an escort, or have been previously cleared, they can go anywhere in the building.'

Buchanan looked back at the entries for the 10th: Nasim and Achmad had arrived at five minutes to one.

'Reg, what time do people here go to lunch?'

'Who knows? There isn't a prescribed time. Inspector, Michael is here.'

Buchanan returned the binder to its shelf and left Reg's office.

'Inspector, how can I help?'

'Is there somewhere we can go to talk undisturbed?'

'The comms room, that's about as private a place as there is in this building.'

'Fine by me.'

Buchanan followed Michael down the stairs to the garage and the comms room. On the way he noticed Zilini's car still parked in its slot: her father's Rolls Royce was missing.

Michael shut the door and pointed to a chair for Buchanan. He dragged another out of the corner of the room and sat facing Buchanan.

'How can I help?' he said again.

'What is Nasim Barazani's involvement in Mastrani?'

'It's nothing technical. I believe he arranges short-term financing with the bank, and I think he's involved in the negotiations for the new building.'

'Does he visit often?'

'I'm not sure, my work doesn't involve financing.'

'Amal said you also look after security matters for the company?'

'Yes.'

'Does Nasim always come to see Amal on Thursdays?'

'Yes.'

'Does he always come alone?'

'He used to.'

'Used to?'

'Lately he's been bringing his son, Achmad.'

'Have you met Achmad?'

'A couple of times.'

'What's he like?'

'I'm not quite sure how to answer that.'

'How old would you say he is?'

'Late teens, maybe eighteen – nineteen.'

'Do you think his father is trying to entice him into following in his steps?'

'Unlikely at this point. From what I've observed Achmad is a bit churlish when he doesn't get his own way. I say this as a few weeks ago I came across him and his dad having an argument. Though, when it comes to computer games, he's a whiz. You know we create award-winning computer games here?'

'Yes, I've been told.'

'Well, as soon as Nasim goes in to see Amal, Achmad heads for the development lab and the latest games under development.'

'Unsupervised?'

'Not at first, but I suppose he became such a familiar face people just ignored him and let him enjoy himself. It wasn't always one-sided – like a lot of young men his age he is very computer savvy. He actually made some excellent suggestions and even helped resolve an issue on a new program.'

'Last Thursday, did you see Nasim here in the office?'

'Yes, but I didn't have time to talk to him.'

'Can I ask why?'

'We started running a stress test on Mustela just before midnight.'

'That would be the 10th?'

'Yes. At first all seemed to be going well, then when we put it on full load it became unstable and crashed.'

'Did it get resolved?'

'Yes, eventually.'

'In simple terms, can you explain what went wrong?'

'It was a simple issue in the end. When a team of software engineers are writing programs, they sometimes write short messages to each other and insert them into the program. In this case, someone had written a short piece of code that would make the program freeze if it became overloaded with input.'

'Sort of like a fuse in an electrical circuit?'

'Yes, you could put it that way. The software has been designed to self-learn and grows with intelligence over time.'

'Is it sorted now?'

'Spinning like a well-balanced top.'

'And you are sure this was Thursday?'

'Absolutely. We began the test just before midnight on the tenth and it crashed about three the following morning. Why are you asking? These issues come up every time a new piece of software is created.'

'Several investors have received letters, dated Thursday the 10th, warning them about issues with the latest programs being developed at Mastrani.'

'That could be an issue for the finance department, but in development we are forging ahead with the next program.'

'Which one is that? Or maybe you are unable to talk about it?'

'It's the track and trace program, a couple of the programmers have nick-named it Lucifer.'

'Not sure it will sell well with a name like that. What is the company calling it?'

'Guardian. Like the newspaper, we think it reveals the truth.'

'The error you found in Mustela – could someone have placed it there deliberately, to cause problems?'

'Are you thinking about the letter? It could just be a coincidence, or a bit of mischief, even.'

'What about the bit of code that caused the trouble?'

'It could have been lying there for weeks just waiting for the stress test to run.'

'When did you decide to schedule the stress test?'

'Three weeks ago.'

'So, if someone knew the date of the test, and they wanted to cause mischief, they could have inserted the code and just waited patiently for it to crash.'

'I suppose so.'

'Who outside the development department knew the test was going to happen?'

'Probably just about everyone in the company.'

'And outside the company?'

He thought for a moment then said, 'I suppose Nasim would know.'

'Is there anything else going on in the company that could cause someone to get agitated?'

'We're going to be moving to a new building on the other side of town.'

'Why would that get anyone agitated?'

'People don't like change. It's in a bit of an industrial area and further away from the town centre. I'm trying to oversee the Mustela test and work with BT to get our data lines rerouted into the new building.'

'Where is this building?'

'Across the road from Parker Building Supplies, it's an abandoned office building, I think BT used to use it, and after them it was used as a storage facility.'

'Who in the company would know about the finances of the company?'

'That would be Constance, she's head of finance, been with the company from day one.'

'Could you introduce me to her?'

'Sure thing. Is there anything else?' said Michael, looking at his watch.

'No, I think we've covered what I came here for.'

Buchanan followed Michael back up the stairs to the reception and Reg to collect his visitor pass.

'Connie's office is at the end of the corridor opposite Charlotte's, Inspector.'

'Logical.'

Michael pointed to the *Private, Knock Before Entering* sign on the door and duly knocked. 'Connie, it's Michael, I have a visitor for you.'

'Come in.'

'Connie, this is Detective Chief Inspector Buchanan, he's looking into the disappearance of Zilini.'

'How can I help with that, Inspector?'

'I was wondering if you can tell me how often Nasim Barazani attends the monthly progress meetings?'

'Never misses one, and a bloody nuisance it is too!'

'Why is that?'

'To maintain our overdraft facilities, his bank requires we provide a monthly cash-flow projection. Takes me hours to prepare them.'

'Is it a large overdraft?'

'The last one we were provided with was five hundred thousand.'

'Can I ask why Mastrani needs such a large overdraft?'

'Our monthly wage bill is more than seventy-five thousand pounds.'

'Does he bring anyone with him?' said Buchanan, glancing at Michael.

'No.'

'What about his son, Achmad?'

'Didn't realise he had a son.'

'Thank you, Constance, you've been a big help.'

'It's Connie, Inspector; Constance is a prissy name.'

Michael gently closed the door behind them. As they walked back to reception, he asked, 'Is there anything I should know?'

'Not at this moment.'

'But you do think something is going on?'

'All I can say is, whoever is in this game, they have already laid their cards on the table.'

◆

'How was the visit to Mastrani?' asked Street, as Buchanan eased himself into his chair. 'Was Michael any help?'

'Yes. It was a very interesting visit. Michael said that Nasim is a regular visitor to Mastrani, as is his son, Achmad.'

'His son? Why is that?'

'Possibly dad reaching out to son, trying to encourage him to follow in his footsteps.'

'And Nasim?'

'Nasim's bank provides substantial overdraft facilities to Mastrani. In return Mastrani is required to provide a monthly profit and loss projection, which Connie in finance hates.'

'I suppose all companies have an overdraft. What will happen if she fails to provide this profit and loss projection each month?'

'The bank would remove the facility and Mastrani would be at the mercy of a hostile takeover.'

'Did you find out anything about the letters that were sent to the investors?'

'Not directly, but I have a growing suspicion that either an employee or someone close to the workings of Mastrani is trying to destabilise the company.'

'What makes you think that?'

'Michael said someone had left a piece of code in the Mustela program that automatically shut down the program as it grew.'

'Was it deliberate?'

'He said it was just one of those things that happen with new programs.'

'But you think differently?'

'Yes. Michael said they ran the program on the evening of the tenth, the same day the letter was written and posted.'

'Do you suspect anyone?'

'The main candidate would be Nasim Barazani, he is in the building once a month on Thursdays for meetings. If it weren't for the fact he has no ambition other than to climb the greasy pole to a senior position in the bank, I'd put him first on my list of suspects.'

'Any other candidates?'

'There's Achmad, Nasim's son, he's about the same age as Zilini. For the last few months, he's been accompanying his father to the meetings at Mastrani.'

'Following his dad into the family business?'

Buchanan shook his head. 'I don't think so. Michael said when Nasim went into the meetings, Achmad would make a beeline to the development lab and the latest computer game. Initially he was seen as a nuisance to be accommodated, but when the techies saw just how good he was they used to have him crash-test the latest games. He even found several faults and made suggestions on how to fix them.'

'Do you think he could have planted the fault in the Mustela program?'

'It's possible, but if he did, what would be his motive?'

'I think we need to have a word with him.'

'I agree, but in the meantime, how did you get on with the phone numbers on Sam Taylor's phone?'

'After quite a few attempts I managed to get responses to the three remaining numbers. The first belonged to Yousef Barazani, the second to someone calling themselves Delilah, and the third belongs to Hiezabel Barazani.'

'Good work. How about Zac's agent?'

'What a waste of time that was! Do you have any idea how many musician agents there are in the UK?'

'No idea.'

'Too many to try, the internet is full of them.'

'So, what did you do?'

'I called the pub where they performed and asked the duty manager. I was fortunate, she said she remembered Zac and Zilini sitting with someone who Zac introduced as their manager. She didn't remember his name, but she said he did leave his card for anyone looking for an agent. I tried the number, but it went to voicemail. I left a message and asked them to call me back, urgently. I haven't had time to contact forensics about the Bulgarians' flat.'

'OK, I'll take care of that after I try Interpol.'

'I've had a thought about the ring box, want to hear it?'

Buchanan put his phone down. 'Yes, certainly.'

'I was lying in bed last night thinking about why send an empty ring box – why not the box with the ring? That's when it dawned on me: I bet they've run off to get married and the empty ring box is her way of telling her father. Remember, you said that he mentioned Zilini wanted to wear her mother's ring at her own wedding.'

'If what you say is true, it still doesn't help us find her and Zac. There's no national weekly register of marriages in the UK, only for deaths.'

'I have an idea,' said Street. 'Most musicians have a YouTube and Facebook presence.'

'What will that tell us? Anything on there would only be in the past.'

'I'm not sure, I'll try YouTube first.'

'Looks like Macalister beat me to it,' said Buchanan. 'The forensic report for the Bulgarians' flat in Eastbourne has just come in.'

'Anything unexpected?'

Buchanan scanned the report. 'Ten 0.1-gram bags of heroin, eight 2-gram bags of cocaine and forty ecstasy pills in the freezer compartment. The only other item that interests us is a broken mobile phone in the rubbish bin, which has been sent off for analysis. What's that? What did you find?'

'A video of Zac and Zilini playing at the Jenny Lind, not great quality, but it is definitely them. I'll try Facebook next. Macalister have much to say?'

'Let me have a read.'

'While you do that, I'll check Facebook.'

As Street scanned page after page of Facebook, Buchanan read down the report from Macalister till he got to the results of the DNA test on the cigar stub.

'This is weird,' he said.

'What is?' Street looked away from her computer screen.

'Remember the cigar stub I removed from Nasim's ashtray?'

'Yes, and remember I said you couldn't use it as evidence, especially since you hadn't actually seen him smoking it.'

'Do you recall what I wrapped it in?'

'Wasn't it a tissue that Hiezabel passed you to wipe up your spilled drink?'

He nodded. 'The report says the DNA on the tissue matches one set of DNA on the cigar-stub I pinched from Nasim's ashtray and it also matches one set of DNA found on the cigar-stub found by the garage in Westham.'

'So, if I understand you correctly, Hiezabel's and Nasim's DNA was found at the garage where Sam was dismembered?'

'Looks that way.'

Street shook her head slowly. 'I just can't see Hiezabel holding a chainsaw and cutting Sam up. So, if it wasn't her, it must be Nasim.'

'That is one possibility.'

'What about the chairs at the Mastrani telecoms room? I don't remember them being tested by forensics.'

'They were tested last week. The report says - samples of green fibres, floor dust, etc. taken from chairs in the comms room at Mastrani do not match those from the body of Sam or any other samples.'

'So, where does that leave us?'

'I think it's time for us to go and see Nasim and ask a few awkward questions. Would you drive? I need to do some constructive thinking.'

15

Friday 18th
Father and Son

Street turned off Marshfoot Lane and parked in front of the open doors of Nasim's garage. There were a pair of overall-clad legs lying on a crawler sticking out from under the chassis of a brightly coloured touring car. The chassis, minus its wheels, was sitting on bright-red floor jacks. The slicks, mounted on aluminium hubs, were stacked in the far end of the garage.

The sound of Buchanan and Street approaching the garage attracted the attention of the body under the car.

'Bahija,' shouted Nasim, from under the car, 'pass me the torque wrench with the fourteen-millimetre socket. It's on the bench beside the box of brake pads.'

Street stepped into the garage, nodded to Buchanan regarding the cigar smouldering in an ashtray, then picked up the torque wrench and put it in Nasim's outstretched hand.

'It's Detective Sergeant Street, Mr Barazani,' she said. 'Inspector Buchanan is also with me.'

Nasim lay the torque wrench on his legs, pushed himself out from under the car and stood up smiling.

'Like it? Just got it back from the paint shop.'

'It's yours?' asked Buchanan.

'Yes.'

'BMW 330i?' said Street.

'You know your cars,' remarked Nasim.

'My husband is a bit of a petrol head; I just watch them race.'

'You surprise me, Nasim,' said Buchanan.

'You thought I was just some sort of boring bank clerk that spent his days looking at figures, am I right?'

Buchanan nodded. 'Yes, I must admit I had you as just that. Do you drive the car as well as maintaining it?'

'I drive, but the tuning of this high-performance touring car I leave to my friend Toby. He's the expert when it comes to tuning the engine, I'm just the monkey on the end of the wrench.'

'An expensive hobby?'

'Yes but, being an accountant, I keep a keen eye on expenditure. And before you ask the obvious questions, I just compete for the fun of it. I have a few trophies for coming fourth and that is all.'

'Something we have in common,' said Buchanan.

'You race touring cars?'

'No,' said Buchanan, 'my ride only had one horsepower. I came fourth in the Castlewood Cup a few months ago. It was a cross-country ride for non-professional riders at Castlewood Country Club.'

'I suppose you are not here to talk about cars. Is it about Zilini? Have you found her?'

'Not yet,' said Buchanan, watching Nasim walk over to the workbench and pick up the cigar.

'Really,' said Nasim, relighting it. 'It's been two weeks since she went missing – what have you been doing all this time?'

'It's a complicated case, Nasim.'

'So, how can I help?'

'This may seem a strange question to you, but does your mother smoke cigars?'

Nasim chuckled quietly. 'If you were to ask her, she would flatly deny it.'

'But you know differently?'

'She doesn't smoke them at home, but I've caught her picking mine up from the ashtray and sneaking a quick puff when she thinks I'm not watching. She's not supposed to be smoking anything anymore. She had cancer and had to have part of her right lung removed a few years ago.'

'What about Achmad? Does he smoke?'

'No, though it doesn't stop him from sneaking some of my cigar stubs I casually leave in the ashtray. I'd rather he did that than smoking full time.'

'Would it bother you if he did?'

'I don't know, never thought about it. Why would you ask that question?'

'Just clearing up some loose ends. Is Achmad at home just now?'

'What's he done to get you two here?'

Buchanan smiled. 'Nothing that we're aware of. We would just like to have a chat with him.'

'Good, you had me worried for a moment.'

'Is he in the habit of causing you to worry?'

'Only about his schoolwork, spends too much time on his computer playing games. I think he's on the patio; if you'll follow me, I'll take you through.'

'Achmad,' said Nasim as they stepped out onto the patio, 'if you can tear yourself away from playing games, the inspector would like to ask you a question.'

Achmad looked up from his laptop screen, eyed Buchanan and Street, then resumed playing his game.

'What's the game?' asked Street.

'Fortnite,' replied Achmad, continuing to stare at the screen while his hands darted across the keyboard.

'My husband plays that with his friends. What tier are you on?'

Achmad looked up at Street. 'You play Fortnite?'

'No, computer games are not my thing. I prefer to watch YouTube videos on gardening.'

'If you like gardening, there are good gardening games you could play.'

'Could you recommend one?'

He shrugged. 'What kind of phone do you have?'

'Samsung Note10.'

'Have a look on Google Play. There's plenty of them on there.'

'Achmad,' said Buchanan, 'when was the last time you saw your cousin Zilini?'

'Months ago, I don't remember the date.'

'Do you have any idea where she might have gone to?'

'Ask her boyfriend,' he said, resuming his game.

'We would if we knew where he was.'

'Achmad,' said Nasim. 'The policeman asked you a question, have the courtesy to look at him when answering.'

'They could be dead for all I care,' he said, smiling at an inner thought and still staring at his screen. 'Then I would be in line to inherit the Barazani empire instead of my cousin.' He looked up from his screen at his father.

'Is inheriting your uncle's company important to you?' asked Street.

'Zilini's just a woman, she should be at home having babies and keeping house for her husband.'

'Do you think her boyfriend is a suitable husband?'

'Him, he's just a musician.'

'Would *you* make a suitable husband?' asked Street.

'If I was, she'd do as she was told and not go gallivanting around the country disgracing the family name.'

'Do you like her?'

'That's a silly question.'

'Achmad,' Buchanan asked, 'when you are visiting Mastrani, do you help them with their programs?'

'What do you mean?'

'For instance, if you see an issue with one, would you suggest a correction?'

Achmad smiled. 'Some of their techies are stupid.'

'In what way?'

He looked to see if his father was in earshot.

'I leave them little puzzles, just to see if they are awake.'

'You mean you sabotage the programs?'

'No, of course not. Why would I do that?'

'Did you leave a message in the Mustela program?'

Achmad turned away and looked down at his game.

'Thank you, Achmad, I'll take your silence as a yes. If you think of anything, your dad has our phone number.'

'Achmad,' said Street as they were leaving, 'have you tried TOCA? I hear there is a 2021 version about to be released. Look it up, you can find it on Google play and the Apple app store.'

♦

'What was all that chat about computer games?' asked Buchanan, as they drove back to the station.

'It's the best way to talk to gamers. At least that's what Stephen's dad says about Olli, Stephen's youngest brother. That and hiding the game charger.'

'Why hide the game charger?'

'Because you can't play the game with a flat battery, his dad says it is a better way to limit time on the game.'

'And the reference to TOCA, whatever that is?'

'TOCA stands for Touring Car Association and is also used to describe a computer game about touring car racing. Stephen used to play it before he got involved in Fortnite.'

'I see what you were up to. Trying to get father and son on the same page?'

'Yep. What did you think about Nasim's statement about his mother smoking his cigars when she thought he wasn't watching?'

'Probably the best piece of information we've had in days, but I can't quite see where it fits into the equation. To use your analogy of computer games, if this case was a game it could be called *Who smokes Nasim's cigars?*'

'I'd stick to the day job,' said Street. 'It's lunch time, I'm hungry.'

'I'll stop at Poppy Seed on the way back to the office.'

16
Friday 18th
Message from Germany

Buchanan unwrapped his sandwich and tapped the mouse button on his computer to check for emails.

'This is interesting,' he said, about to take a bite of his sandwich, 'I have a response to my enquiry about Toma Baretata and Dimitar Lupov.'

'What does it say?' asked Street, as she dipped her spoon in her yogurt pot.

'Quite a bit. They were apprehended three days ago by the German police in a Hamburg nightclub for fighting with one of the customers. Toma Baretata was shot and killed by the customer during the scuffle. Dimitar Lupov survived and is currently in prison waiting on information about any previous convictions and outstanding arrest warrants.'

'I suppose we'll be last on the list for extradition requests?'

'That depends on what there is outstanding. But in the meantime, the German police have been excellent in doing our job for us.'

'Coffee?'

Buchanan nodded. 'Yes, instant will do. I'll have a read of this while you make it.'

Street returned a few minutes later and placed Buchanan's coffee on his desk.

'Thanks, shall I read, or do you want a copy of their report? It's a transcript of the interview, thankfully it was done in English'

'I'd prefer the sound of your voice; promise I won't fall asleep.'

'OK, here goes.

♦

'Det Fernau, 08:00 hours, Wednesday 16th. Interview with Dimitar Lupov, arrested at The Blue Diamond club on Sunday 13th, 01:17

271

hours. Dimitar Lupov, you are charged with attempted sexual assault on Ingrid Becker. What do you have to say about the charge?'

Lupov	Assault her, me? It should be her who is charged, the whore.
Fernau	You deny forcing her into a doorway and attempting to remove her dress in the alleyway outside the club?
Lupov	It was she who pulled me into the doorway.'
Fernau	Why were you outside in the alleyway?
Lupov	You, a policeman, asking a question like that?
Fernau	For the record, please answer my question.
Lupov	She invited me out for some fresh air.
Fernau.	What happened after you were pulled into the doorway?
Lupov	Her boyfriend attacked me, at least that's who he said he was. He said I'd made an inappropriate advance to his girlfriend.'
Fernau.	What happened next?
Lupov	Toma saw the boyfriend had a gun and was going to shoot me. So, he grabbed the arm of the boyfriend and in the scuffle the gun went off twice, killing Toma and then the woman.
Fernau	What did you do after the gun went off?
Lupov	I went to stop the bleeding, but it was a pointless effort, the bullet went through Toma's face. He was dead before he hit the floor.
Fernau	And the woman?
Lupov	She must have been startled by the noise of the gunshot and stepped in front of the gun as the boyfriend fired his second shot.
Fernau	Did the boyfriend try to help?
Lupov	No, as soon as he saw the woman was dead, he ran off. I got the impression it was a set-up. I think we were both supposed to

	die.
Fernau	Why do you think it was a set-up?
Lupov	I've seen those types of killings before. The bullet through the face is a hitman's target designed to obliterate the identity of the victim. Besides, who wears a bullet-proof facemask?
Fernau	Dimitar, I have been asked by the British police to ask you some questions concerning an incident near Eastbourne in Sussex.
Lupov	I have nothing to say.
Fernau	You are refusing to answer?
Lupov	I have nothing to say.
Fernau	Dimitar Lupov, till we investigate further, you will be kept here in custody. End of interview.'

'That's quite a turn-up for the books,' said Street. 'Do you think the shooting could have anything to do with our case?'

'An excellent question, for which I have no answer.'

'Was there anything else?'

'Yes, quite a bit. I am very impressed by the German police's thoroughness of their investigations. Both of them had their fingerprints taken, and identities confirmed. As we previously found out, they are both career criminals. Their DNA has been determined and, according to the information I sent with my enquiry, they are the two who were involved with the dismemberment and burial of Sam.'

'That's a very professional report,' said Street.

Buchanan smiled and leaned back in his chair. 'But that's not all. We also have a phone call found on Lupov's phone. The transcriber doesn't know who was actually phoning, so they just used the names, Lupov and Caller. The message was dated Wednesday 2nd at two thirty-five in the afternoon.'

'Why would Lupov record a phone call and not just delete it?'

'Maybe to blackmail the caller,' said Buchanan, and since you like the sound of my voice, I'll read it to you.

Caller	I need the car, tonight.
Lupov	You want the car?'
Caller	Yes.
Lupov	You realise it's being followed?'
Caller	By who?
Lupov	Some private cop.
Caller	Not the police, is it?
Lupov	No. They are too good for that. These guys are professionals.
Caller	Change the plates and give me the car this evening for a couple of hours then you can have it back.
Lupov	What you want with it?
Caller	It's personal, no need for you to know.
Lupov	Where do you want it dropped off?
Caller	I'll be waiting by the pier.
Lupov	What time? I don't want to be caught with it.
Caller	Nine-thirty, it will be dark then, make sure you're not late.

'I wonder who the caller was?' mused Buchanan. 'I have the number; shall I call it and find out?'

'I'm all ears.'

Buchanan dialled the number then pressed the speaker button on his phone. The phone rang seven times then went to voicemail.

'Hi, it's Nasim. If you get this message it means I'm busy, leave your name and number and I'll get back to you.'

'That's a puzzler,' said Buchanan, 'Nasim's phone – now why would that be? Why – how does he come to be connected to the Bulgarians? It just doesn't make sense.'

'Is there anything else in the report?'

'Several text messages found on Lupov's phone, mostly in Bulgarian between Lupov and someone we yet don't know.'

Street looked at the printout, 'Nothing about text messages to Nasim's phone. You said mostly in Bulgarian – I take it that there are English ones as well?'

'Yes. The Bulgarian text messages are mostly to do with them dealing in drugs and gambling, not part of our investigations, and this English one does. It makes for strange reading. It is timed at just before one the morning of the Thursday 3rd, and I presume that is European time, which would put it at just before midnight on the 2nd here. Let me read it to you:

♦

Other	I need you, there's been an accident here, he's dead.
Lupov	You stupid shit, why you do that? The boy never did you harm.
Other	He tried to blackmail me. Just get here.
Lupov	No good, we not in country, back Friday.
Other	OK, Friday will have to do
Lupov	How bad is it?
Other	I've got sheets and newspapers, but we still need to get rid of the body.
Lupov	It will cost you, disposing of bodies in your country is not easy.
Other	You'll get your money.
Lupov	We want cash.
Other	Don't worry, you'll get paid.
Lupov	Dimi has an idea where he can get a van and where we get rid of body. Where to meet you?
Other	Stupid question. You know where.
Lupov	What time to meet?
Other	After dark, I will leave the padlock undone, drive in and you can use the back door to load up.'

'That's interesting, I wonder who was doing the texting?' said Buchanan

'Now all we have to do is find whose phone that was, and we'll find Sam's killer.'

'Do you still think Nasim is the prime suspect?' asked Street. 'If so, what could his motive be?'

'I don't know. Earlier today we saw where his interests lay; I wouldn't mind having a drive round Brands Hatch in that car. I think we need to return and have further words with Nasim.'

'Shall I drive? Let your little grey cells have a snooze?'

'Yes, please.'

♦

The garage doors were still open when they arrived, but the wheels were now attached to the BMW and it sat on the driveway dripping wet from being washed. The sound of someone singing came from the far side of the car.

'Nasim, it's Inspector Buchanan and Sergeant Street.'

The sound of a sponge being dropped into a bucket preceded the appearance of Nasim from the far side of the car.

'Inspector, back so soon? Did you forget something?'

'Just a short visit, Nasim. Did you get a phone call from me earlier?'

'I wouldn't know, the phone's on the charger in my study. Do you want me to go and check?'

'Yes, please. No rush, we'll come with you.'

'Where are you going with this?' asked Street quietly as they followed Nasim through the garage to his office.

'Not sure at the moment. Let's just play it by ear.'

Nasim's study was directly across a narrow hallway from the internal garage door.

'Here's the phone and is this your number?' Nasim asked, showing the phone display to Buchanan.

'Yes.'

'And you left me a message?' He dialled his voicemail.

'Yes.'

Nasim nodded. 'Yes, got your message. Still want me to call?'

'That won't be necessary. Do you get a regular phone bill?'

'Monthly.'

'Do you review your calls?'

'No. I have a lot better things to do with my time than read old phone bills.'

'Would you happen to have the latest one here at your home?'

'Sure, but it's not printed, it's online. I presume your interest is more than just cursory. Still looking for Zilini?'

'Yes.'

'Would a printed copy suffice?'

'That would be most helpful.'

'Just a minute, I need to turn the printer on.'

Street gave Buchanan an inquisitive look, he put his finger to his lips and smiled.

'I hadn't realised how many calls I make on that phone,' said Nasim, handing the printed phone bill to Buchanan.

'I have the same issue,' said Buchanan, while scanning it. 'Nasim, do you recognise these numbers?'

'Which ones?'

'These three here.'

'No, don't recognise them. I make many calls every month. I'd have to go through my telephone directory to find out who those numbers belong to.'

'Do you carry your phone with you?'

'This is my personal phone. While I'm in the house, I just leave it on the charging stand. My business phone I keep in my briefcase and take with me when I go to work. It's the only way I can separate business and pleasure.'

'I see. Do you keep your office locked while you are not here?'

'No, why should I?'

'So, anyone could use it?'

'I suppose so – why?'

'And your computer and printer?'

'Yes. The computer is a high-spec model. Achmad sometimes uses it for his studies.'

'So Achmad has access to your office, computer and mobile phone?'

'You suspect Achmad?' he said, shaking his head. 'He would have no need to use my phone, he has his own phone, in fact he has several phones. I give him my old phones when I get a new one.'

'How old is your current phone?'

'I usually replace them when a new model comes out. I think I've had this one for about ten months.'

'And you don't recognise those numbers?'

'Sorry, Inspector. I could look them up in my phone directory if that is helpful.'

'That won't be necessary, thank you.'

'Anything else, Inspector?'

'Just one thing. Do you always work from home on Thursdays?'

'Most Thursdays and Fridays. Thursdays are my days to go and visit local customers. I find it is easier to get the pulse of a customer if you see them in action. Inviting them to attend a meeting at the bank sometimes creates too formal an atmosphere.'

'Is Mastrani on your list of Thursday customers?'

'It is.'

'And how were they when I assume you visited them – yesterday?'

'They were fine.'

'Finances OK?'

'Like any business they have their ups and downs.'

'Are they having an up, or a down, movement at the moment?'

'I'd say they are currently having an up movement.'

'Why is that?'

'We, I mean they, are about to complete on the acquisition of new premises.'

'I thought they were happy where they were?'

'They are. It's just with the expansion on the product range they will need to take on more staff. I'm sure you've seen just how congested the offices are.'

'Does that mean they will be leaving town?'

'No. The new building is only about a mile from their existing building, it's an old BT office. It has a remarkable similarity to the existing premises, even to having under-building parking.'

'When do they expect to be moving?'

'We – sorry, I keep saying we. The bank I represent is providing a bridging loan to facilitate a speedy transition from the old premises to the new one. The process should be complete by the end of next month.'

'Thursdays are the days your stepniece has music lessons with your wife?'

'Yes.'

'Do you make many calls on customers on Thursdays?'

'It's always a full day.'

'And your mother visits and bakes on Thursdays?'

'Most Thursdays. We sometimes bump heads, so she takes the opportunity to visit while I'm out.'

'Nasim, when you work from home on Thursdays, do you bring client documents home with you?'

'Yes, sometimes. My home office is much quieter than the one at the bank.'

'How about Mastrani documents.'

'Such as?'

'When I talked to Mr Zhukovski, he informed me his company had been asked to do DBS checks on several prospective employees for a project Mastrani were about to commence.'

Nasim nodded. 'Yes, that is so, we did ask him to do that.'

'When you say we, I'm assuming you are included in the we?'

'Yes, but why are you asking these questions?'

'Let me continue. Am I also correct in thinking you would have a copy of this list in your office?'

'Yes.'

'Would this list of names form part of the proposal to finance the pending new project that Mastrani were about to start?'

'Yes, it is a government contract hence the requirement to vet all prospective employees.'

'And you would have this proposal at home with you?'

'I suppose so, yes, of course I would. Like I said, my home office is more peaceful than my office at the bank.'

'Do you know how many of the names on that list were employed for the project?'

'No, that's nothing to do with the bank.'

'Thank you, Nasim, I think we have taken up too much of your time today.'

'That's all right, you have a job to do.'

'When's your next race?'

'Two months' time, I've got a track day tomorrow. Thanks to you, Sergeant, I'm taking Achmad for a spin. Who knows, maybe he'll see the difference between staring at life through a computer screen to seeing life through the screen of a real race car.'

♦

'Well done, Jill. I do believe you have made a real difference there in the Barazani family. Father and son may finally have found something to unite them, well done.'

'Thanks, I was just saying the obvious, doing what came naturally.'

'Well, whatever it was, I think it worked.'

'Nasim now out of contention for being behind what's been going on?'

'I'm reserving judgement on that case.'

'What about Yousef?'

'Same.'

As they made their way back to the station, Street asked, 'If Nasim is no longer a suspect – and by that, I imagine Achmad is also out of the picture – what is going on?'

'Since we can now assume Zilini is safe and can no longer be used to coerce Amal Barazani, whoever is behind the crime must be getting desperate. They are going all out to discredit him and are now trying to wrest the control of Mastrani away.'

'Any suspects in mind?'

'A couple, but I want to keep that to myself for now.'

'Are we working late?' queried Street, looking at the time on the dashboard.

'No, let's check if there's any messages for us first, then we can have an early night.'

'You call six o'clock early?'

'It is for a policeman who works the day shift.'

Street turned off the office light and was about to shut the door when Buchanan's desk phone started ringing.

'Shall I get it?' she said to Buchanan, who was already three paces down the corridor.

'No, I'll get it, you go on home.'

In spite of Buchanan's suggestion, Street stood by the office door as he answered the call. He listened for a while, then said, 'OK, don't worry, we'll be right over.'

As Buchanan put down the receiver Street asked, 'And where is right over?'

'Amal Barazani's. He's being blackmailed.'

281

17
Friday 18th
Blackmail

Buchanan parked in front of Amal Barazani's house. As he got out of the car the front door was opened by Darsameen.

'Hello Darsameen, we're here to see Amal.'

'Yes, I know. He's in his study.'

Buchanan and Street followed Darsameen along the hallway to Amal's study. She stopped at the door and knocked. 'Mr Barazani, the Inspector and Sergeant are here.'

'Come in, come in.'

Amal Barazani was slumped in his chair, and to Buchanan's eyes he'd aged ten years. His shoulders were drooped, his face unshaved, and his hair looked like it had just had a cat chase a squirrel through it.

'Please sit,' he said, indicating two chairs by the window. 'Jack, what you see is a broken man. I've ascended to heights unknown to many men, and now I have descended into the very depths of hell. I'm ruined, all this will have to go,' he gestured with his hands. 'I just cannot see anyway back up.'

'In your phone call you said you were being blackmailed?'

'Here,' Amal said, passing a typed sheet of paper. 'It's an email I received it just before I left the office. Read it and weep; it's my death sentence.'

> Amal Barazani, I am well aware sc2tbxc2gda2eg is your computer password. Let's get right to the point, you don't know me, and you are most likely wondering why you are getting this email. Absolutely no one has paid me to check on you. Actually, I placed a particular piece of tracking software on the websites you have been browsing and also on your computer. This software has given me access to your

keyboard and webcam. You are a naughty boy, do your family and business acquaintances know just what you get up to while watching those websites on the dark web? I have been tracking and recording your browsing history. The videos of what you were salivating over, if it was known, would get you many years in jail –

'Amal,' said Buchanan, 'this is just another version of sextortion emails. It's a well-known scam, nothing for you to worry about.'

'But they say they will send copies of it to all of my contacts. True or false, I'm ruined.'

'Amal, it's a scam.'

'You didn't read it to the end, try reading the penultimate paragraph.'

Buchanan looked back at the email and read quietly to himself. He read the relevant paragraph then looked up at Barazani, who by now had tears in his eyes.

'It accuses me of beating my wife so badly she took her own life and Zilini, – how could anyone accuse me of doing that to my own daughter?'

'This is worrying,' said Buchanan. 'Someone has taken the wording of a well-known scam email and doctored it to make you out to be a wife beater and paedophile. This has to be someone close to the family. Someone who knows that Zilini has disappeared and is inferring she has run away from an abusive father.'

'But the password, it's my password. If it's a scam, how do they know my password?'

'It's your current password?'

'No, thankfully. Zhukovski advised us all to change them regularly, mine was just changed three weeks ago.'

'Let me be blunt, is there any truth to this email?'

'No, of course not. Pornography in all its forms is anathema to me.'

'If this person was to follow through on their threat to send this email to your contacts, what would be the ramifications?'

'I'd be ruined, people would say there's no smoke without fire. The bank would withdraw financing, my own reserves wouldn't last more than a few weeks. Worst of all, the family would ostracise me. I'd be forced to sell Mastrani, probably at a severely devalued price.'

'If that were the case, who do you see as a possible candidate to purchase the company?'

'Take your choice, just about any one of a thousand companies would be interested in purchasing a top-notch company at a knockdown price.'

There was a knock at the door, followed by Charlotte's voice. 'Amal, can I come in?'

'Yes, it's only the police who are with me.'

The door opened and Charlotte entered, walked over to Barazani, wrapped her arms round his shoulders and hugged him. 'I heard you've been the victim of a scam email. How bad is it, my lovely?'

'It couldn't be much worse. We're ruined, Charlotte.'

Charlotte let go of Barazani and turned to Buchanan. 'Can't you do something about this?

'The email says Amal has seventy-two hours to put the company up for sale, or else the accusations will be made public. I believe this email is a hoax. I believe Amal when he says there isn't any truth to the accusations. So, who stands out as a potential purchaser of the company? Do either of you have any ideas?'

Charlotte shook her head and as she stood behind Amal, massaged his shoulders.

Barazani reached up and squeezed her left hand. 'Thank you, my dear, we'll get through this somehow, I just know we will.'

Charlotte took a deep breath and asked, 'Would anyone like something to drink?'

'Coffees all round,' said Barazani.

'Thanks.'

'If you'll excuse me,' said Buchanan, 'I just need to call my wife and let her know I'll be late for dinner. Jill, you can call Stephen for a lift if you want.'

Street shook her head, 'That's OK. I think it's more important I stay with you. I'll tell him to get his own dinner.'

♦

The door opened and Darsameen entered carrying a tray of sandwiches, followed by Charlotte with a jug of coffee and five cups. Buchanan took a second look at Charlotte's left hand: where once it had been a plain, unadorned hand, it now sported a wedding band.

Charlotte noticed Buchanan looking at the five cups. 'Darsameen is part of the family, Inspector. And since this is family business, she has every right to sit in on the discussions: we have no secrets between us.'

'Fine by me.'

'Where will you start, Inspector?' said Charlotte.

'I think at the beginning would be best. Amal has given me an outline of how the family functions. I've also talked to everyone in the family. But the one part of your family history, the one that is mentioned in the email about what happened to the first Mrs Barazani, I know nothing about. And I did notice, Charlotte,' said Buchanan, nodding towards her hand.

'I thought it was time to end the pretence,' she said, looking intently at the recently added wedding band on her left hand.

Barazani put down his coffee, took a deep breath and began his story. 'I was 18 when Ruth and I met. We were at a dance on Brighton seafront. It was a perfect place for a drink on the seafront. It had a cosy atmosphere inside and plenty of seats outside for enjoying a nice sunny day. We got on well and arranged to meet the next week by the clock near the station. Over the next few months, we would walk the seafront eating ice creams, or, when we were hungry, fish and chips; we shared the fish.

'Occasionally when we could afford it, we'd go to the cinema. I had a part-time job in a shop that bought and sold second-hand phones and computer games, while Ruth, who was a year older, worked as a waitress. Later she moved on to work for a plumbing company as their bookkeeper.

'We seemed to always be broke, but that was all right, we were happy being in each other's company. Entertainment was expensive so we did not go out very often. There was a pub close to our one-room flat. The manager must have realised our situation because he never said anything when we'd nurse one drink all night between us. We got married a couple of years later and just as the UK economy was slowing to a stop, Ruth fell pregnant with Zilini.

'Ruth was very happy when she was pregnant, and I was ecstatic. But soon after Zilini was born, things started to go wrong. Ruth became withdrawn, wouldn't speak and I had to face finding someone to look after Zilini when I was at work. That is when Darsameen joined the family, so to speak.

'Eventually I took Ruth to the doctor who diagnosed severe postnatal depression and prescribed time in hospital. When she came home her personality had changed – she was paranoid, withdrawn and would stare into space for hours. I argued with the doctor that her medications were wrong. He just said when I got my medical degree to come back to him and we'd discuss Ruth's medications. If we'd been in the same room, I'd have throttled him.

'I was devastated, but since I had Zilini to look after, a mortgage for this house to pay, a fledgling software company to keep afloat and Ruth to see in the evenings – I just had to soldier on.

'I don't know what I would have done without Darsameen. When things got really bad, she just stepped in and took over the responsibility of looking after Zilini while I was at work and Ruth was in hospital. She's really the only mother Zilini has known.

'Ruth spent almost a year in hospital, but there then followed a period of several months during which she was living happily at home, taking Zilini to the park, to cafés, and on walks to visit friends. But it wasn't to last. Ruth went downhill fast and was soon readmitted to hospital. I just didn't understand why it could happen again. I thought she'd been cured.

'The fateful day arrived about four months after her second stay in hospital, I was in Germany at a trade show. I got a phone call from Charlotte, she was just my secretary at that point. Darsameen had gone out with Zilini for walk, when she returned, Ruth was dead. She'd overdosed on her medication.'

'So just about everyone in the family knew about Ruth?' asked Buchanan.

'It's such a cruel thing to put in the email,' said Charlotte. 'Amal was dedicated to his wife.'

'Do you suspect anyone in the family of sending this email?'

Both Amal and Charlotte shook their heads; Darsameen sat silently, frowning.

'Darsameen, do you have any thoughts on this matter?'

'No, sorry, Inspector. I only know about what happens in the house.'

'Darsameen,' said Buchanan, cocking his head to one side and smiling at her, 'when was the last time you spoke to Zilini?'

'It was the Friday she went missing.'

'And not since?'

'No,' she said, shaking her head.

'What should I do, Jack?' asked Barazani.

'In the case of blackmail and in this case, when it is mixed with extortion, I'd sit tight and let them show their hand.'

'But they said I have seventy-two hours to put Mastrani on the market, and that was two hours ago.'

'Then that gives us seventy hours to catch them,' said Buchanan, standing up. 'I think it's time to flush the culprit out of hiding. Are you ready, Jill?'

♦

'Back to the office?' queried Street.

'Yes and no. Yes, to drop you off, and the no is, looking at your face, I'd say you could do with putting your feet up. Tomorrow is going to be a full-on day. We've got to knock this case on the head before anyone else gets hurt.'

'Thanks.'

18
Saturday 19th early
Deadline

Buchanan squinted at his bedside clock, at least it was only six-thirty – fifty hours to go before the threat to release the damaging email. He got out of bed, dressed and went down to the kitchen for his breakfast. He'd just dropped two slices of whole-wheat bread into the toaster when Karen, wrapped in her dressing gown, entered the kitchen.

'Not sleepy?' asked Buchanan.

'Not when my man is going into battle.'

'Is that how you see what I do, fighting battles?'

'You fight not against flesh and blood, but against principalities and powers of darkness.'

'A bit early for a sermon, my dear, you're sounding a bit like Travis.'

'It's never too early for prayer, some of the greatest men and women in history relied on prayer. If you had time, I'd go through history's list of great men and women who prayed.'

'Some day, but not this morning. Would you like some toast?'

'No thanks, coffee will be fine. I'll have breakfast with Poppy later.'

'You still going shopping?'

'Yes, and I suppose with you and Jill working this morning, Poppy and I will be going alone?'

'I'm afraid so. This case is turning into a real mess, especially since we now have this deadline to either solve this case, or Amal Barazani will lose his business, his reputation, and all that he's worked hard to build.'

'Do you have any ideas as to who is behind these threats?'

'There are several candidates, one I think fits the bill. But when I try and put the pieces together, the picture looks like Picasso's picture of Adrianna.'

'Well, I hope your day goes well and you can soon wrap up the case.'

'Thanks.'

'You're welcome,' said Karen, yawning. 'I'm off back to bed, see you at dinner time.'

♦

'It's this case, it's so frustrating,' said Buchanan, as he leaned back in his chair. 'Every time I think we're making progress; we end up getting shunted into a siding.'

'Where shall we start?' asked Street, as she dipped her cinnamon roll into her coffee.

'There's a few things that stand out to me,' said Buchanan, 'the first being, who engaged the services of the two Bulgarians, and also, who arranged their payment? Contract killing is an expensive enterprise.'

'What about the garage on Peelings Lane?' asked Street. 'You saw how well hidden the garage door was by the brambles, and why there anyway? It would have been much simpler to have driven out onto the marshes and lose the body in one of the numerous ditches. It would have been months before anyone found it.'

'The cigar stub DNA bothers me. Nasim told us that both his mother and son Achmad sneak occasional puffs on his cigars and all three of their DNA was found on the cigar stubs found at the garage on Peelings Lane. Oh, did you get any response to your enquiry with Zac and Zilini's agent?'

'I just talked to their agent, he said he'd managed to book them for a performance on the Towersey open mike stage as the Taylor Jazz Duo.'

'Where are they now?'

'Their agent said they were going off on a honeymoon to Paris. I don't think it would do any good to call round the hotels in Paris – there must be hundreds of them.'

'I wonder if they have any idea of what chaos they have left behind them? Though it would be good to catch up with the two lovebirds. Zac has the answers to a lot of questions I would like to ask. But since he's not currently available, I guess we'll just have to soldier on.'

'What do you propose we do?'

'I would like to have a quick word with Nasim, then go on to have a talk with Yousef and Hiezabel.'

'We've probably missed Nasim. Remember he said he was taking Achmad for a track day at Brands Hatch?'

'Would you give him a call and see if he's still at home? Tell him it will only take a few minutes. In the meantime, I need to go down the hall.'

'He's still home,' said Street, as Buchanan returned. 'I said we'd be with him in twenty minutes.'

'What did he say to that?'

'Don't be long.'

'Well, let's get going.'

♦

Buchanan had to park in the street on account of a large Range Rover 4X4 with Nasim's touring car strapped down on the attached trailer. Achmad was loading spare wheels onto the trailer.

'Life in the Barazani family is definitely changing for the better,' said Street. 'Is that a cigar Achmad is smoking?'

'Like father, like son,' said Buchanan, removing the key from the ignition.

'Ah, Inspector,' said Achmad, 'we were just about to leave. Dad's in the kitchen getting our lunch, he'll be right out.'

'Actually,' said Buchanan, 'it's you I want to talk with.'

'Oh?'

'Were you home on Wednesday evening of the 2nd?'

'Yes.'

'Do you remember what time you went to bed?'

'I went to bed after I watched West Ham play Chelsea.'

'What time was that? I don't get time to watch TV during the week.'

'The game ended about nine o'clock. After the game I watched the post-match commentary and went to bed after that, about ten-thirty.'

'Did you watch the game alone?'

'Yes. Mum and Dad had friends over for dinner.'

'Your mother made dinner?'

'No, she was in the kitchen doing the ironing.'

'Who made the dinner if your mother was doing the ironing?'

'Grandma.'

'And you are sure this was two weeks ago, Wednesday evening?'

'Yes, Chelsea lost.'

'Thanks.'

'Inspector,' said Nasim, as he walked out of the garage, 'sorry, not much time to chat. How can I help?'

'Two weeks ago, Wednesday evening, you were at home?'

'Yes, we had some friends over for dinner.'

'Achmad was telling me your mother cooked dinner for you.'

'Yes, she's a great cook, especially when it comes to food from the homeland. Also, it gives her something to do when Yousef is away.'

'Did she stay for dinner?'

'No. She said she was going to spend the evening with a friend.'

'Do you know which friend?'

'No. Why?'

'Just tying up loose ends. You and Achmad are off to Brands Hatch?'

'Yes, Achmad is going to get a baptism today. He thinks computer games are better than the real thing.'

'I guess he's in for a surprise,' said Buchanan.

'He certainly is. See you,' said Nasim, as he climbed into the Rover.

♦

As they drove. Street looked at Buchanan. He reminded her of a dog following a scent, determined to hunt until he had tracked down his quarry.

'Looks like they are home,' she said. 'I wonder if they are holding a workshop today?'

'Let's go find out,' said Buchanan, opening his car door. 'There's only one person I really want to talk to.'

'Hiezabel?'

'No, I'm primarily interested in having a long chat with Yousef.'

'Good morning,' said a twentyish female dressed in a tight-fitting white blouse with a black pencil skirt and holding a blue clipboard. 'You're a bit early, the workshop doesn't begin till ten-thirty. Can I have your names, please?' She raised her pen to check off the early arrivals for this Saturday's workshop.

Buchanan winked at Street. 'Yes, it's Detective Chief Inspector Buchanan and Detective Sergeant Street.'

She frowned and shook her head. 'Oh dear, I'm so sorry, but you're not on the list. Do you have your invitation with you?'

Buchanan smiled, reached into his jacket and took out his warrant card. 'I'm sorry, please excuse me, I'm having a bit of sport with you. We aren't here for the workshop, we're here to see Mr Barazani.'

'Oh, I'm sorry, but I don't think he will have time to see you today. He's preparing for his workshop.'

'Miss,' said Buchanan, looking at her name tag while trying not to look at her ample cleavage, 'Miss Annabel, this is police business. Would you please let Mr Barazani know we're here to ask him some questions?'

'Oh, sorry, now I remember you. If you'll just wait a minute, I'll go and let him know you are waiting.'

The door closed and Buchanan and Street were left standing looking at a well-oiled oak door complete with antiqued iron hardware.

'She has lovely hair,' said Street. 'Wish mine shone like hers''

A few minutes later the door was opened, not by Annabel, but by Hiezabel. 'What do you want? Can't you leave us alone to get on with our affairs?'

'We would like to talk to you both about Sam Taylor, we shan't keep you long.'

'You've got five minutes, come in.'

Buchanan followed Street along the entrance corridor to the kitchen. Yousef had his back to them as he arranged food on the large central island table.

'Yousef,' said Hiezabel. 'The police want to talk to you.'

'Ah, Inspector, come to join my class?'

'What are you teaching this morning?' asked Buchanan, looking at the island table. It was spread like it was prepared for a party. There were pastries, cold meats, various cheeses, sliced sourdough bread, and crackers, all under cling-film, and several bowls of fresh fruit for those looking for something a little healthier. At one end of the table there was an automatic coffeemaker and a stack of mugs beside three large jugs of fruit juice with glasses.

'Methods of funding film projects. You wish to join us? We have room.'

'Not this time.'

'Well, coffee then?'

'Please,' said Street.

'Help yourself and have something to eat.'

'No thanks to the food,' said Buchanan. 'We won't keep you long.'

'Fine, how can I help?'

'We are wrapping up the Sam Taylor case. We have just come into some DNA evidence that will lead us to his killer.'

'What makes you think we can help with that? We hardly knew Sam Taylor,' said Hiezabel.

Buchanan's question had to wait as Annabel ushered four students into the kitchen.

'Maybe it would be better if we talk outside,' Buchanan suggested.

'Yes, certainly,' said Yousef, opening one of the French doors onto the patio.

Street and Buchanan followed Yousef and Hiezabel out onto the patio and over to a small retaining wall.

'We shouldn't be disturbed here,' said Yousef. 'What do you want to know?'

'I understand you used to have a gardener?'

'We've had a lot of them over the years we've been here. Is there anyone in particular you were referring to?'

'Sam Taylor.'

'Excuse me,' said Hiezabel, 'I've got bread in the oven that will burn if I don't take it out.'

'Ah, yes, Sam Taylor. You said you are investigating him. What for?'

Before Buchanan could ask his question, Annabel came out onto the patio. 'Excuse me, Mr Barazani. I can't find your wife anywhere. The rest of the students will be arriving soon, what shall I do?'

'Now where's she gone? And we have a near full class this morning,' said Yousef.

'Could I help?' said Street. 'If it's just registering students and serving coffee, I could help with that.' She nodded slowly at Buchanan.

'Yes, you could,' said Buchanan, realising what she was up to.

'Are you sure? You're from the police,' asked Yousef.

'It's what I did at uni to make extra money,' explained Street.

'OK, if it's all right with your boss, it's all right with me. Annabel will show you what to do.'

'This way. What's your name?' said Annabel, as she led Street back into the house.

'Shall we go into the garden?' Yousuf suggested, 'We're less likely to be interrupted there.'

'That's fine by me.'

They stepped down from the patio onto a lawn that would be the pride of any bowling club and walked across to a small summerhouse. Barazani opened the doors and offered a chair to Buchanan.

'It's quite a garden,' remarked Buchanan, 'do you look after it all by yourself?'

'No. We have a local company manage the garden for us.'

'If you have a fulltime gardening company looking after the garden, what did Sam Taylor do while he was here?'

'Not that much.'

'Was he lazy?'

'No, I don't think so, it was just –' he paused, looked around, then let his breath out slowly. While looking straight into Buchanan's face he said. 'You and I are about the same age, we're both married. You look like a man who knows what it's like to be loved by someone dear to your heart. Well, I'm a man who knows what it was like to have been loved by someone dear to his heart.

'After I had my heart attack, I was not the man I was before. My wife, Hiezabel, is a woman who needs to be loved, needs to be held and shown physical love – which I am no longer able to do.

'At first, we just got on with life, but when I began the Saturday workshops, Hiezabel started flirting with some of the students. At first, I just thought it was harmless, a way for her to let off steam. All was well till I noticed that she would always pick one out and, well, sometimes she would make an excuse to ask for help with something around the garden, *just for a few minutes, we won't be long, you go on,* she would say. She would only be gone for about fifteen – twenty minutes.

'At first, I didn't think much about it, after all they were in the garden just outside the lecture room. But it became a regular occurrence and I soon learned the pattern. Eventually her

296

philandering became blatant, she no longer tried to hide what she was doing. She always knew to pick the single unattached males. Sometimes she'd sit at the rear of the class and send text messages to her latest find.'

'Where did Sam Taylor come into the picture?'

'He was a good gardener, we got on well and I enjoyed his company. We would sometimes sit in here, drink a beer and sort out the world's problems. That was when I found out about him and Hiezabel. He was very apologetic about the whole affair, said he'd tried to fend off her approaches, but he needed to earn money for his rent, so –'

'So, he put up with your wife's advances?'

'Yes, sadly. You've met my wife; she can be a bit demanding at times. Her need for sexual gratification was an addiction for her.'

'What happened?'

'I doubled Sam's wages and told my wife to leave Sam alone.'

'Did it work?'

'No.'

'Hiezabel got angry and said if she couldn't have him, neither could I. So, I had to let him go, it was either that or living with a raging Medusa. I'm going to miss him; he was good to have around.'

'When was this?'

'Two, three weeks ago. Is he still missing?'

Buchanan shook his head. 'No, I'm afraid he's dead.'

'Oh, how sad! What happened to him?'

'He was strangled.'

'Strangled?'

'He was abducted, tied to a chair and strangled. Before his body was disposed of, he was emasculated, dismembered, and buried in a construction pit.'

'Who could be so cruel to have done such a thing?'

'That's what we are trying to find out.'

'Are you following any leads?'

'Several.'

'Anything hopeful?'

'Cigar stubs seem to play a big part in the case, though the DNA evidence is a bit confusing. The DNA found on a cigar stub found at the scene points to three individuals, all of whom have perfectly good alibis.'

'How could it be confusing if your suspects weren't at the scene?'

'It could have been in Sam's possession and got dropped or discarded by his captors.'

'Could Sam have been smoking it – you know, if he was allowed one last thing before the execution?'

'His DNA was not one of the samples found on the cigar stub.'

'Do you have any suspects?'

'A couple.'

'Well, I hope you catch them soon,' said Yousef. 'I liked young Sam. Shall we go back? Hiezabel will be wondering where I've got to.'

19

Sunday 20th early
Amontillado?

Buchanan looked at the bedside clock, six-thirty. He reached over for the phone and pressed the answer button.

'Jill, it's six-thirty – so what's got you up so early? Yes, I know where ESK is – sorry, I've never noticed the old BT building – and you think that's where Sam was held – OK, let me get dressed and I'll meet you there.'

'Who was that?' asked Karen, squinting at Buchanan as he got dressed.

'That was Jill, she thinks she knows where Sam Taylor was held.'

'Will you be long?'

'Shouldn't think so. Probably just a wild goose chase.'

'Talking of geese, well not quite geese, more like chicken and ham. I've invited Harry to have lunch with us and Poppy after church today. Would you ask Jill if she and Stephen would like to join us as well?'

'Bit short on notice?'

'That's OK, I've made plenty to eat.'

'OK, I'll ask.'

'Don't forget, you know how you can get wrapped up in your work.'

♦

Buchanan parked behind Street's car and got out to look at the three-storey former office block. As he did so Street exited her car and joined him.

'It's a bit dark just now to look inside,' said Buchanan.

'Sorry, I was so excited. I thought I'd figured out where Sam had been held, I didn't realise how early it was. What do you propose we do?'

'I think I'll call Nasim and see if he has the agent's contact details,' said Buchanan, taking out his phone and scrolling through his contact list.

'Nasim, Inspector Buchanan. Sorry to call this early on a Sunday morning – it's a police emergency. I wonder if you have the contact details for the agent handling the sale of the new Mastrani office building? You do? Great, we'll wait for you at the gate.'

'What did he say?'

'He said he'd be here within the hour. In the meantime, I could do with a coffee and something to eat – is there anything open at this hour?'

'McDonalds in the precinct, it's open twenty-four hours,' said Street.

'Fine, I'll drive.'

♦

'What made you think of the building?' said Buchanan, as they sat by the window of McDonalds drinking their coffee.

'Stephen was driving us to ESK yesterday afternoon and, as we turned the corner past the builder's yard we were held up by one of their lorries as it was backing into their yard. As we waited for it to move, I happened to look at the building and remembered I'd seen a photo of it in the *Eastbourne Herald* a few weeks prior. In the article it said the old BT building had finally been given the green light to be developed. I checked what Nasim had said about Mastrani relocating and put two and two together.'

'And you think it makes four?'

'I hope so. If it doesn't, I'm sorry to have got you out of bed too early on a Sunday morning.'

'That's all right, gets me out of going to church. Nasim confirmed this is the building. He also said he had keys for it. I told him to meet us at the gate.'

'What about a CSI team?'

'Let's have a quick look at the building first.'

'OK.'

♦

'He doesn't look too pleased to be up so early on a Sunday morning,' said Street, as they returned to the building.

'How was Brands Hatch?' asked Buchanan, as they approached Nasim.

'Brilliant – Achmad is a better driver than me. I think we have a champion in the making.'

'That's good to hear.'

'Why do you want to see inside the building?' said Nasim, as he lifted the padlock on the gate, 'That's strange.'

'What's strange about a padlock?' queried Buchanan.

'The padlock is undone. It's supposed to be locked at all times.'

'Who was last here?'

'I was here a few days ago with the architect, but I'm sure I clicked the padlock shut when I left. There's been a lot of vandalism in the building lately.'

'How many keys are there?'

'Just this one set and a spare.'

'Where are they kept?'

'One set is kept in the key safe at the Mastrani reception.'

'You went into the office on a Sunday morning to get the keys?'

'No. I had a spare set cut for me a couple of weeks ago. Saves me having to go into the Mastrani office for it.'

'Where do you keep them at home?'

'On the hook in my study.'

'Not on your key ring?'

'No.'

'Not a very secure way to keep them, is it?'

'No one knows what they're for. Why would you want to know that?'

'Just part of our investigation.'

'Really, I think you are clutching at straws. The entrance is on the far side of the building.'

'Nasim,' said Buchanan, as they approached the main door to the building, 'do many Mastrani employees come here?'

'No, not just now; we've only had the keys for a few weeks. The only people who should be here are, BT, the architects, the builder and Michael, he's head of IT.'

'Thanks.'

Nasim unlocked the main door and pulled it open. 'There's no electricity turned on at the moment, so please be careful as you walk. Shit, they've been at it again!'

'Who's been at what?' asked Buchanan.

'Bloody vandals. They seem to get a lot of fun painting slogans on the walls. Those rollers and paint trays are theirs; I wonder why they left them behind?'

'Maybe they were disturbed and ran off, meaning to come back sometime to collect them,' suggested Street.

'It looks like one of them managed to step in the tray,' said Buchanan, pointing to a set of partial footprints.

'Serves them right. Is there any place in particular you would like to see?'

'No. We'll just wander around the building; we shouldn't take too long. Or you could give us the Cook's tour of the building?'

'Sorry, Cook's?'

'Thomas Cook, he started the tour business.'

'Oh, that Cook. This way then. Through there on the right we have the garages, the target of the graffiti artists and plenty of room for Amal's Rolls Royce. The new reception will be here on the left. Across from the reception there will be a staff canteen and lounge.'

'Is the lift working?' queried Buchanan.

'Sorry, no, as I said there is no power on in the building, and besides, as you can see, the lift doors have been bricked up. On this floor, they will have the main administration, marketing and sales offices,' said Nasim, as he stopped on the first-floor landing. 'Of course, all these partitions will have to be stripped out and rebuilt to the company's requirements.'

'Looks like someone has already started stripping out the partitions,' said Street, looking through a man-sized hole in one of the partition panels.

'Vandals and druggies,' said Nasim. 'They'll soon find somewhere else to shoot up and vandalise. Top floor is where all the development labs will be situated.'

'You seem to know a lot about what is going to happen to the building,' remarked Street, as they climbed the stairs to the top floor. 'What's your involvement with the project?'

'This is supposed to be confidential. I'm working on behalf of the bank as the finance consultant.'

'The building looks sound,' said Buchanan.' Will Mastrani be financing the renovation costs separate from the purchase of the building?'

'The renovation costs are included in the total finance package.'

'Not so much vandalising on this floor,' said Buchanan, looking in at one of the offices.

'You wouldn't say that if you saw the toilets. The water in the building is also turned off due to all the cisterns having been smashed. One of the vandals thought it fun to roll out the fire hose and flood the floor.'

'That's a bit odd,' said Street, as she investigated one of the almost empty offices. 'Has someone brought their green chairs over from the present office?'

'No. I found it odd as well. Turns out BT seems to like green chairs, there's more of them in the other offices.'

'Is there a telecoms room in the building?' asked Buchanan.

'I seem to remember there was a telephone wiring frame on the ground floor. It's on the wall by the main garage doors.'

'How do we get to it?'

'Back down the stairs and through where the new staff canteen will be.'

'Is that the lift?' Street pointed to a partially open lattice gate as they passed a steel door on their way to the stairs.

'Yes, quite out of place in a modern office. The whole thing will have to be replaced before they move in. The architects say these type of lattice gates on lifts are now illegal.'

'Where does this door lead to?' asked Buchanan.

'The lift motor room, it's up a separate staircase.'

'Is there much to see up there?'.

'Just an electric motor that works the lift.'

'Thanks, I'll be back in a moment. Jill, you want to come along?'

'That's why I'm here.'

'I'll go first in case there are any creepy crawlies.'

'I'm not scared of spiders.'

Buchanan pushed the door open to reveal a set of steel-treaded stairs that led up to another steel door on a small landing.

'Will I need a key for the door at the top?'

Nasim shook his head. 'If I remember correctly, there is no lock.' He held the bottom door open to light the staircase as Street followed Buchanan, their footsteps making a ringing sound as each foot set down in the treads. At the small landing, Buchanan turned the handle and pushed the door open.

The room was small, with a winch drum and motor bolted to the floor directly over the lift shaft. The walls were breeze blocks originally painted white, now stained yellow with years of winch oil vapour. The roof and floor were concrete slabs. There was a second door in the wall beside the entrance door. On the opposite wall were some circuit breaker boxes and, in the far corner of the room, stood a solitary green chair with shards of silver gaffer tape still attached to the armrests.

'Should I call for a CSI team?' said Street.

'Yes please. I'd say this room is where Sam Taylor was held, tortured and strangled.'

'Are those what I think they are?' Street pointed to a cigar stub lying on top of the winch motor.

'I think we should get out of here and leave the room to the CSI team,' said Buchanan. 'Let's go down and break the good news to Nasim.'

Buchanan followed Street back down the steps to the second-floor landing.

'I told you there was nothing to see up there,' said Nasim. 'Can we leave now?'

'Could we have a look at the rest of the building while we wait for a CSI team to get here, please?' asked Buchanan.

'CSI team? What's that and why should we be waiting for one? I have work to be getting on with at home.'

'I believe the lift motor room is a crime scene. The CSI's are police specialist teams who search crime scenes for evidence, which should lead to the apprehension and conviction of the criminals involved.'

'Oh, is that necessary? Druggies shoot up all over the place. We had a specialist team in two weeks ago to clean up all the old needles and detritus that went along with the filthy habit.'

'Nonetheless, would you show us the rest of the building?'

'OK, follow me, but be careful going down the stairs – the concrete edges are a bit rough.'

Nasim led them back down to the ground floor, through a dilapidated office into what was the old garage workshop.

Buchanan walked across the floor to where some metal boxes hung from the wall. 'What are these for?'

'I believe it's the main power distribution board for the building. The lift control panel is on the right.'

Buchanan nodded as he carefully looked inside the box. He saw where the main fuses should have been, they were now missing.

'Where does that door lead to?' he asked, pointing to a metal door beside the circuit breaker panel.

'Outside, and the car park, why?'

Buchanan walked over to the door, knelt down and looked at the floor. He turned on his flashlight, then nodded. He stood up and smiled at Street. 'I think we've found where Sam's body left the building.'

'If you are going to wait for your people, can I go? As I said I have a lot of work to do at home.'

'Sure, leave the keys before you go, I'll lock up for you' said Buchanan, smiling. 'Just don't leave town without letting me know where you are going.'

'What are you getting at? Am I a suspect in some sort of crime you've dreamed up?'

'Just don't leave town without letting me know.'

Nasim shook his head and started for the door. He stopped halfway across the room and turned to look at Buchanan. 'Do you suspect Achmad of involvement in this crime of yours, Inspector?'

'I'll return the keys when we're done here.'

'You were a bit hard on him,' said Street, as the sound of the door closing echoed through the empty room.

'He should be more careful with things given into his care.'

'The keys?'

Buchanan nodded. 'Did Control say how long before we could expect the CSI team?'

'Within the hour.'

'Let's wait in my car for them.'

♦

'What have you found, Jack?' asked Littlejohn.

'Torture chamber in the lift-motor room. The trail of the corpse should lead down the stairs to the ground floor, then through the old garage area and out the back door. We'll stay down in the lobby out of your way.'

'Fine, see you later. Dave, Anne, let's get to work. Sorry, you'll have to carry the kit up the stairs, there's no lift.'

'Could you do their job?' Buchanan asked Street.

'No, definitely not. Our job is bad enough without having to pick up decaying body parts.'

♦

'Never inspected a torture chamber before, Jack.'

'What did you find, Henry?'

'The room stinks like an abattoir. Looks like the victim was tied to the chair, naked, with gaffer tape and suffered some sort of masochistic torture routine. We found his male organs on the floor underneath with what looks like urine and faecal matter on the chair. There are also copious amounts of blood. There were cigar stubs scattered round the room. I expect we will find the remains of human tissue in the ash. We examined the stairs leading down to the ground floor and found traces of human tissue and blood on the edges. The large room you said was the old garage area had drag marks leading over to the back door. We also found recent tyre marks on the ground outside the door, we took an image of them.

'Well done. I know it's Sunday, but can you put a rush on with the results?'

'I'll try, but I doubt if we can get anything to you till sometime late tomorrow. What do you want me to do with the keys when we are done here?'

'I'm going to arrange a police presence here on site. Leave the keys with me and I'll hand them over when to whoever is assigned to look after the building. Thanks again for coming out on a Sunday.'

'What now?' asked Street.

'Fancy lunch?'

'I'd rather go home, if that's all right with you.'

'Not quite what I meant. Would you and Stephen like to come to lunch?'

'What would Karen say if we just show up? It's almost two o'clock.'

'She'd love it, she asked me to invite you both. I should have mentioned it earlier, just forgot. Poppy and Harry will also be there.'

'If you're sure.'

'Of course, I'm sure.'

'What time?'

'As soon as you are ready.'

'Perfect, I'll call Stephen, I could do with some normal conversation after what we've just been told.'

◆

Buchanan was chatting to Harry when doorbell rang. 'I'll get it,' he said. 'Hello Jill, Stephen, come in, Harry's in the conservatory, Poppy is with him.'

Buchanan led them through to the conservatory. 'Karen is in the kitchen. Can I get you something to drink?'

'I'm fine,' said Street.

'Do you have a cold beer?' requested Stephen.

'I'll go see, back in a minute.'

'I'll come with you,' said Street.

Buchanan returned a few minutes later with Stephen's beer.

'How are you, Harry?' said Stephen. 'All over your adventure?'

'Being kidnapped, tied up and beaten by two thugs, then almost being trampled to death by a horse is not quite what I'd call an adventure.'

'It all worked out in the end though.'

'Yes.'

'I heard the two of them got a lengthy jail term,' said Stephen, as he took a sip of his beer.

Harry nodded.

'Jill was saying you're off to the USA?'

'Yes. I've been offered a position as stable manager at a stud ranch just outside Dallas. I'm just waiting for my visa to come through.'

'You and Poppy set a date?'

'Probably early next spring, it all depends on my visa application.'

'Morning, Harry,' said Jill.

'I think you'll find two o'clock is afternoon,' said Harry.

'You should be a policeman with that gift of observation, Harry,' said Buchanan, with a grin on his face.

'How's the case going? Poppy said you're working on a missing girl and abduction case?'

'It's almost over, just a couple of loose ends to tie up.'

'Come and eat it while it's hot,' said Karen.

Karen waited till everyone was seated, then said. 'I'd like you all to look round the table and remember this moment. Two years ago, Jack and I came down to Eastbourne from Glasgow not knowing anyone. It was just the two of us, and now we have sort of a family, just the six of us.'

'Excuse me,' said Jill. 'It will soon be seven.'

'I thought something was going on!' exclaimed Buchanan. 'It all now makes sense, you losing your breakfast. Why didn't you tell me?'

'I just did.'

'Did you know, Karen?'

She nodded. 'I guessed.'

'Well done, Stephen.' Said Buchanan thumping him on the back.

'Congratulations, Jill. When are you due?' asked Poppy.

'Next spring.'

'Oh, I hope it doesn't prevent you and Stephen coming to our wedding.'

'I hope so too,' said Jill. 'We're really looking forward to it.'

Just as Karen started to serve the dessert, Buchanan's phone rang.

'Oh Jack, let it ring,' said Karen, as he reached for it, 'we have guests for dinner – surely the call can wait?'

Buchanan looked at the display and recognised the number. 'Sorry folks, but business has to come before pleasure today. I'll take it in the study.'

'Don't be long,' said Karen.

'I'll be with you as soon as soon I've returned this call,' said Buchanan, as he carried his bowl of trifle and coffee through to his study. He closed his door and sat down in his chair. He pressed the call-back and speaker buttons on his phone, and as he waited for his call to be answered, he finished his trifle.

'Hello, Yousef? It's Jack Buchanan, you just called me?'

'Yes. Jack, I don't know what to do.'

'I always find starting at the beginning helps.'

309

Yousef let out his breath and began his tale of woe. 'I've had a blazing row with Hiezabel. She's left the house in a right temper. I worried she might do something silly.'

'Has she come back home?'

'No. I've called her mobile several times, but it just goes to voicemail.'

'Have you called Nasim to see if she's there?'

'Yes, but he said he hasn't seen her all day.'

'What would you like me to do?'

'I – I think I'll wait. She can be quite an emotional person when she gets angry and it takes a while for her to wind down.'

'OK, if she doesn't come home by bedtime, call me back.'

'OK, thanks.'

Buchanan put his cup in the bowl, collected his phone and returned to the dining room.

'All OK?' said Karen.

'I hope so. Yousef and Hiezabel have had an argument, she's gone out for a walk to cool off.'

'Good, at least we'll have you home for the day,' said Karen.

'I hope so too,' said Buchanan, thinking it wouldn't be the last time he heard from Yousef.

20
Monday 21st morning
Home at Last

'Are you sure you should be at work?' asked Buchanan, looking at the clock on the office wall.

'Of course, I should. I'm only having a baby, and that's not for several months yet. Women have been having them for centuries.'

'OK, if you're sure.'

'I'm sure. You can rest easy; I'm not going to take any risks with your first grandchild.'

'Stop that, you'll make me cry.'

'Just teasing.'

'How was your visit to the doctor?'

'Mother and baby doing fine. Now stop worrying and let's get to work.'

As Buchanan hung up from a call, his phone immediately rang again. He picked up the receiver. 'Buchanan. Oh hi, Henry. You have? Hang on, let me put you on the speaker. OK, we're all ears.'

'Yes. Sorry to disturb your Monday morning. There's been a development you should know about.'

'What is this development?'

'The PCSO who was on duty at the old BT building said he heard the sound of a mobile phone ringing, so he went to investigate round the building and found a body.'

'Where?'

'At the bottom of the lift shaft. The door is bricked up on the ground floor but there is a gap for ventilation. The PCSO reached through with his phone and saw the body, not a pretty sight. I'm waiting for fire and rescue to get here in case we have to retrieve the body up the shaft.'

'OK, I'll be right there.' Buchanan released the speaker button and hung up on the call.

'Do you need me?' asked Street. 'I've got a mountain of paperwork to go through.'

'No. You stay, I should be back before lunch.'

◆

As Buchanan arrived at the former BT building, he saw a Fire & Rescue wagon and an ambulance waiting in the car park. He parked beside the CSI van and went into the building.

'Hi Henry, how is the tunnelling going?' said Buchanan grimacing at the noise of a hammer drill in the hands of a builder slowly chipping away at the brick wall.

'Slow, but we'll get there.'

'Do you have a description?'

'Female, looks middle Eastern. That is all I have till we get through the wall and into the pit. Before we started, I had a fireman go down on a rope and assess the possibility of recovering the body. But since she was already deceased, and it may be a crime scene, I thought it best to wait.'

'Has the coroner been notified?'

'Yes, Doctor Mansell is on his way.'

'Fine,' said Buchanan. 'Who found the body?'

'I did,' said the PCSO. 'I heard a phone ringing and went to investigate. My ears led me to a missing airbrick in the wall where the ground floor lift doors once stood. I was able to reach through the hole with my phone and take a photo – that is when I knew there was someone behind there.'

'I wonder how she got in there?' mused Buchanan looking at a blurry picture of the deceased.

'Looking for a cache of amontillado?' suggested Littlejohn.

Buchanan thought for a moment then said, 'Ah, Edgar Allan Poe. I read the story as a kid.'

'Looks like she must have fallen from an upper floor,' said Littlejohn. 'I checked the lift door on the next floor; it isn't bricked up like this one. Didn't have time to check the other floors.'

'Thanks, Henry. I'll go have a look while you do your stuff.'

Buchanan left the builder and the CSI team to get on with knocking down the brick wall and climbed the stairs to the first floor. He looked at the lift door and saw it was shut and secured by a chain and padlock. He continued up to the second floor and, as he was about to approach the lift door, he remembered something that Street had said when they were there Sunday. At the time he was too busy to take in the significance of what she'd said. But now, when he looked at the lift gates, he saw they were slightly ajar, just enough room for someone who wasn't looking where they were going to fall through.

Buchanan took out his phone and turned on the flashlight app. He scanned the floor immediately in front of the lift gates and could just make out two sets of footprints. One smaller than the other, it looked like one set was male and the other female. He did his best to remember what Travis had told him about tracking footsteps. He walked back to the main stairs and could see, between his, Street's and the CSI team's footsteps, two pairs of distinct footprints, one large and one small, both with a splotch of white paint by the big toe of the left shoe.

He followed them from the top step of the stairs to those leading up to the lift room. One thing stood out to Buchanan, the larger of the footprints sometimes obliterated that of the smaller ones. From this information, Buchanan surmised that the male had been following the female. He looked at the first steps going up to the lift motor room and saw the smaller footprints coming back down, with those of the male following. The female footprints, instead of continuing down the stairs to the ground floor, had turned to the right and stopped in front of the lift gates, toes pointing forward; her back would have been to the open door of the lift shaft.

Buchanan looked at the steps coming down and back at the ground. The male footprints had started towards the staircase down, but stopped. What had caused him to pause? Had she made a noise? Had he heard it? He must have, as his footprints went over to the lift shaft, stopping about three feet from the female's. He had taken a short step forward, she back, and, as she did so, had stepped into an empty lift shaft. The male may have said something, or maybe he made an attempt to catch her, but either action would have been too late.

Buchanan stepped to the side of the footprints and got closer to the lift shaft, when he heard the sound of falling masonry. He took two more steps and carefully looked into the empty shaft. The light from the ground floor lobby illuminated the blooded corpse lying forty feet below him.

He returned to the ground floor, thinking about the ramifications of his observations. By the time he got there Dr Mansell had arrived and was at that moment being helped down into the lift shaft.

'Good afternoon, Andrew,' said Buchanan.

'This one of yours?' Mansell asked, looking up at Buchanan.

'Afraid so.'

'Before you ask, she died from the fall, neck broken on impact.'

'Anything else, Doctor?' asked Littlejohn.

'Let me check the jacket pockets,' said Mansell as he carefully reached for the jacket pockets. 'There's a mobile phone in the left one, in the right, a small folding knife, bits of gaffer tape and a cigar stub.'

'Any ID, Doctor?' queried Littlejohn.

'Nope.'

'Her name is Hiezabel Barazani,' said Buchanan. 'Her husband called and made a missing person's report earlier.'

'OK to move the body?' asked Littlejohn.

Buchanan nodded. 'I'll go and inform the next of kin.'

♦

Buchanan rang the bell and waited. He heard the sound of footsteps then the sound of the door lock. The door was opened by Annabel.

'Good morning, Annabel. Detective Inspector Buchanan to see Yousef Barazani.'

'Yes, I remember you, Inspector. Where is Jill?'

'She's in the office. I'm here to see Yousef, I won't keep him long.'

'Yousef is in the garden. If you will follow me, I'll take you to him.'

'That will be fine,' said Buchanan, looking at the assortment of shoes in the rack at the front door as he passed. One pair in particular caught his attention: they were faded blue slip-ons, the left bearing a splash of white paint on the toe.

Yousef was at the bottom of the garden tending a small bonfire. Buchanan smelled the smoke – it took him back many years to his grandfather's farm and the bonfires he had lit when trimming the hedges.

'Yousef,' said Annabel, as she led Buchanan across the lawn. 'You have a visitor.'

Yousef threw a small branch into the fire and turned round.

Buchanan looked at Yousef's face. *He's been waiting for me*, he thought.

'Good afternoon, Yousef. You didn't call – I presumed Hiezabel had returned home?'

'No, she hasn't. We will be more comfortable in the summerhouse. Annabel and I are the only ones here. Would you like something to drink?'

'Tea, please.'

'I'll make it,' said Annabel. 'Yousef, what would you like?'

'A cold beer, there should be some left in the fridge.'

Buchanan watched as Annabel almost skipped across the lawn. Yousef saw Buchanan's face and said, 'It's not what you think, Inspector. Annabel works with me helping with the course bookings. There's nothing else.'

'Your tea, Inspector. Do you want milk or sugar?' asked Annabel, returning with a tray which she placed on the small table in the summerhouse.

'Thanks, just a splash of milk and two sugars.'

'Where's your partner, Jill?' asked Yousef, as he took a swig of beer from the bottle.

'She's back in the office, I thought it better if I came on my own. Yousef, I am the bearer of sad news. Earlier today, the body of Hiezabel was taken to Eastbourne morgue after it was recovered from the bottom of a lift shaft.'

Buchanan looked at Yousef's face – it was poker straight.

'She's dead?'

'Yes, she's dead. What can you tell me about it?'

Yousef pondered for a while, then began his story. 'I see there's no sense in pretending. I know she's dead, I saw it happen. Is your tea all right?'

'The tea is fine, are you all right?'

'Yes, I'm fine.'

'Please go on with your story.'

'Saturday,' he said, shaking his head slowly, 'Saturday, you remember you and I went out to the summerhouse to talk?'

'Yes.'

'And I told you about my marital relationship with Hiezabel and her philandering?'

'Yes.'

'Unfortunately, she heard every word I said to you about her and Sam Taylor. She's always had the bad habit of eavesdropping on other people's conversations. She stayed out of my way the rest of the day and went to bed without saying goodnight.

Sunday morning, she let me have it, both barrels. She was incandescent with rage because, as she said, *I had betrayed the sanctity of our marriage.* Me, betray our marriage, what a joke! I had talked to you about her. We argued for what seemed hours. In the end she went out for a walk, or so I thought at the time. I was still angry and I'm not sure why I went into her office to

316

look for something and that's when I saw the email on her laptop. Thankfully, she was in so much of a hurry to leave, she forgot to send it. Here, I have printed a copy of it.'

Buchanan took the letter from Yousef's hand and looked at it. It was word for word the same letter he'd read a few days prior at Amal's house.

'I was angry that she would stoop so low and decided to have it out with her. I got in my car to try and catch up with her. It took me quite some time of searching until I saw her get on a number three bus. Well, I couldn't stop the bus, so I followed it till she got off in town at the main bus stop. She then got on a number five and got off at the stop near Whitley Road. I managed to follow her to the old telephone building. I parked in the ESK car park and walked back. By now I realised she wasn't just going for a random walk, she had something in mind. I wasn't totally shocked when she opened the padlock at the old exchange and went in. I assumed she had got the key from Nasim.'

'He told me he had his own set hanging in his office.'

'I followed her into the building, it was dark, so I used the flashlight on my phone to see where I was going. I followed her up the stairs to the room at the top. I think it was something to do with the lift. As soon as I saw the chair with the silver tape on it I realised something awful had taken place. I demanded she tell me what was going on, but she just laughed at me and said I was a pathetic image of a man. She went on to tell me, in excruciating detail, what she and Sam used to get up to.

'How did you react?'

'I lost it, Inspector,' he said, shaking his head slowly. 'I don't remember what I said but it must have really shocked her because she threw a piece of metal at me and, while I was distracted, she ran past me and down the stairs. I followed her, but by the time I got to the bottom she was nowhere to be seen. If she hadn't sneezed, I might have missed her altogether. I wish I had because, had I missed her, she might be alive today.'

'What happened when you heard her sneeze?'

'I looked around the corner and saw her crouching in front of the lift gates. I pleaded with her to stop swearing at me. But it was no use, all the evil that was in her was driving her on. I remember taking a step towards her and then it happened; she took one step backwards and fell into the lift shaft. It was awful, I could hear her screaming all the way down. The sound of her body bouncing off of the metal rails is a sound I will live with for the rest of my life. I walked over to the shaft and looked down; she looked dead, lying on her back, face up, with arms spread out.'

'What did you do?'

'What could I do? She was at the bottom of a lift shaft behind a brick wall.'

'You could have called 999.'

'And what would I have said? I would have been accused of pushing my wife down the shaft.'

'You still could be.'

'After what I just told you? You only have my word for what happened, I could deny everything.'

'Yousef, I know what happened. I've seen the evidence.'

'What evidence? I was careful, I didn't touch anything, there are no fingerprints.'

'Maybe not, but there is other evidence, scientific evidence.'

'Oh. What will you do?'

'At the moment, I choose to do nothing.'

'You think I deliberately pushed her down the shaft?'

'Yousef, I plan to let the evidence speak for itself.'

'That's not very comforting.'

'You'll just have to live with it. What did you do with Hiezabel's laptop?'

'You see the bonfire?' he pointed at the pile of brushwood smouldering.

'When you through Hiezabel's laptop in the fire, was it an act of pique? Or was there something on the hard drive that might embarrass or incriminate you and the family?'

'When I returned from that dreadful place, I went straight to Hiezabel's office. I wanted to see if there was anything else I should know about.'

'Was there?'

'Her laptop was open, so I didn't need a password. I found an email she was about to send; it was full of dreadful lies about Amal. I also found emails between her and people called Lupov and Baretata. It was in a crude code but dealt with her drug dealing with them.

'I was horrified when I saw how often she had me little gifts into the country for her. Little did I realise they were packed with drugs. I was mortified thinking what would have happened to me if I had been caught.'

'How did it work?'

'She would say she'd purchased something on the internet and could I bring it back for her.'

'How often did this happen?'

He sighed. 'On reflection, almost every time I went abroad. I was so naive – no matter where I was going, she'd find something to purchase.'

'What did she do with these objects you brought back?'

'She'd sell them on eBay or Etsy. I was only too happy she had a hobby and glad to help. I checked her bank account; it has thousands of pounds in it.'

'Do you realise that is what the police would call tampering with the evidence of a crime?'

'So, arrest me, I no longer care what happens to me.'

'Yousef, I have no intention of arresting you.'

'Thanks for that one small comfort. I suppose I will have to tell the rest of the family about Hiezabel.'

'Why don't you let me be the bearer of bad news? You've had enough of it for one day.'

'Thanks. I didn't push her, I did actually still love her, in spite of what she did.'

'Oh, Yousef, one more thing.'

'What's that?'

'I'd throw your old slip-on shoes in the bonfire; they have paint on the toe.'

♦

Buchanan said goodbye to Yousef and Annabel and climbed into his car. Before he drove off, he took a moment to think. His next task would be to go and see Nasim and tell him about his mother's accident. But he decided against it, he had another and much better idea. But first, it was back to the office.

♦

'Have we heard from forensics, Jill?'

'I'm presuming you're referring to the body recovered earlier today from the old BT building?'

'Yes, would you read it to me?'

'Body recovered to mortuary; Dr Mansell gives the cause of death as a broken neck caused by fall down lift shaft. Body identified by DCI Buchanan as Hiezabel Barazani. Contents of pockets are as follows: broken mobile phone, one folding knife – box cutter type blade, two cigar stubs, various pieces of silver-coloured gaffer tape, woman's purse containing a single five pound note and some loose change to the value of thirty-two pence, a paper tissue, and a bus ticket,' read Street. 'Hardly anything to be taking with you to the next world if you were an Egyptian princess.'

'My, you are being quite erudite this afternoon.'

'Why, thank you, my kind sir.'

'First, we are in Egypt, now southern USA. What's going on?'

'That was Stephen's fault. Neither of us was tired last night so we sat up and watched old movies on TV till three this morning.'

'Practising for the night-time feed?'

'I hadn't thought of that, how odd.'

'What about Zac and Zilini, anything?'

320

'I talked to Zac's agent earlier. He said they will be back later today.'

'Perfect timing.'

'But he said they were worried about their safety. I suggested he tells them to come and see us before they go to the family.'

'What did he say to that request?'

'He agreed and said he thought that would be a good idea. He'll phone Zac back and have him call us when they get to the station.'

'Does Zilini know that her stepgrandmother is dead?'

Street shook her head. 'I didn't say anything to the agent. I figured it would be best coming from one of us.'

'Fine. Could you hold the fort? I'm going over to have a quick word with Dr Mansell.'

'Sure, I've got my maternity leave papers to read.'

♦

It's not a pretty sight, Buchanan,' said Mansell. 'Rats have eaten her eyes, tongue and most of the brain. Still want to see the body?'

Buchanan nodded.

Mansell pulled the drawer out and unzipped the body bag. 'Death was instantaneous. In falling down the lift shaft headfirst, her head struck a protruding metal support bar at the bottom of the lift shaft. The impact broke her neck in three places and caused the injury you see to the face.'

'There go the answers to many unanswered questions.'

'Such as?'

'Why did she kill Sam Taylor, was it a romantic romp that went wrong, or something more sinister?'

'What could be more sinister than that?'

'Her husband told me she used to have him unknowingly smuggle illegal drugs into the country.'

'He didn't know?'

'No, apparently not.'

'If that is the case, what was Sam's involvement?'

'According to what we have discovered, Sam used to sell the drugs for her, and may have tried to blackmail her.'

'So, what do you think made her return to the building?'

'She overheard my conversation with her husband when I said we had DNA evidence that would prove who killed Sam. I think that spooked her into making one last visit to clear up anything that would incriminate her.'

'So how did she link up with Baretata and Lupov?'

'A few days ago, when I talked to Nasim Barazani, he said as part of the upcoming Mastrani government contract and their move to the new office, he was doing work from home. To work efficiently he had some of the financial documents in his home office. Included in those documents was a list of names of prospective employees. Two of the names on the list were Toma Baretata, and Dimitar Lupov. She could have seen Baretata and Lupov's contact details and reasons for not employing them and got in touch.'

'And they are the two responsible for the dismemberment and disposal of Sam Taylor's body?'

'The very same. Nasim also told me Thursdays were his days to work from home. He said that when he wasn't home, he never locked his office. With Hiezabel regularly visiting the house on Thursdays, it would have been a simple job for her to wait for Nasim to go out and then sneak in and have a nosey look around. It would have been easy for her while in the office to take Nasim's keys for the new building and get copies made.'

'I found a set of keys in one of her pockets when I was examining the body in the lift shaft,' said Mansell   .

'They'll probably fit the padlock on the front gate and the rear door to the building.'

'Poor Sam Taylor.'

'Hell, hath no fury known, like a woman scorned.'

'And look where it got her, seen enough?' asked Mansell.

'Yes, thanks.'

'Is it over, or should I expect any more bodies?' said Mansell as he closed the body bag containing Hiezabel Barazani.

'No, no more bodies. I think this sorry affair has finally concluded.'

'That's good to know, I was hoping to have some time off.'

♦

'Any calls while I was out?'

'Yes. Zilini called from Ashford station. She wanted an assurance that they would be safe returning to Eastbourne.'

'What did you say?'

'I said the reason for their apprehension has gone, and that you would explain everything to them when they get here. I said one of us would collect them from the station.'

'Well done.'

'How was your visit to Dr Mansell?'

'Short, he was in a hurry to wind up the case, he's planning on having some time off. Fat chance of that around here.'

'I find it difficult to think of him doing anything other than being a doctor.'

'You might be surprised if I told you he goes fishing, not in the sea, but on rivers.'

Buchanan's explanation of Dr Mansell's hobbies was interrupted by his phone ringing.

'If that's Zac, could you put it on the speaker so I can hear?' requested Street.

'Will do. DCI Buchanan – who is this?'

'Inspector, it's Zac Taylor. Your sergeant said to call you and you would come and get us.'

'That's correct, where are you?'

'Just left Hastings station, we're on the Victoria train. Is it safe for us to come home?'

'Yes, it is now,' said Buchanan. 'Wait at Eastbourne station and I'll come collect you.'

'Could you meet us at Pevensey and Westham?'

'Yes, why there?'

'Because if we cannot see you, I'll know something is wrong and we'll stay on the train.'

'He's a smart one,' said Buchanan, pressing the speaker button on his phone. 'C'mon Jill, let's go meet the train. You go on down to the car, I need to visit the boys room.'

♦

Street drove over the level crossing and turned right into the station car park just as the crossing barriers came down.

'Quick,' she said, 'you go over and stand on the platform so they can see you, I'll park the car.'

Buchanan was in plenty of time as the crossing barriers were for the Hastings train.

'Is that their train?' asked Street.

Buchanan looked down the platform at the departure board. 'I believe it is.'

'A bit weird this,' said Street. 'Meeting total strangers for the first time. Suppose they change their minds and stay on?'

Buchanan shook his head. 'We'd catch them at Eastbourne.'

'But suppose they got off at Hampden Park, then waited for the train to come back out of Eastbourne, got back on and headed for London?'

'My, you are a worrywart today.'

Buchanan and Street watched as the train came to a halt and the doors opened. A lady with a dog got off from the front carriage, two schoolchildren got off from a middle carriage and finally, as the doors were closing, a head looked out from the far end of the train. It popped back in then an arm extended and stopped the door from closing. Next a young girl holding a suitcase stepped out onto the platform followed by an equally young man holding a guitar case.

The doors closed, and the train accelerated out of the station.

'Oh,' said Street.

'What?'

'Look at them. They look just like two children on their first day at boarding school.'

'Welcome home, Zac and Zilini,' said Buchanan. 'This is DS Street; I believe you talked to her earlier.'

'Yes, I remember,' said Zilini, 'Have you told my father that we are here?'

'No, not yet,' said Buchanan. 'We wanted to talk to the both of you first. If you'll follow me, the car is in the car park.'

'Are we being arrested?' asked Zac.

'No, not at all. I just thought it would be best if we had a chat before you go talk to your families.'

'I feel I've been away for ever,' said Zilini, as they drove past the Langney shopping centre on their way to the police station.

'It's only been a couple of weeks,' said Street.

'Still feels like for ever.'

'You got married while you were away?' queried Street.

'Sort of,' said Zilini. 'We met up with some people at Towersey and one of them said he was qualified to marry us. We didn't get a certificate or anything like that. We did say our vows to each other.'

'I hear you performed at Towersey,' said Buchanan.

'Not quite,' said Zac. 'We had a spot at the open mike studio. Towersey is more of a folk festival than a jazz one. Even so the audience liked us, and it was a blast to be performing in front of a large audience.'

'How was Paris? Your agent said you'd gone there for your honeymoon,' said Street.

'It was fantastic. We didn't know this at the time, but when we asked where to go in the evening the concierge suggested the club which was just a few doors down the road from the hotel. We went there on our first night for a drink and to our surprise it was a jazz club. During one of the intervals, Zac got talking to the guitar player, and told him we'd just played at Towersey. I'm not sure what he understood about that, but as a result we were invited onto the stage to perform a couple of songs. We now have a firm summer booking for next year.'

'It helps to be able to speak their language,' said Zac.

325

'This is the police station?' asked Zilini, in surprise, 'I thought we were going to Eastbourne?'

'This is the police station,' said Buchanan. 'The old one on Grove Road is now closed, though there is a drop-in police station inside the council building beside the main library.'

He drove into the police compound and parked the car. Zilini, Zac and Street got out and started towards the front door.

Street showed them into the office and pointed to two chairs in front of the window.

'Would either of you like something to drink? I'm afraid the selection is quite limited.'

'Could I have some water?' requested Zilini.

'Of course, you can. Zac?

'I'll have water as well.'

Street walked over to the office fridge, removed two bottles of water and handed them to Zac and Zilini.

Buchanan waited for them to relax before he began.

'Zac, you are aware that Sam is dead, but what you won't be aware of the circumstances surrounding his death.'

'What were they?'

'Do you remember the night you forgot your guitar and had to take the next train back to Hastings?'

'Yes, and when I got home there was no sight of Sam. Wait a minute, how do you know I went back for my guitar?'

'You left your phone under your mattress in your flat. We were able to follow you through your text messages,' said Street.

'Oh, that's right. I left our phones behind so no-one could trace us.'

'Zilini,' said Buchanan, 'there is one thing that has been bothering me. What happened after you parked your car in the Mastrani garage the Friday evening you and Zac disappeared?'

'I went out the fire door intending to meet Zac by the NHS trailer. When I stepped out onto the street, I was startled to see Hiezabel and Yousef sitting in the back of a taxi, right outside the fire door. I stood for a second hoping they hadn't noticed me.

'I would have got away with it, but the fire door made such a noise as it shut, Hiezabel looked up and saw me. I was going to say hello, but she just ignored me and picked up her phone and began texting someone.

'I waved and stood waiting for a few minutes to see if she was going to open the window.'

'Did she?'

'No. I was puzzled then confused when I saw another taxi stop across the road from Hiezabel's taxi. The driver wound down his window and leaned out. It was strange, but Hiezabel pointed at me.'

'What did your grandfather do?'

'Nothing, I think he was looking at his phone and didn't see what Hiezabel was doing.'

'What did you do?'

'After Sam going missing, and what Zac had told me about the two men in a taxi, I got nervous and walked off towards the road that goes through to the station car park.'

'We were watching on the station CCTV cameras,' said Street. 'We saw Zac, but not you.'

'I hid behind some wheely bins to see if the other taxi would follow me. It is just as well as I did. No sooner had I got behind one of the bins, the taxi drove slowly past and into the car park. I'm sure it was looking for me.'

'That clears that up, but what about Zac's guitar?' said Buchanan. 'We watched the station CCTV cameras and didn't see anyone with a guitar get on a train.'

'We didn't take the train. When I thought the coast was clear, I made my way through the car park dodging behind parked cars. I managed to make it over to the back of the Enterprise centre where I caught up with Zac. He thought it better if we took a taxi, that way we wouldn't be noticed.'

'Zac,' said Buchanan. 'Where did you and Zilini stay after we talked to you in the flat?'

'Travel Lodge by Gardners roundabout.'

'That makes sense, and why PC's Hunter and Dexter met you in Morrisons garage.'

'Yeah. So, what actually happened to Sam?'

'It is quite complicated, but the short version is, when you got back on the train, he was met at the station by Zilini's grandmother, with whom he had been having an ongoing relationship.'

'You're joking!' exclaimed Zilini. 'There must have been at least thirty years difference in their ages.'

'Sam, a toy-boy – who'd have thought it?' Zac shook his head.

'According to your grandfather, Sam and Hiezabel became friends when he came to work for him.'

'Did he know about it?'

'Not at first.'

'I don't understand,' said Zilini.

'I will explain more in detail later. In the meantime, I'm glad you're both OK.'

'What about my grandmother?' said Zilini.

'I'm sorry to say she had an accident and fell down a lift shaft.'

'She's dead?'

'Yes, I'm afraid so. Zilini, can you answer me one question?'

'Yes, what is it?'

'What was meant by you sending the empty ring box to your father, you didn't include a message?'

'Oh that. I did write a letter, but in our hurry, I forgot to put it in the envelope. I still have it.'

'Well, maybe you could give it to your dad when you see him.'

'I'm not sure, he may be angry and refuse to see me.'

'I doubt that,' said Buchanan. 'He may be angry that you ran away, but he'll be glad to see you back home. As will Darsameen – you do realise she has missed you?'

Zilini nodded. 'I did send her a card from Paris, I didn't want her to think we had forgotten her.'

'That was a bit risky, suppose your dad saw it?'

'Unlikely. Darsameen always collects the post, it doesn't arrive till after Dad has gone to work. I'm sorry about Sam.'

'What about the two cretins who were hanging around the flat and picked up Sam in their taxi?' asked Zac. 'Have you caught up with them?'

'One is dead, apparently shot by a gangland hitman, the other is currently in a German jail awaiting trial for various crimes. I'll explain everything when we get to your father's.'

'I'm still nervous about meeting him,' said Zilini.

'You're nervous – what about me?' said Zac.

♦

As Buchanan drove up to Amal Barazani's house, he saw the results of his phone calls. Along with Amal's Rolls Royce in the driveway, there was a car that he recognised as Nasim's and one other he figured would be Yousef's. He parked as close as he could to the front of the house. As they walked up to it, the front door opened and Darsameen came out; she had tears in her eyes. As soon as Zilini saw Darsameen she ran to her; Buchanan watched as they embraced, hugging and sobbing. Eventually they let go of each other and went into the house with Zac, Street and Buchanan following them into the living room. They looked like a bunch of strangers waiting for a train, no one spoke.

Amal was standing with his back to the fireplace, Charlotte by his side. Yousef and Annabel were seated on one of the sofas; Nasim and Bahija were on the opposite sofa with Achmad, looking decidedly uncomfortable, between them.

Zilini stopped at the entrance to the room, and waited for Zac to catch up with her, then burst into tears. Amal immediately came forward and wrapped his arms round her.

Buchanan waited at a distance for Amal and Zilini to finish hugging. Amal looked at Buchanan, teary-eyed and said, 'Thank you for looking after my Zilini and bringing her home.'

'Excuse me for saying,' said Buchanan, 'but it is Zac you have to thank for looking after Zilini. It was he who took her away from danger and kept her safe till it was safe to return.'

Buchanan wited for the congratulations and joyous noise to abate, then said. 'I have asked you all to be present this afternoon so I can explain what has been going on these past five weeks.

'At some point, Hiezabel took into her mind that the Barazani family were not behaving as she felt they should be, not coming up to the standards she held for them. Amal was seen as a derelict father, a playboy with his fancy car and business ideas that were unholy, and Zilini, *dressing like a tart* I believe I heard Hiezabel say, and consorting with a non-believer, who was taking her away from the family values.

'Nasim, her own son from a previous marriage, was not interested in following into the family business, but would rather drive fast cars round in circles. Bahija, Nasim's wife, a teacher of music. Finally, Achmad, more interested in playing computer games than chasing girls.

'That, ladies and gentlemen, is what I have come to believe was driving Hiezabel's demented plan to restore the Barazani name. Her first attempt at restoring order, as she saw it, was to poison Zac. You all know that each Thursday, Zac and Zilini came to Bahija for music lessons. You may also have remembered it was also Thursdays that Hiezabel came to

330

Nasim's to bake. Three weeks ago, she baked a fruit cake, for Zac to take home and eat. What she didn't know was Zac is a coeliac sufferer, so he gave the cake to Sam to eat. What Sam didn't realise was the fruit cake didn't just contain mixed fruit, it also contained belladonna seeds. The night he died from strangulation; he was already dying from atropine poisoning.

'Unknown to all but Yousef, Hiezabel was having a relationship with Sam. I believe at first, he enjoyed the clandestine affair, but a couple of weeks ago, the relationship soured, and Sam did his best to break things off. This enraged Hiezabel, who in a jealous frenzy strangled him. She then engaged the help of two Bulgarian thugs to dismember Sam and bury his body in a construction pit in the village of Westham. The two Bulgarians have been apprehended in Germany, one since shot dead by a gangland hitman, the other currently waiting to come to trial on numerous charges.

'Last week Hiezabel overheard me discussing some aspects of the case with Yousef. She felt threatened and decided to get rid of any evidence at the scene of Sam's murder, the former telephone building. In doing so, in the dark she accidentally took a wrong turning in the building and fell to her death down the abandoned lift shaft.'

Yousef looked at Buchanan for a few minutes, then nodded.

'When Sam disappeared under worrying circumstances, Zac decided it would be best if he and Zilini went into hiding till whatever was going on was brought to a safe conclusion.'

Amal turned to look at Zac, who was standing at the back of the room behind Darsameen. 'Is that so, Zac? Then I owe you a big thank you. I thought I was a good judge of character, I – I'm sorry, I misjudged you. Please forgive me.'

Buchanan saw Zac visibly relax as he walked over to Zilini and took her hand in his.

'I'm sorry Dad,' said Zilini. 'I did write you a note, but I forgot to put it in the envelope with the ring box. She held the note out to Amal.

Amal took it and unfolded the sheet of A4 paper.

Dear Father
I am going away for a while because I am not sure
where is safe. Zac says he thinks someone tried to kidnap
him and his brother, now Sam has gone missing. Zac
thinks something awful has happened to Sam, it's their
twin thing, he feels worried when something is
happening to Sam. I am going to do some singing with
Zac at a music festival, then on to Paris for a few days.
Please do not worry about me if I don't get in contact. I
have left my old phone at Zac's flat; he says we can be
traced by our phone location. Please do not worry about
me, Zac is going to take good care of me.
Love Zilini.

'I wish I'd got this earlier; it would have helped me not to worry about you so much,' said Amal. 'Just one thing, your mother's rings – where are they?'

Zilini raised her left hand and displayed the two rings on her wedding finger.

'You're married? When and where did this happen?'

'It wasn't a formal wedding; it was done two weeks ago at Towersey music festival.'

'I need something to drink,' said Amal, sitting down with Charlotte. 'Are you married, or not?'

'In our hearts we're married,' said Zilini, putting her arm round Zac's waist. 'We would like to make it official, if you'd give me away?'

'Of course, I would! I think a toast is in order – my Zilini has come home with a new husband.'

♦

'Do you think he pushed her?' said Karen, as Buchanan pulled the bedclothes over him.

'I don't really know, and by now it's too late to find out. The CSI's did not see what I saw, in fact they probably would not have noticed if they had looked at what I saw. If it were not for my impromptu lesson on tracking by Travis a few months ago, I'd never have thought to try it.'

'Will you mention your thoughts in your report?'

Buchanan's answer was lost in the sound of his gentle snoring.

The End